AN OPPORTUNE MOMENT

With a bow that impressed her as incredibly graceful when made by a man of his size, he made his salutation. "The Marquis of Tynsdale, ever at your service, Miss Doune," he murmured.

Warm lips burned the soft, sensitive skin exposed between glove and sleeve cuff. It made her feel disoriented and strange, but she quite sensibly decided that the odd sensation must be due to the realization that she'd unthinkingly taken an English peer under command.

"Your servant, my lord," she said steadily. "You have been more than kind, and I won't have you think your efforts are unappreciated. You've only to tell me how I might repay you. I place myself at your disposal."

For perhaps the first time in his life, Marcus Kinsworth allowed his immediate desires to cloud his reasoning. In slow, velvety tones, he offered, "Certainly we can come to some arrangement that will relieve you of any supposed debt, Miss Doune, and one which will undoubtedly satisfy us both in the process. That is, if you think you might find yourself agreeable?"

Made wary by his suggestive intonation, she politely inquired, "And just how, my lord, may I discharge my obligation?"

For answer, his lordship apparently thought it best to demonstrate his meaning. And without warning, Rachel found herself pulled tight against his chest as he bent his head, finding her lips with his. . . .

An Uncommon Miss
Melissa Lynn Jones

ZEBRA BOOKS
KENSINGTON PUBLISHING CORP.

ZEBRA BOOKS

are published by

Kensington Publishing Corp.
475 Park Avenue South
New York, NY 10016

First Printing: February, 1993

Printed in the United States of America

Chapter One

The master's bedchamber lay quiet and somber with only the dying embers behind the fire screen offering an inadequate light. Although it was not yet the hour of nine, the weak March sun had ended its puny efforts some little time before, leaving the room in shadowy darkness. On a side table, their labels just barely discernible, rested numerous bottles and vials of mysterious content, their clutter reminiscent of the physician who had just left.

Resting in the center of a great coach-top bed lay a man brought low by age. Ian Creagh, as canny a Scot as ever drew breath, reposed beneath multiple layers of luxurious quilts and covers. His snowy hair was drawn back into a neat queue in the style of his youth, while his blue eyes showed bright through the gloom. Awake and watchful, he regarded the heavy oaken door to his suite.

"Grandfather?" A well-modulated, feminine voice penetrated the shadows as the chamber door swung open.

"Aye. Come in, Rachel," he rasped. "And come ye here closer sae that I can see ye, child."

Rachel Doune carefully shut the door behind her and moved farther into the room, the array of medicines left by Dr. Fordyce at once drawing her attention. She reached for the unlit candle set amongst the jumble, intending to dispel the room's obscurity and examine more closely the various tonics and potions.

"Nae, leave be," countered the bedridden ancient. "The

5

light disturbs me. Just sit ye down and hear me out, for there be a thing of importance that weighs on my mind: a matter o' great concernment."

The young woman nodded and gracefully settled her long, full skirts into the garnet red velvet of the chair nearest the bed. She sat with her back quite straight and her features composed, the very picture of elegant poise. Her eyes lowered demurely to slim fingers folded relaxed in her lap. There were no anxious looks, no nervous twitchings, to mar the tranquil front she presented.

Mr. Creagh was undeceived, however. He knew his illness was a source of serious upset, and that his visitor had needed to call upon her not-inconsiderable courage in order to disguise such anxieties as she must be feeling, and he admired her greatly for it. Taking a few moments, he studied his granddaughter in the dim glow of the firelight.

Under his care since little more than a babe, over the years Rachel had grown into a remarkably comely young woman with a wide, intelligent forehead, smooth complexion, and with an abundance of dark blond hair, now bright-tipped with gold by the dying coals. Heavy, dark lashes shaded her eyes; still, the old man knew well the odd, blue-green color they shielded, for they were the exact same shade as had belonged to her grandmother. *Yes,* he mused, *Ailsa Creagh had had such eyes.* They were the color of the water upon which shores he'd been born, the color of Loch Fyne.

Rachel's small, squared chin was a miniature replica of his own less-than-delicate jaw and a particular delight to his eye. Even in her distress it showed a tendency to lift to a challenge. Perhaps not a trait ordinarily desired in a woman, it was, nonetheless, a sign of character that Mr. Creagh was especially glad to acknowledge, for he was depending on that little chin to see them through this time of trial. Thus mindful of his purpose, he came to the point of his request for his granddaughter's presence this night.

"Child," he began, speaking slowly, "for these two years and more, ye hae been attending our local assemblies

6

wi'out finding yerself a man to yer liking. And, while ye hae ne'er sat out a dance that I've haird of, ye hae discouraged any to be asking me for yer hand. Yer heart is as yet untouched, I believe, and yer head asks for more than what the young swains hereabouts hae offered. Mark me, I do not disapprove of such discriminating ways, but I am now reminded that I hae not much time left to see ye settled."

At these words, Rachel's gaze flew across to her grandfather's face, and words of denial sprang to her lips. "But surely, Grandfather, this indisposition will quickly pass. It's naught but a chill brought on by the weather! Or, at least, that's as Dr. Fordyce has assured me," she added, less certainly. "Is there something more wrong than—?"

"Nae, nae. Hush now," Ian Creagh interrupted her, his voice enfeebled but his will still strong. "Neither yer wishes nor mine can change my alloted span, and dinna, be forgetting that ye are already twenty yerself!" Agitated, the old man shifted restlessly under the covers. "Dear child," he said after resettling himself and affixing Rachel with his eyes, "ye are aware that it has long been my desire that ye should belong to the aristocracy. Aye, for all that I hae made a bit o' money, and a fair amount as it happens, I am convinced that ye must hae more than that. The security of peerage has long been my ambition for ye—a' well ye know the reason—but the only way to obtain such great elevation is by yer marriage."

Once more Rachel started to speak, but was silenced by a quick movement from his hand. "Rachel," he said, his gruff voice softening further, almost pleading, "please, listen to me. Only those privileged by rank truly hae protection in this world. Think. Ye know that this is true."

Though born the same year as His Majesty, George III, Ian Creagh rightly noted that his birth had not occasioned the gift of a silver spoon. Rather far from it, in truth. Instead, at a tender age, this Scots scion of the working class had been handed a wooden-handled coal shovel with which to make his way. Despite such inauspicious beginnings, however, young Ian had progressed to own not only the first mine in which he'd labored, but soon, other mines and businesses as well. He'd worked hard, cleverly investing each bit of money until he had become a man of substantial wealth—a man, moreover, understandably confident that his efforts had assured him of a full and satisfying life. And so it had been for many good years, until his beloved wife Ailsa had succumbed to a fever, and then, less than a year later, their only daughter and her young husband, Rob Doune, had been killed.

The memory of this second tragedy now determined Ian Creagh on his course, for the story of how his daughter and her husband had lost their lives was not a very pretty one.

When Rachel had been just a small tot, her father had needed to make a business trip to Glasgow. Rob Doune had wanted to inspect a new air-pumping device that promised to effect a substantial improvement over older models, such inventions being to his particular interest. Loath to be separated from his little family, Mr. Doune had brought his wife and his chattering three-year-old daughter along with him. The trip was a success, and the Dounes had made a leisurely return home to Ayrshire, stopping at a busy coaching inn mid-journey to obtain a room for the night.

They'd just completed making arrangements with the proprietor for his last vacancy when another carriage had drawn up behind theirs. An arrogant English earl had descended, belligerently demanding that since the inn was full, he should have the room just let to the Dounes. Being commoners, without even a knighthood to recommend them, Rachel's parents had been made straightaway to bundle up their child and find another, although not nearly so luxurious, resting place.

During the wee hours, a fire broke out at the second inn. Its timbers were dry and crumbling, so it was with incredible, horrible swiftness that the building burned right down to the ground. Only tiny Rachel was saved from the disaster. . . .

Ian Creagh had learned the hard way that in any

dispute, a mere baronet would fare better than he or his kin.

It quickly became apparent, however, that Rachel did not share his fears. Neither did she now hesitate to disagree with the plan just set forth, sure that she had the right. "So, you would have me marry into the peerage, Grandfather?" she chided him, albeit gently, her unaccented English beautifully precise. "We've had this discussion more than once, I think, but I will tell you again that even if such a thing could be done, you are wrong to suppose I would be more secure if bound to some Tom Fool of a lordling."

"But ye must hae position in this world, Rachel. Ye must!"

Rachel shook her head slightly from side to side. "Oh, no, Grandfather. Here, we are known and respected, after all, and times have changed a great deal. Why, in this modern day, a prosperous family has nothing to fear— surely you cannot but agree. Never once have I been shown the least disrespect, nor have you real cause to expect it." She sat back in her seat, confident that any would see the sense of her reasoning.

But Ian Creagh was not so easily swayed. "Ach, no such thing," he averred. "I say that a title is what ye need, *and* what ye will hae!"

"Oh, then, you really believe, Grandfather, truly believe, that I'd be better off with a man who cares more for fashion than sense? Some avid gamester or break-neck Corinthian? Why, only last week I read of two lords who gambled away a vast sum on the outcome of an absurd race between the raindrops trickling down the windowpane of some silly men's club or other. Do you honestly expect that I would be safer in the company of one of that ilk? I hardly think so. Far better to remain a spinster here at Plumwood House, or to marry a day-laborer who knows the value of honest effort." Of its own volition, her stubborn little chin started to tilt itself upward.

But Ian Creagh had other ideas. His craggy features were unyielding in the flickering shadows, and his voice held surprising strength. "Ye will regard my wishes on this, Rachel," he corrected. "I know what I am about and hae decided to send ye off to London as soon as may be."

Rachel's composure slipped just a bit, revealing a stunned expression. "To—to London? *London!* Why, whatever for?"

"To find a proper husband, o' course, so make up yer mind to it. I hae sent for my solicitor, who will arrange for the town house in Bruton Place to be opened for ye; the last renter moved out some months ago, so the house now stands empty and available for yer use. My man will also retain the services of a gentlewoman to gi' ye the proper Society introductions, and she can also teach ye how ye're to go on there; so I expect ye to prepare yerself to leave before the end of this month."

With these words, the old man seemed to have exhausted the last of his energy. He sank back into the pillows, his eyelids drooping in obvious fatigue. In tones scarcely audible, he said, "Child, please leave me now. I hae not the strength to answer yer questions and yer argufyings. We can talk again tomorrow."

They did not meet again the next day, however, nor even the next. Ian Creagh sent word that he needed to rest, but that Rachel should not delay packing. Mr. Mahony, the Creagh solicitor, was seen to come and stay for some time, but all Rachel's entreaties to have herself admitted into her grandfather's room were met with firm refusal. Had Grandfather not been so ill—it was the first time in memory he had been in bed above a day—Rachel would have greatly resented these events. As it was, she clung to Dr. Fordyce's assurances that nothing was seriously wrong. She had only to be patient and not worry overmuch; Grandfather would soon be restored to his customary good health.

And to his senses!

Really, Rachel thought with a disbelieving laugh, distracted from her primary concern, as well as the small book of Italian grammar lying open on her lap, *he could not have meant what he said!*

She loved her home here in Scotland and had absolutely no desire to leave it. Never, not for a single moment, had she considered living elsewhere. Decorated by Ailsa Creagh's fine hand long years before, the rich furnishings of Plumwood House had been chosen for both quality and style, bequeathing a legacy of tasteful timelessness that made Rachel ofttimes feel as though she'd known her grandmother well. Barely educated by enlightened standards—for an exacting course of study had seen to it that Rachel knew her *pi* from her peonies—that unequaled dame had created an atmosphere of refinement and comfortable elegance that no amount of education could rival. And even after marriage, Rachel's parents had continued residence within these spacious, thirty-odd rooms that comprised this house, leading Rachel to suppose that when she herself married, she would do the same. Plumwood House was home.

Abandon everything here? For what? Rachel thought scornfully.

Unthinkable that she should pack up her traps and go haring off to another country entirely—the land of the Sassenach at that— in some ridiculous and, likely, futile endeavor to find a husband from among the English noble houses. All she was apt to encounter in London were fortune-hunting, ne'er-do-well, idling . . . fops! She had known of her grandfather's cherished ambitions, of course, and though in disagreement with him on the matter, she wanted very much to put his mind at peace if she could. But as for this eccentric plan of his? Well, it was just beyond anything!

Leave Grandfather?

It was he who had thrown her up on her first pony, bandaged her childhood scrapes and cuts, and listened to her lessons year after year. More, he had taught her to face life as he himself did, with a willingness to work toward each goal, against all odds and without fear. That is, Rachel thought wryly, *almost* without fear. She was afraid right now and freely admitted it. Not that the idea of travelling to London caused her any great measure of unrest; that was of scant importance once Grandfather was well enough to be brought to see reason. Certainly, he would not persist if she truly did not want it.

No, what really caused her the gravest concern was the threat of losing the wonderful old man who continued so very ill.

To Rachel's enormous relief, on the fourth day of his infirmity, Ian Creagh once again sent for her. Pausing only to hand over the linen list she'd been working on with the housekeeper, she hastened along the upstairs hallway as fast as convention, and her years of training by a strict English governess, allowed. Rachel fully expected this time to see Grandfather looking more the thing, and she was eager for the meeting. Despite all her expectations, though, her hopes dwindled to naught even as she entered his room.

The curtains remained drawn against the thin afternoon sun, leaving the opulent chamber deep in shadow, much as it had been on her last visit. In the near-darkness, Ian Creagh was to be found not only still abed, but most unnaturally pale besides. His face, lying still against white pillowcases, had a bleached, pallid appearance that was everything shocking to his devoted granddaughter. Masking her fears, Rachel concentrated on keeping her voice light and pleasant.

"Grampa?" Unconsciously, she slipped into using the familiar childhood name for this dear, substitute parent. "Are you not feeling any better today? Can I fetch you anything, or perhaps I could read to you for a while?"

Ian Creagh's sharp blue eyes met her own readily enough, but she was disheartened at the weakness of his voice when he answered.

"Nae, though I thank ye for asking," he said. "Ye mean well, I know, but there be other, more important matters we must discuss. There are details relative to yer journey."

"Oh, please, *do* let that wait. Once you are up and about again, I promise to listen to whatever plans you have in mind, but the return of your health is all I care to be concerned with right now."

"My point exactly, child," he reminded. "Were ye thinking that I was wishful to be sending ye off alone? Ye can be sure that I hae considered it from all sides, but there be not another way about the affair."

But it was not in Rachel's nature to allow him, sick or no, to persist in his misapprehensions. With as much calm as she could manage, she said, "Well, I won't leave you, Grandfather, never think it. And do regard what you are asking . . . traipsing off to London in a preposterous quest for a husband, and amongst the haut ton, no less! You don't seriously expect me to tie my future to some horrendously indebted lord who cares only for the cut of his cloth and his own reprehensible amusements— amusements, no doubt, which put him in dun territory in the first place! You can be assured that only such will have me, but I tell you this plain, *I* will not have such!"

Horrified that she should so lose control as to practically shout in a sickroom, Rachel dropped her glance to her lap amost immediately. Consequently, she missed the thoroughly calculating, altogether satisfied look that flitted across her grandfather's withered old face. Giving her no chance to recover, Mr. Creagh responded in the merest whisper, making her all the more aware of the harsh tones she had herself just used.

"Rachel," he said, the words coming softly, "I'm nae asking ye to take to yerself a man ye cannot admire. And yet, surely, wi' all that I hae taught ye, and with yer canny ways, ye can find the means to attract a man of sound principle to yer side. Oh, there are many such, I do assure ye, for over the years I hae often met and done business wi' men of worth and good character. Men who also bore grand names. But only in London are ye likely to find them. Aye, there are those who are naught but what ye say, o' course—I know it as well as ye—but I send ye to find a special lord of whom we may both be proud."

Rachel looked up, her eyes guilt-stricken, but not so much so that she was unable to take in every crease, every line, that marked his expression. Intently, she measured the position of each deeply carved wrinkle, as if, somehow, the signs of his greater experience with life could give her the answer she sought.

Finally, she felt compelled to acceptance. "Very well, then. If it eases your mind, I shall do as you wish. I'll go to England and look about me for one of those paragons you seem to believe in so strongly." She sighed, once, determinedly graceful in her defeat. Then, on a thought, she brightened. "However, Grandfather, since March is only half over, and the social season in London doesn't really begin until May, there's plenty of time yet for you to recover your strength and come with me."

His answer came in saddened tones. "Oh, my dearest one, 'twill nae do, I'm afraid. The journey is a long one, and it would be far, far too much for a man o' my years. We will speak to the doctor when he comes, if you like, but I misdoubt he can tell you any different.

"Now then," he went on more briskly, pushing himself upright against the headboard, "Mr. Mahony has my instructions and will acquaint you with the arrangements as they are completed. Every protection will be afforded— and so I've told him—but I expect ye to be on yer way before it comes on April. Ye will need the time in London to get yerself established and to attend to the makings of a new town wardrobe. We'll have no nip-cheese ways either, mind ye! Spend as much as ye need. I ken here in Scotland we are quite out-o'-date, and ye won't be catching the best man's eye wi' less than the very best dressing."

Rachel caught a note of the old man's eagerness. Of course she was glad if this project relieved some of the tedium of his ailment, still, she was uneasy. Another question came to mind. "So, how long exactly am I to stay in London? I mean, supposing I find no one to suit?"

The white-haired old patriarch appeared to sink lower beneath the dark satin quilting, his features gaunt and stark against the plump, lace-edged pillows. There was a certain rigidity about his expression as he stared upward at the bed-top's ribbed wooden arches, vaulting high above the mattress. "Nae, child. I cannot permit your thinking

14

that way," he breathed. "Ye must have the right attitude, or be doomed from the start." He stopped, then seemed to gather his next words with care, perhaps in fear of placing all he valued at such great risk.

Somehow foreseeing irrevocable danger, Rachel rushed to stop him from proceeding. She was unaware that she gripped her hands together so tightly that the blood was almost wholly squeezed out, rendering the flesh across her knuckles transparent over the bone. She knew only that she *must* prevent his next speech.

"No, please, Grandfather!" she cried, avoiding his eye. "It is not of such moment that we need speak of this today." She jumped up from her seat in certain, conscious dred, anxious to leave the gloomy room and escape whatever it was that seemed to threaten. Despite her efforts, however, and before she could take so much as a single step, her fears became reality as, relentlessly, he pushed on to the finish.

"Tis done, Rachel. Nothing ye can say will change it." He spoke in flattened voice, snaring her eyes and holding her motionless with the intensity of his light blue gaze. "I hae finalized my will, and by its terms ye shall fully inherit, *providing* ye contrive the marriage I desire. For if ye should fail, Plumwood House and all else I own will be reverted to the Crown, less two hundred pounds ye will receive each year of yer lifetime. So. I depend on ye to keep this from happening, but I intend to see ye properly wedded afore I die."

Rachel felt as if the very air vanished from her lungs, leaving a vast emptiness in its place. She sank back onto her seat, her eyes glazed and unfocused, it being all she could do to suppress a whimper. *Surely this isn't happening*, she protested within her mind. Could this dearest of men, this only kinsman, actually do this to her? Could Grandfather really cast her out, bar her from Plumwood, and from her rightful heritage?

His next speech proved the matter.

"I dare not give ye more time, Granddaughter. This shall be the greatest test of yer abilities, I dinna' doubt; but

I hae worked hard for each farthing, and that should stand for something. And now? Now 'tis up to ye to earn the right to it. I can gi' ye till the first of July, and not a single day longer, to complete yer task and make the announcement I desire."

Wholly numbed at this ultimatum, Rachel stumbled out and made her way to her own rooms. As it was, when she closed the door behind her, she missed seeing the mendacious old Scotsman as he sat up in the bed . . . to treat himself to a sly, triumphant grin! She would have been yet more astonished to see him then push back the mounded covers, and—with amazing agility!—hop over to the marble-topped washstand to begin removing a thick dusting of white powder which he had earlier applied. His granddaughter had long known him for a clever old devil, but even she, who knew him best, would have cavilled to believe him capable of such horrendous, bald-faced duplicity.

Entering the bedchamber not ten minutes behind her, Dr. Fordyce was quicker to believe and so was swift with sharp criticism for his patient. "Ach! You old faker!" He rounded on the old man. Dr. Fordyce had suspected for days that Ian Creagh was shamming it, but he quite boggled at the proportions of the crime now uncovered. "I've a good mind to go at once and tell Miss Rachel the truth," he cried. "For if you think I will sit quiet and condone the misery you're putting that girl through, why, I tell you, I won't be any part of it!"

"So, ye'd have her set on the shelf, then?" Ian Creagh snorted from his place on a small settee where he sat at his ease. "That's what it comes to, think on." Behind him, branched candlesticks, newly lit, gave out a cozy light, betraying the decidedly healthy glow across his recently scrubbed cheeks. His expression turning serious, he explained, "If Rachel had found herself a man like her da', I would nae have taken this course. Rob Doune was a fine man and my best mine manager, ye'll recall, and ne'er once did I regret her mother having him. But, since none of the local lads hae taken my granddaughter's fancy, why

16

should I not now hae my way?" He propped one quilted-top slipper over the other in comfort.

The good doctor sank into an opposing chair, a sense of righteous condemnation warring with his genuine respect and affection for his patient. "But, Ian," he protested. "Must it be done like this? The girl thinks you are practically at death's door!"

"That she does," Mr. Creagh said dismissively. "But my Rachel hae the optimism o' youth, and a wee little worry won't hurt her. Otherwise, she would argue with me for weeks—ha! more like years—before I might convince her that what I want is best. It be a harsh thing, I know; but I tell ye, 'tis the only way."

"A wee little worry won't . . .! And so you would toss her out and threaten her with disinheritance?"

"I would," answered Mr. Creagh. The decisive set of his pugnacious jaw left no room for any doubt on that head.

Dr. Fordyce was privately unsure that such deception was entirely unjustified, either, especially since he'd known the strong-minded Miss Rachel from the cradle. Still, he conscientiously tried his best to mitigate the sentence that his old friend seemed set to impose. "In that case," he begged, "will you not at least go with her, Ian? The greedy lords with their shabby titles are likely to be at her like—like wolves on a sheep!"

"Nae, I cannot go, and so ye must tell her," Mr. Creagh frowardly dissented. "Her old gramps would hardly add to her consequence before the London ton! Nae, I intend that my gold should be its own attraction, but it would nae do to be constantly reminding the tattlers of its source. And as for the wrong sort of fellow, there be a good head on my granddaughter's shoulders, and she's well aware o' the dangers. We can trust her to find a right 'un," he stated blithely.

Helpless in the face of such singular resolution, Dr. Fordyce found himself surrendering, but only after extracting a promise that there would be no more talk of dying. "Or I promise, Ian Creagh, I will myself tell Miss Rachel the whole!" he warned.

Chuckling at the scruple, Mr. Creagh gave his word.

Even as this discussion was being carried on, away down another hallway along the second floor, Rachel stood in her room, staring out the window as she tried to recover her balance. Staggered by her grandfather's demands and the penalty for failure, she worried about the prospect of leaving Scotland, alone, and for the very first time in her life. She fretted about all the arrangements that must be made while fighting down her fears for her grandfather's health.

What she could least understand was why she must stake her entire future on these coming few months. Suppose she could not find a suitable man in the time allowed; and what if she did, as her grandfather thought possible, and the man would not have her! She knew no one in London, had not a single acquaintance there, much less anyone among the beau monde. Rachel fervently hoped that the promised chaperon would know her business, for the idea of receiving no invitations, or, worse, of being snubbed in company, was enough to daunt even the staunchest young miss.

Rachel groaned aloud as myriad questions and doubts rushed in to overwhelm her. She knew that two hundred pounds per year would see her in modest comfort, and she understood that she could live as a pensioner at Plumwood for as long as Grandfather lived—and, surely, that would be for many years yet, *wouldn't it?* But even if he lived to be a hundred, she hated to think of letting her beloved grandfather down. He had applied himself diligently these many years and had made himself a man of substance; the idea that such gains should be lost repelled her.

At that very moment, Rachel resolved that she would not only go as her grandfather asked, but that she would succeed!

With only two days left remaining in the month, Rachel announced herself ready. It was arranged that she and her maid would sail south through the Irish Sea and down around to Bristol, thence hiring a suitable carriage to complete the trip to London. Duncan, their longtime family coachman, would go along as both driver and bodyguard, charged with seeing them safely installed in the city. Duncan would then return to Ayrshire when he was satisfied that Rachel was secure in the company of her chaperone, Mrs. Beekham.

These plans established, on the eve of departure Rachel asked for a final admittance to her grandfather's rooms. They were to leave Plumwood House quite early the next morning, since the trip to the docks was a long one. She sat down once more in the velvet-cushioned, garnet red chair, heaving a deep sigh as she did so.

"Grampa?" Her eyes opened wide in the dimness of the room. "Are you really quite, *quite* sure that you want me to do this?"

The beseeching look that accompanied this question almost undid the old deceiver, but he straightened his thoughts at once. "Oh, my child, I dare nae let ye delay. I'm nae saying that my death is imminent, um—" His conscience threatened him for an instant as he remembered his word to Dr. Fordyce, "Um, that is, I only remind you that everyone's demise is, er, inevitable." Satisfied that Rachel remained unaware of the slip, he continued. "I am six years past seventy, ye know, and yer rise is my dream; it is now up to ye to accomplish my aims. Ye must do this for me. But, nae! Ye must do it for *yerself.*"

"But—but what if something should happen here? What if you need me whilst I'm gone?" Her voice trailed off helplessly.

"Ye are frightened, I know, but ye need nae be," he soothed her. "Ye've but to use the strength, the resourcefulness which I know ye hae, to find a fine lord and bind him to ye." Grandfather Creagh reached across the covers and wrapped Rachel's slim fingers within his own gnarled, work-hardened fists, everything in his mein honest and true. "Rachel, my dearest, dearest child," he said gently, "I hae learned in my dealings that with

19

perseverance, one can accomplish whatever one wishes. I hae full faith that ye will win out."

The firelight flickered behind the screen, the only light in the room. Moisture glittered in blue-green orbs as Rachel leaned over to kiss her only family good-bye. With effort, she prevented even a single tear from spilling over.

And early the next morning, seen through a cold and misting rain, the Creagh family carriage left for the coast of Scotland as planned. Ian Creagh watched from behind parted curtains, contending with a very real sense of misgiving; he continued to stare outward, long after the equipage had passed from sight. Though never so ill as he had pretended, as he stood there at the window, he had to quite sternly remind himself that he really did not have so much time left that he dared let Rachel fight him too long. His decision to put this scheme to the test had not been lightly made. Even so, he could not prevent the shiver that shook him when he thought of the consequences should his granddaughter fail.

Then, with a gesture not unlike his willful descendant, his jaw squared at his doubts.

Chapter Two

Grosvenor Square boasted the elegant London addresses of Society's most fashionable members. Behind the bright-finished brass knocker of one of its Greek columned, porticoed entrances, an impeccably groomed retainer paused in his duties at the sound of an arriving carriage. Hastening to swing wide the panelled front door, he stepped back as Lydia Cheeves, wife to the viscount of that name, made to enter her brother's house.

"I am expected," she said hurriedly as she tip-tupped in, taffeta skirts rustling about her full figure. "Well, where is Marcus? In the library?"

At the butler's affirmative reply, Lady Cheeves, that socially prominent and modish woman, divested herself of her sable-trimmed muff and pelisse, as well as the orange-and-white-striped and ruffled umbrella she'd brought to combat any wayward rain shower, it being that time of year. In a swirl of burnt orange and highly contrasting peacock blue, she then quickly made her way through to the inner regions of the house. She rushed down the appropriate hallway ahead of the butler, scarcely stopping long enough to allow herself to be announced.

As she approached the library's large, precisely centered desk, however, the lofty space above her head proved more effective in slowing her steps. The coffered ceiling soared a full fifteen feet above her smart bonnet, causing Lady Cheeves to wilt somewhat. She hunched her shoulders, much in the manner she had adopted as a girl when summoned to this rather awesomely proportioned room by her father, most usually, as it was, for a well-deserved scolding. Fretfully, she removed her gloves and began toying with their decorative trim.

"Marcus, whatever are you wanting of me?" she groused, attempting to regain her confidence. "I know it cannot be anything I wish to hear. It never is! Although, why you couldn't come to see *me*, I'm sure I just don't know."

The faint whine in her voice grated across her host's ear, leaving him to wonder for the umpteenth time why this particular sister always managed to sound like such a beastly child. Marcus Kinsworth might be eight years her junior—he was the youngest of the three Kinsworth children comprising their generation—but he neverthe-less had no hesitation in exerting his authority over this frippery, complaining lady. He was the Most Honorable, the sixth Marquis of Tynsdale, and the acknowledged head of his family. Concomitantly, he held to all of the rights, privileges, and responsibilities that his position entailed.

But for all of that, it was true that Lord Tynsdale rarely sought out his eldest sister's presence. He preferred that the harmony of his home remain undisturbed by the chaos that reigned wherever Lydia moved—Susan's efforts not-withstanding. Thus reminded of Lady Susan Kins-worth, for indeed, their middle sister was the reason for this meeting, Marcus forthwith asserted himself to call Lady Cheeves to order.

"And I bid you a good morning as well," he greeted, his expression unreadable from behind his desk. "Although, perhaps, I should better say 'good afternoon,' as it is somewhat beyond the hour I recollect suggesting for this appointment. Surely, I must remember incorrectly in thinking you were to be here at eleven of the clock." Marcus lifted one dark, sardonic eyebrow.

"Well! I'm sure you did mention the time you preferred, but I don't know what that has to say to anything," Lady Cheeves answered peevishly. "I do have my own concerns

22

after all, and it is hardly possible for me to drop everything at an instant's notice."

"Ah, but I believe that my note advising you of my convenience was sent early on yesterday. If the time suggested was inappropriate, you had only to say so then, I think?"

Upon seeing the hapless gloves further mangled beneath her ladyship's restless fingers, Lord Tynsdale desisted in further censure and came at once to the point. "Lydia, your son called to see me yesterday, at about this hour as it happens. It would appear that he is once again in debt, and he politely informed me that as my heir presumptive, he would like an advance on the Tynsdale inheritance. He gave me to understand that you had outspent yourself and were unable to . . . I believe he said, 'sport the blunt,' and he then proceeded to tell me that his Aunt Susan had already given him the loan of her income for this quarter. It seems he next considered it up to me to satisfy his more pressing creditors." Marcus paused in obvious disgust. "Do tell me how it is that you and Lord Cheeves have allowed this state of affairs," he directed.

For a moment, Lady Cheeves had the grace to look properly chastened. The expression did not last long, however, as within seconds she returned to her customary posture of believing herself ill-used. "But, Marcus," she insisted. "You know we haven't the income to properly provide for Gilbert. A young man's wardrobe costs the very moon these days, and I *will* have him move in the first circles!"

The marquis cast a lazy eye over his sister's richly embellished gown with its expensive, accenting silk scarves, pausing to peruse the recently purchased bonnet of Italian chip straw, crimped in the latest shape as declared *dernier cri* for this spring's fashion. He finally allowed his appraisal to linger over the various brooch-pins and bracelets which adorned her person.

"What a charming ensemble," he finally drawled. "Dare I guess it the work of that very fine new modiste on Bond Street?" The criticism implied was unmistakable.

"What, would you have us all in rags, Brother?" Lydia's whine became even more pronounced. "You cannot mean we shouldn't dress according to our station? We have a position—must uphold certain standards! Certainly you would not be so unfeeling as to disagree?" Feathers were set to trembling, and armlets were all quite a-jingle with the older woman's agitation.

"Somehow," the marquis remarked dryly, "I don't think a clothing allowance was what your son had in mind. I rather had the idea that he needed funds for—what shall we call a young man's penchant for deep gambling and drink—*entertainment*?"

The viscountess looked immensely shocked that her brother would draw such fine lines. "Well, of course, he must keep up with his friends!" she protested. "And I think it no more than proper that Gilbert should come to you when he wants a little assistance. After all, you are quite thirty-and-four years of age, and it's not as if you had any plans to start your nursery! Gilbert is your heir, and you should naturally be expected to accommodate him."

From behind his well-polished rosewood desk, the Marquis of Tynsdale silently rose to his feet, completely indifferent to the high ceiling above. A tall man, he moved with the relaxed grace of some huge and very dangerous predator as he came forward to stand before his sister's chair. Well-delineated muscles slid smoothly beneath his beautifully tailored coat and dove gray pantaloons, worn above impeccably polished Hessian boots. His wide shoulders dimmed the watery April light filtering through the library windows behind him, the clouds which had threatened since the morning serving to emphasize his mood.

"Lydia," he spoke in soft, velvety tones, "whatever gave you reason to assume that I would not one day marry? I have, as it happens, decided to undertake matrimony before my next birthday." He allowed these words to sink in before continuing. "While as for young Gilbert, I will repeat to you what I told him. *Never* again is he to approach his lady aunt for money. Her quarterly sum is due her by our father's will, and it is intended for her sole use. If it should again come to my ears that your son has made free of Susan's monies, I will hold her funds in trust and have all her bills sent directly to me. It is by her request she lives in your home, but I will demand her removal to this house should she be further annoyed."

Lady Cheeves inhaled sharply, drawing back in her chair. "Take Susan from under my roof?" she blustered. "You would not dare! And besides, where else has she to go?"

"She will be welcomed here," Marcus stated flatly.

"Well!" came Lydia's rather petulant response. "I'm sure she is *welcome*, but she's told me ever and often how she's happy to stay where she's needed. Just what you think she could do here, I cannot for the life of me imagine." She glanced about at the spacious room, spotless in all its portions. "In any case, what is all this nonsense about marriage?" she then pressed, suddenly recalling that most important of points. "You've shown no one a particular preference that I've heard of; indeed, you haven't been seen at Almack's for eons! So, unless you have developed a recent partiality for some opera dancer you have in keeping," she added snidely, "I can hardly think who your intended might be."

Lord Tynsdale's eyes turned on her, dark brown and as hard as any stout English oak. "You are not to concern yourself as to the specifics of my plans," he quelled her in a voice so deep it sounded as though brought forth from Stygian depths. "You may, however, tell that less-than-perceptive viscount you call 'husband' that he should henceforward keep his own house in better form, for I will not be looked to for any further support."

With a negligent wave of his hand, he dismissed his sister—very much as if she were some Cit come on business, she thought. She flounced her way out, leaving it to the butler to quietly close the library door behind her.

Marcus merely sighed and returned to his seat. He forced his attention to the current batch of papers neatly aligned on his desk, where not less than three estate matters awaited his decision.

He stared unseeingly at the neat stack before him, pondering the very question to which his sister had demanded an answer. The fact of it was, he had absolutely no idea with whom he would care to link his name! Until today, he'd not really considered that it was his duty to assure that the title stay in the Kinsworth line; he'd only formed his intention to marry when Lydia had goaded him to it.

On the town for well over a decade, Marcus had always deplored the simpering, Society misses paraded before him. Much sought after among the muslin company for his generosity—and for his well-defined, masculine features, if he but knew it—he'd taken his share of female companionship without the attendant danger of falling into those inevitable snares set for him by the many ambitious Society mamas. Contrary to Lydia's mocking supposition, however, he had no mistress currently in keeping. His last *inamorata* had bored him every bit as much as had her predecessors with her chronically clinging female emotions and tears. At the most, he had felt scarcely more than a mild exasperation at her histrionics, exasperation which had readily turned into relief when she had accepted his last, parting gift.

Perhaps that remembered feeling of relief, when combined with this morning's irritations, had precipitated today's sudden resolution. Marcus supposed that a wife would be more comfortable than a mere fancy piece and would, in due time, also provide the added benefit of giving him the means to prevent the irresponsible Gilbert from expecting to follow in his stead.

Yes, of a certainty, there must be a Kinsworth to uphold the Tynsdale honors.

What was wanted, he decided, was a lady of sense, an attractive lady, and one of good family, of course. His father had impressed upon him the importance of superior breeding, but to make matters easier, Marcus needn't consider the financial prospects of any one candidate, since the management of his properties was well in hand, providing him an income sufficient for every luxury. A girl of good background was all that was necessary; among this year's crop of debutantes would be some young miss who would suffice to the purpose.

Satisfied that the problem of his nephew would soon be taken care of, Marcus settled himself deeper in his chair, wondering if perhaps he ought not invite his middle sister to come and live with him in any case. After he'd entered the wedded state, she could surely be of benefit to him when the children began to come. Although always shy in company, gentle Susan would be an asset, bringing order and tranquility in her wake. He knew that it was through her influence that the Cheeves' household functioned even halfway efficiently around Lydia and her undisciplined brood.

In his musings, Marcus recalled that Lady Susan had been but a young woman of seventeen years when the fifth marquis had died, while he had himself been a mere schoolboy of fourteen. Susan had left soon after the funeral to take up residence in their older sister's home, leaving her brother to return to his schooling. Heretofore, he had presumed that his sisters were content with the arrangement, but, after twenty years with the Cheeves, Marcus wondered if Susan might now be amenable to a change. He had no desire to compel her, nor to influence her against her wishes, but he did think he should like to have Susan with him. He resolved to speak to her about it at the earliest opportunity.

While Marcus continued at his desk thus contemplating the future, some blocks away at Cheeves House, one of the subjects of his deliberations was in the process of attempting a strategic retreat to her small, upstairs bedroom. Unfortunately, the slight swish caused by one dragging slipper gave her defection away.

"Auntie *Su-u-ue . . . !*"

Lady Susan Kinsworth barely restrained a wince at the unpleasant diminution of her name and family title in the high-pitched voice of her eldest niece. It seemed she was discovered by Edwena Cheeves. *How very frustrating,* she inwardly mourned, *to have escape denied.*

"You aren't thinking of going to your room at this time of day!" Edwena accused, hustling up the steps to confront her aunt. "Mama said you were to help me practice my scales and aria this afternoon. Did she not tell you?" The heavyset twelve-year-old fixed her slightly bulbous blue eyes square to Susan's own soft brown ones.

"Well, we do often practice at this time, Edwena," Lady Susan said quietly, "but I thought that today we might skip. Wouldn't you like to pass up your scales just for once?"

She was somehow unsurprised when Edwena refused the proffered dispensation. All three of Lydia's daughters loved to sing before whatever audience they could contrive, though not even their aunt's most strenuous efforts at instruction could quite remove a certain common shrillness in their voices. Privately loathing the compulsory sessions, Susan, for the most part, usually managed to endure them with grace, ever optimistic that someday the girls would become more pleasant adults.

And so, swallowing her disappointment, Susan dutifully descended the staircase, condemned to the music room, regretful of the horrid limp that had trapped her. Unable to dance or even to stroll like other people, she had no hopes of marriage, nor even a home of her own. Instead, she was forced to take shelter with her sister, and as the years had steadily passed, she believed herself resigned. But there were times—times like today—when she felt a tiny spark of resentment that her life should be so circumscribed.

As the pair reached the front hall, Lady Cheeves was at the same time returning home from her troublesome visit with their brother. Susan thought her sister looked much put about by something when she stepped inside the house, but since that in itself was in no way unusual, Susan didn't feel overly concerned at first. She never considered that she was herself involved in whatever it was that had Lydia out of temper.

As orange taffeta skirts swished over the threshold, however, Susan discovered otherwise.

"Sister!" Lydia snapped. "You will attend me in my dressing room. At once, if you please!" The viscountess's ire had found its direction.

"But, Mama—" Edwena bleated. "You said Auntie was to work with me on my voice lessons today!"

"I am so sorry, darling, but there is something I must immediately discuss with your Aunt Susan. I'll send her to you as soon as I can. Please be patient for Mama, we shan't be long."

Edwena huffed off, most probably to the kitchens to pester the chef, her aunt shrewdly speculated. But Susan mentally shook herself at the unkind thought, smothering her annoyance by sheer will. Once again she began the climb up the stairway, this time in Lydia's ample wake.

Upon her marriage, Lydia had displayed as neat a figure as one could wish. She loved to pamper her family, however, and to pamper herself, as well. By now, Lord Cheeves was in contest with the Prince Regent for his girth, his proportions very nearly as gross, though his wife and daughters were as yet what one might call "plump." Of the Cheeves family, only Gilbert, the eldest and only son, had kept a trim figure, even though, in face, he most resembled his father. Lady Susan, too, had remained as slim as a girl, but then, she and Gilbert had slight appetite for Chef's rich sauces and desserts.

"Close the door, Susan," Lydia said when they reached the grand apartments. "I must cry shame upon you, and you will not want the servants to overhear."

Susan reluctantly did as she was bid before taking up a seat on a stuffed chair, covered in an unpleasant shade of orchid. Lydia commanded a Rococo-styled chaise longue, newly gilded and lavishly upholstered in bright pink plush. Susan patiently observed as her sister then carefully arranged herself to a pose of long suffering, first removing her bonnet, and artfully rearranging her several scarves, her burnt orange skirts in disagreeable contrast with the pink plush.

"I have just come from our brother's," Lydia started in, "where I learned that you refused Gilbert additional funds to meet his needs. Marcus dared to lecture me on this unfortunate situation—if you can believe it—and told me that it was not his place, nor yours, to provide for my dear boy. Lord Cheeves and I have not the wherewithal to properly keep Gilbert up to the mark, as you very well know, for we *do* have the girls to consider."

Lydia then switched to a high, wheedling tone. "Now, Susan, *dearest* sister . . ."

The object of this importuning flinched at the whining note.

"We have given you a home and made you a member of our little family . . ."

Susan bethought the years of lessons she had provided the three lumpish daughters of the house.

"You've sat at our table countless times . . ."

Susan remembered the lonely suppers in her room whenever guests were expected.

"And we have given you our protection and included you in all our activities."

Her only outings had been to take the girls to the park, or to Gunter's for one of the confectioner's special cream and fruit ices. But even those jaunts had been curtailed when Edwena complained that her aunt's awkward steps had caused some to stare; thereafter, a maid took the girls out for their treats. Only once, and that over a year ago, Susan had cajoled her charges to the botanical gardens at Kew, but she'd learned her mistake soon after arriving, when her nieces had commenced whining and carrying on about the long walk and how they were thirsty, and bored, and so forth, until Susan had sworn never to attempt a similar excursion.

Before Susan could become quite sunk in depression by these recollections, Lady Cheeves came to the purpose of her discourse. "Now, Susan, my dear," she said, recommencing, "your income is a great deal more than you need, and, by helping Gilbert, you have your rightful duty in mind. Very properly, too! But since Marcus has forbidden you to give my boy any more money," Lydia stopped to remove one scarf from about her neck, fiddling with another still draped across her shoulders, "we must contrive a way for you to help your nephew without it coming to our brother's attention. So, and nothing simpler, if you will just give over the money to me, I will see that Gilbert receives it." The viscountess's face lit up expectantly, sure that her sister must be satisfied at the solution thus proposed.

But Lady Susan was far from persuaded! She had to make Lydia understand that while she felt certain that Gilbert was basically a good sort, and she wanted to help all she could, she really thought Marcus was right. It was time and more that their nephew outgrew such pecuniary embarrassments. The boy was lately persuaded to too many extravagances and was greatly in danger of spoiling. More, she had emptied her purse so often—and so rarely with thanks—that she truly did not have more than four or five pounds available to call her own.

Susan took a deliberate, calming breath and attempted to explain the situation. "Lydia," she temporized, "I am very sorry Marcus has cut up stiff with you—"

"Oh! If you only knew! For I tell you that it's *totally* beyond belief how our brother has caused me to suffer with that cold, odiously offhanded way of his. So excessively unconciliating, so *hard* and *unfeeling!*" Lydia scrabbled for the vinaigrette normally tucked somewhere beneath the pink cushions.

But Susan felt disinclined today for a show of her sister's histrionics. "Yes, yes, Lydia, that's as may be. But I do think it just possible," she persevered in her gentle tones, "that some of today's unpleasantness might have been avoided if Gilbert had first asked my counsel. I would have perhaps been able to dissuade him from applying to his uncle, for that was surely not at all the thing to do. I am unable to give Gilbert any more at present, but, Lydia, I fear your constant reminders of what he is owed as the current Tynsdale heir are likely more to blame for this trouble than any shortage of mine. Marcus will someday take a wife, and the expectations you have raised could lead to a mischief."

Realizing that she was being thwarted, and thus put in mind of her greatest injury, Lydia at once flared out. "Oh-ho! So you knew about the nuptial plans, yet would dare tell me that *I* am to blame for my poor boy's disappointment?" she cried. "Cheeves has warned me forever that you are a sly one, and now I see *just* what he means."

Lady Susan had never had any illusions regarding her constant state of disfavor with her brother-in-law, for she knew that Lord Cheeves mistook her customarily self-effacing manner for weakness and guile, preferring the brash assertiveness of his own family. Not that Susan minded the viscount's attitude overmuch, nor should her sister's words be taken too seriously either, for Susan knew that Marcus was prone to deliver a stinging set-down when provoked.

"Please, Lydia," she said in tones meant to mollify, "do let us cry peace between us. I've said I am sorry for the upset, although I am naturally most happy to learn of it, if Marcus plans to wed. I misdoubt it is to anyone I've met, but I would be glad if you could tell me more about his intended."

"Such stuff, Sister!" Lydia sneered. "Do you expect me to believe that you knew nothing about it? Though one might naturally regret seeing the Kinsworth name die out, I *had* hoped, or rather, what I mean is . . ." Her voice trailed into uncertainty; Lydia then seemed to remarshal her thoughts. "But that is nothing to the point, Susan. What I want to know is why you insist on this pretence of not knowing about Marcus's intention to marry? And I won't be tricked into accepting any *crammers*, I do assure you! *I* was told only that his decision was made, so it is obvious to me that *you* are the one not giving out the whole!"

"Indeed," Susan interposed softly, "I know nothing more than what you've just told me, for I haven't seen

Marcus since he supped here on Boxing Day." Then, in a voice softer still, Susan continued in a tone reminiscent of Marcus's warning notes heard less than an hour earlier. "And do not even think to question my word, for you know that I do not tell lies," she cautioned.

"I know nothing of the kind!" Lydia recklessly screeched. "I am convinced you knew all about it; in fact, I think you have used your influence to convince Marcus to take this way to disinherit my son. You have masked behind your quiet ways and your crippled leg one time too many, I say!"

The utter unfairness of the indictment was too much for Lady Susan this day. It was unbearable that she should be so blamed! At the age of thirteen while mastering the sidesaddle, she had been thrown from her horse and had sustained a bad break, leaving the bones in her leg ill-knit, though the physician in attendance had done his best at the time. The pain had ceased after many unpleasant months, and she quite disregarded her injury in the ordinary way, unless somehow reminded as she had twice been today. Since she knew herself not prone to complaint—*never* did she try to take shelter in her infirmity—Susan concluded that her sister's accusation was made from plain spite.

"Lydia, really you do go too far," she said carefully, her tolerance pushed to the limit. "I will surely not stay where I am accounted nothing more than a liar or an encumbrance."

Lydia, however, was too caught up in her own perceived wrongs to heed the warning. Thoughtlessly, she indulged her rage. "Well, then, let me tell it to your face that I see you as both—a petty liar and a clumsy, worthless cripple!"

"But, Lydia, I've told you I did not know Marcus's plans—"

"Oh, yes, you did!" Lydia shrieked, sounding much like a headstrong child. "You did. You *did!*"

Susan started, shocked by the outburst. Was this really her life? All of these years, living with people who used her good nature, but who did not truly know her at all? Of course, she understood that her sister was speaking in anger; she wanted someone to blame after Marcus's scold and had turned on an ever-present, convenient "Auntie Sue." But the injustice of Lydia's denying her honest word, of accusing her of playing for sympathy, was more than Susan could bear.

"Very well." She spoke quietly. "I can manage to be gone on the morrow. There is no need to put yourself into such a taking, when the remedy for us both is so simple."

Though spoken on the moment, Susan suddenly realized that the words she pronounced caused her to feel a sensation of such phenomenal lightness that she thought she could float with the clouds. In dawning comprehension, she discovered that she desperately wanted to leave this house, along with all of its clamoring, self-indulgent inhabitants.

And she just might do it at that!

She stood up quickly and made to quit the room. Her mind more than half made up, she wanted to get out and away before prudence sapped her nerve. "Farewell then, Lydia," she managed to say coolly. "You will understand if I don't feel much like joining the family for supper tonight, but I'll take my leave of the children before their bedtime. I shall be off at first light tomorrow."

Oh, how she rued the uneven footsteps that seemed to so impair the dignity of her departure! She wished she could move with more elegance, with more an air of control. As it was, she could only be glad that Lydia said not a word as the door closed between them, although Susan did not turn around to look.

Had she done so, she might have enjoyed witnessing her elder sister's look of gaping, disbelieving surprise.

Once in her room, Susan rapidly assessed her belongings with a critical eye. She called for a housemaid, making arrangements to put most of her things in temporary storage after deciding it best to carry only the one portmanteau. She also requested that a hired hack await her at seven o'clock the next morning.

The maid bobbed a curtsy at the receipt of these orders, before rushing from the room to apprise all belowstairs that Lady Susan was taking her freedom at last!

While delving into the drawers of her scuffed wooden clothes press, Susan's triumph-gained momentum suddenly flagged. She was struck by the sheer audacity of what she had done. She straightened and reached for the back of a chair as her knees grew quite wobbly and weak. *Gloriful heavens!* she marvelled. With such little money, just where did she plan to go?

She had tried to merit her place in Lord Cheeves' home by quietly ordering his house and giving his children their lessons. Gilbert, of course, had studied under his own tutor, though she'd many times assisted her nephew with a difficult exercise. But Gilbert was now a young man with bachelor lodgings, so she could not like to intrude there. While as for her brother, Marcus had a home where everything already ran with great smoothness; moreover, she didn't know Marcus terribly well. The three years that separated their ages weren't so very many, she knew, but their lives were quite different, making her brother practically a stranger to her.

She really could not go through with it! This whole thing was but a tempest in a teapot! She must go at once and beg Lydia's forgiveness, for surely her sister had not meant to wound her so deeply.

Before she could make a move, however, Susan's innate honesty required she admit the truth. Such maliciousness could not be reasonably excused. The barbs flung her way were not always careless, and her continued presence could only encourage more of the same. Had she a choice, though? With almost no funds at hand, she could not keep herself for long: possibly a week, no more than two.

As first-born, Lydia had claimed all of their mother's jewelry many years before, and Susan had been disinclined to argue when the items had seemed so vastly important to her sister. Marcus had been too young at the time to note and protest the injustice in such a non-division of property, so that now, Susan had nothing to take to the moneylenders to help carry her over until her finances were renewed next quarter-day. Then she would be able to set up her own establishment, perhaps in Margate, or Leamington, or some other smaller resort, a place with a well-stocked lending library and just such quiet society as she had always preferred. Certainly, she had been in caps long enough that propriety would not be offended.

Not that Marcus would begrudge a first request for an advance on her portion of their father's estate, should she ask it. Susan knew enough of her brother to know that he was a fair man, one who would give her whatever she asked for as soon as the request was made. And yet, the idea of petitioning Marcus was particularly repugnant. She would not have him know that still others of his kinsmen were incapable of managing their affairs. Not even Lydia suspected how many hundreds of pounds a doting aunt had given Gilbert over the last months, nor did Susan think that such knowledge would have made any difference, did she know. Lydia would still have berated her sister for not having more to give, though Lady Cheeves never so stinted herself.

Susan slackened her grip on the chair back. It occurred to her that rather than give her the money to set up on her own, Marcus was more likely to insist she remove to his house. He would take her in out of pity, the same as Lydia seemed to have done. Like Lydia, too, he might well resent the intrusion, though Susan expected Marcus had far better manners than to ever show his annoyance.

The thought of being *tolerated* pleased Susan no better than the idea of remaining where she was. She would just have to make do until next payment day.

Or seek employment? a little voice in her mind asked slyly.

"But, of course," Susan whispered in answer, a tiny smile curving her lips. "Why, I could give instruction in music, become a governess, or provide companionship to some lovely old lady. There's no need for me to hang on to anyone's sleeve!"

With a rare burst of exhilaration, Susan spontaneously

twirled round the room. It must be admitted that it was done somewhat clumsily, but she was aware only of a strengthening of a certain euphoric feeling that had been steadily building since making her momentous decision to leave. The opportunity for adventure—her first!—was entirely too precious to lose. Susan set about packing with her enthusiasm renewed.

Chapter Three

"We've arrived. At last!" breathed out the golden-haired traveller, blue-green eyes wide at the sight of the countless carriages, surging hordes of humanity, and block after bewildering block of burgeoning buildings. London in this year of 1814 could boast over a million inhabitants. But as to that, Miss Rachel Doune was easily convinced that she must be seeing at least twice that many. After eleven days of continuous and unexpectedly arduous travel, Rachel and her two loyal servants were finally entering the city's West End.

It was rather late in the afternoon, overcast and gray, but not raining as it had done every day since the start of their journey. Nevertheless, they were all of them still suffering varying degrees of discomfort: Mrs. Tully, Rachel's middle-aged maid, due to a squall-ridden and singularly unpleasant voyage in which the belowdecks' lurchings had left her clinging to her bunk in nausea for days on end, an experience from which the faithful abigail was not quite recovered; Duncan, their Scots coachman, upon finding that the subsequent two-day coach drive across the south of England had stretched into five because of a relentless, slogging rain which left him soaked and somewhat less than his usual, stoic self; and Rachel, both the least and the most of them all, suffering no physical bad effects from their trip, but anxiously chafing at each new delay brought by the untoward weather. She worried about her grandfather so many miles behind, and she worried nearly as much about whatever lay just a short distance ahead. Until, that is, the actuality of Town gave her new life.

Their destination was Bruton Place, a short street just off Berkeley Square. However, even with the help of the postboys, Duncan couldn't seem to find the right turning. The fashionable western section of the city was like some great house vine gone mad, the area sprouting in small parks, arcades, and shops without end. Worse, the thoroughfares seethed with horses under saddle, swarmed with sprightly pedestrians, and churned with every type and variety of chariot and dray that could possibly be imagined.

But Rachel was too intrigued by the new sights and sounds to be immediately concerned at the added delay. It hardly seemed of moment when so many new excitements and wonders spread before her eyes. She all but hung out of her window so as not to miss a thing.

As she sat, facing forward, one carriage in particular caught her eye as it approached. It being an unprepossessing equipage, painted all over black and drawn by two horses of negligible breeding, Rachel remarked something rather interestingly furtive-looking about the vehicle's driver. As they passed it by on the crowded street, she craned her neck to better observe the sight, noting as she did so that its black interior shades were drawn, disallowing her view of any occupants within.

Then she heard it, almost as if she'd known to expect something of the sort. A thin, desperate-sounding scream came from behind the closed curtains of the opposing carriage.

"Duncan, stop!" Rachel called up to the box without the least hesitation. "Turn us around and catch up with the carriage we just passed!"

Accustomed to following Miss Doune's orders, Duncan instantly began wheeling their big, rented berlin around, using a fortuitous gap he spotted in the flow of traffic. But as luck would have it, at just that same moment, a fast-

40

moving curricle, drawn by two high-mettled creams, moved to enter the exact same space from a side street, driven by a smartly dressed man of obvious means. There seemed no way this side of heaven that a collision could be avoided.

Duncan fought to control his hired foursome in hopes of at least minimizing some of the inevitable damage. Still, he felt himself fortunate, indeed, *privileged*, when he witnessed the other driver exhibiting such a skill with the ribbons as was but rarely ever seen.

With the phenomenal dexterity of a true virtuoso, the driver of the smaller two-wheeled carriage neatly pulled his bloods to an orderly halt off to one side, managing to sidestep the ensuing melee, wherein an ale wagon tipped and shed its load of flat wooden kegs which rolled and spilled out every which way onto the pavement. Several of the casks burst into frothy clouds of fragrant white foam, all but hiding the cobblestones across the width of the street, as, simultaneously, a tilbury carrying two gentlemen came to grief against the berlin's front axle hub, adding greatly to the chaos.

The curricle's driver made the single, calm exception in the cries of "Whoa! Watch it there! Watch it!" resounding from every driver on the street. Indeed, the curricle experienced not so much as a single scratched spoke.

Poor Duncan did not fare half so well amidst this confusion. His horses lunged and reared in their soon-tangled harness, emitting excited squeals and snorts that could be heard even above the exhortations of those enthusiastically vocal bystanders that seemed always to be present for such incidents. One of Duncan's leaders plunged his leg over the traces, the other nearly went down, while his wheelers backed and sidled and rolled their eyes, threatening to bolt at the first opportunity presented. His postboys scrambled to safety, too frightened to be of real use.

If not for the help of the other driver, the Scots coachman might never have got his nags under any sort of control. The stranger sent his tiger, a small groom dressed in immaculate livery, to his own horses' heads with a simple gesture. Wasting no time whatsoever, he then dashed across the street to grab the bits of Duncan's leaders, pulling them forcefully into submission. Soon, the gentleman's low, deep-voiced croon had the job horses quieted and the berlin standing still.

Put in mind of the jostling his two passengers must have suffered, Duncan set the brake and let go his reins, scrabbling down from his seat to hurry round to the curved door of the coach. Just as he reached it, however, Miss Doune threw back the panelled door and jumped down, without even waiting for the steps to be lowered.

She made a quick survey of their predicament—and a sorry one it was—noting that they were wheel-locked with the tilbury, and that minutes would be wasted in relieving the situation. Having been a spectator to the accomplished maneuvers of the curricle's well-dressed driver, she had no qualms in addressing the Fashionable Unknown.

"You, sir! You must take me at once to catch up with the coach we were trying to reach. It's a matter of the utmost importance!" Without further ado, she then darted across the street, stepping nimbly around the spirituous puddles and kegs littering her path, reaching the sporting vehicle virtually unhindered. She climbed lithely up to its high seat unassisted.

Thus addressed, but thinking the matter most urgent, the owner of the curricle handed Duncan back the now-gathered reins to the rented team. Motioning to his tiger to resume position, the gentleman quickly joined Rachel and took his creams into hand, at once starting them through the cluttered street at a smart clip, skillfully avoiding the assorted hazards.

"Describe the coach we must find, Miss . . . ?"

"Doune," she supplied, scanning the traffic before them. "It's a black brougham with the curtains drawn, and there are red scrollwork designs on the rear luggage cover."

While he maneuvered through the traffic, his eyes keenly focused, Rachel's new-found assistant wondered briefly at what manner of young person it was who would so boldly appropriate a seat in his curricle. His was not a vehicle meant for the taking, after all! For no matter how pressing her business, such behavior from a female was altogether shocking—almost as shocking as the fact that he'd seen none but servants in her train. In truth, there was only one kind of woman who would dare to careen the streets in such harum-scarum fashion, only one type of woman he knew of. And, after paying due heed to Miss Doune's obvious attributes, he bethought himself more than willing to offer his aid. Who could know what else her acquaintance might bring?

But before he could frame a question to clarify the young woman's status, Miss Doune spotted their quarry. "There, just in front of that donkey cart," she crowed eagerly, pointing out the way. "Oh! Do you happen to have with you a pistol, by chance?"

Wholly startled, the curricle's driver pulled back on his reins, hard. He spun around to stare in amazement at the young woman seated beside him. "Do I have a . . . a *what!*" With a look of sheer incredulity, he leaned back in his seat to make a more thorough examination of his uninvited passenger!

He'd been too taken up with the exigencies of the moment to have been very particular before, but the sight that now met his eyes proved even more disarming. He was quite distracted, in fact. An honest man, he had to modify his initial appraisal to conclude that he beheld not merely a Diamond, but a Diamond of the very First Water. Eyes of a green that was not quite blue, framed by long, long, dark lashes—these things caught and held his attention. Flawless skin, seen close up, showed peach tints at high cheekbones, beautifully positioned above full, coral red lips, golden blond hair. . . .

Loud curses at the obstruction came from a wagon behind them, bringing the gentleman back to the present with a snap. He ruthlessly squelched any further reverie, forcing himself to the matter at hand. "And just exactly what do you require with a pistol?" came his deep-pitched notes as he started up his team once again. "Would you also be so kind as to satisfy my curiosity, Miss, er, Doune, and tell me precisely who it is that we pursue? And why?"

Had she more experience, Rachel might have taken greater notice of the softening in his voice and, thus, been warned that her accomplice had begun to rethink the wisdom of their entire undertaking. She was too disconcerted by the close scrutiny to which she'd just been subjected, making her aware of the intimacy of sitting on a high, narrow seat, so *comfortably* near to a handsome, dark-haired stranger. As it was, she paid no heed to the gentleman's suddenly speculative look.

"There's a woman in some trouble in that carriage," she managed, waving toward the brougham which was just turning the corner up ahead, "and we are on the way to her assistance." The warmth radiated by his shoulder then served to set her to urging, "And, please, do hurry lest we lose them in this crowd!"

Given to understand that his passenger knew the particular occupants of the vehicle they followed, Rachel's driver pushed his suspicions aside and showed no further hesitation in giving chase. Using that same dexterity with the ribbons as had earlier inclined Rachel to insist on his involvement in this venture, he soon caught up with the black coach.

As they approached the near side of the brougham, it did indeed look a sinister sight with its seamed leather curtains drawn shut, and its driver a hunched figure in a black woolen tricorn pulled low over his face. Forcing the larger vehicle to the curb by a deft movement of his team, Rachel's companion may have had a premonition similar to her earlier one, for he reached under his seat and tossed his tiger a brass-headed cane. He then leaped to the ground, wrenched open the door to the silent coach, and beckoned the occupants to exit. "Out," he demanded with authority.

A beefy man tumbled out first, his neckcloth and jacket awry, and Rachel noted that he had at some time become separated from his hat. She watched as the man first peered up at his unarmed assailant, then dismissively took note of the liveried tiger holding the creams. Finally, he swung his gaze around toward Rachel on the curricle's seat. He looked for all the world like a fat goose studying a scattering of fresh corn, she thought.

"Tynsdale," the bare-headed man gleefully responded to his blunt treatment, causing Rachel's eyes to widen with surprise. "I see you've a little poplolly of your own, heh-heh! Were you thinking to trade?" His gaze returned avidly to Rachel's shapely figure outlined against the gray, fading sky. "Why, I have no objection to that—none at all!" he chortled. "Come down here, girlie, come down and let's have a look at you, then."

Horrified by what was implied, for Rachel was wise in the ways of the world, she was nonetheless too shocked to make protest at the man's vile assumption. She resolutely remained firm in her seat, gripping the side rail tightly while bracing her toes against the mud guard at her feet. She was not about to allow herself to be intimidated by one such as this. Carefully steadying her voice, she called down a request to have a word with his other, as yet unseen passenger. To her further astonishment, the disheveled man readily agreed, allowing a tiny girl to emerge from the coach.

Rachel judged the little maid to be scarcely into her teens, of ten years, plus three or possibly four. She was dressed in a faded dimity of ill-fitting cut, black worsted stockings, much darned, and heavy old brogues that were cracked and broken with use. Beneath her large mobcap, ugly red blotches marred her tear-streaked cheeks as she ran to Rachel as though to salvation.

"Please, mum, don't let 'im take me!" she cried. "I only sweeps up the floors and tote slops from that 'ouse; nothin' else, an' I tell you true. This 'ere gentlemun thinks me a 'ore—but I'm not, I swear!—an' I don't never want to be neither. But 'e won't listen to me, mum. Please, please help me!" she pleaded in the gathering twilight.

If Marcus Kinsworth, better known as Lord Tynsdale, had at first concluded that Rachel must be acquainted with Lord Ripley's victim, or perhaps with the baron himself, he now must understand that such was not the case. It was apparent that Miss Doune had no previous experience of either. And, for some unaccountable reason, he was enormously glad this was so. He returned his attention to the baron.

"Lord Ripley?" His soft question broke through the dimness of the cloudy, late afternoon. "It appears that my guest is uninterested in your invitation, and your companion seems likewise reluctant to continue in your company. You will not mind it, then, if we replace your escort?"

The older man blustered and denied any mistake, grabbing for a hold on the slight little maid. A grip of iron took his arm instead, and the baron found himself shoved back forcefully against the side of his scuffed black carriage and every ounce of breath knocked from his lungs. Lord Ripley bravely croaked to his driver to lend assistance, yet, before that worthy could gather his wits, Lord Tynsdale had moved even faster.

Quick as thought, the marquis' tiger tossed the brass-topped cane into his master's awaiting and outstretched hand. With a practiced twist of the wrist, a gleaming rapier appeared, which Lord Tynsdale applied gently to his opponent's pained and still-heaving chest. Lord Ripley's driver needed no further warning, sure that if he moved an inch, he would see his master promptly affixed to his very own carriage—likely in a somewhat messy fashion at that!

"I think you will have to seek amusement elsewhere, Lord Ripley," the marquis rumbled through the waning light. A sweetly amused smile followed this. He added, "The ladies do seem rather set upon placing themselves in my care, and so, of course, I must abide by their wishes. Do you not agree, my dear sir?"

Lord Ripley momentarily ceased his struggles for air, his eyes dropping to the deadly slim blade pressed just below his mussed cravat. He gave an assenting jerk of his head.

"Allow me to give you good evening, then," said Lord Tynsdale with quiet finality.

The marquis turned abruptly and tossed the little servant girl up with Rachel, quickly moving around to the other side of the curricle to take up the reins. The tiger hopped to his customary perch, and as Marcus adjured the horses to make their return, they passed Lord Ripley, wheezing and gasping in helpless frustration.

Rachel took the still-shocked and sobbing girl onto her lap. Though not above average in size herself, and the petite maidservant was very much smaller, Rachel found that the seating brought her again into close contact with her driver. Her awareness of him was unwilling, but conscious nonetheless.

This time, it was a hard-muscled leg that held her attention, pressed tightly as it was against the length of her own. The single seat of the curricle was designed to barely hold two people, so that in such close confines, it was impossible for her not to notice the union. But Rachel needed whatever support she could garner against the jogs and jolts as the curricle rolled over the cobblestone street. Turning her thoughts away from the disturbing sensation, she braced her charge with one arm and held fast to the seat rail with the other.

After making less than a block, Lord Tynsdale seemed to realize the precariousness of his passengers' positions, for he slowed his team to a walk, reducing the chance that they should become dislodged. Rachel could not but appreciate his thoughtfulness and so smiled her thanks across at him, never realizing that her open smile, combined with her earlier intrepidity, served to revive her driver's suspicions regarding her station in life. How should she have known that in England, at least, the delicately nurtured female was expected to have long since given way to a severe attack of hysterics? How could she have suspected that her dispatch and calm in a difficult situation—qualities she ordinarily accepted with pride—were the very virtues that now condemned her?

The return trip was accomplished in short order. Soon

enough, they drew up alongside the heavy travelling coach where Rachel's servants anxiously awaited; the hired horses stood thankfully calm in their traces with the postillions chatting unconcernedly at their heads. The ale cart was nowhere in evidence, with only the fumes from its leavings tainting the air with a reminder of the day's earlier disaster. It seemed to all as if they had been separated for hours, when, in fact, they'd never been more than a few streets apart.

Rachel handed her prize out of the curricle. She then accepted the stranger's help as she herself moved to climb down from the high, button-tufted seat, feeling remarkably relieved at the opportunity to step away from the unsettling physicality of the gentleman's presence. Inexplicably, she felt further discomfited to notice that the bustling traffic of just minutes ago had disappeared with the end of the business day. She hustled the little maid over to the berlin where her abigail could assist her in calming the overwrought girl, wanting for a bit of calming herself. Mrs. Tully at once added a volume of concerned cluckings to Rachel's more soothing tones.

While they were about this task, Duncan apparently was busy at a task of his own, taking the measure of the man his mistress had brought into her toils. "Miss Rachel," he awkwardly interrupted, "just who be this *Tighearna* ye've pulled under yer banner? 'Tis an ill-omened thing, I'm thinkin'."

Mrs. Tully ceased her fussing, and she and Rachel peered through the gathering darkness to see who it was that Duncan had so respectfully called a chieftain in his native Gaelic.

The gentleman stood in a posture of easy repose, leaning lightly against the curricle. He was a tall man in a high-crowned beaver hat with a deep, curly brim that dipped low, front and back, his hat positioned exactly above dark eyes. Beneath his beautifully shaped jaw rested a fine, white muslin neckcloth, intricately starched and tied, the precise folds lying undisturbed by his earlier exertions. His drab driving coat sported no coachman's-

48

style series of descending capes, but was, instead, a luxurious single-fall cloak, thrown back like some regal ceremonial robe to frame thick, broad shoulders. Taller than Duncan's solid six-foot length, the gentleman was yet lean of hip, and Rachel's eyes lingered along his heavily muscled, leather-encased thighs.

Looking back to the gentleman's now-hooded eyes, Rachel was glad for the late hour and the cloudiness, which she most fervently hoped hid the color she could feel creeping into her cheeks. Why on earth she should suddenly be fascinated by a man's body, she just could not understand! She forced her thoughts into order and boldly stepped forward, intending to shake the man's hand in proper thanks for his timely assistance. She prepared to remove her right glove to that purpose.

Before she could do so, however, the curricle's owner took her gloved fingers into his own. Gently, he turned her hand palm upward. With a bow that impressed her as incredibly graceful when accomplished by a man of his size, he made his salutation. "The Marquis of Tynsdale, ever at your service, Miss Doune," he murmured in a deep, rumbling voice.

Warm lips burned the soft, sensitive skin exposed between glove and sleeve cuff. A tingling vibration seemed instantly to shoot along Rachel's arm to a place deep inside her chest, making her feel disoriented and strange. Quite sensibly, however, she decided that this odd sensation must be due to the realization that she'd unthinkingly taken an English peer under command. She'd begun to suspect that the gentleman was of the nobility when he had addressed the other miscreant lord by name; still, she was not such a ninny as to allow herself to be overly upset by the elevated company. When he finally released her hand, she accepted its return as if nothing untoward had occurred.

"Your servant, my lord," she said steadily, dipping a curtsy right down to the pavement of the now-deserted street. "Permit me to offer my gratitude for your help in rescuing this unfortunate maid—" she nodded at the child being helped into her coach—"indeed, we are in your debt." Concluding that her speech sounded rather too stilted, too cold, after all the trouble he'd been set to, she added more sincerely, "Truly, you have been more than kind, and I won't have you think your efforts are unappreciated. You've only to tell me how I might repay you. I place myself at your disposal, my lord."

For perhaps the first time in his life, Marcus Kinsworth permitted his immediate desires to cloud his better reasoning. Ignoring the possibility that a respectable young woman might travel with only a common maidservant in attendance because of circumstances unknown to him, and recalling how Miss Doune had not denied Lord Ripley's presumptions as would any well-born lady of his acquaintance, Marcus instead chose to read his own wishes into his understanding of Rachel's words. In slow, velvety tones, he offered, "Certainly we can come to some arrangement that will relieve you of any supposed debt, Miss Doune, and one which will undoubtedly satisfy us both in the process. That is, if you think you might find yourself agreeable?"

With the day's light all but gone, Rachel could not quite read his lordship's expression. Nonetheless, she was made wary by his suggestive intonation, following as it did after his too-personal kiss on her wrist. She felt confident, though, that customs here could not be so very different from those of her homeland—*or could they?*

Uncertain, she politely inquired, "And just how, my lord, may I discharge my obligation?"

For answer, his lordship seemed to consider it best to demonstrate his meaning. Without warning, Rachel found herself pulled tight against his chest . . . as he bent his head, finding her lips!

Shocked into immobility by the unexpected onslaught, Rachel did not at first resist. Ages-old instinct stilled her as firm lips met her own in a kiss that could not be described as gentle, but which soon changed and softened to become something very much warmer, bringing with it the most surprising response. Without thought, she gave herself up to the powerfully whirling pool of emotion which swirled up and through her, her senses reaching out for the new pleasure they'd found. An eternity later, when he raised his head with a questioning lift of his brow, she too raised her head—to stare at him with the purest incredulity!

She couldn't know it, but in the dark, she simply looked expectant, as if she were waiting for him to speak further. In a voice low and deep, resonating softly through the shadows, he reassured her. "I intend that your least wish shall have the utmost priority in our arrangement, Miss Dourie. You will have the advantage of me wherever possible. So, may we proceed to your address where we might discuss the requirements in comfort and, ah—" he looked over her head at the occupied servants behind her— "some privacy?"

For several seconds more, Rachel merely stared. Her every effort was required to first master her shaken senses, to next comprehend his meaning, and then to finally respond. Keeping her voice low, due more to an excess of indignation than for any reasons of discretion, she hissed, "And I, too, believe we can manage something 'advantageous,' my lord! I shall start by arranging never to come into your sight again, as I am sure you will please me, doing us the same service! You . . . you *vicious rakesshame!*" she then exploded.

Belatedly, she turned to see that her servants had been too occupied to have noticed her disgrace. And indeed, the time elapsed must not have been nearly so long as it had seemed, for the postboys were busily arguing over whose cap had been lost in the earlier melee, Mrs. Tully was still inside the coach, comforting the loudly sniffling, young servant girl, while Duncan was busy at lighting the candles within the glass-cased carriage lamps.

With her turning, Rachel completely missed seeing his lordship's look of appalled dismay. When she turned back around to face him, he had erased all signs of reaction.

She glared up at him through the shadows. "And to think," she gritted out, "I came all the way to London just to deal with one such as you. But, and no matter *what*

51

Grampa says, I'll give it all up—every bit of it!—before I choose from amongst your kind."

Before Marcus could think to question this last and altogether intriguing declaration, Rachel whipped about and marched over to her hired coach. She dug in her heels with each step, her clear voice demanding that Duncan see them off without further delay.

With a tug at his cap, the Scots coachman looked over and nodded to the fine lord before signalling to their postboys and mounting to his box. Obediently, he cracked his whip over the job horses' heads.

Neither of Rachel's servants had quite caught the introduction when the gentleman had given his name, but Duncan had seen his mistress when she came storming back to their carriage with her chin up in the air. Now Duncan found himself hoping that the laird had rung a righteous peal over the lassie's head for this afternoon's ramshackle doings. High time, in his opinion, that someone steered Miss Rachel to the rightabout. But since not even Mr. Creagh could easily manage her when she took the bit between her teeth, it was of all things unlikely that his lordship had fared much better.

The proper direction having been earlier supplied by a helpful street lad, they arrived at the Creagh town house without further mishap. A glowing circle of light from the entry lamp seemed to bid the travellers welcome, although it was a greeting that soon proved deceptive. The door was opened by a pinch-faced servant in traditional butler's garb—black cloth coat, black knee breeches, and vertically wide-striped vest—whose countenance did not sweeten a spoonful when Rachel identified their party.

Introducing himself as Jenks, the Bruton Place butler stood blocking the doorway while Rachel advised him that whatever footmen were available would be needed to see their trunks unloaded and safely brought inside. In turn, Jenks informed his new mistress on a lofty sniff that he was capable of seeing to the business, before he finally stepped back a pace to allow her admittance.

His look of disapproval upon the clustered group as

they filtered past him into the house caused Rachel to wonder at such high-handedness. She made no comment though, being entirely too exhausted.

Unnoticed by all, a certain curricle and creams stood at some distance down the street. Silent in the shadowy darkness, with his team quiescent at their bits, the Marquis of Tynsdale sat in wary observation. He couldn't actually hear the exchange between Miss Doune and the butler at the door, but he did observe the servant's rude and disdainful manner. From it, Lord Tynsdale drew certain conclusions.

Plainly, Miss Doune was an unwanted guest, or at least, unwelcome to the resident servants. But since she ultimately was given entry, however grudgingly, it must be by the owner's orders. Now that Marcus considered it, too, hadn't Miss Doune told him the way of it herself? She had come to London to "deal with" a man, as she so euphemistically put it. The master of this house must be the man she had spoken of. That would explain her apparent lack of interest in a liaison with himself, a marquis of at least *some* personal attractions; evidently, Miss Doune had already had a protector when he had made her his offer. She had already committed to another.

Marcus was surprised to feel a sharp pang and an accompanying feeling of loss at this knowledge. He suffered the oddest desire to go up and knock on the now closed door and confront Miss Doune, in hopes she would refute his conjectures. After all, he possibly could be wrong, for in that moment when he had kissed her, he'd thought, just for a moment, that her reluctance stemmed from inexperience and her subsequent anger justly caused.

But, no. The situation was all too obvious. Miss Doune was what she was, condemned by her very own words. It was just as he'd supposed from the first.

Resigned to the truth, Marcus turned his horses back toward his own home. In his disappointment, he did not remark the house number.

Chapter Four

The next morning, Rachel awakened to bright sunshine highlighting a tightly gathered, yellow chintz canopy stretching high over her head. *But really,* she thought muzzily, staring at the rippling fabric, it was not at *all* familiar! She lurched up in confusion before accounting for her location. She then relaxed and plumped the pillows higher behind her. She leaned back to study her new surroundings by morning's light.

Last night, Rachel had been too tired to do more than see to it that a few dresses were hung before she'd tumbled into bed and fallen soundly into sleep. She was pleased to see now that her room was of an agreeable size with a large dressing alcove off to one side and a huge pair of matched armoires set between spaciously wide windows. Otherwise, admittedly, the furnishings were what some would call sparse. A straight-back chair was placed beside her bed, while a washstand stood at an angle in one corner, but there was not a dressing table, nor a rug, nor a single mirror within sight. Rachel thought these omissions most peculiar.

She was particularly concerned to notice that the small fireplace in her room lacked for a screen. Thankfully, no welcoming fire had been lit for her the night before, so there was no immediate danger, but the nearness of the Thames would make some additional warmth occasionally needful, even in the springtime.

At least wood fires weren't used in the city. Rachel thought those were the worst. Sea-coal was the fuel of choice in London, quite possibly coal from her grandfather's mines. But whether it was Creagh coal or not, the mere thought of an unrestricted flame was not to be considered.

In the general way, Rachel had no problem with candlesticks or flambeaux, but open hearths ever caused her heart to pound, her breath to come short, and a nasty panicky feeling to envelope her. Almost as early as she could remember, the sight of unprotected, crackling red flames left her feeling shaken and wholly unnerved. Definitely, her first order as the new mistress of this house would be to have fire screens set firmly into place in front of every hearth.

Thinking back to what dealings she'd had with the house servants the night before, Rachel recalled certain other shortcomings. The butler had acted very much as if she and her party were some sort of intruders, and later, when she'd requested a tray be sent up for her dinner, not only had the food arrived stone-cold, but she doubted it had ever boasted tasty. Perhaps this morning, Mrs. Beekham could explain. Her chaperon had been out when Rachel's party had arrived last evening, so their meeting was postponed until today.

Before Rachel left the comparative comfort of her bed, though, there was one other subject requiring evaluation. Not that Rachel had lost any sleep over yesterday's events—oh, most assuredly *not*—but she would like to arrive at some explanation for the marquis' strange behavior. Lord Tynsdale had seemed so supportive of her efforts against the lecherous baron, but then had himself made her an indecent proposal. Why? He'd shown only concern for the little housemaid's predicament and had acted willing enough in assisting against Lord Ripley's misdeeds, and this, just before he offered Rachel a carte blanche, and in an impossibly deep, seductive voice! Such a change to downright licentiousness could not be rationally explained.

No more could Rachel supply reason for her own unprecedented reactions. Remembrance merely brought her a muddled brain and strange sensations of tingly warmth, which she felt right down to her toes. Sitting up and shoving these same offenders into her slippers, Rachel decided that her response was simply an odd aberration, one unworthy of further analysis. And as for handsome, dark-eyed noblemen, it was undoubtedly just another case of those infernal aristocrats forever trying to take advantage. It was a waste of time to give it more thought, and so, if a worm of cowardice inclined her to gather up her trunks and return at once to Ayrshire, she would certainly not give in to the weakness. Of a surety, the encounter would have meant less than nothing to his lordship; he was not to know that as her very first real kiss, the contact had made a deep impression on her.

So why am I smiling like an idiot? Resolutely, Rachel snatched her mind back to the day ahead.

She would begin by meeting Mrs. Beekham and taking a tour of the house. Since this would be home over the coming weeks, its possibilities needed to be investigated without delay. Whatever changes were required must be ordered, beginning with the matter of fire screens. On this expectant note, Rachel took up her wrapper and went to give the bellpull a tug.

In a very few minutes, she recognized a familiar tattoo on her door, followed by the entry of her maid, who whisked into the room with a freshly ironed dress draped over one arm. Her expression put Rachel in mind of yesterday's thunderclouds, looking ready to burst.

Mrs. Tully, in typical Gaelic tradition, apparently felt free to speak her mind. "You'll not tell me I'm to be talked down to such as I have been this very morning, Miss Rachel," she declared in obvious resentment. "Hoity-toity London lot. They refused me my breakfast, saying I wasn't to eat until you had done. And then, that purse-mouthed butler said as how I could be at dusting the back parlor until you were needing me, just as if I wasn't already full busy, what with all your dresses to be unpacked and aired!

It's a bad house you've brought us to, miss, a bad house, I say!" The redoubtable maid fairly swelled in her indignation.

"Yes, yes, Tully," Rachel said soothingly. "I've already noticed that things are done a bit differently here. But, no, you are not to dust any parlors nor have your breakfast delayed. Help me to dress, and I will make things clear with the staff."

Mrs. Tully bobbed her head positively at this, satisfied that Miss Rachel would soon have the situation in hand.

"What do you make of Mrs. Beekham?" Rachel soon asked, changing the subject as she stepped into the newly pressed muslin brought by the obliging abigail. "I've only the solicitor's account of her; in fact, I don't believe I even know her age. Does she seem pleasant?"

Mrs. Tully scowled as she did Rachel's buttons. "Mrs. Beekham? I can't tell you anything on that head, miss. Seems the lady hasn't come down yet, what with her being out so late and all."

"Oh?" Rachel had rather expected that her sponsor would be anxious to look over her new charge, for *her* curiosity was certainly aroused. "Well, no matter, Tully, I daresay we'll meet her soon enough."

Twenty minutes later, Rachel and Mrs. Tully descended the wide front hall. They were greeted by Jenks, who, looking somewhere over Rachel's shoulder, inquired as to how he might be of service. Rachel promptly informed him that inasmuch as he'd not seen fit to introduce the staff in form upon her arrival, and in truth, she'd been too thoroughly fatigued to much care the night before, he was to see to the oversight at once.

"And afterward," she said crisply, not allowing his response, "I will expect you to accompany Mrs. Tully and me on a tour of the house so I can see what changes to make. When we've done, you are to ask Mrs. Beekham if she would be so obliging as to give me a time when she can make herself available."

At her brisk, authoritative tones, Jenks deigned to bow just slightly, disclosing that the house held two housemaids, one footman, Cook, and himself. He went on to say that Mrs. Beekham had been given charge of the domestic arrangements, and that *she* had expressed herself satisfied.

Ignoring this last, Rachel instructed, "Then, please bring everyone forward so that we may begin, Jenks. Oh. Before you do, I had best make a few things plain. Mrs. Tully,"—she nodded at the abigail—"is my personal servant. She will not be assisting anyone but me. Furthermore, she is used to start the day with an early meal, and I expect her to be accommodated."

Rachel regretted that she dared not take the time to break her own fast just yet, but if she was to set this house in order, she would have to leave personal needs till later. Grandfather had taught her to always attend important matters first, undeterred by lesser distractions.

"Is that understood?" she prodded when the butler remained silent.

Mr. Jenks sucked in his already-hollow cheeks. He nodded abruptly, then turned to do her bidding.

Rachel stood composed and unmoving while the employees were called in and assembled. However, a strong sense of disgust formed in her mind as they lined before her in the hall. The footman leered in a conspicuous and overbold manner, the housemaids looked slovenly and wore identical sly expressions, and Cook actually smelled like something unwashed! Rachel heaved a deep sigh after acknowledging the introductions. She wished each a good morning before motioning to Jenks to dismiss the lower servants so that they could commence their tour of the property.

Purchased since her mother's death, the town house had been bought furnished by way of an investment. It had been let at a goodly rent for the past several years and, after Rachel's use, would probably be rented again. Rachel was glad to see now that the rooms were generally light and well-proportioned, with every evidence that the previous tenants had taken very good care. The wallpaper looked new, while the hardwood floors showed to be recently varnished. She did observe that the best rugs and tables adorned the rooms of the staff, however, and Mrs. Tully was heard to sniff at this obvious over-extension of privilege.

They did not enter Mrs. Beekham's chamber, of course, but Rachel insisted upon inspecting every other nook and cranny in the building, including even the attic with its narrow dormer windows. There, in one of the smaller compartments set aside for the servants, she found the little mobcapped waif she had rescued the day before.

Rachel had ordered the girl a separate room in which to recover, and she was pleased to see that the young maid was up and about this morning, if still somewhat heavy-eyed. Wearing the same faded dimity of the day before, its ill-fitting folds fairly swallowing her, the girl also suffered a wide, drooping ruffle around her cap that very nearly covered her brow. The sight made Rachel wish that she'd thought to send up a fresh change of clothing.

Saving such concerns for a later time, and wanting to have speech *sans* audience, Rachel sent Tully off to make up for her missed meal. By now, the morning was already half over. She also dismissed the obviously interested Jenks, making sure he closed the door behind him.

Rachel glanced about the room. She noted that the bed was already neatly made, and also saw that with the exception of the cot and a two-drawer, paint-chipped chest of a rather dismal shade of green, the room held not another item of comfort. Compared to the other servants' quarters, the room was positively Spartan.

"I gaive you good day, Flora," she began, having learned the girl's name the prior evening. "May I trust that you slept well?"

"'Deed I did, miss," the little maid replied. "I slept ever so good, and I do thanks yer fer askin'. I never thought to sleep a wink neither, but next I knew it were past sunup. It's sorry I am to be still a bother, and after all yer kindness, too, but I can be out of 'ere in no time, you'll see."

"But is that really what you want?" Rachel asked, dismayed. "To leave here, I mean? Surely, you cannot intend to return to your employer after what nearly happened. Why, I should think you entirely too young for that sort of place . . . that is, if I understand the circumstances of your previous employment."

Flora gave a rueful little shake of her head. The edging on her mobcap quite obscured her vision; with a quick gesture, she pushed it back from her eyes. "Oh, I knows I don't looks it, miss, but I'm a full seventeen a'ready and been on me own fer years. An' I won't be going back to that 'ouse again, fer it were never a job I shoulda take'd from the first." The little maid's brave front wobbled precariously when she added, "Leastways, this 'ere's me only dress and shoes, so there's nothin' for me to go back fer." Rachel caught sight of woe-filled eyes before Flora dejectedly ducked her head.

"Well then, may I suggest you remain here, Flora? At least for the next few weeks while I'm in town. I'm newly come to this address myself," she said encouragingly, "so it would be of great help to me if you would stay and stand my ally, don't you agree?"

At this, Flora looked up with an awed expression. "You can't never mean it, miss? Ooh! I would likes that ever so much, fer it's an angel, you are! I'm stronger than I looks, and I'll work as hard as you *ever* saw, if you'd let me stay fer true." Watery tears, this time of joy, rolled unchecked down the little maid's cheeks—making Rachel glad for the impulse that had brought Flora safe to her home.

"Then, it's settled," she declared. "Dry those eyes and run along, and tell Cook I said she is to serve you your breakfast right away. Oh, and if Jenks—he's the butler—or anyone else should ask, you may say it is by my order that you are not to be given any duties today. You may use the time to familiarize yourself with your new surroundings and to get some more rest."

"Ooh, miss!"

"Now, now. Not another word, Flora. Just give me the best service you're able, and I'll be satisfied." Shooing the tiny maid ahead of her, Rachel followed her down the stairs as far as the second floor. When Flora continued on down to the kitchen, Rachel turned off toward her own bedchamber, thinking to tidy her appearance before meeting with Mrs. Beekham.

Upon entering her room, however, she was immediately reminded of one of its particular shortcomings: the lack of a mirror. Thankfully, Tully had the knack of pinning her heavy gold hair securely, so a few careful top strokes of the brush should be all that was needed to set it to rights.

"Botheration," Rachel next muttered, when she looked down and saw the dust marks imprinted on her skirts, caused by poking into too many places the servants had missed in their cleaning. And if that weren't enough, her stomach rumbled out a complaint that missed meals was severe mistreatment. Her mood a trifle testy, she damped a cloth from the washstand and began carefully brushing away at the spots on her dress.

While she was busy at this task, one of the serving maids came with a message that Duncan requested speech with her at her earliest convenience. Rachel realized that she had not seen her Scots coachman during her survey of the town house, so it was with a sense of foreboding that she promised to come down immediately. She could scarcely believe it when she then sighted a devious smirk on the servant girl's face as she left to deliver her mistress's reply.

Somehow, Rachel was sure, the maid took pleasure in the promise of any new misfortune. "Oh, a plague take the lot!" she swore in growing exasperation.

She finished cleaning her skirts and hurried down to meet Duncan at the hall bench. And indeed, to judge by his look, all was not well with him. Outwardly cheerful, Rachel gave him her best smile and essayed a bright greeting.

But he started right in.

"I'm yer grandfather's man, that I am, Miss Rachel, and ye knoo I'm nae one to fuss. But when the high-nosed butler-fellow takes to ordering me aboot, well, I'm nae here to please Mr. Jenks! I offered to make meself useful howsomever I'm needed, o' course, and sae what does he do? He's had me off since early this morning, scouring the stalls for eels. *Eels*, I say! As if I dinna' know ye'd never eat such great, nasty things!"

Rachel's stomach gave another growl at this juncture, but not, she thought, in anticipation of such fare as Duncan promised.

"And if tha' weren't enow'," continued her dour-visaged protector, "yon shifty-eyed footman dared suggest that what with him bein' such a handsome gillie, would I knoo if ye might be needin' him fer some 'extra' duties. *I* told him to examine this fist tha' I would plant in his phiz while I threw him out on his . . . !" Duncan flushed beet red as he choked back the words that threatened to follow.

"Lass," he finally recovered himself enough to say, "I'll be askin' ye to be on yer guard with that one. Better if ye should send him packin' this verra day!"

Astonished more by the coachman's unprecedented garrulity than by his disclosures, Rachel assured Duncan she would rectify the problem as soon as may be. She sent him off to the kitchen, thinking it likely that he, too, had lacked for an opportunity to feed himself, a sore aggravation to any man. Deciding this idea had definite merit, Rachel hastened down the hallway, intent upon easing her own hunger before some new disaster befell.

Inside the breakfast room, she found Mr. Jenks positioned like some thin black grackle by the sideboard. He said not a word as she came forward; he just stood in his place with a haughty expression while she stepped over to the buffet. Neither did the butler make a move toward assistance when she picked up a plate; Wedgwood-designed and known as "Queen's Ware," the creamy-glazed, basket-patterned dishes had come furnished with the house.

Rachel ignored the lovely tableware, though, deliberately putting the plate back onto the stack with a snap. "Thank you, Jenks, that will be all," she bit out. She clenched her jaw as he left the room, preferring in this instance to be left alone with her meal.

The food displayed, although plentiful, looked to be about as unappetizing an assortment as any Rachel thought she had ever encountered. Vegetables, limp and faded, failed to tempt her to try their flavors despite their attractive containers. One dish held what might have been meat—*perhaps it was those loathsome eels!*—while a matching deep-dish platter contained floating globs of what looked like grease, clinging all along its sides. Even the bread was repugnant, spotted with what was almost certainly mold.

Finally, Rachel took up a plate to hold a portion of stewed preserved pears which did not look too bad, adding to this a slice of judiciously trimmed cheese. She decided to leave the remaining comestibles for some more valorous soul. Seating herself at the table, she made what she could of her repast.

Almost as soon as she was done eating, and it didn't take long, Jenks opened the door from the hallway to let in a rather large woman of perhaps fifty-odd years. Hideously overdressed for the hour, she billowed in wearing a velvet-swagged gown of a dull, mossy green color, much embellished by bunches of grosgrain ribbon and positively *wads* of multicolored lace. Thick pinkish powder covered what was surely a wig, piled high in the style of the last decade, sporting at its apex an artificial bird that looked suspiciously like a macaw.

"Missus Beekham," Jenks announced, respectfully bowing in the newcomer.

The apparition smiled broadly, displaying an incomplete set of teeth. "It's Calpernia, dearie. And I'll just call you Rachel. There's no need for any silly formalities between us, is there? Now, now, don't you get up!" Mrs. Beekham then protested, misapprehending the purpose of Rachel's sudden stiffening. "Just you keep to your seat and I'll be with you in but a moment."

This last was certainly true, as Jenks immediately drew back Mrs. Beekham's chair with a sweeping gesture, everything solicitous in his manner, as he went to prepare a plate with selections from each dish on the board.

"I'm glad to be meeting you at last," Rachel managed politely, repressing a shudder when the disgusting assortment of foods made its way back to the table. "I do regret, ma'am, not having the opportunity of making your acquaintance yesterday evening, when we arrived, but I felt it best to retire early after our long trip." Deliberately, Rachel's next words took on a note of question. "But I must suppose that whatever took you away last night, it was of some importance? Especially since you knew I was momentarily expected."

Mrs. Beekham gave a high, twittering laugh. It was a most surprising sound, coming from someone of her size. "Oh, 'deed it was!" she cried, preening importantly. "For you might know I was engaged to the Theatre-Royal in Covent Garden, and it was everything flattering when I found myself in the most distinguished company! Why, between us, my escort and I knew quite half the personages there!"

With this pronouncement, Mrs. Beekham turned her attention to the large helping of eels Jenks had set out on her plate—for so that mysterious dish turned out to be— with every sign of relish.

Rachel watched in grim fascination as the utensils were employed with exaggeratedly refined motions, all the while Mrs. Beekham chatted about her evening and her plans for further glittering social outings which would, presumably, include her young charge. Sipping sparingly from her none-too-clean water glass, Rachel listened to gushing descriptions of the great ones whom she would soon be privileged to see and the fabulous entertainments London held in store for her. The widow's heavily sprinkled references to Lady *this* or Lord *that* failed to engender much enthusiasm in the listener, however. Her suspicions growing apace, Rachel determined to get to the truth of her companion's exalted connections.

"So, do I understand you correctly? You went to the theater last night and were invited into Lady Knightley's box?" she asked.

"Oh, tee-hee!" Mrs. Beekham laughed. "Did I say that? No, no. Lady Knightley and I aren't yet acquainted to such an extent. But I certainly do know the baroness, for anyone of my discernment would recognize her ladyship, if merely for those priceless diamonds she always wears around her neck. Of course, being new on the town, you have a great deal to learn, dearie, but don't you worry about it. I'll have you right up to snuff in no time!"

This obvious tergiversation sat ill with her employer. "In other words," Rachel said, "it might be more correct to say you have a, er, 'nodding' acquaintance with the baroness, and with the Lords Parington and Harcress, and . . . who was it else you spoke of? Oh, yes, a Lady Bridmonds."

"And a host of others, don't forget!"

"Oh, no, I shan't forget," agreed Rachel dryly. She managed to stifle a natural dislike for Mrs. Beekham's rather horridly pretentious manner, then directed, "That being the case, though, ma'am, would you be good enough to explain just how you thought to gain the invitations you promised for us to go about in Society? But perhaps it is your escort of last night who will actually see the thing done."

Again Mrs. Beekham emitted a high, girlish titter. "Oh, that's rich, it is. Mr. Simpson is one of the city's most highly respected professional men—an apothecary, no less!—but surely you understand, it is the money which will see us admitted. The haut ton are very conscious of the value of money. So, just as soon as I get out the word, I expect we will be quite covered up in requests for our presence. And I must say that I, for one, can hardly wait!"

Dismayed that her grandfather's solicitor had been so taken in as to be gulled by this tuft-hunting woman, Rachel grimly held her own counsel. She, too, realized that her financial prospects were the one thing that might render her acceptable to the Polite World, but she certainly had no wish to puff the facts so blatantly as to give offense to anyone of refined sensibilities. She had no desire to encourage those who might be attracted solely to her purse, those whom Mrs. Beekham would be most likely to encourage.

She willed herself to every outward show of interest as Mrs. Beekham rattled on and on, then rang for the butler when the meal was done. Saying all that was polite to Mrs. Beekham, Rachel excused herself, maintaining that she had a small errand to discharge. She told Jenks to retain a hackney carriage, as she would be leaving with her maid after changing to warmer outdoor clothes.

Mrs. Tully came to assist her in dressing. Before all else, though, Rachel requested to see the day's copy of *The Times*. She had noticed the paper on the entry table when she had come downstairs earlier, but she wondered that she had not seen it since. And only after searching at length did Mrs. Tully locate the desired item; it was discovered in the deserted butler's pantry with its pages scattered and mussed. The abigail gathered them up and smoothed them as best she could, returning to her mistress, flushed with her success.

Rachel eyed the disordered news sheets distrustfully. "Gracious, Tully, what's all this?" she asked, amazed.

Her dainty jaw squared at the maid's explanation, but without making further comment, Rachel resolutely turned her attention to the classified columns on the front page of the daily. Seating herself on one corner of her bed, she studied the advertisements for a moment, then took up a pen to add a few notations to the list of priorities she'd begun on shipboard.

New clothing stood at the top of her list, and farther down were such items as subscribing to the *Gazette* for the social news and a tour of the city, should time permit. Scribbling away, Rachel rearranged the guide.

Time was her greatest enemy. The misadventures that had dogged her steps were costing her precious days. She knew that she must move quickly, or be defeated right from the start.

Depositing the revised list, as well as a supply of coins and bank notes into her reticule, Rachel donned a fresh gown, her most imposing bonnet, and her best fox-trimmed pelisse. She instructed Mrs. Tully that they were off on an errand of some importance: a commission Rachel vowed to complete before the day grew very much older.

Jenks was lingering in the front hallway when they came downstairs, but he did bestir himself sufficiently to call Rachel's attention to a letter as she passed. She easily recognized her grandfather's sharply spiked handwriting, but she waited until she and the abigail were seated in the waiting hackney carriage before attempting to break the wax seals. She also thought it prudent to withhold her instructions to the driver until Jenks had closed the front door, so it was not until the carriage started up that Rachel felt free to read.

A single folded sheet was all therein contained. Ian Creagh's style was always direct and to the point. But as Rachel read through the lines, she felt herself greatly heartened by his words.

"Oh, listen to this, Tully!" she exclaimed some moments later. "Grandfather says here that he is feeling much better and soon expects to be 'victualling in the dining room.' Oh, Tully, is that not of all things wonderful?"

When no immediate answer seemed forthcoming, Rachel looked up to discover that there were other equally wondrous appeals to her maid's attention. The melodious cries of a plethora of street vendors drifted in through their carriage windows.

Catching the meaning of one song in particular, Rachel at once ordered a halt and motioned the singer over, a pieman with his wares stacked high. Selecting two rich-smelling examples of the hawker's generous product, she offered her maid the choice.

"Oh, blessed be!" the good woman exclaimed gratefully. "I'm as near to starving as makes no difference, and not a bite fit to eat since yesterday noontime!"

Ravenously, the two women proceeded to wolf down the purchase, their handkerchiefs held at the ready to keep the delicious drippings at bay. Finishing at about the same time, they relaxed back against the seats in a state of marvelous repletion.

It was not so long after that when they came to the address specified. Rachel thought the old bricked building would be better for having a bit of care, for the sign designating its purpose could certainly profit from a fresh application of paint. On the whole, though, it was most satisfactory with its well-worn front steps and freshly cleaned glass windows. Confident that here her needs would be met, she paid out their driver and included a tip, requesting that he return for them in an hour.

Inside, they found a large reception area fronted by a cluttered desk which was manned by a harassed-looking clerk. Around the room sat and stood men and women of all ages, apparently in patient wait for a summons. Rachel felt encouraged to see so many people on hand, for she was steadfast in her intentions to sustain no delay. She silently wished them well, knowing that her needs would not support them all.

She approached the desk and addressed herself to its occupant, noting as she spoke that the man's face assumed a fixed, slightly idiotic expression. "I am here to engage a companion and some domestic servants," she said quietly, hoping he was more intelligent than his appearance would suggest. Mrs. Tully's jubilation could be felt just behind her, and Rachel had to fight to hide a smile. Then, aware of the attention she must have drawn from those others in the room, Rachel further lowered her voice to add, "And I should like to discuss my requirements in private, if you please." Ever considerate of those less fortunate, she had no wish to cause the supplicants any unnecessary anticipation.

Rachel could not know it, but it was her own dark blond beauty which had rendered the clerk absolutely speechless, thus causing his absurd expression. Her self-contained air and refined speech soon brought him to his senses, however, sending him scurrying away into the building's inner reaches, thinking he knew gentry when he saw it.

Returning almost immediately, the clerk motioned for her to follow him through to the next room. Telling Tully to make herself comfortable in the waiting area, Rachel advanced into a smaller room, housing the owner of the employment registry. The overcome subordinate then bowed himself out, reluctantly closing the door behind him.

The proprietor seemed to Rachel a singularly unctuous man; he bowed too deeply, and she remarked his beady eyes as he assessed the quality of her apparel. "Well, well, my lady!" he cried upon rising. "I understand you are interested in reviewing our applicants. I'm Josiah Potter, your most obedient, and I'm delighted to be of assistance. I know that such a lady as yourself will appreciate our careful selection of prospects, and obliging you is our earnest ambition. Let us start with your name and go on from there, shall we?" He waited for her to seat herself before he sat back down, his pen at the ready and an ingratiating smile on his lips.

Unmoved by such toadying, Rachel quickly disabused Mr. Potter of the supposition that she was of the nobility. She gave him her name and restated the requirements as she had given them to his clerk.

"And what is that address, Miss Doune? For you may know that you can rely upon me to send out only those persons whom I personally recommend."

But Rachel decided she knew nothing of the kind. "No, Mr. Potter, that will not do at all," she said forthrightly, "for I intend to complete my business this afternoon, if not here, then at another agency." Significantly, she pulled out the list of alternate addresses from her reticule.

"But . . . but, Miss Doune! Surely, for a decision of this magnitude, you will want someone in authority to, to—?" Mr. Potter seemed aghast at the implication that any young woman proposed to do her own hiring; more, that she seemed set upon doing it today! But as his eyes took in the meaning of the paper she held, it entered his head that he might just be whistling a commission down the wind. Best he proceed with caution. "Er, that is to say, who am I to bill for this service," he ended weakly.

"Oh, there is no need for any billing, Mr. Potter." Rachel pulled another set of notes from her reticule, this time of the ten-pound variety. Reading his thoughts, Rachel concealed a smile as she intentionally furthered his interest. "My grandfather is Ian Creagh of Ayrshire, you must know, and he has entrusted me with this duty. But perhaps you know of him?"

Totally amazed by this revelation—for who *hadn't* heard of the phenomenally rich Creagh mining properties!—Mr. Potter thanked his stars that he'd not voiced his disapproval. Aloud, he said merely, "Certainly, Miss Doune, to business then! And if you would care to use my office, I shall go out and select those I think suitable before sending them in to you."

Satisfied with this offer, Rachel sat back to await her first interview.

In a very few minutes, a remarkably stout young man peeked inside, a deferential smile dimpling his round, ruddy cheeks. Rachel asked him to come forth and be seated, giving him a short statement of her needs, followed by a more thorough questioning of his background, accomplishments, and ambitions.

In soft country accents, he gave her his name as one Will Slats, and a less likely name Rachel could hardly imagine, and he said as how he'd just come from his home village looking for work. The fourth son of a baker, he told her that times were hard in the county, so feeding an able-bodied, seventeen-year-old son was beyond his father's means. Young Will added this last rather self-consciously.

From the pocket of his smock, he next produced a letter written by the local vicar, attesting to his honesty and willingness to work. Will Slats said he hoped someday to become a gentleman's gentleman, for to be a valet was his idea of reaching the pinnacle of success. His face reddened after his admission; apparently, he realized that she could have little use for such. But he assured her that he was hers to command, as any employment was welcome.

"I own myself glad to hear it," Rachel responded. "Regrettably, I will have no need of your services after June's end, as I've already explained, but I can assure you of obtaining at least some of the training needed to advance in your calling. I expect that my maid, Mrs. Tully, can put you in the way of understanding a good many household matters, and should you prove disposed to learn what she can teach you, I'll be most happy to add my own letter of reference, augmenting that of your vicar's."

To this promise of an employment that would ease his way in moving up in the world, Will Slats promptly agreed. Pledging to render himself useful however he might, he left to wait outside with the abigail, thence to accompany them home.

The second knock at the office door was made by a small-statured, but very handsome woman, followed by a distinguished-looking, yet obviously much older man. Rachel noted that the woman had a sharp, aggressive look about her, while the man merely looked tired. Perhaps it was the weight of the hemp basket he carried by its thick leather straps.

The woman offered her name politely enough, calling herself Mae Fullerton, before introducing her companion as her husband Samuel. At this juncture the couple's eyes happened to meet, and Rachel noticed that there passed between them a look that was undeniably affectionate. Mrs. Fullerton's softening lasted for only the briefest instant, however, before her features hardened back into lines of the greatest severity. Rachel was made curious at the transformation. She set herself to study the woman while Mrs. Fullerton answered her several questions.

Somewhere in her forties, for the afternoon sunlight exposed the first signs of silver that laced its way through jet-black hair, Mrs. Fullerton was not quite five feet in height, while Rachel, not overly tall herself, stood some four inches taller. But Rachel recalled that the woman had moved with a certain elegant precision before being seated. She leaned forward with interest to hear how Mae Hodge-that-was, was used to ride in the horse exhibitions of Astley's famous circus.

Mrs. Fullerton paused after making this revealing statement, as if expecting Rachel to protest. Receiving no response, she continued her descriptions of the attainments of both her husband and herself in a flat voice, at one point, presenting Rachel with a thick stack of laudatory references.

Her husband of three years was two decades older, Rachel learned, his shiny bald pate an attestation of this fact. He bore a dignified paunch, consonant with his years, and Rachel could only be impressed. Mrs. Fullerton said then that they two must work together, and, indeed, she would be happy to serve as a parlor maid or even do scullery work, for lack of other domestic experience. But her husband had for many years been butler to no less than a duke, she finished proudly, so Samuel Fullerton's fine qualifications were the only ones Miss Doune should consider.

After this elevating statement, a slight cough was heard, and Rachel turned to Mr. Fullerton. His first words were in the sonorous tones she'd somehow expected from such a dignified personage, though the information he felt compelled to impart left her feeling rather flustered.

"Mrs. Fullerton has not yet told you all, I'm afraid. For you see, Miss Doune, my Mae has cats," he said.

As Rachel tried to form the question that might lead to her further enlightenment, Mr. Fullerton sighed and raised the leather-strapped, hemp-woven basket onto his knees. He folded back the top, and two triangularly shaped heads emerged. Four round, yellow eyes studied Rachel in smug dispassion.

"They are very good cats, I do assure you, miss," sighed Mr. Fullerton. "But not what some like in their homes."

Rachel began to comprehend the reason for Mrs. Fullerton's defensive attitude. But before she could convey to them that she would have no objection, Mr. Fullerton continued speaking. "These two are our favorites, Miss Doune, but you must needs comprehend the whole. We have three others at our lodgings that must also come with us." Rachel met Mr. Fullerton's eyes, reading resigned acceptance there.

Just then, the two felines gracefully, if unexpectedly, slid out of their enclosure. While one moved unhesitatingly onto Rachel's lap, the other hissed away and, after swivelling its gaze round the room, decided that its place was atop a certain bookcase. A bound ledger had been positioned close to the edge of the topmost shelf, and when the cat's weight was added to this, ledger and cat began a wild tumble to the floor! Howling shrilly in alarm, the animal dug in its hind claws, scoring the shelf wood as it regained a precarious purchase.

Mrs. Fullerton jumped up with a hastily suppressed exclamation, quickly lifting the indignant cat into her arms. Her husband, moving nearly as fast, removed the other from Rachel's lap, making her his deepest apologies. After some little effort, they finally managed to return the errant felines to their bag—Mrs. Fullerton wringing her hands as she examined the damage to the bookcase, digging into her pockets for money to reimburse Mr. Potter.

The couple, taut, and both pale of countenance, began moving toward the door. They thanked Miss Doune for her time. Realizing that they intended to leave for thinking their chances spoiled, Rachel stood and halted their progress.

"Could you be at No. 12 Bruton Place by six this evening?" she interposed. "I am in need of a butler, *and* a housekeeper, I think."

"Miss?"

"Yes! Certainly, Miss Doune!" Mr. Fullerton's voice resonated over his wife's incredulous cry. Mrs. Fullerton's stony look disappeared like magic, and Rachel was happy to shake their hands, welcoming the couple to her employ. To have such a lofty personage as Mr. Samuel Fullerton order her house—more, a couple who were so obviously of tender hearts—made the salary they requested seem but the merest pittance.

The next few knocks for entry brought in aspirants reminiscent of those servants Rachel most wished to be rid of, and so she kept these conferences short, ever mindful of the time. Mrs. Tully came in once, and Rachel gave her a few coins for the returning hack driver, along with a request that he come again after thirty minutes more. At yet another knock, Rachel bade the petitioner to enter, hopeful that this chore would soon be done.

A slight, dark-skinned individual bounced in. He had huge black eyes and shiny white teeth, displayed from ear to ear. "May I please to come in, missy?" he asked musically.

Rachel heard the intriguing thrum of a sitar in his voice. To one of her limited travel experience, it held all the romance of the East.

Bowing with his dark hands held palm-to-palm before his face, he chimed, "Permit me to have the introducing of myself to you, please! I am Sujit Rajenderabhan."

An Indiaman, unquestionably, the little Hindu looked strange in knee breeches and his wide-lapeled coat, although Rachel had little or no idea of his proper native dress. But his smile was contagious, and she found herself answering with a wide grin of her own. She beckoned him to a chair which he quickly refused, pleading that it would not be correct for him to sit while in her presence. "For I am but the most lowly of persons, and undeserving of such honor," he humbly objected.

"That's nonsense, Mr. Rajablee—that is, Rajabla-bla . . . Oh, my goodness, I am so sorry! I seem unable to repeat your name," Rachel finished lamely.

"Not to be concerning yourself unduly, missy! I am indeed bearing an unfortunate appellation, so you must therefore be calling me 'Sujit.' But, no, please be excusing the familiarity, as I am forgetting that the English are so rightfully being offended by our Hindu names. So, I think, 'Roger' will be pleasing me most wonderfully. Please! My old master is calling me 'Roger,' and I am not minding," he rushed on, still with an open smile on his brown face.

"Ah, but I am a Scotswoman, and not English," said Rachel in the face of his verbiage. "It is for you to say how you will be called, after all. Well," she said next, uncertain as to the position he sought, "may I ask what function you wish to fulfill?"

"I am hearing that you are needing a cook, missy," he answered earnestly. "I am happy to be telling you that I have many years serving in that capacity and can shop for the freshest produce, and am getting the very best prices for

75

everything, too. My old master is teaching me himself every day, the giving of the very highest perfection! He is being the second son of a most noble house, so naturally, he is to have only the finest. And for my experience, I am knowing the preparation of such a great many dishes that it will set your mouth to salivating in anticipation of each meal!"

"Why, then, have you left this nabob's employ, Sujit?" She pronounced the name without hesitation.

"Oh, the worst of bad karma, missy," said the little man woefully, "for in his most greatest kindness, my master is bringing me to this country when he is returning here two years ago. He is not a young man, please to understand, and his health is also not so very good. Then my master is dying with his cane rising up over my head as he is instructing me in my correct duties—" the slight figure drooped—"and his very bereaved relatives are not giving me references for their grieving of his death. I am very needful of a house now, for the streets are not safe places in this country."

Rachel frowned in concentration, trying to decipher this strange explanation. With budding perception, a look of horror swept over her face. "You are saying that your employer was *beating* you when he was falling . . . er, when he fell dead?" She frowned at herself for her use of his style of grammar, then frowned still more deeply at his affirmative nod. "But, surely, Sujit," she protested, "you don't mean to say that the daily lessons he gave you were in the form of striking you!"

"Certainly, oh, yes, most certainly!" the little Hindu exclaimed. "Not many masters are taking such trouble to be making sure that I am having the best training. I am truly fortunate that he is giving me so much effort. For my late master many times is telling me that 'pain is the reminder of life,' and I am honored to be coming from a very lively household, indeed." He looked sincerely proud after this enunciation.

Fervently, Rachel regretted that she could not protect this small man from the heartless cruelties of the

Sassenach forever. He made her feel almost maternal; he was so innocent and full of optimism. But she vowed to herself that she would do her part to see to it that no one ever battered him again. In comparison, her own problems seemed suddenly rather small.

She asked if he would be prepared to leave with the others after she'd completed her business, and was reaffirmed in her pledge when his face lit up, tears of gratitude filling his eyes. When he left, Rachel had to wipe the moisture from her own eyes as well, now turned a dark, lake green color with her compassion.

The sycophantic proprietor came in next to inquire if everything was thus far satisfactory, her positive reply causing him to rub his hands together at the thought of his fees. For some reason, he seemed disposed to linger.

Rachel was having none of that. "Mr. Potter," she made the stern reminder, "I've yet to find a companion, and I expect there are several more applicants awaiting a word with me." Rachel pointedly looked at the delicate, chased-gold watch pinned to her pelisse.

"Oh, well, of course, miss. But it seems we may have a slight problem. There are no older women registered with us who are suitable to your needs at the moment. Possibly by tomorrow I can . . . ?" His voice trailed off at the gathering storm he saw in her eyes.

"That will not do at all, sir," she said crisply. "I must insist on the matter being attended without delay." Mulishly she jutted him a look. The thought of retaining the shabby-genteel Calpernia Beekham for a single day longer was not one that Rachel felt herself prepared to face. She had to have someone to play propriety. Obdurate, she insisted, "I reiterate: I am in immediate need of a chaperon, and it is urgent that I find someone today, Mr. Potter."

Worried that Miss Doune would take her business, *all* of her business, elsewhere, Mr. Potter promised to check his files again and look over those outside once more.

Chapter Five

Lady Susan Kinsworth sat quietly in the busy waiting area of the Potter Domestic Registry, fervently wishing she had thought to bring a book along with her . . . and a cushion. After long hours of sitting rigidly upright on a hard wooden chair, she found herself longing to lean back against its dubious support, if only for a moment. But of course, she knew it would not *do*. A lady absolutely never touched the back of her seat, and under these crowded conditions, she must feel herself fortunate just to *have* a seat.

She would still be standing, too, had it not been for that uncommon-looking, dusky-skinned man who had so kindly given up his own place to her. At first, Lady Susan had expressed some reluctance to accept the courtesy, but upon seeing his honest concern, she had thanked him for his offer and taken up her current position. His eager, answering smile had made her doubly glad of her acceptance, for there was something about the dark little man that made her want to please.

Like everyone else in the room, Lady Susan had remarked the beautiful young woman with the honey-blond hair when she had entered the hiring hall with her oh-so-respectable maid, yet she could hardly believe her ears when she'd overheard the young woman's request! A parent or husband always saw to these matters; it was an odd sort of gentlewoman who would present herself at an agency to fulfill her own requirements, after all.

But upon understanding that among other needs, a companion was wanted, Lady Susan forgot all about the conventions. She, like her fellows, wished only to find a position of employment as soon as possible. Otherwise, she would have to impose upon her brother, a thing she could not like. She did wonder, though, which of the young woman's family needed a companion. Her mother? A grandmother? Perhaps an elderly aunt?

That thought sent her into a deep brown study.

She was brought to recall yesterday's strife and the good-byes she had made to her nieces. Edwena had simply given her a dry-eyed stare, seeming to think her aunt's plan to leave a very poor sort of joke at best, while the two younger girls had showed no signs of interest whatever. But she'd hugged them all anyway, begging them to remember their studies, and promising to write to them when she could. While as for her sister, Lydia, neither she nor her husband had cared to see her off.

Lady Susan smothered an unladylike sigh and adjusted the veil of her velvet poke bonnet. Deep-brimmed, its puce-brown color threw a sallow cast over her features, dulling her complexion and the soft brown of her eyes. It, along with the matching pelisse, had been a Christmas gift from Lydia a few years before, but despite cleverly woven black-braid trim embellishments, neither hat nor wrap flattered Susan's subtle coloring. Susan knew it but had no need for fashion, especially when the items served so well against the crisp, unheated air in the hiring hall.

An hour passed, then another. One by one, various applicants were sent away on prospectus while some few more were called into the office presumably to interview with the young gentlewoman. As the minutes crept slowly past, however, Susan felt herself losing hope. She watched interestedly when the dusky-skinned man was called to the inner office, and when he came out, she saw him join the thickset youth beside the young lady's maid on the bench. Obviously, they were of the chosen, and Susan was happy for that much.

When next the office door opened, it was only with the greatest difficulty that Susan kept her composure. The proprietor scanned the room and immediately came forward, apparently bent on approaching *her* seat. Susan felt a strong urge to wipe at her suddenly heated brow; with desperate effort, she forced herself to appear calm and self-possessed.

Mr. Potter motioned for her to follow him. While smoothing her skirts and gathering up her reticule, she worried whether or not her portmanteau would be safe if left behind. The only item of possible value amongst her possessions was a daintily crafted porcelain, depicting a chevalier of the last century, a funny little figurine that Lydia had always derided. But it held fond memories for Susan, having once adorned their mother's dressing table. She hated to risk it.

As if sensing her dilemma, from across the room the dark man who had given over his chair to her earlier twinkled her a look. He motioned to let her know that he would watch over her things. Gratefully, Susan smiled back her thanks.

As she trailed along behind Mr. Potter, Lady Susan was conscious of the many eyes upon her. She so rarely went out in public, that now the slight shuffle in her step embarrassed her. But she forced her shoulders straight and her head level, determined that her halting gait should not be allowed to arouse anyone's pity.

"Miss Worth?" Susan heard herself greeted as she stepped inside the office. "Please come in and sit down. I am Miss Rachel Doune, late of Ayrshire."

Susan started at the use of her newly adopted name. She'd abbreviated her surname, hoping it would not be too much of a falsehood for her conscience to bear. Yet now, she felt dreadfully ashamed at the deception, even one that had seemed so necessary when she had written the particulars on Mr. Potter's application. She consoled herself by remembering that the scandal it would cause if her real name became known was simply not to be thought of.

"Thank you, Miss Doune," Susan replied in her soft voice, moving across the floor to the seat indicated. She was relieved that the younger woman made no comment on her limp; perhaps, if she was lucky, the affliction would not affect her employability.

"Now then, Miss Worth," Miss Doune said briskly. "I see that you've written here that you 'Can have an Undeniable Character upon Request.' Would you care to tell me who it is that approves you so highly? For I must tell you here at the start that since the position is that of companion to myself, I had someone older in mind."

Susan's smooth, fine skin and warm brown hair were as yet unmarked by time, but she certainly had not expected that anyone would consider her young! She took just a moment to digest this unexpected assessment. "I find myself flattered," she finally said, feeling shy, "for I am all of thirty-and-seven years of age, and have not lately considered myself youthful by any measuring. And as for the statement you refer to," she paused once more and drew a deep breath, "I must make my own commendations, actually."

"I beg your pardon? I'm afraid I don't quite understand."

"What I mean," Susan said nervously, "is that only I can confirm my character, since I am unknown for personal reasons. Reasons I am not prepared to disclose. Oh, dear heaven, how very difficult!" Lady Susan flushed and sat up straighter. "Miss Doune, pray forgive me. This is not going at all in the way I had thought. But you see, I have never looked for a situation before and do not know quite how it's done."

Susan was completely nonplussed when lovely, silvery-light laughter rippled out in response. "So! You are telling me that you are here under false pretenses, Miss Worth? But how delightful! For I may then feel free to tell you that I am in something of the same case."

With that, Susan was treated to a very candid description of Miss Doune's concerns in London, her problems with the servants chosen for her, and lastly, her fears about

82

her grandfather's health and about his plans for her future—plans which Miss Doune did not seem to much care for, since she was required to pretend, at least, an interest in a level of society she did not seem overly to admire.

"But it all sounds so exciting," Susan softly marvelled at the end of the telling. "I must say that I am everything impressed that you should even think to do this on your own, Miss Doune. Why, I could never—"

"Oh? Could you not indeed?" This interruption came accompanied by an ironical, challenging gleam in Miss Doune's turquoise-colored eyes.

"Yes, well," Susan prevaricated, "I suppose it is true that I'm out on my own, but, disregarding my past, or even my current circumstances, it is clear that what you are needing most is someone who can help you to get on in Society. And for that," she admitted despondently, "I am not perfectly qualified."

Susan realized that she hated thus sundering her prospects, for she found herself quite drawn by Miss Doune's spirit. And wasn't it odd how their cases held such similarities: both being away from home for the first time, and neither quite welcome to return? Susan hated to lose this small chance for adventure. About those awful servants for instance, they sounded so deliciously vulgar! Susan quite longed to see them for herself.

Something of these yearnings must have shown in her face, for an answering sparkle seemed to grow in Miss Doune's eye. "Then, permit me to tell you, Miss Worth, that you are wrong. Grandfather may have set me the task, but since *I* am the one closest concerned, *I* shall be the one to decide how to get about it. And you, Miss Worth— Susan, if I may—shall come to Bruton Place with me!"

There was no hesitation on Susan's part. "In truth, I too have the feeling that we should suit!" she breathed. "So if you are certain that you want me, Miss Doune—"

"Rachel!"

"Indeed, Rachel, then," Susan agreed modestly. "I can at least lend you the countenance you need, if you will agree to have me. Possibly, too, can I but manage it, I can even gain you an introduction or two."

Whether Miss Doune was impressed by the potential of this statement, Susan could not tell. But she was certain of the Scots beauty's sincerest goodwill from the warmth and air of confident good cheer Miss Doune exuded. Together they went to join the others outside, and after Rachel made arrangements for everyone's fees, the small group left the building.

Squeezing herself into the hackney coach with Tully and three of her newest dependents, Rachel felt herself positively elated by the day's success. Miss Susan Worth was her especial prize, for Rachel felt an immediate affinity there. And while it was obvious from the well-modulated voice and the ladylike demeanor that Miss Worth was a gentlewoman of some background, Rachel did not credit that it would give them any particular entrée. It was more likely that straitened circumstances had long since closed tonnish doors on the gentle spinster, but that was no great matter. Rachel was accustomed to finding a way.

Like her grandsire, Rachel enjoyed outwitting her adversaries. She found herself looking forward to the upcoming confrontation at No. 12, and she would see those odious servants out of her house in a trice. Then she could go to work on her other difficulties, difficulties of no mean order. But, hadn't she routed that horridly presumptuous not-so-noble nobleman of last night?

Rachel's tiny gold timepiece showed five of the clock as the carriage started up. She took the opportunity permitted by the drive to explain to those as yet uninformed in her group something of the situation they would find upon their arrival. Rachel assured everyone that they were themselves in no way involved, but if Will and Sujit would be good enough to assist her by helping the unsatisfactory occupants to remove their possessions from her home, she would be very appreciative. She wanted the thing done as quickly as possible.

They entered the house by way of the front door, and Rachel asked Jenks to assemble the staff, "At once, if you please," as she had an announcement to make. Only Duncan and Little Flora were exempted from the summons. "No, on second thought," Rachel amended, "I will have Duncan by me." She might feel herself brave, but not foolish.

After observing those they were about to replace, the new employees had an inkling of Miss Doune's reasons for wanting them gone. Jenk's show of insolence had Sujit and Will Slats bristling in defense of their new mistress, and the footman young Will was to replace could only be described as *insinuating*. When the maids and Cook had joined with their fellows, the grounds for their dismissal were completely apparent.

Not unexpectedly, at the news of their fate, much outcry ensued among the supplanted employees. The two housemaids began screeching to the rafters about the injustice of the affair, the footman began to make more threatening gestures, while Cook stood right in Rachel's face, yelling and shaking her fist.

Restraining Duncan for the moment, Rachel allowed the uproar to continue for some few minutes before entering the fray with her customary clear tones. "There is nothing for any of you to say in the matter. You forget, this is my house and you have no right to question my ordering of it. Not today, nor at any other time."

Her firm insertion into the contretemps silenced the hall. Rachel continued uncompromisingly. "Now, good people, my coachman and these two men I have brought with me will help you see to your things. When you have finished your packing, come into the library where I will have a full quarter's wages awaiting you, as well as a bonus of two guineas apiece to compensate you for the trouble."

At these words, the indigenous domestics disappeared quicker than a conjurer's scarf! No longer resentful before such generosity, they became most anxious to take themselves off before Miss Doune could change her mind.

Glad of their prompt acceptance, Rachel then asked Susan if she would care to be shown to her room. Expressing herself grateful, Susan followed her employer up the stairs and down the wide second-floor hall.

The passage was not long, as there were only four equal-sized chambers for the family on the second floor. At the end of the hallway, Rachel opened the door into a charming room, outfitted in soft pastels and ivory tones, joined by a dressing area as big as the entire apartment Lady Susan had enjoyed with the Cheeves. Rachel's apology that the room was not really prepared for a guest was met with denial; Susan exclaimed that she had not had such rooms to herself since she was a young girl.

Leaving her new companion to collect herself after her event-filled day, with sure steps, Rachel crossed the hall to Mrs. Beekham's room to knock upon the light-painted door. Receiving permission to enter, she wasted no time in telling the woman that she was making certain changes. She told Mrs. Beekham that although her attendance was no longer needed, she was welcome to wait until morning before removing herself from the town house.

Like the servants, Mrs. Beekham seemed to take exception to Rachel's summary dismissal. Then, at the severance pay named, her powdered face shone with greed. She asserted that she, too, would pack her traps at once, leaving Rachel free to skip downstairs to the small, book-lined library to await her departing crew. In just over an hour, all were off the premises with their promised wages in hand.

The Fullertons arrived even as the last housemaid was making her departure, and in his open way, Will Slats explained to the newly come pair what earlier had occurred. Seeing the too-fine chairs and accessories that had accumulated in the servants' quarters, the Fullertons did not wonder at miss's way of cleaning house.

They met Sujit in the kitchen, elbow-deep in suds, chanting some foreign song as he worked swiftly to set his domain to rights. Mr. Fullerton praised this industry, although thinking that an Indiaman was a strange sort of cook for a proper household. But the slightly built man won Mrs. Fullerton's heart when he dried his hands to stroke and hum to a just-released cat.

The new butler of No. 12 traversed the rooms with staid steps to find Rachel in the library where she was just putting the cash box away. He bowed deeply to inquire of her most immediate needs.

Suddenly feeling tired after all the to-do, and barely suppressing a groan, Rachel pressed her knuckles to the small of her back and said candidly, "Fullerton, I would like nothing so much as an early supper. Do you suppose we could have two trays brought in here? One is for my new companion, Miss Susan Worth, who is still resting, but as soon as she appears, you could ask her to please join me. Oh. And one thing more, Fullerton. Before we are done eating, I think her room may need some freshening . . . she was not earlier expected, you see." So saying, an imp danced gaily in Rachel's odd-colored eyes.

"Very good, miss," the butler replied solemnly. "And may I say that Mrs. Fullerton and I are very happy to be here? We look forward to serving you and will soon have things running smoothly." The faintest trace of commiseration tinged his voice.

"Why, thank you, Fullerton," Rachel acknowledged, touched by his concern. "I shall rely upon you and Mrs. Fullerton completely."

With stately tread, the butler nodded respectfully before he quietly left to effect her commissions.

Returning to the library desk, Rachel sat down to pen a short note to her grandfather. She had written to him last from Bristol and was encouraged by such quick receipt of his response. His familiar spiked handwriting, and his assurances that he was feeling much more the thing, had lessened the worst of her fears; now, in her own neat hand, Rachel wrote to apprise him of the domestic adjustments she had made. She trusted that he would approve.

Some little time later, Susan came in, looking much restored in a silken gown of some uncertain color from which she'd shaken most of the wrinkles. A nicely worked lace collar lay primly around her neck; a cap, also edged in lace, covered most of her brown hair. "Good evening, Miss Doune," she said softly.

Rachel stopped her at once, with a reminder that they were already on a first-name basis. "For I think that we shall be fast friends," the younger miss declared. "Why, as soon as I learn as much about you as I have told you of myself, we will be nothing less than the closest of bosom companions!"

Susan gave a diffident smile and agreed to the terms straightaway.

They sat in companionable silence for a time, both too taken up with their reflections of recent happenings to notice that the only sound in the room was the tick of the mantel clock and the crackling pop-pop of the fire behind the screen—for Rachel had confided her preference for protective coverings to Mrs. Fullerton earlier and was assured by her new housekeeper that henceforward nary a fireplace in the house would ever be left exposed.

After Fullerton placed their plates and napkins, the quiet accord continued into their meal. The butler had seated them across from one another at a walnut refectory table positioned in the library's center, where Sujit contrived to provide them an excellent dinner with what he had found on hand. Rachel was satisfied to see that the water goblets sparkled spotlessly in the glowing light from the oil lamps.

At the meal's completion, Fullerton brought forth a sweet and aromatic malmsey wine. The ladies accepted this offering from their places in the two matching red-leather library chairs, set to either side of the table's narrow width. So comfortable were these last, that both glossy heads began to nod before the last of the wine was consumed.

After checking to see that Susan's room had been readied, Rachel said her good nights. Then, being very much wearied, she turned her steps to her own door. Mrs. Tully already had the covers pulled back invitingly, and

Rachel crawled beneath snug quilts, falling asleep even before her amiably prattling abigail quit the room.

Both Rachel and Susan slept on far into the morning. But the servants arose betimes and were soon bustling about. Fullerton and young Will rearranged the confiscated furnishings from the servants' quarters with Duncan's able assistance, the coachman having decided to wait a few days longer before returning to his master. Good pieces were found for the domestics' rooms, and with due consideration, Fullerton directed that their more grand predecessors be returned to their rightful places on the first and second floors.

Sujit had left quite early to shop for fresh stores, but soon was back in his kitchen preparing all a tasty breakfast. Mrs. Fullerton was nothing less than delighted to have Flora to help her in the morning's tasks, since it was not often that Mae Fullerton had anyone to supervise, much less someone like Flora, who was smaller in inches than herself. As for Mrs. Tully, she was so greatly impressed by "that nice-mannered Miss Worth," that she busied herself in the laundry room, fussing over that lady's few dresses.

When Rachel finally awakened and came downstairs, it was to find Susan just come down and making her morning selections from the sideboard. "A fine day!" Rachel greeted, pleased to note that *The Times* lay beside her own place at the head of the table, having been neatly ironed to prevent ink-smudgings, before being refolded and correctly set by her plate.

"It promises to be warmer, too," said Susan shyly. "Though it will likely be a few weeks yet before we can count on real comfort." After filling her plate, she squeezed the edges of her dish. "And nothing feels so welcome of a morning as a hot plate in one's hands," she added fervently.

"Right you are!" Rachel agreed as she, too, took up a plate.

Fullerton, with the mysterious timing of the truly superior servant, chose this moment to enter with an aromatic urn of steaming hot chocolate. Intrigued by the spicy smell, Rachel and Susan both accepted a sample. A bare hint of cinnamon and something else met their palates in a most pleasurable combination. Before emptying their plates, they refilled their cups twice more, unanimously agreeing to send word to Sujit that his brew should be a regular part of their breakfast thenceforth.

The wiry man popped his head through the door at the compliment, a huge smile spreading whitely across his face. "I am very pleasing that my poor preparations are meeting with the missies' approval," he chirruped. "I am making every endeavor to be following your desires, and I am only hoping that you are continuing to be much satisfied," he finished brightly.

After he left, Susan caught a glimpse of Rachel's barely suppressed grin, bringing laughter bubbling to her lips. Rachel joined in the rising sound, and soon their laughter brought answering smiles from everyone close enough to overhear them.

"He really is an utterly charming man," Rachel finally got out between giggles, "but he is sometimes so hard to understand!" She then described to Susan the interview of the previous day, and her difficulty in comprehending meanings, when Sujit seemed always to prefer speech in the present tense. When she went on to explain the circumstances of his last employment, Susan's eyes grew large with sympathy. Rachel noticed, and was renewed in her confidence that in Miss Worth, she had discovered the perfect companion.

Rachel next turned her attention to her list of priorities which she had brought down with her to breakfast. She extracted the guide from her pocket, and while sipping at the last of her chocolate, she went over each item and explained their sequence to Susan. The older woman nodded approvingly at the enumeration, then added her own recommendation that a subscription to an opera box be included. Rachel quickly saw the sense in this suggestion, convinced that it might prove helpful in expanding their acquaintance.

Of the two, neither had ever had a close friend before. Rachel had enjoyed her grandfather's company, of course, but Tully was forever rattling away and had rarely stopped to listen. Rachel had acquaintances aplenty in Ayrshire, but now that she considered it, no one had been a close friend. Too educated for the common run, and not well-born enough for the elite, she hadn't ever found anyone with whom she felt really comfortable.

For her part, Susan had not shared many interests with her sister over the years, so she merely had held her own counsel. Accordingly, she agreed with Rachel that they should spend the day just resting and getting to know each other better. They looked forward to having a little time together with events at a slower pace, or at least, compared to their several earlier ordeals. The idea of sharing confidences with another woman was pleasing to them both.

They repaired to the small back parlor, where Susan's quiet attention soon had Rachel telling more about her life in Scotland. She spoke of keen debates between Dr. Fordyce and her grandfather, debates which sometimes included herself, of Plumwood House, and even of how her parents had died. She explained this last as being the reason for her grandfather's insistence that she come to London and marry into "the big-wig nobility," as Rachel termed it.

In a day when estates customarily passed through the male line, Susan felt no surprise at hearing of Mr. Creagh's ultimatum. She could not fault his ambitions for his granddaughter; he wanted Rachel to have the best in life. It was unfortunate that Mrs. Beekham had only empty pretensions to offer, but Susan was gratified to have found a place for herself as a result of that disappointment. She put her mind to recalling every society matron she'd met at her sister's over the years.

Rachel went on to impart the tale of Flora's rescue. She took particular delight in recounting the details of Lord

Ripley's frustration and defeat, making Susan glad she had never met the hideous baron. Rachel then described how she had been subsequently insulted by the curricle's driver—also a peer—without mentioning either the kiss he had stolen or his precise title.

Susan somehow sensed that she had not heard the whole, but her nature was not at all prying. She respected the younger girl's reticence without any questions or comment. Rachel's apparent indignation at her treatment by the mysterious aristocrat did, however, serve to remind Susan that it was past time to make her own confession.

Her planned disclosures were delayed, though, when Fullerton discreetly coughed at the doorway, asking if they would care to partake of the luncheon now prepared. Surprised that it could possibly be so late, Rachel and Susan felt like naughty children to have let the morning hours pass them by unnoticed. They returned to the small breakfast room to find a tempting array of cold meats and cheeses awaiting them, as well as several piping hot vegetable dishes and freshly baked breads.

"Delicious!" exclaimed Rachel, nibbling as she filled her plate. "It pays to follow first impressions, I vow. Sujit told me he was a marvelous cook, and I never doubted his word!" she crowed.

Guiltily, Susan agreed, resolving there must be no more delays in exposing her real circumstances to her new employer. She greatly dreaded doing so, fearing that the gallant Scots miss would only feel disgust at her previous prevarications.

But Susan would not shirk what she regarded as her duty. The younger girl had given out her confidences so trustingly, and on such short acquaintance, that Susan felt she could hardly meet such candor by withholding the truth of her own circumstances. She felt confirmed in her opinion that Rachel was deserving of whatever help she herself could offer, and she only regretted that a retiring nature had not given her a more useful acquaintance with the beau monde.

Resolved to make a clean breast of it, Susan brought the

subject around and launched into an account of her misdeeds. She began by apologizing for using a false name and modestly admitted that she bore a 'Lady,' before her first name, since she was the daughter of a marquis. "Not that you should now feel you must stand on ceremony and address me by title," she begged Rachel earnestly.

She went on to explain that while temporarily without funds, she was by no means destitute either. And, like Rachel, she found herself with a good listener, soon even telling about the accident that had left her impaired, revealing more than she intended about the life lived subsequently in her sister's home. Not yet knowing her employer very well, Susan did not attach any particular meaning to Rachel's growing stillness, nor to the slight rise of the Scotswoman's chin.

The meal was forgotten during the long recital. Susan told her story simply, calmly, yet completely. That Susan still loved her sister, Rachel did not doubt, for tears stood and held in the older woman's eyes as she related how she had parted from Lydia.

And is there no outcry at my Lady Susan's disappearance?

Rachel asked this very question, and the spinster aunt with the soft brown eyes flushed with remorse in giving her reply.

"That's my fault, I'm afraid, for my brother Marcus certainly cannot know that I'm away. He sees us so seldom that he would not yet have had occasion to ask after me. As for my sister, Lydia would suppose that I've gone to Marcus, and she will thus try to avoid a meeting with him, hoping to keep a peal from being rung over her head. It will be days, possibly weeks, before I am found out." Susan sighed. "At some point I shall have to notify them of my whereabouts," she added softly, her head bowed, "but I saw no reason for hurry."

Agreeing that she need not rush to make her new address known, Rachel privately was so incensed by the family's neglect, that she longed to tell them all just exactly what she thought of such Turkish treatment! She inwardly shuddered at the idea of this gentle maiden, with but a few pounds in her pocket, going out alone and unprotected to seek a situation of employment.

Susan's trepidations about repulsing her newfound friend were thus proved groundless. In fact, her courage had earned Rachel's respect. And Ian Creagh's granddaughter wasted no time in reassuring her new companion that she was proud of her for making the daring escape, for so Rachel considered the deed. Rachel's admiration was unmistakable as they parted to rest before dressing for dinner.

Alone in her room, the mine owner's granddaughter again went over her companion's revelations. How very sad to be so used by one's own family! She understood that Susan's only brother was a marquis named Marcus Kinsworth, but Rachel wondered at what manner of man it was who could so ignore a sister's hardships? Just what kind of man would leave the afflicted but generous Susan to languish a slave to the eldest?

Rachel mentally recounted the dates she'd been given, and concluded that at the age of thirty-four, he must be either totally heartless or else remarkably dull-witted. That Susan was afraid of him she did not doubt, for although she hadn't spoken of any particular fear, why else would Susan refuse to go to him for help?

"Really," Rachel spoke aloud to herself, "these aristocrats are worse than animals. Not only do they prey on the weak, but on their own, as well!"

At the appointed hour, Rachel and Susan again came together, this time to take their places in the formal dining room, for the very first time. The long walnut table, with its twelve matching chairs, glowed a friendly welcome beneath the pendant chandelier. Rachel sat at the table's head, and Fullerton seated Susan close beside her. He'd moved the other chairs to line the walls, so the room looked more inviting for its two occupants. The polished sideboard, also of walnut, was larger than the one in the breakfast room, and Mrs. Fullerton had placed Holland blooms in a low vase in the center of the sideboard, with a similar arrangement completing the table.

Fullerton supervised Will in serving their meal, another appetizing assortment of dishes from which they took their fill. At the meal's finish, they withdrew to the cozy little parlor behind the library to sit before the fire, built up to ward off the late-spring chill. Soon the coffee was brought in. Both had a preference for that drink after dinner, and the two talked companionably for a time before retiring for the night. The subject of Susan's kinsmen was not reopened.

Chapter Six

The following morning Viscount Cheeves sat down to his breakfast and was presented with a rack of toast, toast which showed distinct signs of having been scraped. Unaccustomed to such defects, his lordship bellowed his disapproval. The offending burnt items were taken away, and he settled himself to enjoy his usual soft-boiled egg. That article was also discovered unfit, being closer described as hard-boiled, and so, with no hesitation, the egg-cup was loudly ordered back to the kitchen, as well. And when his lady wife entered the breakfast parlor shortly afterward, it was to be told in no uncertain terms that she must attend to her house at once, or her husband would be pleased to know the reason why!

Lady Cheeves dared not to tell her lord that an untried under cook was in charge of the kitchens, all because their fine French chef had marched out in a huff the night before. Her husband had often commented with approval on her table, never realizing that it was Susan who planned their fare while Lydia improperly, if understandably, took credit. Instinctively, Lydia knew that her husband would be unsympathetic to consider how she'd reneged on her wifely duties. She *had* told her sister what were the family's preferences, but it was Susan who always had made the arrangements.

Then, last night, Lydia had asked that the menu be changed and that raspberries be served for dessert. But with typical Gallic temper, the *chef de cuisine* had taken insult that she'd not known the fruit was impossibly out of season. He had told madame that Lady Susan would never have made such an *imbécile* mistake. "*C'est très, très stupide!*" he had shouted.

Lydia had become furious at having her authority thus questioned and had not hesitated to remind the enraged man that *she* was in charge. If she wanted raspberries, it was his duty to provide them, and she had demanded that he do so at once.

To be fair to the chef, it must be noted that for these many years he'd taken his direction from the unmarried sister, and that this was the very first time he had spoken more than a few words to the actual mistress of the house. He was more accustomed to Lady Susan's soft persuasions, and such peevishness from Lady Cheeves, combined with the fact that he'd not seen a raise in pay since the youngest daughter was born, pushed him past his limit. He'd received many good offers from other housholds which might better appreciate his talents, and so he'd notified her ladyship.

Now Lydia must find a new cook, when all she wanted to do was to cry. It was so unjust that she should be left to fend for herself; how horridly selfish of Susan to leave after all of these years! And to make matters worse, all three of her daughters had come to her room early this morning, bored, and expecting their mother to amuse them. While prideful in considering herself an indulgent parent, Lydia was not at all used to the reality of having children underfoot. Better they should stay in their wing until sent for. She further despaired of her household budget at this proof that a governess must needs also be found.

Lady Cheeves knew herself greatly wronged by these misfortunes, although she could not help wondering what her dear Gilbert would say to the news that his favorite aunt had left them. His decided partiality for Susan made it likely that he would not approve; moreover, he might fail to understand why his mother should not bear the blame. But since Gilbert's establishment was some distance away in Clarges Street, Lydia thought that with luck, he might not find out about his aunt's defection for some time yet.

She prayed that the same held true of her brother, Marcus. For there was little doubt about what *his* attitude would be; the only question was how long she had before her brother sent for her to read her a scold. Lydia trudged up the stairs to seek sanctuary in her room, certain she was about to fall into a serious decline.

The sixth Marquis of Tynsdale was at that same moment sitting down to break his own fast. Succulent ham slices steamed on his plate, and no fault could be found with his morning egg nor with his crisply browned toast. Sunlight streamed over the immaculate linen tablecloth spread before him, and freshly cut flowers graced his table.

Amidst this well-ordered perfection, his lordship was considerably startled when Harold Beaumont, earl of that name, suddenly burst into the room without warning.

"Marcus, you'll never guess!" the earl exclaimed, his long strides bringing him into the room at speed, the Tynsdale butler hard upon his heels.

"My very dear Lord Beaumont," drawled the owner of the house, cloaking his surprise with exaggerated politeness. "Do you sit down and join me." He motioned for the beleaguered butler to set out another plate for their unexpected guest.

"Bosh, Marcus! Cut line. I heard how you shot the cat last night. But, I must say, it is not at all like you to go off on a binge, is it?" Lord Beaumont examined his friend closely after making this remark. "Oh, well, at least you don't look *too* bad," he added perkily, his handsome face brightening. "Anyway, you're sure to feel more the thing when I tell you the latest!"

"Harry," Marcus sighed, wincing only slightly at the earl's ringing tones, "I can assure you that I enjoy the greatest good health and have not the least need to, ah, 'feel more the thing.'"

Privy to most of the marquis' concerns, Lord Beaumont ignored this obvious misstatement. He blithely proceeded to fill up a plate while giving out a tale of phenomenal luck at the tables enjoyed by the Honorable Gilbert Cheeves, just the night before. It seemed that young Gilbert had made quite a showing at Brooks's Club.

"Dicing, was he?" Marcus asked at the end of the narration, critical.

"I'll say. And every rattle of the bones netted him a neat profit, too!"

"Drinking deep, no doubt?"

"Cold sober, Marcus! Damme if he wasn't!" the earl denied, eyeing his friend in possibly disapproving comparison. "Why, I watched his game from start to finish, and he was cool as you please when he gathered his winnings. I tell you, that boy has promise!"

"We'll know more about that when we see how he hangs on to the proceeds," the marquis responded dampingly. "Young Gilbert has never been out of dun territory for very long at a stretch. You know it as well as I."

Marcus scowled at the thought of his nephew and heir. His fork half-raised to his lips, he ruminated on Gilbert's affairs and his own plan to find himself a wife during the Season. He had come to realize that it really would not do to forfeit the Tynsdale marquisate; those honors had followed the name of Kinsworth for generations! So it was the prospect of ending his much-enjoyed freedom that had sent him into the bottle last night and not the tantalizing memory of a golden-haired miss asking him if he carried a pistol.

But despite this judgment, Marcus acknowledged that he had found himself, again and again, trying to recall if the young charmer had had blue eyes or green. In the gathering twilight, they had seemed some strange combination of both. His mind slid quickly past the question of just why he had kissed her without waiting for her to express her willingness to accept his proposition. For if he *were* to allow himself to consider it, he would have had to

100

own his misdeed. It had not at all been the thing, as anyone would know.

His thoughts slowed further at the recollection of her response to his kiss. She had seemed almost improbably innocent as to method, at first, giving him some rather uncomfortable doubts about her experience, even as he reconsidered it. But he then reminded himself that the young woman had as good as admitted her calling, and, of a certainty, those later moments of unresisting enjoyment could not be denied. No gentlewoman would have permitted the pleasure, he decided.

In honesty, Marcus had to suppose that Miss Doune's rejection of his proposed alliance possibly might, just might, have been the cause of some unrest—the discomfiting words, *vicious rakeshame*, continued playing round inside in his head—yet he was unaccustomed to the idea of a woman inducing lingering thoughts of any sort. His was a world of politics, properties, and sport; women were, for the most part, mere nuisance.

If he'd turned his curricle onto Bruton Place only yesterday afternoon, thinking to discover the number of a certain house in the daylight, he'd done so from simple curiosity. And even before he had completed the turn, he had become disgusted with himself for his apparent interest in a female, more especially one who was in all probability no better than a straw damsel. He had given up his quest and turned back around, going on to his club without further detour. An excellent Madeira had gradually soothed his memory and his lacerated feelings. Before the desired result was achieved, however, he had, in truth, drunk more than was his usual.

"Woolgathering, are you?" Lord Beamont broke in.

Marcus quickly lowered his fork, laughing softly at his lapse. "Something like that, Harry. I was just thinking of myself under the nuptial yoke."

"So that's what got you jug-bit! Well, it cannot be so bad as all that. I may even join with you in a last survey of the ladies—before I consign myself forever to a life of bachelorhood, don't you know. Of course, I don't have to

101

get myself an heir like you do; we've plenty of young Beaumonts to take the title after me."

"Lud! You, Harry? I'd have thought you content at your age."

"And just what's my age to say to anything?" the earl abjured, looking offended. "I may be a few years older than you, my friend, but I believe I can still strip to advantage." Harry Beaumont drew himself up straighter in his chair and squared his shoulders beneath his well-cut coat. Marcus had to chuckle at this unexpected reaction to his comment.

In point of fact, neither gentleman needed to resort to padding nor lacing for their figures, both being well-known Corinthians: crack whips, and noted regulars at Gentleman Jackson's Sparring Saloon. And, unlike some of their ilk, they were always perfectly correct in their dress and in their manners, as well, though preferring the more strenuous outdoor activities to the routs and balls of refined society.

Physically, Marcus was slightly the taller and heavier of the two, but Harry's quick left was widely respected by proponents of the Fancy. The older man's hair did show conspicuous signs of silvering at the temples, but such an addition must be considered to have definite appeal, accompanied as it was by a thick, black wave dipping romantically low over his forehead. Nearly as dark, Marcus's own hair was revealed in the morning light to be actually composed of a rich, rare brown, with mahogany tints displayed here and there, making him no less attractive than his friend. Together, they were as handsome a pair as ever gladdened the heart of any match-making mama, out to catch a title for her daughter.

"Advantage, indeed," Marcus agreed. "But no need to go puffing yourself up for me; after all, I am the one needful of a wife. Not you."

"Who's to say?" Harry remarked cheerfully, relaxing into his seat. "A warm bed of a night, and a beauty at the breakfast table—why, it might be just the thing!"

Brought into a better humor by his friend's teasing,

Marcus suggested they put off further connubial discussion for the moment. There was plenty of time for them to visit Tattersall's before lunch, a far more gratifying activity. Oh, most certainly.

Over the cups at a third breakfast table this same bright morning, sat two young women, deep in consultation.

"Wardrobes," Rachel pronounced, looking over her list. "You cannot have enough dresses to go into company, Susan, and everything I have to wear is sadly out of vogue. I shall send Will out at once for the latest issue of *La Belle Assemblée*, and we'll use the afternoon to make a study of the newest styles and colors. We must be at the shops just as soon as they open tomorrow."

"Oh, but I really cannot afford to do more than add a few small items to my dress," responded Susan uneasily. "Besides, it is your apparel that we must concern ourselves with, for it can hardly matter to anyone what I wear."

"Nonsense," Rachel countered. "It is the duty of any proper chaperon to make a good appearance. By having you dressed in the latest mode, I add favorably to my own notice, you understand. While as for the cost, Susan, you may consider such gowns as I require for you to be merely a form of livery. Unless I'm very much mistaken, 'tis customary for an employer to provide such, is it not?" She twinkled a smile across the table.

"Only if the clothing is to remain with the house," Susan said anxiously.

"Why, what absolute twaddle, Susan. If you think I mean for anyone to wear some hemmed-up, let-out rag. . . !"

"But, Miss Doune, I—"

"It's Rachel. We agreed, remember?"

"Oh, yes, of course. Rachel." The older woman looked rather pleased by the reminder. "However," she continued on a more self-conscious note, "I cannot like your putting yourself out so. I am, after all, merely someone in your employ and for a very short term at that."

"Ah, but I intend to have new dresses made up for our housemaid, and *she* is to keep them afterward. What difference, Susan?" Rachel argued.

"Well, then perhaps there is another solution. Do you keep an accounting, and I can repay you for my purchases after I receive my next quarter's allowance. It is a generous amount, so I'll have more than enough to make you a full reimbursement."

Rachel looked unconvinced. "I tell you, it will be no such thing. You must have whatever clothing I require, and at my expense!" She paused to examine her new friend with a speculative eye. "At any rate," she mused, "those dark-colored dresses are not at all what I would like to see you wear; they quite overwhelm your true beauty. Furthermore, as I consider it, that horrid cap simply *must* go. I realize that it is consonant with a mature woman's years, but I think we can do very well without it." She scowled ferociously at the lacy wisp atop Lady Susan's head.

A stricken look followed this piece of plain speaking. Rachel was horrified at what she had wrought. "Oh, my stupid runaway tongue," she groaned in dismay. "Please, forgive me, Susan; I should never have spoken so. Certainly you may wear your cap if it makes you more comfortable. I *do* beg your pardon, and—"

"No. You are quite right," Susan gently interrupted, her expression relaxing even as she waved away the apology. Sounding thoughtful, she offered, "As you say, it would never do for me to appear too much the dowd beside you, lest we cause unfavorable comment. I was the one being stupid about this; I was thinking more of myself, wanting to avoid a fuss being made over me, than I was of our actual purpose. Of course I would be grateful for your help in selecting new clothes. In fact, I might take advantage of this opportunity to try a new style altogether."

A shy smile reassured the offender of Susan's real sincerity. Rachel felt completely forgiven when Susan next expressed herself interested in the new shorter hair styles: "For I've often admired their carefree look," she admitted on a somewhat wistful note.

"Then, so it shall be!" Rachel exulted, vastly relieved. She cocked her head and gave her companion a critical look. "Then, and with your permission, Susan, I'll add a coiffeur to my list. Yes, I rather believe that a shorter cut will do you very well. Very well, indeed!"

Thus restored to harmony, young Will was sent to fetch them the latest fashion magazine. And the next day, when Fullerton was consulted for the locations of the best shops, he was happy to recommend a certain Madame Hautlieu for designs most à la mode. The helpful butler then promised to call them up a hackney carriage, Duncan having left to return to Ayrshire after seeing the household adjustments settled in a satisfactory manner.

Fullerton directed "miss and my lady" to the appropriate address, attended by Mrs. Tully. Fullerton even allowed himself a tiny, dignified smile at their quite noticeable excitement, confident that "his" ladies would outfit themselves in a style that could only engender pride.

Rachel had earlier informed the butler that there had been a small misunderstanding, and that Lady Susan Kinsworth was her companion's actual name. Fullerton had rightly surmised that there was something more to the story than had been explained to him, so when he had informed the staff of the change, he had advised them not to discuss the matter outside of Bruton Place. The servants, although in all ways amazed by this piece of news, had loyally agreed that it was best to keep it mum among themselves. It was a tribute to the house that neither Rachel nor Susan suspected the degree of domestic curiosity surrounding them since.

When the eager shoppers finally arrived at Madame Hautlieu's establishment, they found it to be situated in a neat, white plastered building, with Madame's appellation lettered on a small panel beside the doorway in fine gold-leaf script. They stopped at the sacrosanct portals, pausing in admiration, since few commoners were worshipped like the couturieres of the day.

For this was no mere mantuamaker. The trio felt as if they were about to enter some consecrated shrine. In its way, the notion was appropriate.

When they stepped inside and onto the thickly woven, light gray carpet, as one they fell silent in the hushed, stilled atmosphere. Elegant groupings of small sofas and ebonized tables were scattered about the room, where miniature lighted chandeliers overhead distinguished themselves by their construction in the finest of gilt-work and Venetian crystal. Rachel was glad she'd thought to bring her letter of credit, for surely she otherwise would not be accepted here as a client.

A pretty, dark-haired salesclerk came forward to greet them and beg they be seated. After Rachel made known their object in coming, the girl deigned a small, albeit not unfriendly smile before leaving the room, taking with her the bank reference Rachel had discreetly offered.

In less than a minute, Madame herself glided out and effusively bade them welcome. Dressed in a severe black gown of the same chic cut as that worn by her minion, there was no doubting Madame's singular air of authority. A Frenchwoman well-known in Paris before her escape from the Terror, she had risen to the top of her profession in London by her talent for design. It was her business acumen, however, that kept her there.

Madame Hautlieu was unerring in the assessment of her clients. She noted the fine fabrics, yet outmoded styles worn for the occasion, and correctly concluded that entire new wardrobes would be needed. Women always donned their best clothing before being seen in *her* shop, so if this was their best, there was much work to be done!

Leafing through the pattern book set out on a table, Rachel quickly showed Madame the lines she most favored. She stated her preference for bold shapes with flamboyant colors, finding the current rage for pastels altogether insipid. The prevailing little-girl-precious styles were not for her; she wanted strong, sharp contrasts and clean, crisp tailoring.

Madame took note of Rachel's youth and reminded her

that white was de rigueur for a debutante. After noting the determined set to Rachel's chin, however, she then allowed as how they might contrive a satisfactory compromise. "For the mademoiselle's looks are not of ze *ordinaire*," she said, scrutinizing her new client with shrewd black eyes. *"Mais oui!* I think there ees much *caractère* besides—so we may, perhaps, *excuser* a small departure."

Using elaborate emerald green embroidery on the bodice and sleeves of a white gauze-silk model, followed by the same rich green in a heavy satin sash which was fitted tightly just below the high waistline, Madame rapidly devised a gown that was pleasing to her customer, yet which would be unexceptionable to Society's dictates. Walking dresses with high, crisply folded lapels were sketched and approved; morning round gowns, tea gowns, cloaks and pelisses with rich fur linings were quickly added to the order for needed apparel.

Nor was Susan ignored as these decisions were made. Taking note of her more subtle coloring, Madame recommended lightweight silks and jaconet muslins, using soft, feminine shapes. Neither bows nor too-frilly trims were to distract the viewer from seeing the lovely woman within; not for her the bright sprigged muslins Rachel so adored. Instead, Madame insisted on demure lustrings in sorbet colors and soft gray-blues to attract the eye to Lady Susan's sweet face.

At a signal from the owner, the pretty brunette assistant then brought out a long, elegantly slim redingote, completed for a client who had discovered herself in a delicate condition shortly after its commission. It was of a pale pearl gray color, in the softest wool imaginable, fashioned with an upswept mandarin collar. A curly lamb turban and muff had been made up and dyed to match, and though the price named for the three pieces was not exactly low, it did reflect a considerable discount when one considered their luxury. However, as Madame herself was honest enough to point out, the weather for such outerwear was very nearly over.

"Susan, do you come and try on this coat," Rachel instructed, stroking the big fluffy muff delightedly.

"Oh, no," came the answer. "It would be much more becoming on you, and my own things are well enough." Susan stole a glance across to her puce-brown pelisse and poke bonnet lying discarded in a lumpy heap on one of the dressing room chairs.

"Well enough for the old Susan, perhaps," Rachel scolded, intercepting her look, "but hardly becoming for the Susan of today. At least let us see if it fits you. I insist!" Rachel quickly put the muff aside and held up the coat invitingly.

"*Oui*. It ees your color," coaxed Madame.

"Yes, very well," Susan said, giving in. "Oh. Oh, my!" she then breathed as the material slid smoothly over her shoulders. "It is rather nice, isn't it?"

Rachel adjusted the sleek turban into place and handed Susan the matching muff before positioning her before the mirror. "Very nice, indeed," she said reassuringly. "The perfect ensemble, I think." Turning to the shop owner, she asked, "Madame, your opinion?"

"*Vraiment*, the fit could not be better."

Still, Susan tried to protest. "But, Rachel, you cannot be serious! The terms of my employment hardly warrant—"

"Terminated," Rachel roundly declared.

"But I cannot—"

"I mean it, Susan. We'll have no more talk of wages or debts owed between us! Expenses I will pay, since you are my guest. Gifts I will give, since you are my friend. And as for the wages I had originally promised, I've decided, will you, nill you, that the amount shall serve as your pin money, money such as any proper head of household is bound to dispense to its members. We are now officially and forever to consider ourselves friends. Agreed?" At Susan's shy nod, Rachel signalled their acceptance to the modiste. She gave Susan a hug and a shake. "So this is a little gift to you," she whispered, "because you are my very good, my very dearest friend!"

Misty-eyed, with an answering smile, Susan returned

the embrace. Leaving the old brown coat and bonnet to be returned to the town house along with the first shipment of new gowns, they exited the shop.

Mrs. Tully followed along behind them, busy with a handkerchief used to swipe moisture from her eyes. The abigail told Lady Susan that she looked a very *fine*, and Susan glowed at the compliment.

From there, they traversed the shopping district for gloves and shawls, fans and feathers, discovering such items as only could please. At Mr. Hodson's renowned warehouse, they found supple kid slippers abounding in a rainbow of colors, and at still another stop, they found an array of stockings so sheer as to make Susan blush.

Once, Rachel thought she glimpsed a familiar tall figure in a curly-brimmed beaver striding along the footpaths lining the fashionable West End streets. But when the man turned down a side street, thus allowing her a view of his face, she realized it was no one she knew. Inwardly, she chided herself for feeling so concerned. It was of all things ridiculous to think she should have any interest in seeing the Marquis of Tynsdale again. Surely!

After refreshing themselves at a tearoom in the area, they next took a hackney to a milliner Madame Hautlieu had recommended. A multitude of spring bonnets were displayed in the shop, along with an incredible variety of marvelously inspired trimmings. Chip straws were adorned with huge bunches of ribbons and pert, artificial cherries, while the more seductive toques interested the viewer with their matching scarves and mysteriously provocative veilings. Clever Italian weaves were also savored and selected, Rachel resolutely ignoring Susan's pleas that one or two hats were sufficient for a mere maiden aunt.

"For how can you think to desert these enchanting confections?" Rachel questioned in a no-nonsense tone. "They are used to being in company, just as you see here—" she gestured at the walls, festooned with dozens more hats—"so I think we must give our new bonnets plenty of companionship. Otherwise—overnight!—they will but pine and wilt in our closets." With that, Rachel added another stringed hatbox to Susan's growing stack.

Susan couldn't help grinning at the whimsy. In the drollest of tones, she responded: "Imagine. And for all this time, I thought drooping brims came from the moisture of our English climate. I'm very glad to be put in the right of it, Rachel, for now I understand that the solution is simply in buying oneself another hat."

"It's worked for Miss Rachel these many years." Mrs. Tully spoke up. "Not once has anyone caught *her* wearing a limp bonnet, and I can swear to that!"

This analysis brought everyone's laughter to the surface. Gaily completing their purchases, they returned to the town house at the end of the day, thoroughly tired but prodigiously gratified.

Rachel dismissed Tully for a short rest, telling the abigail they would attend to the unwrapping of those items brought in hand after dinner. She then slipped off to her room for a brief repair, anxious to remove her jean half-boots and the outerwear which seemed to have grown twice as heavy after so many hours in the wearing. She tossed these last onto the bed in relief.

Not really sleepy, Rachel went over to the small *escritoire* Fullerton had supplied her from the booty uncovered in the servants' quarters. He had also unearthed a proper dressing table and a lovely wheat-and-lemon-colored Aubusson rug, as well as a fluted-edged, bevelled-glass mirror. Rachel sat herself down at the desk, and after trimming her pen and unstoppering the inkpot, she set herself to marking off the items on her list that were now attended to.

She found it necessary to light a taper before the task was completed. The activity set her to wondering why it was that her every return to Bruton Place seemed to be just at dusk.

Her first evening in London, not quite a week ago, still hung in her mind. In particular, she recalled her treatment by Lord Tynsdale; memory of that disastrous encounter again stirred her to anger. And yet, perversely, she found herself recalling the man's unstinting assistance against Lord Ripley and the subsequent consideration he'd shown in escorting his two passengers—two unasked-for, rather troublesome passengers—as he'd brought them to safety. Those memories held her, along with the recollection of his intriguing, resonant voice, issuing from firm lips, lips whose soft touch had sent a languorous warmth rushing to fill her with longing, a longing for—

But what can I be thinking of?

Of course, she did not want to see that arrogant lord again! He would only insult her further! He was no better than all of the rest of his kind, taking every opportunity to prey on those less fortunate. But *she* was no weakling to fall to his wiles. If she should happen across his path again, she vowed she would give him the cut direct!

If only I could listen to him speak a few words first. . . .

Rachel jumped up from her chair in abhorrence at her wanderings. She resolutely pulled the pins from her hair and snatched up a brush from the top of the dressing table. She began pulling the brush through her long, tumbled tresses—"Peagoose. Ninnyhammer!" she growled out loud.

Entering the room with a rap on the door, Tully began scolding as she took the hairbrush from Rachel's tight grip. When she saw the angle of the girl's clenched jaw, though, she reduced her words to meaningless cluckings. She began untangling the snarls her mistress had caused; with soothing strokes, she dressed Rachel's hair for the evening.

Chapter Seven

"Another delivery has come for you, miss."

"Oh, thank you, Fullerton. That will be the gloves Susan and I ordered. If you would, just have Will take the package up to my room for Tully to sort through later. That is,"—she turned to her companion—"unless you would like to go up now?"

"Not I!" Susan moaned in mock-horror. "They may have seven fingers to the pair for all I'd care at the moment, and be dyed chartreuse with my blessing!"

Rachel nodded her agreement. For the past two weeks and more, the door knocker had constantly seemed to be in use, as bandboxed confections and silver-tissue-wrapped finery had arrived in a steady stream. Mrs. Tully had several times more accompanied Miss Rachel and Lady Susan on their forays to the shops, until the big wardrobes in their respective rooms overflowed. Not surprisingly, the novelty of acquisition had finally begun to wear thin.

"Well, at least now we have clothing and to spare, even if we've no place to go," Rachel said gloomily. "It was the worst of bad luck that I couldn't secure a subscription to the Royal Italian Opera House. Who would have thought that they'd be all sold out, and after the price increase, too?" She gave a small sigh, despairing of any immediate solution.

"But there must be some way we can obtain seats," said Susan, "for I don't know how we are to bring you into

113

notice otherwise. We can hardly expect introductions to come from the ether! No. We *must* go, and that's all there is to it. Even if it means taking seats in the pit."

"Ugh," Rachel groaned, wrinkling her nose. "Somehow, that particular plan fails to enthuse." She thought of the oranges popularly sold along the aisles among the common seats . . . and of the squashed, juicy-sweet discards which would no doubt litter the floors.

"No, I don't suppose it would accomplish much," Susan conceded grudgingly. She heaved a deep sigh of her own. "Oh, what a perfectly horrid coil this is turning out to be."

With glum faces, the two sat and considered Rachel's plight. Susan had already explained the reason for insisting that they attend the opera; it was the most likely place to encounter Society's members, specifically those hostesses Susan had chance-met in Lydia's salon over the years. Could Susan but manage to renew an acquaintance or two, for none would actually snub one of her rank, the ton might also accept one whom she sponsored. That would, in turn, lead to invitations for those elite functions where the gentlemen might gather: the properly eligible gentlemen who would qualify for Mr. Creagh's approval.

Their plan was simple enough, but only if an opera box were to be had.

To Rachel's bewilderment, Susan suddenly started chuckling deep in her throat. "Why, I daresay I know what will answer, dear," she responded to the younger woman's puzzled look. "Supposing I, um, *availed* myself of my Lord Cheeves' booth?"

"What? Susan, you can never think to do such a thing!"

"Oh, and just why not?" Susan looked unusually stubborn. "Consider, Rachel. Opening night is tomorrow, and everyone who is anyone is certain to come for the usual first-night gala. But if memory serves, it will be the only evening my sister and brother-in-law attend, excepting special invitational events. True, on occasion the viscount obliges a friend by offering the use of their seats for an evening, but it is a rare occurrence, I assure you. I

114

think that if we were to go, say, on Thursday next, none would be any the wiser!" Susan sat back with an air of high expectation.

Since having had her hair snipped short, Lady Susan had become more inclined to overt assertiveness, as this latest suggestion wholly proved. The older woman seemed to have shed some of her shyness, right along with her hair. The newly shortened ringlets, warm brown, and without a thread of white, now bounced about her head in artful disarray. She looked to be scarcely more than five-and-twenty years, making Rachel honestly delighted by the change. But even *she* quailed to think of the bumblebroth their uninvited appearance at the Royal Opera House would cause.

She urged Susan to caution. "You forget something, something important, Susan. If we were to do as you suggest, someone would be sure to report us. This town positively thrives on gossip. And if that weren't enough, have you forgotten we have no escort? It's all very well for us to go about during the daytime with only Tully at our side, but even I know we cannot go out at night by ourselves."

"But at my age—"

"Which is in no wise apparent."

"Thirty-eight my next birthday."

"The years do not matter!"

"But—"

"It does not signify, I tell you!" Rachel was very firm. "Look to your mirror if you doubt what I say. We'd leave ourselves open for all sorts of insult, did we not have the proper accompaniment."

With a jolt, Rachel's words replayed in her head. Better than anyone, she knew what might happen in the streets of London and before even it came full dark. "No, certainly, we cannot go unescorted!" she said again.

Susan looked quite cast down by these animadversions on her plan, but she seemed to duly regard the truth of Rachel's words. Then her face cleared, apparently with another thought. "Oh, but I have it!" she cried excitedly.

"Do you not remember me speaking of my nephew Gilbert? I believe that if I were to ask him, he would be happy to offer us his support. And should he agree to come with us, none could find fault in our use of the Cheeves' reservation, since there would be nothing for the gossips to discuss! So, what do you think? Shall I invite him to tea tomorrow and put it before him?"

"Well," said Rachel, able to see some sense in this proposal and anxious to get about her main business. "I should, of course, like to meet this young man you're so fond of, whether he cares to give us escort or not. But, Susan, are you sure you don't mind giving away your direction? Others of your family will soon hear of it, and who knows what might be the result?" Rachel worried at the sacrifice her friend seemed about to make.

For a moment, a slight frown puckered Susan's brow. "I think that no one is more to blame for my problems than I am myself," she responded slowly. "However, there's time and to spare before we need worry on that account, for it is more than likely that our appearance at the Opera House will pass without comment. Even should that not be the case, I think you must leave any difficulties to me. My family should be my own concern, after all."

Rachel made no more demur and tried to look forward to the planned outing. She had been to the famous Edinburgh Opera in her grandfather's company several times in years past, and had enjoyed herself immensely; but to attend such an event in London, and with their particular purpose, might be a very different thing! She was not so certain, either, that she would like young Gilbert, for she'd had the story of his importuning ways.

At precisely four of the clock the next afternoon, the Honorable Gilbert Cheeves was received into the front drawing room of No. 12 Bruton Place. Larger than the parlor, the room held a certain air of formality, due to the arrangement of its furnishings as charted under Fullerton's discerning eye. Graceful scroll-back seatings alternated with exquisite Grecian sofas, and from some-where, the butler had even managed to unearth a magnificent trio of buhl tables, adding to the look of luxury.

And if those rare examples of the cabinetmaker's art, with their beautiful marquetry of ebony and lighter woods, had suffered for their shamed positions before being released, none was to know of it but Fullerton himself. If quiet hours were spent with a soft cloth and white vinegar in an effort to remove those stains left by the previous custodians, not a word was spoken about it. The refulgent sheen brought out by careful polishing was all the compliment needed, for it was Fullerton's opinion that if his efforts were remarked, he had badly failed in his office. Successful butlering, to him, meant service so smooth as to go unnoticed.

Both ladies had donned new dresses for the occasion, and Susan positively glowed in a soft, mulled muslin, dyed to the palest shade of daffodil yellow. Mrs. Tully had threaded a matching ribbon through her short, fluffy curls, giving her a piquant aspect that was altogether fetching. Susan rose with alacrity, yellow skirts all a-swish, to greet the young Exquisite as he entered from the front hall.

"I say there, Aunt Susan!" Mr. Cheeves exclaimed in surprise. "What's towards?" He conscientiously dropped an obligatory kiss on his aunt's smooth cheek, before stepping back in awed admiration.

A round-faced, but well-favored young man of medium height, Mr. Cheeves had the same fine brown hair and light brown eyes as his aunt. He was carefully groomed and pressed in a tan-colored coat of Stultz's making, sporting the nipped-in waist and the wide, dark velvet lapels that those in his set deemed superior. His waistcoat was a smartly striped affair of lime green and spring pink, while his shirt points, starched and ironed, came right up to his ears. He wore no additional lace nor jewelry, howsomever, excepting a single gold fob, hanging discreetly at his side. Definitely stylish, he yet was not too *outrè* for Fashion's decree.

Susan hugged her nephew tightly, fighting an unexpected burst of homesickness. "So good of you to come," she said, giving him an extra squeeze.

"Well, of course I came," Gilbert responded. "You're m' favorite aunt, ain't you?"

"Your only aunt, I think." Susan smiled fondly.

"Yes, and that's what makes you my particular favorite." Gilbert chuckled, then surveyed his aunt with approval. "But what is it you've been doing to yourself, Aunt? Oh, I say! That cropped 'do' makes you look quite the dasher, too! Why, I'd have taken up the scissors m' self if I'd known how pretty you could be. Who'd have thought that my own Aunt Susan would pay so well for the dressing?"

Susan blushed prettily at this accolade. "Good heavens, Gilbert. It was not such a great decision as all that. I merely concluded that it was time to try something a bit different. I've scores of new gowns in which I intend flaunting myself at every opportunity; after all, there's no reason for you to claim top honors as the trend-setter in our family." This last was appended modestly as Susan pinkened still further.

Conscious that his compliments were embarrassing his lady aunt, Gilbert added one more hug before glancing about the room. His sudden stillness reminded Susan that she was behindhand in making the third occupant known.

"Forgive me, Gilbert, my wits have gone begging it seems," Susan apologized quickly. "Do let me make you known to Miss Rachel Doune, a dear friend of mine with whom I've been staying."

Rachel came forward to acknowledge the introduction. Gilbert bowed deeply over Rachel's hand, struggling to maintain his well-schooled aplomb. But for all of having passed three-and-twenty years, nothing had prepared him for the magnificent turquoise eyes, the wealth of rich, dark-gold hair, accompanied by *such* a face and form. He felt himself quite overwhelmed! But like all young men with claims to a particle of sophistication, it was of paramount importance that he maintain his poise. "I am truly honored to have your acquaintance, Miss Doune," he managed finally.

"I am happy to meet you as well, Mr. Cheeves," said Rachel. Aware that something had discommoded the young gentleman, she thought him merely concerned at his aunt's changed circumstance. So thinking, she sought to put the young man at his ease. "You must know Susan has spoken of you often and quite fondly, and, as her nephew, you are most welcome to come and visit whenever you like. Ah! Here we are." She moved to accommodate Fullerton's quiet entry. "Do let us be seated for some refreshment." While they made themselves comfortable in the elegantly arranged chairs, Rachel turned her attention back to their guest. "May I pour you out tea, Mr. Cheeves, or perhaps you would prefer to take sherry?"

But Gilbert was distracted yet further by an exotic scent wafting its way over to reach his sensitive nostrils. Fullerton was just in the process of setting down a wide, wood-and-brass-work tray, the fragrance seeming to emanate from a tall, painted china teapot centering the embroidery-stitched tray cloth.

Observing the situation, Rachel hid a smile and supplied answer to the young man's unspoken query. "Our cook brews us a special leaf that comes from the isle of Ceylon. Please feel free to sample it, for we think it's especially good."

"Truly, Gilbert, you should at least try a small sip. It has a touch of citrus that I think you'll appreciate," Susan encouraged.

"Well—" He hesitated.

"Of course, if you'd rather not, you must not feel obligated," Rachel entered good-naturedly. "I find that what one *should* like, and what one actually *does* like, are often two entirely different matters. It is a fact that came to my attention quite some time ago."

"As to that, I believe I can put myself a few years ahead of you," Gilbert corrected. "Though such beauty as yours, Miss Doune, cannot have come about overnight."

"Oh, gallantly said!" Susan twinkled softly. "But before the pot grows cold, and we *all* grow much older, you must make a decision, Gilbert." She nodded to Rachel, who promptly poured her out a cup.

Gilbert wavered for a moment longer, then apparently made up his mind. "'Faint heart ne'er won fair lady,' and all of that. So, yes, please make mine a cup of your tea, Miss Doune. I'll not have it said that I cried craven before attempting something new."

"I profess myself obedient to your wishes," Rachel rejoindered, tipping the pot with a practiced, smooth motion. Turning the handle of the cup around in the saucer, she passed the tea across.

Gilbert stared at her in amazement. "Now, just how did you know I lead with my left?" he asked, accepting the drink. "Caudge-pawed is what we fellows call it, don't you know. But, Miss Doune! No one's ever thought to accommodate me before, excepting my aunt, that is."

"It's really nothing so very magical." Rachel smiled conspiratorially. "I just happened to notice that you favored your left hand when I gave you that napkin."

Gilbert cast a look to the linen square now resting upon his lap. "So that's the trick! And why can't more hostesses manage the same, I wonder? You've no notion how awkward it is to be handed your cup and saucer to hold while balancing still another plate on your knee and, then, trying to straighten out a misturned handle without spilling the whole onto the floor!"

This description of genteel service, accompanied as it was by a singularly rueful look, sent Rachel and Susan into gales of mirth. "But, Gilbert," Susan finally got out, "surely it cannot be so bad as all that!"

"Ho! You think not? Give me your cup," he bid, unoffended but apparently determined to make his point. With that, he set his own cup down on a side table and took Susan's teacup from her hand. He revolved it at a half-turn in its saucer before handing it back, leaving her to correct its position.

With both hands free, Susan rotated the cup, thus repositioning the tea with very little ado. "You see, it's easy," she said.

"No, no. Not like that. Here, let me show you." Gilbert took a large serving of baked goods from the tea tray and placed it on a small plate. He added a sampling of the sliced fruits offered, along with one of Sujit's crisp macaroons, then a scone he first slathered with a thick coating of butter, muttering, "Fork!" as he placed the denoted utensil off to one side on the china. Finally satisfied, he perched the entire heaping plate onto Susan's knee.

He then turned her cup in its saucer. "Now try it," he advised smugly.

This time, the feat did indeed prove more difficult. Susan steadied the plate on her lap, using her thumb to anchor the fork beneath the scone, next raising her hand to turn her teacup about. But before she could quite achieve the move, the fork showed suspicious signs of instability, necessitating that she return her attention to her plate. Shoving the utensil deeper under the scone, she tried it again with no better result. "I begin to understand," she admitted reluctantly, surveying her predicament. "Henceforth, I cry curses on all misturned cups."

As one, the trio burst into laughter, renewed apace when the fork, unattended for the moment, chose to leap off onto the floor, propelling the scone before it. The latter landed facedown, of course, bright yellow butter just showing at the pastry's edges.

While Rachel went to the bellpull to summon assistance in tidying up the mess, Gilbert took the opportunity to extract a pretty morocco wallet from his inner waistcoat pocket. Assuring himself that his hostess's back remained turned, he passed the leather envelope on to his aunt. Susan started to question the gesture, but after catching his look, she quietly tucked Gilbert's offering into the cushions instead. Gilbert's merry wink assured her that she had done just right.

Their shared laughter having made everyone more comfortable, Susan next brought up the reason for her summons. She began her speech by saying merely that she'd had a disagreement with Lydia and had left her sister's house "not too long ago." She went on to explain that in consequence, she was left free to come to Miss Doune, her very dear friend who was now sadly orphaned.

For his part, Gilbert was quite shocked. Not really the fribble he often seemed, he *had* lately begun to suspect something of how circumscribed his aunt's life had been under his mother's thumb, but here was an entirely new notion. For the first time, he realized that beneath Aunt Susan's gentle manner there might also lie a deal of courage! Braving his mother's wrath could not but have been unpleasant; still, it was everything amazing that Aunt had actually pulled up stakes and gone her own way; this, from a lady whose usual wont was to travel the path of least resistance. But Gilbert saw that his aunt certainly looked the better for her exchange of abode. While he, for one, was glad for it.

Thinking he understood the matter, he offered, "Perhaps I can talk Mother around, Aunt Susan. If I convinced her to call on you here, so she could see how well you go on, she'd have to give up her objections to your staying with Miss Doune." He turned an admiring and uncritical eye to his hostess.

Before Susan could think of a way to respond to this potentially misplaced bit of enthusiasm, Rachel took over in her stead. "Mr. Cheeves," she entered, "the fact of the matter is, Susan hasn't told her sister that she is here with me. You see, my forbearers are nothing out of the way; all are commoners, through and through, and for as far back as you'd care to go. Susan fears that her ladyship will not countenance our association, especially our being on such close terms."

"But never think that we are either of us ashamed of Rachel's background," Susan broke in at once to say. "She is the granddaughter of the most exceptional man I have ever heard of, Mr. Ian Creagh!"

"Good gad!" Gilbert cried. "You don't mean that fellow who has all those coal mines off in the north somewhere?

Rich as Croesus, ain't he?"

"Well, Grandfather is not exactly a *meikle* crofter," Rachel said wryly. "Er, that means we're not poor," she explained, observing the blank looks this received. "Not," she added proudly, "that the money should signify for anything all by itself, but the ingenuity and persistent hard work it represents should be rated, I think."

"Well, I should say it *does* count for something!" Gilbert said guiltily. It occurred to him that his own earlier inroads into Lady Susan's monies might have precluded his aunt from expending the price of the gown she now wore, and the others she'd spoken of as well. But he consoled himself, knowing that he had done the handsome today.

"Count for something? Yes," Rachel said quietly, "but neither pedigree nor wealth can stand in the place of honor—or loyalty—to be sure."

Given his mother's usual method of judgment, whereby one's ancestry was everything, Gilbert at last began to understand their predicament. He said, "Well, whatever the world's opinion, Miss Doune, true friendships are indeed a better measure of worth than any family tree. But what of Uncle Marcus? What has he to say about this?" Gilbert could not quite bring himself to believe that Lord Tynsdale would be so tolerant.

Susan answered softly. "Well, you see, Gilbert, Marcus is as yet unaware that I have left the family, unless Lydia has told him, which I somehow take leave to doubt. And if you don't mind too much, I would prefer to be the one to tell them of my whereabouts and in my own time."

Gilbert shook his carefully brushed curls in dismay. "M' word Uncle won't learn anything from me. I'll not blow the gaff. Promise you!" Knowing there would be a regular blow-up when Lord Tynsdale learned of Lady Susan's defection, Gilbert was nothing loath to let his aunt be the one to tell the tale. He greatly admired his Uncle Marcus, truly, he did, but knew him for a man who also set great store in the inviolable supremacy of lineage. And, while Gilbert had no such reservations about Miss Doune's quality himself, he held the utmost respect for the wrath he knew this news might inspire in the marquis.

Rachel levelled her aquamarine eyes on their visitor. "Please help us, sir, for I do so want to keep Susan with me. Without her, I do not know just what I would do, for there's no one else to befriend me." This was followed by such a winning smile that the bedazzled young man promptly gave his consent.

Susan went on to solicit her nephew's escort for the opera the following week, saying that she felt it her duty to see to Miss Doune's entertainment. Gilbert professed himself delighted with the scheme; the thought of accompanying such a prime article as Miss Doune, whatever her background, made his acceptance speech all but incoherent. He soon made his departing bow, anxious to find his cronies and tell them of his good fortune.

He reminded himself to be discreet about his aunt's inclusion, however, lest he give away her secret too soon.

"What a nice young man," Rachel exclaimed as soon as Gilbert had gone.

"Yes, he is," Susan agreed with quiet pride. "And I'm so glad you liked him, for he seemed quite taken with you, as well."

At this, a pensive look settled on Rachel's face. "But that makes me feel all the worse, Susan, for we've practiced deceit today. Not that your nephew needed to know how we began as employer and paid companion, for that relationship ended the moment we cried friends. But about the length of our acquaintance, I mean. We left him thinking we'd known each other for ages and ever!" She sighed, a tiny frown marking the distance between her brows. "Truths must be faced, though, and I must not edge my way into anyone's acceptance with a lie. We should tell your nephew the whole at the first opportunity."

Susan appeared to give the matter some thought. "Well, I truly do feel as if you were a friend of long standing, although the actual time since we met is not so very long ago, by most standards. No," she considered, "we've said nothing really so far from the truth. Or, that is, if you can agree that we are as close as we've claimed."

Rachel's frown gradually eased, and a smile took its place. "Fair enough! Even Grandfather has been known to emphasize one truth over another when he saw nothing but good to come of it," she quipped.

Relieved to obtain her friend's agreement, Susan relaxed back onto the sofa cushions. In doing so, she felt of the packet Gilbert had earlier handed over. Digging it free, she made to examine its contents, her efforts exposing a thick wad of new Bank of England notes. A short letter of gratitude was also enclosed, which she quickly read in silence. Wordlessly, she handed the missive over to Rachel.

Rachel scanned the lines which professed to thank that "very dearest of aunts" for her timely assistance. The writer's sincerity could not be misconstrued, and Rachel promptly declared Gilbert to be the best of good fellows.

"And, Rachel, he's even added to what he owed!" Susan exclaimed in amazement, after examining the currency. "Imagine!"

"Well, well," Rachel said slowly; "mayhaps Grandfather was right. If there are more men such as your nephew, I can, perhaps, make a good marriage after all."

Chapter Eight

The last Thursday in April saw the Creagh town house engaged in an unusual degree of activity. Dinner had been served early, and Rachel's abigail was seen several times, first climbing the stairs, then descending, then climbing again. . . .

Will Slats manfully lugged the big copper tub up from the kitchen, the footman's puffs and grunts bringing Sujit over to help. The two worked well together, taking turn about in bringing up the heated cans of water needed to fill, empty, and refill the tub. Mrs. Fullerton and Flora were both called into additional service, too, helping Rachel and Susan prepare for their initial entry into the Polite World.

Mrs. Tully brought the curling irons into play, their skillful use causing Susan to smile dreamily into her mirror. Rachel's honey gold lengths were brushed until they sparkled against the light, then softly pulled back and coiled high on her crown. Frothy silk gowns spread over the counterpanes, awaiting the magic moment when they would slide into position over slim figures.

Finally, the last button was fastened, the last ribbon tied, and sleeves were carefully patted into place. Fans were gathered in nervous fingers, and voices throughout the house hushed as, arm-in-arm, the lovely pair descended the front staircase. At its base stood their minions, all standing in silent attention.

Susan shimmered in a gown the color of angel-skin coral, the tiny puffed sleeves cupping her smooth, bared shoulders in the most flattering way. The bandeau gathered below her breasts was made of creamy, ivory-colored satin, but it was in no wise creamier than the soft skin exposed by the low bodice. Daring, but proclaimed by Madame Hautlieu to be *au courant,* the bold display of so much untouched flesh caused a becoming spot of color to rise in Susan's cheeks. She had never dressed so brazenly before, though even the staid Mrs. Tully had approved it without reserve.

But it was Rachel who literally drew gasps from their audience. She wore a deceptively simple gown of virginal white, the sleeve caps sharply pleated instead of gathered, as was the long, slim skirt beneath the high waistline. The shocking white silk seemed to glow apart from the bright candlelight, and the only color seen was that of her lips and cheeks, her topaz-bright hair, and her marvelous eyes.

She wore lengths of thin gold chain studded with twinkling yellow cairngorm entwined throughout her hair, but no other jewels did she allow. She had loaned Susan a pair of dangling, filigreed drop-gold earrings, and had insisted her friend wear the matching, teardrop-shaped pendant, though Rachel had chosen for herself only the single piece. Both wore long kid gloves to complete their ensembles, one pair in soft cream, the other in luminous white.

Arriving at the bottom of the staircase, Rachel wondered briefly if it was just her imagination, or if Susan's limp had improved. The drag of her right foot seemed somehow less pronounced, making Rachel question whether it was possible that their recent habit of walking each afternoon through the city's royal parks had helped. Perhaps, her friend's leg was strengthening along with her confidence.

Fullerton was the first to speak, his dignified manner and sonorous tones lending pomp to the occasion. "May I congratulate you on your charming appearance, Miss Rachel? And, if I may be permitted to say it, Lady Susan, I have never seen you look lovelier. On behalf of all the staff, we wish you both a very good evening." He executed a deferential bow to each.

"Why, thank you!" Rachel encompassed everyone with a radiant smile.

"We do appreciate all of your help," Susan added happily.

At a rap on the knocker, Mr. Cheeves was duly admitted, and after pausing to take in the absolute splendor set before him, he paid his own extravagant compliments on their appearance. Not usually in the petticoat line, Gilbert readily admitted that his Aunt Susan looked very fine indeed, and that Miss Doune was surely the most beautiful woman he had *ever* seen. He proudly tucked his lady aunt's gloved arm under his own before turning to add Miss Doune to his escort. The three then removed to the drawing room for a cheerful glass of wine, there being just enough time for a small refreshment before they must needs set out.

Fullerton brought them a fine white Tokay, served in delicately etched crystal glassware. A toast seemed called for, and Gilbert was the first to raise his glass. "To the two fairest ladies in England," he proposed. "Slap up to the echo! Really prime, I say!"

Not to be outdone, Rachel raised her own glass next, her clear voice sincere as she offered, "To my best friend, Lady Susan Kinsworth . . . and to my newest acquaintance, who I hope will stand my friend, the Honorable Gilbert Cheeves."

"Who surely outshines us all!" Susan added with a ready grin, lifting her glass in her nephew's direction.

Attired in satin knee breeches of darkest burgundy, with gay, powder blue rosettes tied at the knee, Gilbert affected the same powder blue in the color of his waistcoat and in the lining to his burgundy-colored evening cape. He took his aunt's teasing well enough, the light jests following one upon the other as they drank down the sparkling wine.

In continued good spirits, the three soon made their way

out to the coach Gilbert had hired for the evening. It was an elegant equipage, not an ordinary hack; they were ready to see and be seen.

When they entered the King's Theatre, Hay-market, better known as the Royal Italian Opera House, Rachel was instantly struck by the sheer, immense size of the building. The Opera House was built to accommodate some 3300 persons, although, to her, it looked capable of housing several times that number. The large, circular vestibule was lined with huge mirrors, increasing the apparent spaciousness, but the low red sofas which were set around the room's perimeter could hardly be seen for the glittering personages who flowed through the doors.

Gilbert carefully led their party through the swirling throng, ushering them around the vast, lyre-shaped auditorium. He guided them to their seats, placed on the third tier halfway round.

By unspoken, mutual agreement the two ladies sat close to the front of their box. For several minutes they simply marvelled at the scene. Tiered layers of boxes rose high in the air, with a gallery above topping that, and down in the pit marched rows of seating which Rachel guessed would hold at least a thousand guests. New Argand patent lamps had recently been installed on the overhead rims of the boxes, which, in combination with the stage lights, provided enough illumination for the entire glorious scene to spread before them in a fantastic feast of encircling, moving color.

In the pit below, the earliest arrivals soon caught their attention. The ticket holders entered in twos and threes to hail and join their fellows, while it seemed to their audience that the congregating costumes progressed from the merely absurd to the positively outrageous. Young gentlemen wearing colors that nature never fashioned, in shapes much exaggerated by buckram wadding and corsets, vied with each other in striking the popular poses known as Attitudes. Gilbert instructed his two ladies in recognizing the formal postures, with names such as *The Anchorite* or *A Victorious Jason*—this last especially in

130

favor since Napoleon's abdication.

Studying the swarming pit with a delightfully wicked look, Rachel thought up her own names for the poses. She decided that *The Drooping Dandy* and *A Belligerent Bantam* were more appropriate names, by far.

Rachel was even more impressed by the dress of their neighbors in the surrounding booths. Tall, fluttering ostrich plumes, dyed to every hue, stood upright in the center of one lady's head, while another exhibited what appeared to be a whole collection of ivory combs topping her coiffure, and a man with a huge, triple cravat tied in a bundle that practically covered his mouth made even Gilbert stare. Precious jewels boasted their owner's status as the deeply colored gemstones glistened and danced in their settings, throwing brilliant shafts of light a-skitter from one side of the auditorium to the other. And as the seats filled, the volume of sound rose accordingly, until little could be heard above the escalating roar.

Susan, too, felt quite overpowered by the display. The blatant exhibition of wealth—and by such numbers!—was awe-inspiring, to be sure. She was relieved, however, to see that her neckline was quite discreet in comparison to many she observed. And despite their party's more modest dress, she thought that they looked very well.

Other attendants seemed to agree. Curious glasses were swiftly raised to study the newcomers. Speculation was rife as to their identities, for while the young Mr. Cheeves was recognized, his two companions, most definitely, were not. Those in the ton who might have been introduced to Lady Susan at one time or another could have no suspicion that the lovely woman in the exquisitely cut, pale coral gown was the same inoffensive lady occasionally glimpsed sitting quietly in some corner of Lord Cheeves' home.

"Now *this* is splendid," Rachel volunteered over the noise. "I can scarce believe my eyes! So many people in one place, why, it's just beyond anything."

"Oh, nothing like it," Mr. Cheeves remarked with spirit. "Looks like we'll have a full house tonight, too.

Why, half the beau monde must be here!"

"And I was worried that it might be an off night," Lady Susan softly added. She gave Rachel a meaningful look. "Instead, it would appear we are in luck."

"Do you mean . . . ?" Rachel traded her a look.

"Well, let's just say that circumstances are favorable," came the cryptic response. Susan then smiled in apparent content.

Rachel followed her friend's glance across to a box on the end near the stage, where a party of élégants was just removing their wraps. She was surprised at her friend's apparent calm; for her part, she felt like the greenest stage player, awaiting her first turn on the boards!

While Rachel contended with unfamiliar feelings of inadequacy, on the other side of the house, one quizzing glass was raised and held in their direction. For long seconds it remained unmoving. Finally, its owner allowed the glass to fall back on its silk grosgrain ribbon; the gentleman then settled in his seat to consider what he had seen.

That one of the party was his nephew, Lord Tynsdale had no doubt. But Marcus could scarcely credit his recognition of Miss Doune in Gilbert's company, while the third member of the group looked to be, yes, another fancy article! Oh, Marcus knew his heir to be a trifle cork-brained, but it was beyond belief that the boy could be such a *spooney* as to bring a pair of lightskirts to the opera. And then, to honor those fancy articles with a place in his parents' own box just as though it was all perfectly unexceptionable—well!

"That boy hasn't the good sense God gave a dromedary," Marcus avowed within his mind.

Certainly, Gilbert had shown himself first on the spot to consider the Tynsdale heritage when it came to his financial needs, but with all the heedlessness of youth, he had obviously forgotten everything else due to the name. And to make matters worse, Marcus knew that it would be up to him to disengage the foolish young man from a course surely destined for scandal. Once again, it would be left to Gilbert's beleaguered uncle to rectify things, since Lord Cheeves had never held the reins as he ought and so could not be relied upon to show the proper interest in his offspring's latest peccadillo.

Marcus barely stifled a groan, wondering what sort of apple-blossom twaddle Gilbert would offer by way of excuse. "One-quarter flash, and three-parts foolish. The hoddypoll!" he silently decried.

As the lights were lowered and the singers came onto the stage to begin the evening's program, with effort, Marcus held himself in check. He knew he must wait for the intermission to confront the improper trio lest his interference add to the spectacle already drawing attention from far too many in the audience, as witness the sea of faces still turned in their direction. Society loved a *buzz*, and the scenario seemed set to provide it without him doing anything to make matters worse. His jaw clenched several times more during the next sixty minutes, those minutes spent speculating on just how and *why* Miss Doune had ensnared the foolishly naive Gilbert. The young stripling was not at all up to her weight!

At last, the expected break came, and Marcus excused himself from Lord Beaumont, who had accompanied him for this evening's entertainment. The marquis made no comment about his intended destination, thus to avoid Harry's questions.

The passageways were crammed as Lord Tynsdale moved across the theater; nonetheless, he made good time in reaching the appropriate box. When he arrived and pulled back the curtain, however, he found that the seats were no longer occupied. Frowning at this turn of events, he resorted to his quizzing glass to restudy the crowd.

Methodically, he examined every booth, in every row, until he spotted his quarry. Young Gilbert, the woman in coral silk lustring, and the rich golden curls and that oh-so-deceptive white gown that outfitted Miss Doune were across the house and two tiers down. She was just leaning over to converse with someone . . . and that someone was none other than Sarah Sophia, Lady Jersey.

Totally astounded by the unmitigated audacity—at his nizy nephew's unbelievable imprudence!—Marcus made haste across the great auditorium to the other side of the building.

"Of all the people for Gilbert to introduce those jades to," he muttered under his breath, "why did it have to be the one who is foremost among Society's leaders? And *the* foremost gossip to boot!"

Housemen were just dousing the lamps by the time he reached the first level. The intermission had ended. With grievous frustration, Marcus resigned himself to further delay while he worked his way back to his own box. "Silly young cockerel. . . . Scheming hussy!" he growled, much aggravated, as he reentered his booth and sat down.

"What's that you say?" prompted Harry. Lord Beaumont leaned over to peer at Marcus through the dimness. "What's got into you, man?" he next whispered, as the orchestra recommenced playing. "First, you fly out of here like a shot from a bow the instant the lights are raised. Now you return with an unhandsome look and sit there mumbling away to yourself! Give over and tell me what's toward," he quietly demanded.

Disconcerted to have so revealed himself, Marcus took hold and deliberately lounged back in his chair. He, too, kept his voice down so as not to disturb their neighbors. "It's nothing, Harry. Sorry. Just thinking about the program tonight."

"Oh? I daresay tonight's performance is not anything inspired, but I hadn't thought it completely contemptible, either. However, I was just on the point of suggesting we take ourselves off. Better doings at White's, I'll be bound."

"Well, you must do as you like, of course," Marcus rumbled, settling himself deeper into his chair. "But I think I'll stay on a bit longer if you don't mind."

Surprised, Harry began to take issue. "How is it that I

haven't an inkling of what goes forward here? Why are you so set on remaining when the time could be better spent! It's not like you to tolerate a mediocre production, Marcus, which is all tonight's looks to be."

"Perhaps I'm persuaded that I'll enjoy myself before the ending," Marcus answered him softly. His expression was enigmatic. In a stronger light, only a slight glitter about the eye would betray his real sentiments, for his posture depicted a man relaxed and at his leisure.

"Then, I suppose I may as well keep you company," Harry whispered uncertainly.

Marcus merely nodded. With eyes half-lidded in concentration, he kept his attention on the opposing box, his determination to catch up the bold miscreants unimpaired. Far from appearing bored, Marcus further baffled his friend by continuing seated through barely competent arias and repetitive choruses without any sign of impatience. They stayed until nearly the end of the finale, at which time the marquis abruptly signalled his willingness to leave.

With Harry Beaumont trailing in his wake, he glided swiftly along the carpeted back hallways where other theatergoers were just beginning to gather in numbers. The earl stopped to chat for a moment with an acquaintance who eagerly hailed them, but Marcus was undeterred by all such calls of recognition. He was interested only in making his own interception. He knew his nephew's little group couldn't begin to make their way through the teeming corridors with his same proficiency, and he continued undistracted by anything that might prevent his overtaking the brass-faced Miss Doune.

Sometime within the last two hours, and without his active awareness, Marcus had managed to transfer all blame for the evening's mésalliance onto the Scots miss's shoulders. He'd at some point decided that his young puppy of a nephew was hardly to be censured for being manipulated by an expert; with that thought in mind, he surveyed the crowd, not so much for his erring nephew, but for the opportuning Scots miss.

Having no reason to consider herself the subject of anyone's particular attentions, Rachel was meanwhile craning her head in search of her two companions. They had become parted somewhere between the third and second levels, separated by the crush.

She suspected no danger as she gradually made passage down to the vestibule. For efficiency of movement, she elected to keep to the inside wall where the numbers were less, making her way past the booths situated between each succeeding stairwell. Prevented from moving much faster than even the veriest garden snail, she noticed that the noise level seemed to increase substantially in the low-ceilinged area, as the gaily chattering throng inched toward the last set of steps. Her ears ringing with sound, she wondered if she should slip into one of the now-abandoned boxes to wait for the mob to thin a bit before attempting the final staircase.

But the decision was quite ripped from her hands. She felt herself being pulled—actually *pulled!*—through the curtains fronting one of the booths, just as she thought to pass it by. Before she could protest, or even think to shout for help, inexplicably, she found herself released.

"So pleased that we should meet again," a familiar deep voice addressed her. In the feebly lit confines of the private box, Rachel whirled round to meet her opponent face to face.

"Wh-why, confound you, sir!" she sputtered. "What do you mean by assailing me in this manner?" Her eyes opened wide with alarm. She then quickly stepped back, prudently taking firm hold of the draperies just behind her. The brightly faceted cairngorm scattered throughout the coils of her hair trembled at the sudden movement.

Startled by her reaction, Lord Tynsdale also backed up a pace. He'd not expected such a strong response to his gambit; to be sure, Miss Doune looked set to effect an immediate and hasty exit! When he had first spotted her coming down the corridor toward him, he had blessed the opportunity and decided to step into one of the un-occupied boxes, both for its convenience and its privacy.

He somehow hadn't thought about how his actions might be interpreted; he'd concerned himself only with being discreet. The realization that her fear was justified shocked him absolutely no end.

He shut his eyes in resignation. He waited for the inevitable shrieks and protests which would come raining down on his head. But when no sound followed, he reopened his eyes, half-afraid that Miss Doune had fainted away. Instead, he beheld the stalwart young miss, still in her same position, warily eyeing him. He felt more discomposed than if she'd fallen into the strongest hysterics.

"Er, I suppose I can't blame you for thinking me every sort of brute, Miss Doune," he began uncertainly. "I—I really don't know what to say! That was incredibly thoughtless, wasn't it?" He shook his head in disbelief for his own clumsiness.

"Oh, I'd say you've done very well with your choice of words," she answered him sharply. "*What* a way you have with language. Why, I'm all admiration, Lord Tynsdale! Indeed, I could not have stated it better."

He was relieved to see that she held to her ground; still, he heartily regretted her stinging tones. As he regarded her wary stance, he was also most uncomfortably reminded that she had cause for taking fright. Much stricken, he offered, "Miss Doune, I didn't mean to give you such a scare. Truly, I am sorry for it. My only thought was to have speech with you without bringing it to anyone's attention."

"Oh, yes? Well, you certainly obtained *my* attention," she said wryly. With noticeable reluctance, she loosed her grip on the curtains. After making him a careful and measuring look, she then seemed to relax a bit. She made a show of readjusting the drape of her heavy satin evening cape, before politely clasping her hands in front of her, apparently willing to await his explanation. "Come, come, my lord," she encouraged. "Don't disappoint me now, just when I thought you such a master of dialectic!"

At that, he was surprised into a chuckle. Here he'd come

137

to chastise her for her indecorum, and had, instead, been found guilty of unbecoming conduct of his own. The sly minx had completely diverted him from his objective, he realized, and unless he was very much mistaken, she was also deliberately putting him at his ease by teasing him. How very singular it was.

In homage to her *savoir vivre*, he made her a bow, carefully keeping his distance so as not to alarm her again. "Ah, but surely, Miss Doune," he said on an appealing note, "one might make some little allowances for a fellow dragon-slayer. We once worked together to rout a nasty beast, if I recall. Er, men of action, don't you know!"

He was delighted to see a slight twitch at the corner of her mouth. Nothing definite, but still a good sign.

"Hrumph!" she muttered trenchantly, her tone in variance to a rather mischievous expression. "It seems that not only a dragon can prove itself a *scaly* creature."

Marcus was sure he could feel her grin shining out at him, though there was no telltale movement. He didn't try to stop the wide, answering smile that spread across his own face, though. "Well, that certainly puts me in my place!" he conceded, his big shoulders shaking with laughter. "I'll have to admit that I've given good cause for you to wish yourself well away from me. But, please, believe that my intentions are entirely honorable. In point of fact," he added significantly, "it is of honor that I would speak."

"Honor, you say?" The words came out in a whoosh, all sign of Miss Doune's earlier playfulness gone upon the instant. "Do you dare to even mention the subject in my presence?"

Stepping forward, she folded her arms stiffly before her and squared her chin as she glared up at him. She then lowered her voice, apparently sharing his distaste for attracting vulgar interest from the traffic yet behind her. "Insolent man!" she spat, her eyes flashing blue ice through the dimly lighted space. "What new sort of arrogance is this? For you to speak of *honor*, is rather like the jester speaking of statecraft, is it not?" Lady Jersey herself could not have appeared more sublimely outraged.

Again he felt compelled to soft, rumbling laughter, even while Miss Doune looked at him askance. He couldn't but appreciate the farcical aspects, though; his previously peaceful and predictable existence seemed little match for this rather irregular young woman. From his earliest years, Marcus was much more accustomed to persons who behaved as expected, falling neatly into their prepared slots. Miss Doune quite defied the conventional categories, leaving him *bouleversé*.

"My lord." She recalled his attention. "I think perhaps you should cease those ridiculous giggles and explain yourself, and at once, if you please!" Her face remained frozen in a look of haughty disdain.

"Oh, not *giggles*, surely." He managed to look wounded and affronted, both at the same time. Valiantly trying to regain control of this wayward humor, he endeavored to pacify her. "Yes, well, possibly I deserve your censure," he agreed. "I did overstep a bit during our first encounter, so I suppose you have me there."

"Overstep? Overstep, is it!" Drawing herself up to her full five-feet-and-four, Miss Doune spoke in the most damping of accents. "My dear Lord Tynsdale, would you be good enough to tell me what, exactly, it is with you? Just what kind of man grabs at every woman who comes within his ken?"

That got his attention.

"Grabs at . . . ? Well, of course I don't!" It was his turn to feel outraged.

"Then, it's only me you hold in such low esteem?" She paused and seemed to study his face, her expression changing to reveal a look of genuine dismay. "But why?" she implored. "I've done nothing, *nothing* to warrant your mistreatment! Oh, I know I shouldn't have taken over your curricle like I did, or at least, not without asking you first. But, under the circumstances, was that really so very bad?"

Without thought, he reached out one hand as if to comfort her, but he caught the movement before she noticed and quickly pulled his arm back to his side. He feared upsetting her further. "No, no, of course it wasn't," he tried to reassure her, realizing at the same time that he spoke no more than the truth. "In fact," he added gruffly, "I'm sure I should make you an apology for that first evening." He struggled with his explanation. Finally, he sighed and shook his head. "Was our kiss then so offensive, Miss Doune? I had rather thought you might have enjoyed it. As I did. You see, at the time I had rather hoped—"

"Oh, give over, do!" she said fiercely, cutting him short. "You are the one who spoke of being reasonable, yet you fail in considering the particulars! This makes but the second time we have met, and yet, upon both occasions, you've—you've *assaulted* me! Dare you think to deny it?"

Seen in that light, he couldn't. And it rankled. "Well, it's not as if I were holding you here," he countered stiffly. "All I really wished was for a moment of your time."

"I think not," she said firmly. "Indeed, my lord, I have had enough of this conversation—if that's a proper term for this singularly preposterous encounter!—and I'm no longer in the slightest interested to hear whatever petty excuses you might contrive for your actions. Now, if you will excuse me, I have friends waiting."

Put in mind of his primary objective, his lordship at once returned to his purpose. He knew he *must* regain control of the situation to accomplish what needed to be done. He stayed her with a deep-voiced question. "And who, precisely, are these friends of yours, might one ask?"

"I am escorted by the Honorable Mr. Gilbert Cheeves," she returned promptly.

"Ah, yes. Young Gilbert. And . . . ? Another of the fair sisterhood, perhaps?"

Something in his voice made her answer with a certain caution. "The lady who accompanies us is none of your concern. However, I think you must realize that Mr. Cheeves will raise the alarm should I not repair to them soon, so I suggest we permit of my leaving here without any more delay."

Marcus felt sorely tried. "Discovery or no," he warned, his voice low and resonant, "you will understand me, Miss Doune. I sought you out to inform you that you are not to go out in Gilbert's company again, nor seek to contact him for any reason whatever. I meant it when I spoke of honor. Go back to your protector and stay there!"

His bell-deep tones hung between them, resounding with the knell of finality.

Taking in the full import of his meaning, Rachel felt hot anger replace all previous concerns. "So! A protector, is it?" she gasped. "*That's* what this has all been about? Well, small enough wonder that so many Englishwomen have them, my *lord*, for the women of your country seem to need every possible defense from their despotic, oppressive Betters! Just look at you. A perfect example of those men who haven't yet learned the meaning of simple civility!" She also recalled his reference to a certain "sisterhood" and understood at last what was meant. She forgot that she'd ever wished to hear Lord Tynsdale's voice again, instead forced to wonder why Duncan—normally a man of sound judgment—had called this beast *Tighearna*. A laird was at one with his people, never snide or overbearing!

"Be that as it may," the marquis interrupted, "I want your word that you'll not encourage young Gilbert. Miss Doune?"

But Rachel didn't answer. She made him one long, scathing look, more eloquent than any words. She then turned on her heel and slipped away through the curtains.

Disdaining to check behind her, Rachel conscientiously regulated her pace to the vestibule. Perhaps she should have been afraid of being followed, but somehow, she was not.

And when he reached the bottom of the staircase, she saw that the large room still swarmed with noisy people who were seemingly in no great rush to leave. Lady Susan and Mr. Cheeves stood off to one side with a group of fashionable young Bloods, obviously of Gilbert's acquaintance, so she slowed her steps further—not yet feeling herself fully in command, nor yet ready to face the world. Yet Gilbert's friends, apparently on the watch, almost immediately sighted her. They began surreptitious nudgings, prompting Mr. Cheeves for an introduction to the exquisitely beauteous young woman.

Reluctantly, Rachel joined them.

Chapter Nine

Susan and her nephew carried most of the conversation on their way home from the Opera House, Rachel sitting rigidly straight and quiet in the carriage. The only time Rachel spoke was when a question was put to her directly. This caused Susan an increasing degree of worry. A discerning woman, Susan had noticed her friend's faint air of distraction when she had rejoined them in the vestibule—twice she'd caught Rachel peering around as if looking for someone—but she had thought it merely Rachel's excitement over the evening's surpassing success. Now she wasn't so sure whether that was all there was to it.

After they said their good-byes to Gilbert, Susan became yet more concerned when Rachel clutched her arm and implored permission to go with her up to her room. After assuring Fullerton that they had enjoyed their evening immensely, Susan followed her friend up the stairs, wondering what was causing the younger girl so much upset. Usually, Rachel was such a composed and level-headed girl! But as Susan closed the door to her bedchamber, she saw that Rachel was already restlessly pacing across the rug, obviously in the grip of some strong emotion.

"What on earth is wrong, Rachel?" Susan inquired gently. "When we were parted by the crowd leaving the theater, did it frighten you? We didn't mean to abandon you, be assured, but I thought it best to wait in the front after I'd realized you were not with us."

Rachel stalked around the pastel-decorated bedroom, picking up objects and putting them back down in the most distracted manner. "He can be *bigger* than a dragon and handsome as *bedamned*, but he still couldn't frighten me," the younger girl muttered angrily. "And how anyone's shoulders can grow twice as wide as the rest of him, I just don't understand!" she added inconsequentially.

"Who—what?" Susan asked, confused.

"Oh, it was that ridiculous man again, didn't I say, Susan? He was there, at the opera, and he waylaid me in the passageway after we became separated. I tell you, he is a positive *menace* to my peace!"

"Oh, no, Rachel! You cannot mean the same man who helped you in rescuing Flora? The one who then offered you insult?" Susan was completely dumbfounded at this news.

"The very same," Rachel announced. "And, would you believe it, Susan, tonight he demanded that I never see your nephew again. The man is mad. A lunatic to believe he can order me about so! But I must say, his brains are wanting if he thinks he can succeed by such tactics. Ha! Tuppence for a nobleman!" She snapped her fingers disparagingly. "They all seem to think they can throw their weight around however they like. But no one will tell *me* what I can do, or who I can see!"

"You don't mean to say that he hurt you? I mean, you are all right, are you not? Oh, Rachel, tell me this instant what happened!"

Rachel ceased her pacing and bent her head, ostensibly to examine the craftmarks on the base of a small figurine. A French piece Susan had brought with her, Rachel seemed to examine it with interest, just as though she hadn't often before praised its delicate workmanship. Her thick, dark lashes served to hide her expression.

"No," she said finally. "I was surprised, that's all. He snatched me from the corridor into one of the empty theater booths. He loosed me almost at once, and, to be fair, he did apologize for his method of staying me. I suppose I was more startled than anything else. Anyway, we weren't three feet from the most prodigious numbers of people, you know, so I wasn't truly worried." The golden head remained bent over the china-piece. "But it was the most peculiar thing, Susan," she went on, rather pensively, "he kept mentioning 'honor,' as if somehow he held sole claim to that virtue."

"Well, of all the—! His attic indeed must be all mops and brooms!" Susan shook her head disbelievingly, becoming anxious for her young friend's safety. If this was indeed some madman, they must take every care! She counselled Rachel that precautions were in order, and that she must never be alone for an instant. She then thought over Rachel's words and asked if her attacker had said why Gilbert was mentioned.

"My fault, I'm afraid," said Rachel with a grimace, looking up. "He asked who my friends were, so I named your nephew, hoping to inspire more respect for my person. And, Susan! Another very odd thing!" she then exclaimed in recall. "The man thought we were a pair of Phrynes! High-flyers!"

"A pair of . . . *what* did you say!"

Suddenly, Rachel broke into a swift tide of laughter. The absurdity struck Susan at the same moment; with her cheeks flaming, she joined her friend in appreciation of the utter ridiculousness in any such idea. And while not for worlds would Susan have admitted it, she privately felt rather flattered that she should ever be considered one of the fascinating demimondaine.

"But whether you were actually endangered or not, we still must be very careful with such a man on the loose," Susan advised. "For who knows what he could next get up to?"

Having already been returned to a better humor, though, Rachel gaily dismissed these words. She wished Susan a good night and retired to her own room. Mrs. Tully was awaiting her mistress, and that good woman was pleased to hear how Lady Susan had introduced

Miss Rachel to none other than that most eminent of Society's hostesses, Sarah, the fifth Countess of Jersey.

It seems that Susan had once been Lady Jersey's attentive listener at a small dinner party Lord Cheeves had hosted, and the two had got on well. Trusting that she would be remembered, and knowing that none could spread the word of London's newest Incomparable better than the countess, Susan had tonight taken a somewhat nervous Miss Doune across to her ladyship's box.

Lady Jersey, like everyone else at the theater, at first didn't recognize Lady Cheeves' sweet younger sister and was very much intrigued. Deciding it would not be politic to ask questions outright, she decided on the instant to extend invitations to her rout party on Friday next, the first really grand event of the Season. A hostess of well-earned renown, the countess, who was known as "Queen Sarah" to her contemporaries, could not but realize the advantage to herself in bringing out the much-altered Lady Susan. Sure that Miss Doune's remarkable good looks would add quite a *hum*, Lady Jersey rightly supposed that the two would make an unparalleled sensation. Her rout party would be the source of gossip for weeks to come: quite a coup in the social world. And nothing, but nothing, could have appealed to Queen Sarah more.

Mrs. Tully carefully put away Rachel's finery and helped her climb into her night rail. She then went on to Lady Susan's room, assisting her in preparing for her bed as well. The abigail chattered and fussed as she straightened Susan's room, for Rachel had rather completely disarranged the table tops in her earlier agitation. Finally, content with her efforts, Mrs. Tully blew out the candle, leaving both her charges to their rest.

Sleep eluded Rachel that night. She lay fully awake in her bed, her mind playing endlessly over and over her encounter with Lord Tynsdale. She didn't mean to let her mind wander so at will, but her thoughts twirled round and about in her head like the elusive thistledown on the wind. Fragments of half-remembered words spun and whirled, one moment tickling her sense of fun, the next filling her with ire.

Intermingled were regrets for protests she'd not made, words she could have spoken to his lordship while she had had the chance. Now that she recalled it, too, he hadn't actually apologized for kissing her either, or not exactly. "I'm sure I should make you an apology," he'd said. Then, there was that last, uncompromising look on his face just before she had left the box; it left no doubts as to the sincerity of his belief that she was some kind of fallen woman.

So! she mused, *he really does think me a woman on the town. He believes me a catting sort of creature, even as he stood there asking me for my* word. She laughed humorlessly at the absurd incongruity. "What a simpkin!" she declared to the empty room.

If asked precisely whom she meant to name by this last, Rachel probably couldn't have answered. Her thoughts had already led her on to a reconsideration of the marquis' embrace on the cobblestones of a West End street.

Understanding now what he had thought of her that night—and what he still thought!—went a long way toward explaining his actions. But a fool's notions could have no real importance, Rachel quickly reminded herself. Her only concern must be her own reactions.

Oh, she was far too knowing to suppose that her surrender to enjoyment of his lordship's kiss had any deep, romantical implications. While a less strong-minded young woman might have felt herself somehow bound, or even at fault, Rachel merely thought herself *stupid*. Plainly, the man held some attraction for her, for he was undeniably handsome and had quite an engaging way about him. But such attraction was merely a fact of nature, perfectly understood to commoners like herself. No doubt any well-practiced seducer could obtain the same result from any healthy young lady, she decided.

But as for this particular fellow, well, she would just have to see to it that future opportunities for further meetings were prevented. Not that she had felt herself truly endangered tonight—a ripple of pleasing, male-deep laughter rang in her memory—but as Susan had said, avoiding him would most certainly be prudent. Her goal was to find a principled, upstanding man who would make her a good husband. The man whom she sought must have a title to satisfy her grandfather but must have much more than that to satisfy her.

Despite her resolve to ignore the subject, Rachel next began wondering what could have caused the handsome marquis to think her a lightskirt, as apparently he had from the first. What gave him the right to assume that she was not entitled to common respect? And why should the man treat her as if she were so utterly far beneath him, when her ancestors had worked while his had known only leisure! Restless, she jerked and tugged at her covers.

"Just another arrogant aristocrat," she reminded herself sleepily. "Nothing to signify in that," she whispered to the darkness.

Drowsily relaxing at last, Rachel closed her eyes for what seemed but a minute or two. It was the dark of the hour just following midnight . . . when she became uncomfortably aware that something in her room was not right. After her earlier scare at the opera, with nerves still tight and jittery, she bounded from her bed before her eyes even had the chance to fully reopen. Standing barefoot on the rug, Rachel tried to think what had sent her flying from under the covers. "Who's there?" she called out bravely.

But no sound met her ears.

Reaching out for her bedside candle, Rachel thought she heard a soft, scuffling sound close by. This, followed by a *thump*, then silence stretching endlessly through the darkness. She cautiously stilled her movements, only to have something warm, warm and *very* furry, brush lightly against her shins. She leaped back in fright, painfully landing the soft underside of her foot across one of her own bedroom slippers.

A questioning "Mrr-eow?" sounded in the darkness.

Rachel slumped, loose-limbed, in relief.

Apparently, one of Mrs. Fullerton's cats had managed to find its way into her room and had decided to join her by invitation or no. Fumbling her way back to her bed, Rachel patted the covers to encourage the creature to come up beside her. She rather liked cats and had no real objection. Perfectly willing to take advantage of the soft coverlet offered, the cat began purring as it settled itself in for the night. Comforted by the sound, Rachel soon drifted back into sleep.

The next morning, Rachel opened her eyes to meet with the unblinking yellow-green orbs of her midnight visitor. Grinning in welcome, Rachel reached over to stroke the cat's long, satiny fur—black, with smatterings of white in the oddest places—and was rewarded by a deep-throated purr. She realized that she'd rarely seen any of Mrs. Fullerton's pets about the house, though she had observed a few telltale hairs on the furniture now and again. Singularly silent creatures, the animals seemed to prefer remaining unnoticed.

When she entered the breakfast parlor some little time later, Rachel told Susan about the incident. Susan smiled, looking embarrassed, before admitting that she, too, had taken a large gray-striped tom into her own bed every evening since her arrival. She explained, "We never had cats when I was a child. They always seemed to make Marcus sneeze, and Lydia never could abide any sort of animal inside the house, so I just couldn't resist the opportunity to have a pet of my own." This last on a wistful note.

Overhearing her remarks, Fullerton excused himself for interrupting, saying he was sure as how Mrs. Fullerton would be pleased. "She has tried to find homes for them, you know, but would not let them go to just anyone," he repined.

Susan at once replied that she would like nothing better than to have the big tom when it came time for her to set up her own establishment.

This morning's weather seemed particularly fine. After pouring herself another measure of Sujit's spicy hot chocolate, Susan then suggested to Rachel that they might celebrate last night's success with a trip to Messrs. Budd & Calkins' bookshop in Pall Mall. Rachel had never been to the famous bookseller's before, and eagerly agreed they should go that very afternoon.

"*Not* that I am interested in the newest titles, of course, like *Beggar Girl and Her Benefactors,* that new novel by Mrs. Bennett." Rachel assumed a false-sanctimonious expression to accompany her declaration.

"Oh, good gracious heavens, no," Susan declared. "Nor would we so sink ourselves as to be tempted by *Bandit's Bride:* Louisa Sidney Stanhope's latest, I believe? Such dramatic fluff is not for us." A naughty grin passed her features.

"Two well-educated women, serious-minded like ourselves, could *never* by tempted by, say, Mrs. Llewellyn's newest romance," Rachel agreed, facetious. "No, no. Most assuredly not!"

In a mutual shower of light laughter, Rachel thought again how fortunate she was in her new and dearest friend. Little Flora heard the sounds of jocularity from down the hall, and she, too, was reminded of her own good luck in being taken into such a fine and cheerful house.

Susan's face then turned solemn. "But do not forget, Rachel," she warned, "we must have Mrs. Tully's company. It would be foolish in the extreme to leave anything to chance, for who can tell when that madman might again pop up out of nowhere!"

Not nearly so worried, Rachel nevertheless agreed, appreciating her friend's concern.

Prophetically, just minutes after they set out to walk the few streets over to Piccadilly, Marcus Kinsworth knocked at the door of No. 12 Bruton Place.

Susan had written to her brother and sister only that

morning, wanting to head off a confrontation when it was learned, which it surely would be, how she'd attended the opera the previous night and had made free of the viscount's box. In these messages to her family, she had briefly stated her new direction and had written that she was staying with a friend, one whose name she deliberately omitted. Lydia, she expected, would not seek her out, for such had been the way of their parting. But in the note to her brother, Susan had included a promise to come and visit with him soon, hopeful that he would take the hint and wait for her to call.

In truth, Marcus hadn't attended the day's mail until well after lunchtime. This marked a singular and unprecedented departure from his regular custom, but after suffering an unusual night of restless tossings and turnings, he had necessarily withstood a disruption in his normal habits.

The marquis had spent an uncomfortable morning besides. He had continued to mull over the events of the night before, unable to derive a satisfactory explanation for his very odd behavior whenever in Miss Doune's presence. Ordinarily, Marcus knew, his every action was easily accountable, certainly irreproachable, and un-exceptionally logical, in fact. Yet on both occasions of meeting with Miss Doune, admittedly, he'd made a rare mess of it.

Over lunch, Marcus reminded himself that all he'd wanted to do last night was to warn Miss Doune away from his nephew. He had an obligation to interfere when one of her stamp cast out lures to the boy. Then, how was it, exactly, that he had been brought to behave so badly? He had acted like the veriest cad by pulling her away from the theater crowd as he had.

And then what had happened? He'd forgotten his anger, his very righteous anger, and allowed her to set him to laughing. Remarkable.

The only excuse he could give himself was that he couldn't remember any woman teasing him so before. Neither his mother, nor sisters, nor even one in his succession of *chère amies* had ever dared. His closest friends were allowed such license, to be sure, though rarely did anyone choose to do so. Yet, Miss Doune had twitted him without hesitation and had, moreover, actually opposed him.

The thought had brought a scowl to his lordship's handsome face. He knew that most anyone else, man or woman, would have thought twice before challenging a Marquis of Tynsdale, while Miss Doune had quite easily disarmed him, charmed him . . . and *then* had defied him. Small wonder if he'd felt set upon his ears. Where every other woman of his acquaintance would have set up a screech, or whined, or cried, or *something* after he'd obstructed her, Miss Doune had merely lifted her head and given back as good as she'd got. And she'd done just as cool as you please! Remarkable, indeed, though he couldn't agree to approve it.

But all such concerns were swept from his mind when he'd uncovered Lady Susan's letter. Reading it, he'd ordered out his curricle at once, anxious to learn why his bashful and timorous sibling had seemingly quit their family. Likely, the letter meant only what it had said, and Susan intended a perfectly ordinary visit with friends. But if that was all there was to it, why had she removed from Lydia's home? Certainly Lydia had said nothing to him about it—making yet another thing which worried him— so it was clearly his duty to inquire further into the matter, and at once.

When he pulled into Bruton Place and located the brass numbering of the address Susan had specified, Marcus was subjected to still further disquiet. The brightly polished, cast-metal numerals were mounted on a town house that closely resembled the one he'd marked some weeks earlier as Miss Doune's lodging. Certainly he knew it for being on the same street and within the same block of housing, but it was impossible to tell the entrances apart, since the fronts all looked the same.

He was distinctly relieved to have his doubts laid to rest when an impressively correct and thankfully unfamiliar

MORE PASSION AND ADVENTURE AWAIT... YOUR TRIP TO A BIG ADVENTUROUS WORLD BEGINS WHEN YOU ACCEPT YOUR FIRST 4 NOVELS ABSOLUTELY *FREE* (AN $18.00 VALUE)

Accept your Free gift and start to experience more of the passion and adventure you like in a historical romance novel. Each Zebra novel is filled with proud men, spirited women and tempestuous love that you'll remember long after you turn the last page.

Zebra Historical Romances are the finest novels of their kind. They are written by authors who really know how to weave tales of romance and adventure in the historical settings you love. You'll feel like you've actually gone back in time with the thrilling stories that each Zebra novel offers.

GET YOUR FREE GIFT WITH THE START OF YOUR HOME SUBSCRIPTION

Our readers tell us that these books sell out very fast in book stores and often they miss the newest titles. So Zebra has made arrangements for you to receive the four newest novels published each month.

You'll be guaranteed that you'll never miss a title, and home delivery is so convenient. And to show you just how easy it is to get Zebra Historical Romances, we'll send you your first 4 books absolutely FREE! Our gift to you just for trying our home subscription service.

BIG SAVINGS AND FREE HOME DELIVERY

Each month, you'll receive the four newest titles as soon as they are published. You'll probably receive them even before the bookstores do. What's more, you may preview these exciting novels free for 10 days. If you like them as much as we think you will, just pay the low preferred subscriber's price of just $3.75 each. *You'll save $3.00 each month off the publisher's price.* AND, your savings are even greater because there are never any shipping, handling or other hidden charges—FREE Home Delivery. Of course you can return any shipment within 10 days for full credit, no questions asked. There is no minimum number of books you must buy.

4 FREE BOOKS

TO GET YOUR 4 FREE BOOKS WORTH $18.00 —MAIL IN THE FREE BOOK CERTIFICATE T O D A Y

Fill in the Free Book Certificate below, and we'll send your FREE BOOKS to you as soon as we receive it.

If the certificate is missing below, write to: Zebra Home Subscription Service, Inc., P.O. Box 5214, 120 Brighton Road, Clifton, New Jersey 07015-5214.

FREE BOOK CERTIFICATE

4 FREE BOOKS

ZEBRA HOME SUBSCRIPTION SERVICE, INC.

YES! Please start my subscription to Zebra Historical Romances and send me my first 4 books absolutely FREE. I understand that each month I may preview four new Zebra Historical Romances free for 10 days. If I'm not satisfied with them, I may return the four books within 10 days and owe nothing. Otherwise, I will pay the low preferred subscriber's price of just $3.75 each; a total of $15.00, *a savings off the publisher's price of $3.00.* I may return any shipment and I may cancel this subscription at any time. There is no obligation to buy any shipment and there are no shipping, handling or other hidden charges. Regardless of what I decide, the four free books are mine to keep.

NAME _____

ADDRESS _____ APT _____

CITY _____ STATE _____ ZIP _____

TELEPHONE (___) _____

SIGNATURE _____
(if under 18, parent or guardian must sign)

Terms, offer and prices subject to change without notice. Subscription subject to acceptance by Zebra Books. Zebra Books reserves the right to reject any order or cancel any subscription.

GET
FOUR
FREE
BOOKS
(AN $18.00 VALUE)

ZEBRA HOME SUBSCRIPTION
SERVICE, INC.
P.O. Box 5214
120 BRIGHTON ROAD
CLIFTON, NEW JERSEY 07015-5214

butler responded to his use of the knocker.

"If you would care to step inside, sir?" the servant invited, recognizing the quality of the visitor.

"Yes, I would, thank you." Marcus glanced about at the wide, graciously appointed front hall with an assessing, then appreciative, eye. "I've come to see Lady Susan Kinsworth," he explained. "You will please advise her of my presence."

"Er—that is, sir, if I may be informed as to your name?"

"I take it my sister failed to anticipate my coming," Marcus said in ironic tones, alert to the upper servant's hesitation. "I am Marcus Kinsworth, Lord Tynsdale. And since my Lady Susan also neglected to tell me the name of these friends with whom she's been staying, perhaps, in turn, you would be so good as to supply me the name of the owner here." He quirked an eyebrow, as if to say, *Aren't women the silliest things?*

The butler bowed to precisely the proper degree. "We are honored, my lord marquis," he said graciously, the title promptly accorded from the listings of letters patent studied from youth by every successful aspirant to select service. Punctilious to a fault, he next attempted to answer his lordship's questions. "Lady Susan, regrettably, is not at home just now. Everyone left not a quarter hour past, nor do I expect them back for some time. As for this residence," he provided with meticulous care, "it is the property of an elderly gentleman, Mr. Ian Creagh."

Not at all enlightened, Marcus stood in some uncertainty. There was no doubting that the house was of the highest respectability, though, for few could command such a superior servant without themselves being everything worthy. Coming to a decision, from an inside pocket, Marcus removed an engraved card from an elegantly slim gold case. "Then, if I may be allowed to leave my card?" He crimped one corner of the stiffened square to indicate that he had come in person.

"Yes, of course, my lord marquis. You may rely upon me to call it to Lady Susan's attention at the earliest possible moment."

"My thanks, ah—"

"Fullerton, if it please your lordship."

"Very well then, Fullerton. And if you would, also tell Lady Susan that I'll be back. . . . No. Never mind. Just tell her that I called." Marcus had thought to leave a message that he would return on the morrow, but upon reflection, he decided to leave the matter open. Obviously this was a genteel establishment, so perhaps he needn't concern himself further. No, he decided, there was nothing out of the way after all.

In short order, Marcus was back in his curricle, guiding his creams through the streets with his usual skill. After completing a neat turn onto Bond Street, he tossed a casual question over his shoulder. "Whitson, do you happen to recall the evening we had that turn-up with Lord Ripley?"

"Aye, milord," his tiger carolled back up at him. "We treated that there Captain Queer-nabs with a taste of yer poker in bene style, I'd say. And a fine to-do it was!"

"Just so, Whitson, just so." Marcus's comment came in carefully disinterested tones. He then eased his pair a bit to the right, to provide more room for an oncoming fourgon, its sides bulging with a miscellany of boxes attached to each other with twine. After allowing it to pass, he straightened up his team. Again, he proposed a question. "I don't suppose, Whitson, that you would also happen to remember which house the travelling carriage retired to, would you?"

"Oh, I remembers it well enough," the groom called forward. "Yer meanin' the house where the young lady went in. Yes, I recalls it per'xactly, an' no mistake."

When no further intelligence followed this answer, Lord Tynsdale returned his attention to his driving, reluctant to press the matter. It was not as if he really cared; he resolved that if he should never see Miss Doune again, for him, it would be too soon.

Whitson, on the other hand, held to his groom's rail on the back of the curricle, a puzzled look on his face. But of course, a servant did not question his master, as the tiger was quite well aware.

＊   ＊   ＊

Some two hours later, the springtime sun warm at their backs, the merry excursionists returned with wrapped parcels of books tucked tenderly under their arms. Mrs. Tully deftly added their packages to those she already carried, going off to make proper disposition of the purchases, while Fullerton brought Lady Susan's notice to the calling card entrusted to his care. Its folded-down corner was apparent.

Glancing over engraved script, Lady Susan looked suddenly rather spent. Her shoulders drooped a fraction as she pocketed the card, and it seemed she had to force herself just to meet the butler's eye. "Did Marcus say when he might next call?" she inquired in a subdued voice.

But it was Rachel who pressed the question. She had watched the proceedings in growing indignation, taking the greatest exception to it all. "So!" she broke in. "I take it that your brother came here looking for you? And after you've been gone for what—some four weeks now? Oo-o! *How* I wish I'd been here to receive him. Yes indeed, Fullerton." She turned to the by-now confused butler. "*Do* tell us when we can expect his most estimable lordship." Sarcasm positively dripped from each word.

But Rachel's righteous anger was not such that she was blind to her servant's corresponding expression of totally perplexed dismay. "Oh, dear," she exclaimed by way of apology. "I daresay, Fullerton, you are left quite in the dark. I should have thought to warn you that Lady Susan only just notified her family of her move to join me here, having left them after she suffered far too many of their unkindnesses."

"But Mr. Cheeves—?" Fullerton started to question.

"My nephew agreed to refrain from making mention of me," Susan interposed in soft tones. "While Lady Cheeves, until today, assumed me to be living with our brother, Marcus thought I was still with her." Her doe-soft eyes pleaded for understanding.

Drawing himself up to his full five-foot-and-ten,

155

Fullerton rushed to reassure. "I comprehend completely, my lady! We, many of us, have suffered past wrongs, but we do come about, you know. And as to the question of his lordship's return, I can report that he gave no indication that we should expect him again. Or at least, he seemed to feel no urgency about it. However, if his lordship should call again, shall I say you are unavailable, my lady?" he asked hopefully.

"Better still, you might just let me have a word with him!" Rachel squared her chin pugnaciously. "But of course, it is your decision, Susan," she added with due deference.

"Well, I don't suppose we need dodge the beadle just yet," Susan replied. Then her cheeks suffused with bright color. The canting expression she had just used, derived from the language of thieves and miscreants—but never of ladies—had been learned from her nephew and had tripped from her lips with unexpected ease!

She seemed to have to struggle to regather her forces, ultimately collecting herself enough to say, "Besides, I think I can predict what Marcus's next step would be: he will have left here and gone on to Lydia's." That thought made her shoulders to straighten and her eyes to begin to dance. "And just wouldn't I like to be a mouse inside the wall?" she mused softly.

"Oh, famous!" Rachel agreed. "How nice that your brother should be put to the trouble, and Lady Cheeves be somewhat repaid. Just deserts! Although you may well take exception to my saying so."

"Oh, no. Not at all." Susan looked very much cheered. "You'll get no scold from me, for it's what I am thinking myself!"

Rachel then turned back to the butler. She was compelled to a question of her own. "So then, what was your impression, Fullerton? Susan tells me that her brother can ice a jug of water with naught but a single look. Do you suppose, having met him, that he has that capability?"

"Indeed, miss?" came the butler's dignified response.

He paused, appearing to give the matter his serious consideration. He finally said, "Well, his lordship might be just the man to do it at that. Hmmm. Oh, I say, you don't recall if the marquis was in town this January past, do you, my lady?"

His question, directed to Lady Susan, was said with such a bland, angelic air that it sent both her and Rachel right into the whoops! The winter had been unusually severe, causing the Thames to freeze solidly for a period lasting several days. Water mains had frozen and burst all over London, leaving hazardous sheets of ice to cover footpaths and streets alike. The city had been in a state of dangerous havoc for no small part of the month, as temperature records were broken everywhere from the Highlands of Scotland to the southernmost coasts of Cornwall.

Fullerton maintained his look of comical innocence as the laughter proceeded apace. While he was everything judicious in his dealings with outsiders, within The Family, he was not averse to a little funning discourse.

Harking back to the butler's words, however, Susan's misgivings returned. "Did not my brother seem angry, then?" she inquired rather nervously. "Marcus can be so really off-putting when he is vexed."

"No, no. Not at all!" Fullerton replied bracingly. "I merely meant, my lady, that his lordship appeared to be the sort of man who knew his own way, if you know what I mean. Not belligerent, certainly, but a man one would hate to cross." Turning back to his mistress, his face became more somber. "There is one thing more though, Miss Rachel. His lordship did ask whose house this is. I took it upon myself to give him your grandfather's name and may have led him to suppose that there were, er, older persons in residence. I trust it was not ill-done of me."

"Oh, perfectly satisfactory, Fullerton! I, too, have the feeling that the less Marcus Kinsworth knows, the better it is for us all. We have reason to suppose that with the exception of her nephew, Susan's relations will not approve of her being here with me, or indeed, anywhere

157

away from their influence, come to that. Although, and I cannot stress this too strongly, Fullerton, we will *not* have her bullied."

"Rachel!" Susan excepted. "That's coming it much too strong, don't you think? Marcus is just inclined to be a bit overbearing, that's all."

Rachel gave an ironical grin. "Remember January, Susan?"

"Oh, yes—*January*," Fullerton put in, eyes a-twinkle.

"January, indeed!" Lady Susan conceded on a giggle, resigned to an acceptance that her fears would be put to rest, even without her own effort.

Having ascertained a return of Lady Susan's good spirits, Fullerton went off to attend his other duties. Susan's mood remained untroubled throughout the evening, and talk was animated over dinner, being highlighted by a story Rachel contributed about her very first horse. The tale she told left them both quite in stitches.

It seems that when she was seven years old, Grandfather Creagh had decided that Rachel must have her own pony to ride. Duncan had been commissioned to find her a steed suitable to one of her years, but after scouring the countryside markets, the only animal found that Grandfather would deem safe enough was an ugly brown cob with one drooping ear.

Much embarrassed by such an unhandsome beast, Duncan had made the little girl ride for five and six hours every day. "Fer ye'll ride 'til ye drop, lass, the sooner to get ourselves shed of this *aitsbag*," he'd said. Rachel admitted that it had been weeks before she'd learned that the awful-sounding word meant only "oat-bag."

After telling her story, Rachel realized with a sinking sensation that she might have been horribly unfeeling again. She begged Susan's pardon if her mention of horses had brought back bad memories, but Susan assured her that nothing could be farther from the truth.

"True, I have not ridden since the accident," she said on a pensive note. "But I was so long in recovering, and then, later, no one thought to ask me if I would care to ride again." Susan stopped, wondering to herself why it was she had thought that someone *should* have asked her. *Why had she not indicated her wishes at the time?*

"Rachel, do you suppose—?"

"Susan, why do we not—?"

"—we could ride together!"

"—find ourselves mounts!"

The two laughed again as their words continued tumbling each over the other's.

The hire of saddle horses was the new topic released, both in agreement that they should like nothing half so much as riding out to the parks. Susan's infirmity had indeed continued to improve, for Rachel had not just imagined the change, and Susan now thought that she might manage horseback very well. She advanced, however, that she would need a gentle nag to start.

"But nothing with lop-ears, if you please!" she instructed firmly.

Gilbert was chosen to make the selections after Susan's assurances that he could be trusted to bring them just what was wanted. And the very next day, Mr. Cheeves found himself petitioned to search for a pair of suitable mounts, making him quite goggle at the prospect. Upon realizing that his aunt thought herself ready, however, he saluted Lady Susan and pledged every assistance.

Mrs. Fullerton soon learned about the plan and furnished her own brand of help. She took Lady Susan aside, showing her a series of exercises that were purposed to strengthen the riders at Astley's. The housekeeper cautioned her too-willing student to avoid anything that led to signs of strain, but after guiding Lady Susan through a demonstration, she pronounced her ladyship surprisingly fit. "Take no more than an hour's ride at the start, though," she cautioned.

Two days later, Gilbert returned to Bruton Place, his commission completed. For his aunt he had selected a dainty sorrel mare which came recommended as "a prad with manners mild as milk," and for Rachel he brought up a strong-looking bay which reminded her happily of her mare at Plumwood.

So it was that on the last day of April, the Honorable Gilbert Cheeves, Miss Rachel Doune, and Lady Susan set off down the street a-horseback. And in her shapely new riding habit, Susan was put to the blush when Gilbert proclaimed that his best of all aunts had "a mighty fine seat!"

Chapter Ten

The Marquis of Tynsdale sat at the great rosewood desk in his library, every item around him systematically grouped. Not a paper, nor a pen, nor a single pencil was out of its proper place. Two large Axminster rugs graced the polished wood floor—both laid exactly *so*—while the several furnishings displayed about the room were in their usual designated positions. The rows of books lining the lengths of library shelving were correctly arranged and categorized, aligned side-by-side, without one spine standing less than perfectly upright. Nary a speck of dust marred a single surface in the room.

His lordship's appearance was likewise ordered. His hair was freshly trimmed and brushed, his cravat arranged to perfection, and even seated, his coat of darkest blue superfine cloth showed no hint of an undesired crease.

But discord there was, nonetheless, represented by a pair of twin lines marking the space between his lordship's brows. With intent, dark eyes, he pinioned his reluctant visitor. "What do you mean, you 'do not know'?" he ground out.

"I mean that I have never met this Creagh family you say Susan is with—I am certain they're no one *I* have ever heard of," came the petulant response. "As I've already told you, Marcus, I was out on the day her letter came, and didn't get the message until yesterday. Oh, why do you not go and ask *her* these things?" Lydia whined.

161

Marcus scowled still deeper. "I did. She wasn't in, however. I had thought it odd when I didn't recognize the family name but didn't attach any particular significance to that, since I assumed they were friends of yours. I only asked you to call on me when I began to wonder why she had gone off visiting, bag and baggage, when you live not twenty minutes distant."

Remembering his fruitless attempt to contact either sister two days before, and combining it with Lydia's professed ignorance now, Marcus began to feel distinctly uneasy. He could not quite picture gentle Susan in unknown company, while something in Lydia's tone made him sure she knew more than she was telling. On this conviction he asked, "Precisely how could Susan have met these people, if not through you? It hardly seems likely that she's taken up with strangers, you must agree. And what made her to leave you in the first place?"

Choosing his first question to answer, Lydia sniffed, "I'm sure I couldn't say *how* she became acquainted with them, for you must know she never goes out."

"Never?"

"Well, of course not, Marcus. She cannot want everyone staring at her, and you know how perfectly awful people can be!" Lydia affected a shudder. "But it's really too bad that she's somehow made confidants without anyone knowing."

"Yes. Yes, it is too bad, too unutterably bad if we've neglected her." At his sister's incensed look, he modified his statement. "I don't mean to imply that you've been cruel, Lydia; I'm sure you've done your best to make Susan comfortable in these many years since Father died. But I referred, rather, to another sort of neglect whereby we take people for granted." Marcus sighed deeply. "And I am the greatest offender, am I not? While you gave Susan a home to share, I've done nothing for her. Nothing. Poor Susan, I never really stopped to consider before what her life must be like."

"Poor Susan?" Lydia cried. "I am the one who—"

"Yes, *poor Susan!*" Marcus growled. "Think of what

162

has happened to her, without regarding your own litany of sufferings, for once. Our sister is at this moment sharing a house with persons we haven't even heard of before; this, in preference to our company. She has shunned the protection that we, you and I, should have offered!"

"Well, I'm hardly informed on every point!" Lydia snapped back. "Why, I've not dared to leave my room of a morning without first checking the announcements in the *Gazette!* If even one of my acquaintance should learn the name of your intended before I do—well, it would be too entirely *lowering.* Why I am not allowed to know who the addition to our family is to be, I really do not understand, Marcus!"

Lord Tynsdale shook his head, feeling much beset and suddenly very tired. "Well, you can stop studying the gossip columns, Lydia, at least on my account," he said dryly. "I've not yet fixed upon a bride; in fact, I've scarcely begun the search. But how could you believe that I would leave you to learn such intimate details from the newspapers?" He looked up to study her face. "Did you really think I would neglect to first inform my own family, once the choice was made?"

"And how, pray, should I have thought otherwise?" Lydia whined. "No one thinks to tell me anything; not even Susan trusts me." Brought to consider just who had claimed not to trust whom, Lydia winced and instantly forced her wayward thoughts off to another direction. "And I was so sure she would have come to you," she wailed piteously.

"When? When were you so certain that Susan came to me? How long, specifically, has she been away from Cheeves House?"

Lydia gulped and nervously fidgeted with her purse strings. "Not so *very* long a time," she said, beginning a search through the contents of her reticule. "We argued, you see, and perhaps I said some things I've since come to regret, and then the—"

"How *long?*" Marcus's deep voice rumbled with purpose.

At that well-known tone, Lydia dumped her purse out onto her lap, anxiously sorting through the assorted bits and pieces, doubtlessly for the vinaigrette she always carried. "Four weeks," she squeaked, grasping the located bottle and holding it up to her nose like a talisman to ward off his reaction.

"*Four—?* Good God! Lydia! Why didn't I know of this sooner?"

"And why ever should you?" Lydia stopped and suddenly accused. "You're always wrapped up in your own business to the exclusion of all else. You have *your* activities, *your* friends, all the things that are most important to *you!* We only see you a few times in a year, so how could you hope to know what goes on?"

Marcus heaved another deep sigh, this one more like a groan, and leaned slightly forward in his chair. He steepled his fingers under his chin, speaking almost as if to himself. "A telling point, indeed," he said softly. "It seems I am guilty of constricting my concerns to the moment, without considering the consequences."

"And I, too," Lydia whispered, unexpectedly shamed.

But it was beyond anyone with her particular nature to remain remorseful overlong. Rallying, she entered further reproaches. "But it's too, too unfeeling that you should want to punish me further, Marcus, for Susan had no right to up and leave me like she did, no matter what I . . . no matter what was said. My lord has since been mightily displeased that our meals are no longer up to his standards, and even the girls now blame me that their dear aunt is gone. It's not my fault. She should have come to you!"

Self-condemnation slammed through Marcus's system with unbelievable force. He suddenly realized, even if Lydia did not, that shy Susan would never have come to him with her problems. To his middle sister he must seem a virtual outsider. Indeed, he *was* little more. With his damnable assumptions that all was going along splendidly, he had left Susan to feel much closer to the mysterious Creaghs than to her very own brother. So, if she had a problem, and it seemed apparent that she did, he was the last person she would call upon for assistance.

The knowledge bowled him out.

Finally satisfied that he had learned all he could from Lydia, and impatient to get about his own investigations, Marcus stood and walked his eldest sister out to the front of the house. He did his best to reassure her that she was not to blame herself too much; he reserved the greater portion of guilt for himself alone.

After straightening her wrap and adjusting her bonnet, Lydia looked up and hesitantly said, "Marcus, you will try to learn more about these people Susan has gone to, then, won't you? Find out if they're acceptable, I mean?" With unprecedented charity she added, "But, if she's happy, we must not judge too harshly." She began pleating the lace edging of her handkerchief between fretful, watery snufflings.

"Yes, yes," answered Marcus absently, helping her to adjust a shawl that seemed determined to slide off one silk-covered shoulder. He handed her into her carriage. "They are obviously a family of some importance, at least. Brummell lived just two doors down until very recently, so the address is a good one." Reminded that Miss Doune resided in the neighborhood as well, he muttered, "Or, at least, it *was*."

The first week of May brought the date for Lady Jersey's rout, the first really important gathering of the ton since the winter hiatus. The occupants of No. 12 were again all a-bustle with their preparations for the night's festivities; every one of Rachel's dedicated servants rushed about his duties with diligence. Miss Rachel Doune and Lady Susan Kinsworth had accepted their summonses to the party, the latter as excited as Rachel, having never in her adult life received an invitation all to herself before.

Rachel had written to her grandfather right after Lady Jersey's promise to include them. She knew that by now he would have received her letter, and he would exult with her in the achievement. She had every hope that tonight, yes, this very night, she might meet her husband-to-be.

Sujit added his efforts to make their evening perfect. He carried them up trays of refreshments filled with light but sustaining foods to see them through the planned festivities. He included in their menu a frothy white sauce he called *dadhi*, which he assured them would not interfere with the fit of their new evening dresses. They found its taste tantalizingly piquant, and he was pleased when the dishes were returned to him emptied.

Their gowns were carefully pressed by Will Slats with Mrs. Tully's detailed directions. Young Will was learning his future profession with great assiduity, and was proud of the abigail's confidence in his efforts. Next week, he thought, while applying the iron to a difficult spot, Mrs. Tully had even promised to induct him into the secrets of clear starch!

Ready at last, Susan and Rachel gathered up gloves and shawls. Soon after, they ascended the Jerseys' great staircase amidst a crowd of elaborately dressed guests. Gilbert accompanied them and gave them the rumor that Prinny himself was expected a little later, making Susan glad of the perseverance that had made such glory possible. Having led a retiring life, Lady Susan had never before actually seen the magnificent Prince of Wales, England's Regent.

At the head of the receiving line, their hostess greeted them with effusive expressions of delight at their coming. Her long, dark curls bobbing restlessly about her shoulders, Lady Jersey drew Mr. Cheeves aside and said that she hoped he would introduce his two companions about, as it would be some time before she was available to mingle. Gilbert was happy to agree, and before long, their party was surrounded. Astonished matrons seemed anxious to renew their acquaintance with Lady Susan, and young men accumulated in number, devastated by Rachel's good looks and open smile.

Susan was charming in a gown of delicately shaded mint green silk, trimmed in point lace, while Rachel wore a white lace overdress, topping a mallow pink underskirt. They had chosen their gowns to give contrast and complement, each to the other, and from the growing press surrounding them, they believed they had selected well.

The crowd grew ever larger as the evening wore on. It seemed no one wanted to leave before the Prince Regent made his entrance. The rout was proclaimed a sad *squeeze*, making their hostess smile widely in triumph. And when the announcement was made that the twenty-first Prince of Wales was about to join them, everyone faced the doors where Lady Jersey proudly maintained her station.

Rachel looked up, but could see no more than the top of the Royal head through the press of people when he entered with his retinue. He was followed by his favorites, including that most fashionable, up-and-coming leader of the Dandy set, that most notable Man-About-Town, Charles, Viscount Petersham. Gilbert whispered this last information with suitably awed reverence.

Ever with an eye for a beautiful woman, the Prince Regent stopped before Rachel and bade her rise from her curtsy. "And who have we here?" he asked, smiling with the ineffable charm that had from his early years earned him the sobriquet "Prince Florizel."

Gilbert hastened to make the introductions, bringing forward his sister, as well. Studying Susan in turn, the Prince graciously gave her the nod. With his well-cultivated eye, he acknowledged the true beauty she held within. "We are pleased at your presence, dear lady," he murmured gently. He was rewarded with one of Susan's soft, pretty smiles.

As His Royal Highness passed on, Lord Petersham remained behind to chat in his lisping way. A connoisseur of no mean order himself, Lord Petersham made it his business to depress the pretensions of those with no real quality or worth who were ever trying to broach the ranks of the ton. Mostly, he wanted to learn if the gorgeous

Unknown was worth his taking up. "Misth Doune," he ventured after their introduction. "You musth be a trifle overwhelmed to find yourthelf out among the great ones tonight."

"Oh, great ones, indeed," she sparkled back, her eye following the Prince. There was no mistaking her meaning, for as the Regent's broad form retreated, his blue satin coat showed definite signs of stress by way of the marching rows of little pleats pulling up and down the seams with each Royal step.

"Er—yesth. Jutht so." Manfully, Lord Petersham had to suppress a smile.

"But, so very unhappy," Rachel then added sympathetically, startling his lordship no end. "I suppose being thwarted in one area adds to the need for excess in another. How sad, for His Highness seems a kindly man, withal."

Lord Petersham looked more than a little surprised. "What a novel view, Misth Doune! Though I doubt Prinny would thank you for it."

"Nor should he," laughed Rachel with a friendly smile. "No more would I appreciate being reminded that I am speaking out of turn. Which I am. My apologies to you, my lord." She executed him a brief but graceful curtsy.

The famous Dandy found himself much intrigued! Here was a combination of clever wit and warmth tied up into as neat a package as he'd ever before seen. Thrilled by his find, Lord Petersham made a private vow to assist in bringing the unusual girl into vogue; although, in catching yet another glimpse of her winning smile, he doubted that she really needed any help.

He did think to inquire of her heritage, however. He'd found in times past that the subject brought out the pretender in most. But without resort to evasions, Rachel forthrightly told him of her grandfather's business in Scotland.

Lord Petersham admired her frank and open manner. After daintily taking snuff from one of his famous collection of boxes for same, he spent the rest of the evening declaring to all listeners that he should be credited with the discovery that Diamonds did indeed come from coal! The adroit rejoinder soon made the rounds, and Rachel's reputation was *made*.

And the loyal Bruton Place servants knew of it by the first thing the next morning.

The knocker began sounding at an early hour as invitations fairly poured in, by messenger, by errand boy, and post. The number of those with lozenges on their corners was enough to make even Fullerton swell with pride, and when Lady Susan came down and examined the growing mound, she was sure there were not a few cards from people they had never even met!

Over their chocolate, she and Rachel began going through the stacks, calling Fullerton over to assist them with his greater knowledge of the elite. With his greater experience, the butler had no difficulty in deciding which affairs they should attend, and both Rachel and Susan felt grateful for his advice. Notes of acceptance were soon written for the preferred choices, and regrets were sent to those whom Fullerton had declined to approve.

They began their social rounds that same afternoon by making calls on each and every hostess who begged for their appearance. Susan believed that despite Rachel's adulation by the gentlemen met the night before, it was imperative for her young friend to be well thought of by the ladies. It was the ladies who were responsible for the issuance of those most important of invitations: invitations to parties where eligible gentlemen might be found.

Mothers of impecunious sons seemed especially eager to welcome the very interesting Miss Doune into their circle. Before the day was over, in fact, the gossips agreed that Miss Doune was a very pretty behaved miss, to be sure!

"So honored to have you, Lady Susan. . . . So pleased to meet you, dear Miss Doune. . . . Creagh Coal? *Such* a reliable old firm!"

Of course, not quite everyone was so enthusiastic, for as luck would have it, on the morning following the Jerseys' rout party, the story of the singular honor paid to Lady

Susan by the Prince Regent was carried to her brother's ear by the Earl Beaumont. He brought the news when he met with Lord Tynsdale for an early ride in Hyde Park, but to Harry's considerable amazement, the news engendered not so much interest, as it did disbelief.

"Impossible," Marcus snorted at once. "My middle sister would never go out on the town, especially not into that company of revelers."

But Harry was positive of his facts and didn't hesitate to relate them. "It's the truth, Marcus," he insisted. "I tell you, I had it from Reginald not two hours into the morn. You know him; he's my youngest brother, and *he* had it from his wife, who was there when Prinny acknowledged them. Maria told Reggie that she was never so surprised in all her life, because Lady Susan didn't look anything like herself."

"Now what is that supposed to mean? Who else should she look like?"

Harry shook his head. "Well, how should I know?" he asked plaintively. "I'm merely telling you what Maria said."

Marcus pulled up on his reins and sighed, obviously all forbearance. "Oh, Harry, you just don't know Susan, or you would understand. She is a good, gentle sort, but the kind that goes unnoticed in a crowd of three. Too shy by half, if you want the truth; she'd never think of consorting with the Regent's set. No, the idea is ludicrous. There must be some mistake." This last came dismissively, the judgment of an obliging brother.

"Well, there is no mistake, and you can take my word on that, Marcus." Harry didn't know why his friend insisted on doubting him; they had known one another quite long enough for Marcus to know that he never spread tales carelessly or merely for fun. Put on the defensive, he said, "I tell you that Lady Susan went to the Jerseys' with young Gilbert and a new Diamond that Petersham proclaimed. It's no cobweb pretence, I assure you!"

"Oh? My nephew, did you say?" Marcus seemed to tense just slightly.

"Just so. Maria also told Reggie that their friend was a perfectly unexceptionable and lovely girl, an heiress come to town. Miss Rachel Doune by name."

To Earl Beaumont's astonishment, the marquis looked for all the world as though he'd just sustained a solid blow to the body in some prizefight. For a moment, he even looked down and out. To Harry's further surprise, Marcus then cursorily excused himself, wheeled his big stallion around, and headed for the park entrance with unseemly speed. At a full-out gallop, in fact.

In open-mouthed wonder, Harry stared after him. He was entirely incredulous—altogether amazed!—that Marcus could have so forgotten himself. If anything, the earl had often considered his friend Marcus a bit too high in the instep: staid, sometimes haughty, over-conscious of his dignity. . . . But now Harry just didn't know what he was to think. No one, *no one*, went charging pell-mell through Hyde Park. His friend, Marcus Kinsworth, least of all.

His lordship's butler thought much the same thing when the marquis returned to Grosvenor Square at a pace one might necessarily call hurried. When Lord Tynsdale next shouted aloud for his valet to immediately attend him, and for his curricle to be brought round "damn fast," the dignified butler, for all his many years in service, was shocked to his very toes. That worthy had never seen his master in such a state before, and he hastened to send for the vehicle specified as his master flew past him on up the stairs, taking not merely two, but three steps at each bound.

For Marcus had at last understood why that house in Bruton Place had looked so very familiar. He even knew who had made the mysterious third person at the Opera House with his nephew and Miss Doune. But the thought that galvanized him, sent him flying back out in a barely controlled, ice-cold fury, was the knowledge of his own stupidity. His negligence, his *carelessness*, had provided the conniving Miss Doune with yet another victim for her trap, and her latest victim was Susan!

While he threaded his curricle through the traffic, Lord Tynsdale's subsequent thoughts alternated between a very real anxiety for his sister and his total disgust at Miss Doune's base and ignoble nature. Even as his fears grew and expanded, an implacable, grim expression settled across his features. So intent was he upon his own concerns, he hardly noticed his fellow drivers.

They marked him well, however, making haste to pull out of his path.

At the imperious knock on the front door of No. 12, Fullerton, too, took note of the gentleman's disposition. He reluctantly stepped back to allow Lord Tynsdale entry. Privately, Fullerton gave generous thanks that neither of the ladies was at home, for upon receipt of the marquis' dark look, he knew this was no occasion for Lady Susan to meet with her brother.

"Is my sister here?" Lord Tynsdale asked softly, very civilly, as he stepped inside the house.

Not for a moment was the butler deceived. He'd too well observed his lordship's demeanor to be fooled by the mild-sounding query. "Unfortunately, she is not, my lord," he answered, not altogether truthfully. Indeed, Fullerton thought it a very *good* fortune. "The ladies are out this afternoon, though I shall certainly tell them you called."

Rather than the leave-taking that Fullerton expected, however, his proclamation was met with a length of silence. Lord Tynsdale's next address came in precisely enunciated, low tones, recognizably ominous in nature. "Be so good as to tell me, then, does a Miss Doune also happen to reside here? A Miss Rachel Doune?"

This last came out scarcely above a whisper, yet Fullerton never noticed. Every syllabication sounded more than distinct to his hearing; unaware of it, he drew himself up in stately defense. "Yes, my lord. We serve Miss Doune," he answered carefully.

"Ah, do you indeed?" came the guttural response. "In that case, you will tell the *ladies* that I shall return here in exactly two hours."

"Yes, my lord, though I don't know if they'll be back

172

here by—"

"Furthermore," came the low, overriding voice, "you will request my sister to have her bags packed and ready, for she is to leave with me at that time."

Without another word, Lord Tynsdale returned to his carriage.

Chapter Eleven

When Rachel and Susan returned home, they nearly burst through the doorway in exuberance for having been welcomed and feted at each of their stops. And at some point, Susan was pleased to discover that she had been so busy guiding Rachel's steps through the haut monde that she herself had never had time to revert to her normal, self-conscious timidity. Her confidence had grown accordingly throughout the day, and she was gratified to find herself and her charge so accepted. Susan marvelled at having received so much of the attention on her own. Most particularly, from one certain gentleman. . . .

Their last call had been to Lady Cowper, an open and friendly sort of woman whom no one could dislike. There had been a good many others chatting in that lady's drawing room when they arrived, and the newcomers had been introduced to those they'd not met before. On each of their previous calls, Rachel had quickly been surrounded by the gentlemen, while Susan had found herself mostly in the company of the ladies. But this time the routine was different. They were presented to a very good-looking man of middle years who acknowledged Miss Doune prettily enough, but then, the Right Honorable Earl Beaumont had moved to *her* side and remained there for the entire length of their visit.

Lady Susan had been dumbfounded to realize that the distinguished-looking lord was soliciting her conversation. She was even more surprised to realize that she felt no shyness at his attentions. He admitted to being an intimate of her brother's, although, now that Susan recalled it, he had seemed strangely nonplussed to discover that she had not seen Marcus in several months. But his conversation had not been intrusive, and never for a moment had Susan felt uncomfortable. She was, of a surety, so warmed by the gentleman's attentions that she had lost all track of the time, until Rachel gestured to her that it was time for them to leave.

And so, flushed with their triumph, the two now bounded up the stairs before Fullerton was able to impart his own intelligence concerning their irate caller. Thinking the matter of definite import, the butler left Will on duty in the hall, climbing the stairway himself to knock upon Lady Susan's door.

Susan was struck by the gravity of the butler's expression, and her own eyes grew serious as Fullerton explained his errand. "Fullerton," she responded, frowning worriedly while looking to the timepiece pinned to the waist of her short, fitted jacket, "I don't see how this situation can be decided in the next fifteen minutes. I remember Marcus as a child, when his deathly quiet rages would send us all into a spin. Merciful heavens! The more furious he was, the sterner he became, making everyone positively quake in their shoes. But, did my brother give no indication of his reasons for ordering me to be prepared to leave with him? Even at his angriest, Marcus was always crystal clear about telling one what was wrong."

When the butler could shed no light on the matter, Susan thought for a minute and said, "Well, what say you, then, to a delaying action?"

The butler raised his eyes skyward in manifest agreement. "Oh, a very good suggestion, my lady. Shall I tell his lordship when to expect your, ah, 'return'?"

"Well," she said slowly, absently drumming her fingers against her watch case, "how would it be if you were to tell Marcus that I have sent a note telling you not to expect us for the next several days. I am, at least for this moment, planning to accept the invitation to the Holloway houseparty, the one you recommended against our attending. I will write you just such a note, so you need not lie, and I won't change my mind about attending. At any rate, not for the next thirty minutes. That way, I can put Marcus off for a few days, giving him time to repair his humor. It will also give me the time I need to think what next to do."

Fullerton looked thoughtful, in turn. "If I may be allowed to make a suggestion, my lady?" he said finally. "Rather than mentioning the Holloways in your note, perhaps you could be, er, *forgetful* on that point."

"Oh, very good, Fullerton. Very good indeed!" she replied in admiration. "Yes, I do believe I shall omit any mention of the specifics, and you might do so as well."

With the promised, hastily written note in hand, Fullerton returned to his station in the front hall. He appeared very much on his dignity as he awaited his lordship's return.

In the meantime, Susan hurried across to Rachel's room to forestall the possibility that that young lady would go downstairs before the butler had time to deny a certain unwelcome visitor. As Rachel gaily recounted the afternoon's pleasures, Susan mumbled what she hoped were appropriate comments, all the while trying to fix on a reason for Marcus's reported ire. She really could not for the life of her imagine what the trouble might be. Marcus wouldn't take exception to her going into Society, would he? But no, she decided, for her brother had always been one to wish her well. There had to be something else.

Susan also worried about whether she should suggest a change in the plans made for that evening. She and Rachel had accepted an invitation for an assembly at the home of Lord and Lady Desborough, and Rachel had already engaged herself for dances with several of the younger men whom they'd met that afternoon. Susan had also received one such request, a request she had agreed to at once. She had promised a waltz—her very first!—to her afternoon admirer.

With Mrs. Fullerton's good offices, Susan had been exercising her leg regularly. She knew the waltz steps from the dance master Rachel had insisted they have, and Susan thought she might just manage that *risqué* new dance, since it allowed her to favor her weaker limb almost unnoticed. The mere thought of being held by the gentleman with snow-white hair gracing his temples swayed her decision. She resolved that they would go to the Desboroughs' as planned. She had been on the shelf before even she'd had a chance for making the usual formal come-out, true . . . but maybe, and just perhaps, she was not quite at her last prayers.

Innocent of all the goings-on in her house, Rachel soon shooed Susan from her room to start readying herself for their evening's entertainment. She must wash her hair and buff her nails, and she had yet to decide what to wear.

The Honorable Gilbert Cheeves would not be coming with them tonight. An evening spent "sporting a toe" was not in his style, he'd said, and Rachel was secretly rather relieved to hear it. For some time she had been aware that Gilbert felt a certain fascination for his aunt's protégée, and although Rachel liked the young man very well, she had no wish to encourage him in his infatuation. She had long since discovered that he was far too youthful to seriously consider for herself. Apparently he was tiring of doing the pretty now, and Rachel was glad if Gilbert was ready to return to the more energetic activities of his friends.

Young men were really rather wearying, Rachel thought, rubbing vigorously at one long, oval-shaped nail with her chamois. Gilbert's constant ebullience was not actually unpleasant, but she had discovered she preferred a more sober bearing in a possible husband. In time, Gilbert would surely settle, but his starts of enthusiasm and his irrepressible high spirits were, for the nonce, a bit tiresome. Rachel had no intention of committing herself to a few more years of indulging in all-night festivities such as the young man seemed so much to enjoy.

So, for tonight, Lady Susan would act as her chaperon. Unlike going to the opera, it was regarded as perfectly proper for two ladies in company to attend a private party, especially when one of them was known to be of a mature age. Rachel was determined to prevent Susan from sitting too long on the sides, though. She, too, had noticed the interest of a certain gentleman at Lady Cowper's and so had every hope that Susan would join in with the dancing tonight.

While Tully put the finishing touches to her hair, Rachel mused upon the possibility that her companion might find a *beau idéal* before she did herself. She was reminded that she had less than eight short weeks remaining to find and secure a suitable *parti*, but fortunately, the status conferred upon her by Lord Petersham's cognomen had increased her prospects enormously. Then, too, the news of her financial condition would doubtless bring still more suitors flocking to her side.

Rachel's pretty chin squared at this reminder. "I'll set up housekeeping in any out-of-the-way spa with Susan— and happily!—before I take up with some money-hungry rattle," she declared to her confused abigail as she adjusted her wrap and prepared to go downstairs.

The Desborough party was pronounced a success, although not such a crush as the Jerseys' rout. And while enjoying a glass of lemonade during the playing of a waltz number, Rachel happily observed her companion in the arms of the same, strikingly handsome older gentleman they had met that afternoon. She recalled his name as Harold, Lord Beaumont, and surrounded by her own circle of beaux, Rachel raised her glass in a private toast at Susan's smooth, unfaltering steps. "To you, dear friend," she said softly.

Rachel regretted that she could not join in the swirling movements of dance herself, but only those young ladies approved by the patronesses of Almack's were permitted to waltz in company. It was unexceptionable for Susan to take the floor, of course, as her years made such permission unnecessary. Observing the couples gracefully swaying to the music, Rachel quietly sighed at her fated exclusion from the famed assembly rooms known as Almack's. It was, however, beyond even her elevated aspirations. Only the *crème de la crème* were invited to enter those select portals, only those with the very highest connections.

Not that she was ignored. No less than four gentlemen chatted at her side while the waltz continued, and Rachel had to congratulate herself on having so many eligibles in her attendance. It made her head quite swim at trying to remember who was who. She danced all the remaining sets offered, leaving one pair of slippers in tatters.

It was unsurprising when, the next morning, Rachel received any number of nosegays in filigreed gilt paper from her many dance partners of the night before. Susan turned beet red when Fullerton also presented her with a gift *du compliment*, a huge basket of fragrant spring lilies, topped with a bow of stiffened satin. Attached was a note which Susan read with fiery cheeks, turning her face away in discomfort.

"I am so embarrassed," she confessed to an interested Rachel. "Here I am supposed to be assisting you, rather than going about for my own pleasure. I was forgetting myself—acting like some green girl, I daresay." She hung her head in shame, cradling the big basket within her arms.

"Doing it altogether too brown, my dear." Rachel laughed outright. "I thought we were agreed upon the terms between us, were we not?"

Rachel then frowned and shook back her long, waving lengths of honey-colored hair, worn down about her hips so early of a morning. "Susan," she continued sternly, seriously, her aspect severe as she waggled a finger beneath her friend's still-downcast eyes, "you know very well that you could have gone from here any time these last weeks. You won't make me believe that you've stayed merely from some misplaced sense of obligation, either. For once, I think you have been enjoying yourself. Yet now? Now you insist on enduring some absurd sense of guilt! Why you should think you don't deserve to act upon your own wishes, I do not know, but it's time and past that you do precisely as *you* desire."

At this, Susan glanced up to see Rachel's chin set high, looking down at her in passionate indignation. Nervously, Susan said, "You remind me of Tynsdale when you glare like that. And just like him, you are infuriatingly in the right when you do so. Marcus can forever be going on and on at one, and—" Susan fell silent as she realized Rachel had gone deathly pale. "Great merciful heavens! What on earth is the matter?" Susan dropped her basket of spring lilies in distress at Rachel's altogether ghastly look. She grabbed her friend by the shoulders. "Rachel? Rachel, what *is* it!" she cried.

"Marcus . . . Tynsdale? Your name is Kinsworth!" Rachel could barely get the words out as her turquoise eyes found her friend's. "Lord Tynsdale was the man at the opera," she choked out.

The two were standing in the front hall all this while, and both jumped and broke from their paralyzed stance when the knocker unexpectedly sounded. Fullerton had left them alone to gloat over the flowery tributes each had received, so there was no one on hand to open the door.

Gathering her wits, Rachel called to the butler while she and Susan quickly retired to the small, street-floor parlor. Both were horrified at what had been revealed and were excessively anxious to question each other to unravel this quite appalling mystery. Surely, someone had miscomprehended!

A few moments later, Fullerton came to them to inquire if they were at home to their visitor, Lord Beaumont. Impatiently, Rachel began to deny him, when the earl himself stepped into the room. He came bearing the basket that had been spilled onto the hall floor, the tumbled contents straggling from its sides, the crisp satin ribbon askew.

"Lady Susan, am I to accept my congé already?" He smiled disarmingly at the ladies.

Susan was put to the blush yet again, rising and offering her hand as she tripped and stumbled over her words, even as she attempted to explain how his gift had met with an accident.

A frown gathered itself tight upon Rachel's fine brow. The younger woman deliberately made no move, not about to make her curtsy in the face of such rude invasion. Pulling his gaze away from Susan's soft lips as that lady tried to explain, Lord Beaumont bowed extravagantly before Miss Doune and offered his apologies for intruding at an inopportune time.

But before Rachel could effect the cutting remark she felt the earl deserved, Susan softly interrupted her. "Lord Beaumont has told me that he is friends with my brother, Rachel. Perhaps he can help us untangle this affair?" She gave Rachel such a speaking look that Rachel had not the heart to refuse the request with its accompanying silent plea.

Rachel sighed and allowed their caller two fingers to shake, although she still refused to rise. At her subsequent, albeit reluctant nod, Lord Beaumont seated himself, choosing a place beside Lady Susan on the sofa. Patiently, he waited for someone to begin.

Susan started by saying to Rachel in her soft-voiced way, that while titles did indeed follow family lines, they were almost never of the same name. She offered that Lord Beaumont—Earl Beaumont—was one of those rare exceptions. More usually, families of one name held title to another. The Howard family boasted the title of Norfolk, for example; the Seymours held to the Somerset dignities; while the family named Somerset, oddly, were styled Beaufort. Susan pointed out that Lord Petersham's actual name was Charles Stanhope, and that, should his father precede him in death, Charles would then rise to become the Earl of Harrington. Thus it was in England.

Rachel felt foolish for not having quite understood all of this before. Under the old law in Scotland a laird could be *Tighearna,* or chieftain, only of his own clan. She supposed that with Scotland now so firmly under English rule, such might no longer be the case, but so it had been in the old days of which her grandfather had often spoken.

She shuddered to recall Duncan's accompanying premonition: "*'Tis an ill-omened thing,*" he'd said. And so it seemed to be.

Rachel then recounted the tale of her arrival in London and of the man who had confronted Lord Ripley on Flora's behalf. Lord Beaumont, never having heard the story, thought he now understood why the baron had seemed to dodge Marcus whenever they'd encountered him lately, but he did wonder why Marcus had not explained from the first. But as Rachel continued her narration, and briefly described the dishonorable offer she'd received, he agreed with Susan, sure that there must be some misunderstanding. None agreed with Rachel that Marcus could possibly be involved in such a despicable act.

Next, Rachel rendered an account of her scare at the opera, rendering Harry's attention complete. Sitting forward in his seat, he recalled that night, and remembered uneasily how Marcus had not seemed himself. But for the life of him, Harry couldn't imagine Marcus snatching a young lady away from her friends to threaten and frighten her. He was not about to believe that Lord Tynsdale could so have forgotten himself as to behave as Miss Doune suggested. He intervened to attest that he had known Marcus for donkey's years, and that Marcus could never behave as described, especially to a friend of his sister's.

"I think that Marcus, if indeed it was he, did not recognize me that night at the Opera House," Lady Susan interjected rather self-consciously. "Rachel said her attacker thought we were both members of the . . . well, the Fashionable Impure."

Susan could not meet their caller's eyes after this admission, but did give out how her brother had twice visited Bruton Place—the last time just yesterday—and she shamefacedly told of her deceit when Marcus would have confronted her. "But I cannot think that it has anything to do with Rachel," she added nervously.

"Tall, broad-shouldered, clean-shaven," Rachel broke in to say. "Very dark hair that is cut full but not long, eyes dark and monstrous piercing. And he wears his clothes as if he *commands* them," she added tersely.

With this physical description, all doubts were thrown into jeopardy. At Rachel's insistence, Fullerton was called in to describe the man he knew as Susan's brother, then Flora was sent for in order to confirm Rachel's recollections of the man who had helped them against Lord Ripley.

All doubts were thus finally laid to rest—though unpeaceably. For there were now three very angry, very incredulous people sitting in the parlor of No. 12. The discussion continued apace for some time while the unsuspecting Lord Tynsdale was ripped for his villainy.

Seeing the late hour, Lord Beaumont was finally reminded he had stayed far longer than good manners dictated. He did, however, allow himself to be persuaded to return to them for dinner that evening. At Lady Susan's pleased look, he bowed himself out, giving Susan his assurances that he would not let their problems go unheeded.

Over a superb meal some hours later, Rachel maintained that Marcus Kinsworth simply had no respect for women in general. "Just look at how he treats Susan," she remarked to the company. "Can you deny that the man is a shabster?" She glowered over the covers, daring anyone to excuse Lord Tynsdale's perfidy.

Lady Susan fixed her friend with a rueful look. She felt compelled to disagree and said so. "Oh, Rachel, I think it unfair for Marcus to be reviled for my particular situation. No one forced me into it, and I allowed my own wrongs, actually. You see, it occurs to me that I never once encouraged Marcus to visit me, not really, neither did I go to see him when I might easily have done so. There was no reason why I couldn't have taken the lead in building a relationship; as his elder, I should have made more effort.

No," she continued softly, almost as if to herself, "there is no one else, including Lydia, who should be held responsible for my position. Although," she added on a stronger note, "I find his treatment of *you* to be beyond such forgiveness."

Rachel owned that she was glad to learn Susan was not actually fearful of her brother as she had originally supposed, but there was no gainsaying that the marquis had failed to encourage his sister as he should have. That was what families were for! But Rachel was not about to present what she thought of as her most damning piece of evidence; she would not speak of it, not even in this sympathetic company. Moreover, unlike in Susan's case, Rachel knew that her participation in a certain activity *had* been forced, at least at its inception. And stolen kisses were not to be countenanced, after all!

Occupied with these private grievances, Rachel methodically worked her way through her dinner, never really tasting its excellence.

While taking their ease in the drawing room at the meal's end, Lord Beaumont chose a place in a deep-cushioned, scroll-backed chair, apparently thinking through all he had heard. Finally, he rose to stand by the fireplace, now screened with potted ivy in the warmer weather. His brow furrowed deeply in concentration.

"Why, damme!" he suddenly shouted as the elements fell into place. "I know what it is. The man's dead smit!" he cried. The earl then hastily begged pardon for his language before the ladies, but they both ignored the slip to pounce on his preposterous notion. Despite their protests, though, he stuck to his opinion, explaining the facts as he saw them.

Only a man could appreciate such logic, Rachel quickly decided. Lord Beaumont seemed to think himself intelligible, yet she could make no real sense of his words. The earl went on so about a wild gallop across Hyde Park, secrets kept back from friends, excessive drinking by a man known for sobriety . . . as if these proved a thing. And Rachel was no hen-wit to suppose that two disastrous meetings could possibly—not by any stretch!—result in love.

"Oh, I know my man," Earl Beaumont insisted. "Moved by softer feelings, don't you know! It makes a Tom Fool of us all at one time or another, what?" In proof of which, he murmured a few words to Susan as he prepared to make his exit, words that Rachel did not quite overhear. Subsequently, Lady Susan dreamily floated up the stairs to her room, apparently unconscious of Rachel's quizzing attempts to recapture her attention.

Gritting her teeth at her friend's retreat, Rachel went up to her own bed with footsteps decidedly more pronounced. *Everyone has gone noddy*, she thought disgustedly. *Those two smell of April and May, and then think the entire world has entered into that same state!*

For her part, Rachel hardly thought that Lord Tynsdale's actions added up to any feelings softer than those felt by a schoolyard bully.

Chapter Twelve

Thwarted in his endeavors to confront either his elusive middle sister or the audacious Miss Doune, Lord Tynsdale at last concluded that it was high time he confronted his nephew. But Gilbert proved equally elusive, as a boxing match, scheduled a few days hence, had lured the young man off to Salisbury with friends. A proponent of the Fancy himself, Marcus already had declined an invitation to the same event, having decided he had too many cares in the city to permit of his leaving at just this time. Marcus's sense of aggravation climbed with each new delay in attending those cares.

There was little to be done about it, though. Gilbert was not expected back until late Wednesday or possibly Thursday, so Marcus had to restrict his immediate actions to sending off a note to his man of business, who should begin certain inquiries into the matter of Miss Doune. He also directed not a few questions as to the ownership of No. 12, specifically requiring answers about the involvement of one Ian Creagh.

Scarcely content, and knowing Susan was off somewhere under Miss Doune's thumb where he couldn't reach her, on Saturday, Marcus went to his club. He decided to fill in some time with a bottle of hock in an atmosphere of gentlemanly bonhomie. Making himself comfortable, he had just been served up his beverage, when Lord Ripley entered the seating area from one of the club's inner rooms.

The baron's recent evasions of the marquis had been noted and commented upon by several of their fellows, so an expectant hush fell over the company as the clubmen became aware of Lord Ripley's latest predicament. The baron from Essex was despised by a good many of the members of White's exclusive club because of his crass and vulgar manners, not to mention the baron's habitual slowness in repaying his gambling debts. Still, the antiquity of the baron's title was not easily ignored. Thus, the observers gave their attention to the situation with a variety of smirks and whispers, not a few of them hoping to see Lord Ripley receive a good setting-down.

Realizing his audience and perhaps suspecting their sentiments, Lord Ripley apparently made a decision to face down his adversary. "Well met Tynsdale!" he promptly boomed out in over-bold and hearty tones. "Still have the same two ladybirds in keeping, do you? I'll be happy to help you out, particularly with that little honey-haired beauty, heh-heh!" He leered meaningfully, then cast an eye to his audience. "Not fair to keep all the sweets to yourself, now is it?"

The marquis, to all appearances relaxed and very much at his ease, raised his quizzing glass to his eye. Slowly, infinitely slowly, he allowed one dark eyebrow to climb. He lazily inspected his adversary, from the top of Lord Ripley's brown beaver hat to the toes of his wide, dull boots.

Marcus let the room fall into complete silence. Languidly, he addressed his opponent in a voice both low and deep, yet he made himself heard clearly throughout the room. "If I recall our last meeting, my dear Lord Ripley," he drawled, "you had a servant girl trapped in your coach, who fled the instant you opened the door. Now what, I do wonder, is it about some men that makes them unable to inspire the coquetry for which the fair sex is known?" Marcus then paused, permitting his quizzing glass to drop and dangle from his fingertips. He cocked his eyebrow still higher. "Really," he said, still more slowly and with great care, "it is most unusual! For you do look a very ordinary, truly *common* fellow to me."

The guffaws and laughter that exploded across the room at this sally sent Lord Ripley, red-faced, into a hurried retreat. Laughter chased him all the way out to the street, and as the baron waited for his coach to be brought round, he could see the club members in White's bow window still nudging one another and laughing uproariously at the setdown. Enraged, Lord Ripley spasmodically clenched his fist, swearing vengeance on the man who had bested him.

For his part, Lord Tynsdale would say nothing more on the subject. Even so, he was sponsored to one drink after another and far into the evening, furnished by the stimulated club members.

By the time Lord Beaumont came upon him some hours later, Marcus was rather the worse for these munificent ministrations. Not that he was any less immaculate in his dress than usual, but to an old friend like Harry, there was a slight looseness in posture, an added fixity to the eye, which, together with the sight of any number of discarded glasses on the tabletop, told the story.

"Damme, Marcus, you look a treat." The earl pulled up a chair and sat down.

"Would you care to join me?" came the response. There was no slurring of the marquis' speech, only a certain discreteness as each word was pronounced.

"Don't mind if I do," Harry said, motioning for a waiter to bring him up a fresh glass. "Oh, I say, Marcus, Higgenbotham just told me how you took the whip hand to Ripley this afternoon. Well done, man! It's high time someone sent that rackety dog to the rightabout. 'Common fellow,' indeed." He grinned infectiously.

Lord Tynsdale merely quirked a faint smile, saying nothing.

After a glass or two, Harry decided that the time was propitious to begin a subtle interrogation regarding those events that more closely involved Miss Doune. The opportunity for putting his questions, and while the marquis was elevated above his usual prudence, was just too good to waste. Despite his best efforts, however, Lord Tynsdale remained reticent and revealed little to the point.

Harry was not at all disappointed. Instead, he felt the most complete and utter satisfaction. This, because a man who was truly a gentleman never bandied a worthy lady's name about in the all-male environs of White's. And, since Marcus *was* a gentleman, however deep in his potations, to Harry's mind, it made the meaning perfectly clear.

Much later, as they parted on the pavement outside the club, Lord Beaumont smiled into the darkness with a look of *quite* unholy glee. He knew beyond doubt that his all-too-*high* friend was headed for a fall, and Harry felt in every way content to know that his would be the privilege of seeing it.

When the Lady Susan Kinsworth awakened the next morning, she, too, was filled with a profound sense of well-being. Who would have believed a month ago that she could actually perform a waltz without disgracing herself? Twice! Who could have predicted that she, spinster that she was, would just yesterday receive a basket of spring lilies in token of a gentleman's favor? Not so much a fool as to think her first flirt ready for the altar, Susan was nonetheless thrilled to be singled out for such particular attention, and from such a recognized *nonpareil*.

Her gaze travelled over to her dresser where the basket of flowers now rested, lovingly restored to its original, pretty arrangement. She recalled Lord Beaumont's whispered words of parting last night, causing her to shiver on this warm spring morning with sheer delight at the memory. The earl had told her that he hoped she would be home for his calls hereinafter, as he had every intention of running tame as a housecat, did she but permit it.

Thinking of which, Susan scratched behind the ears of her favorite tom, then turned her thoughts to her brother. She had learned from Lord Beaumont that Marcus had not yet formed any particular attachment—she'd several times wondered about that—but the earl did affirm that Marcus was resolved to marry, and that he intended to select someone appropriate before the Season ended.

While she did not for a moment believe Marcus's treatment of Rachel added up to anything like courtship, she could at least agree with Lord Beaumont that it did appear that her brother was not completely immune to Rachel's charms either. Oh, she knew her brother was prejudiced about "good blood," and that Rachel was nearly as bad about "arrogant aristocrats"—but wasn't there some saying about the attraction of opposites?

So thinking, Susan mused upon certain possibilities.

Not too much time was given over to such thoughts, however. The following days were taken up with drums and Venetian breakfasts, dinner parties and soirées. Lady Cheeves did not appear at any of these functions—in no wise surprising if one considered how many entertainments were offered day and night during the Season—though Susan continued in hopes that she and Lydia might one day be reconciled. When Susan had written to her sister on that day after the opera, she had not really wanted Lydia to immediately come calling, but neither did she expect Lydia to maintain her pique forever.

And lately, Lord Beaumont was always on hand to escort them, since young Gilbert was declining most social invitations for more sporting pursuits of his own these days. Neither did they encounter Marcus; apparently, he had not yet discovered Lady Susan's Banbury tale about leaving town. And that lady, for one, was truly glad for it.

On Wednesday morning, a scant week after the Jerseys' rout party, Rachel and Susan met in the cozy back parlor to spend some time with their books. Like most dedicated bibliophiles, they found it necessary to thus refresh themselves from time to time. Two of Mrs. Fullerton's cats had become bolder, and while the first sat in a window seat, intent upon a study of their small back garden, the second was curled up, tail to nose, amongst the sofa cushions. Happily dispersing themselves in similar comfort, Rachel and Susan took up their reading.

After a while, Fullerton quietly entered to bring them the morning's post. Rachel spotted her grandfather's familiar, spiky handwriting on one of the letters just come, and she hastened to pluck it from the pile. She took it over to the window seat to read, leaving Susan to go through the assortment of newly arrived invitations.

Engrossed in her grandfather's missive, Rachel did not at first notice Susan's attentions to one particular dispatch. She was far too concerned to learn that Grandfather was still too unwell to join her in London. As Rachel finished the letter, feeling helpless in her concern, she was distracted to hear a soft, triumph-filled cry. She looked over to see Susan's sweet face light with pleasure, holding aloft two identical-looking cards.

"Lady Jersey obliged me in this, I think," she said in her low-voiced way. "And one of them is for you."

Not knowing what to think, Rachel reached for a card, studying the elegantly printed message some moments without comprehending. But as its significance became clear, she sank to a chair, her eyes clouding with disbelief. Reverently, she clasped the card by its edges and read through its content one more time.

"Almack's," she finally breathed. "Her ladyship sends us vouchers for Almack's!" Bereft of further words for long minutes, Rachel stared at the coveted ticket of admission to the select assembly rooms, and for that very evening. Finally, she said, bemused, "You, I can understand, Susan. But, why me, when so many others of far better lineage are not admitted?"

Susan's reply was thoughtful. "Well," she said softly, "it may be because Lady Jersey likes to set Society on its ear. You see, Rachel, her maternal grandfather was a remarkably successful banker, a Mr. Robert Child of Osterley. It's known that she inherited an incredibly large fortune from him; in fact, after Sarah inherited, Lord Jersey petitioned to add his wife's family name to their own. When granted, it will make Child-Villiers their cognomen. Far from being ashamed of her background, I suspect that Lady Jersey simply could not resist fostering you as someone in similar case."

The household was energized by the spread of this news belowstairs. Even Sujit understood the accolade paid to his dear mistress. His beaming smile broke into the lunchroom when he came to add his own effusive congratulations.

"Oh, I am being overjoyed to be having such a great honor in serving my two missies!" he chimed. "Good fortune shines down upon this house, and I am daily giving thanks to the gods for their most kind interest in my beautiful ladies. I am never before knowing so very many people who are so greatly caring for each other—" he solemnly bowed to his mistress, then to Lady Susan—"for I am telling you, it makes me wonderfully proud to be standing here behind you."

Long blond tresses and short brown curls bent to their plates in attempts to smother such grins as this speech provoked. Voices a-quiver, they both choked out their thank-yous.

In preparing for the evening, Rachel didn't hesitate over her decision about what to wear. She chose the magnificent formal dress created of white silk gauze and intricate emerald green embroidery: the gown Madame Hautlieu had designed for her. Lady Susan decided on a Grecian-styled gown of a cool, Venetian blue silk, the fabric's soft folds draping her slim figure in a most pleasing manner. Volute headdresses, specially made up by Ross's in Bishopsgate, were worn to match each gown. Susan's was in blue, threaded with silver, and Rachel's of deep green with gold.

Although entitled, Lady Susan had never attended an Almack's assembly before. Her barely suppressed excitement did not stem from her invitation, however, so much as it did from the knowledge that a certain gentleman would again be their escort. During his now regular visit earlier that afternoon, Lord Beaumont had promised to accompany them and had given out the assurance that Lord Tynsdale would be elsewhere occupied for their

193

début, at an out-of-town boxing match, as it happened.

"Oh, I am glad," Susan had replied upon being given the news. "For I know Lydia will be there tonight, since she considers Wednesday at Almack's a social requisite. Marcus rarely puts in an appearance, as I'm sure you're aware, my lord, but I am relieved to know that I needn't contend with him and my sister, both at the same time. But then," she had said, recollecting the reason for her good fortune, "that means you have given up your own pleasure on my account, I think." She had looked an anxious question at her guest.

Lord Beaumont had been swift in his response. "You think I might have liked to attend the boxing match? Oh, no. I give up nothing," he had said with tender meaning.

And for the rest of the day, Susan had felt lighter than air, laughing easily at anything and everything.

Rachel noticed and responded with several knowing chuckles of her own. She felt particularly glad for her friend.

When later they arrived at Almack's spacious assembly rooms, they nervously paid their respects to the hostesses nearest the door. Rachel was dismayed to realize that Lady Jersey was late in her attendance, for their benefactress's presence would certainly have eased their entry. As it was, Rachel thought that Mrs. Drummond-Burrell and the darkly lovely Countess Lieven were less than overjoyed to make her acquaintance, even though both ladies were meticulously polite in their greetings.

Lord Petersham minced his way over to Rachel. Apparently, he'd noted the somewhat frosty reception she'd received, and always amiable, he soon had Rachel laughing away her discomfort. "Mrs. Drummond-Burrell isth merely being *exclusthive*," he commented, "while Dorothea isth unhappy because Queen Sarah stole a march on her by introduthing you firsth! Dorothea vies with Sarah for preeminence in brunette beauty, you understand, and they both tend to favor you fair-haired maids who will besth set off their coloring. It isth nothing to do with you, Misth Doune! You needn't give it a

194

thought," he advised her sagely.

If Charles Stanhope evidenced everything that the Scots miss had thought she deplored about the nobles of the day, she couldn't help but find the affected English Dandy with his come-and-go lisp quite likeable. True, he spent enormous amounts of time and money on his dress, his tobacco- and tea-leaf mixes, and on sessions at the green baize tables. But together with this, he was also, without exception, courteous—often kind—and never cruel in his amusements. Ridiculous and silly, yet congenial and harmless, she discovered.

Of a surety, Rachel had come to realize that most of the absurdities of Fashion which she had so deplored before coming to London were harmless. Boredom lay at the root of most of the aristocratic antics, yet more than a few of the persons she'd met were also rather wonderfully generous. Lady Jersey had extended them a kindness with her invitations, Lords Petersham and Beaumont had been liberal in their courtesies, and nearly everyone else whose acquaintance she'd made had seemed to want to make them welcome. Even young Gilbert was far from being the hardened gamester she'd expected. He'd turned out to be a surprisingly thoughtful and loving nephew. Surely from among such people she could find a suitable mate.

Remembering her grandfather's admission in this afternoon's letter about how he still hadn't fully regained his strength, Rachel was doubly anxious to leave off needless criticizing. She most urgently wanted to get on with her main business.

Fifteen minutes or so after their arrival, Lady Cheeves entered Almack's with a small party of friends. Privy to the private expectations and concerns this aroused, Harry immediately noticed when Lady Susan stiffened with discomfort at his side, knowing full well the reason for it. The musicians were just tuning up for a waltz, and so, bowing low before her, he led Susan onto the floor.

Lady Susan tried to protest his move, wanting to avoid her sister's attention for as long as possible. But Harry firmly denied her, believing it best to get over rough ground quickly.

As the dance ended, they saw that Lydia had moved to stand right up against the red velvet-covered cordon dividing the dance floor from the visiting areas. Her lush figure was draped in an oversized shawl of fine, ecru-tinted hand lace, knotted and fringed, and her mouth hung agape beneath eyes as round as dinner plates. Busily, Lady Cheeves' fingers shredded away at an unfortunate tassel of her wrap.

Lord Beaumont drew Lady Susan over to the swagged ropes to face her sister. Before words could be spoken by either one, however, he smoothly offered his compliments. "We are well met, Lady Cheeves. I was quite hoping to greet you this evening, for I owe you a debt of thanks! Your singular accomplishment in returning your dear sister to our society has not gone unnoticed, nor is it unappreciated. I know—positively everyone must comment on it!— that it was your push which has accomplished the deed. How very gratified you must be at seeing your good advice heeded and your sister turned out in fine style." Harry beamed down upon the viscountess with such good will that none could fail to mark his approval.

Lydia remarked it, certainly, and stared back at him in the purest astonishment! Heretofore, such lights as the Earl Beaumont had scarcely seen fit to give but the barest of nods in her direction, and as for his assigning her the credit for Susan's appearance, well, it was just preposterous. But it was not in Lydia to outrightly refuse such high praise. Nervously, she turned to her sister and blurted out the very first thing that came into her mind.

"I do so like that haircut, Susan!" she exclaimed, sounding rather shrill. "I must have my dresser take note of it, though I'm not sure I'm brave enough to try such a short length myself."

"Brave? Why, of course you are, Lady Cheeves," the earl interposed. "I've no doubt it was your excellent influence which afforded your sister the courage to take up dancing, so don't think of trying to diddle me into believing you're not up to absolutely anything, dear lady."

196

"Well, I cannot quite claim the honors for *that*."

Lydia began to look flustered—while Susan had all she could do to swallow dangerously imminent, and likely hysterical, laughter.

"Now, let's have no false modesty, Lady Cheeves." Warningly, Harry increased a stifling grip on Susan's arm, well-aware of her barely suppressed mirth. Smoothly, he continued. "Actually, my lady, we all think you are most thoughtful. So obliging a mentor! And so magnanimous in sharing your sister with the orphaned Miss Doune. The Creagh heiress, don't y' know," he put in pointedly, "for indeed, I profess myself quite overcome by your sisterly affection." Harry swept her a graceful bow.

Lady Cheeves could only choke out her acceptance of this tribute as Susan strove, and strove mightily, to present an ingenuous face. Then, when Lord Petersham, that most tonnish man of the ton, brought Rachel over to complete the introductions, Lady Cheeves was so flattered that her resentment ended before it had truly begun. Never before had Lydia had two words addressed to her by that greatest leader of fashion—or at least, the greatest after George Brummell—so that now she must own herself prodigiously privileged to have speech with not only Lord Beaumont, but with the ever-so-exclusive Lord Petersham, as well.

The viscountess did not forget her obligations, howsomever. She was both glad and relieved to see Susan looking so well, but as her brother had been at some pains to point out, she had a further part. "Susan," she asked in hushed tones when an opportunity for privacy allowed, "are you *truly* happy where you are?" She anxiously picked at a plume decorating her fan. "I mean . . . well, Miss Doune seems quite unexceptional, of course, and certainly the Countess Jersey seems to approve, but you must know I have missed you. I am so *sorry* we had words. Really, I shouldn't have. . . ?"

Susan reached over and lightly squeezed her sister's shoulder. "And I miss all of you as well, Lydia. Very much. I should like to come for a visit, and I want you to come and see me soon, too. Do you think you will do that?"

"Oh! Yes, of course!" Lydia brightened and let her fan drop on its cord, quite forgotten.

Having overheard this last, Rachel prettily excused herself from their number. By this time her dance card was more than half-filled, and she saw her partner for the next set approaching. Lydia returned to her own group of friends to make sure they were aware of the notice she had received and was soon telling everyone who would listen, how she had been the one most responsible for her sister's coming out.

Lord Beaumont elected to remain near Lady Susan, giving the news-gleaners to conclude that he was caught at last. Lady Jersey, when she eventually arrived on the scene, supposed that such a handsome admirer would bring out the best in anyone. Gleefully, the countess was soon heard adding her speculations to the rest.

As for Harry? He did not seem to mind it in the least.

Chapter Thirteen

Not excessively interested in the predictions surrounding Lady Susan and the Earl Beaumont, Lord Petersham happened to be standing near the doorway of Almack's when Lord Ripley came in some fifteen minutes before the hour struck eleven. The Dandy pursed his lips in disapproval. For, in his estimation, the patronesses were highly remiss to give a man like the baron a voucher for so much as a single night.

At this, Lord Petersham determined to keep an eye on Lord Ripley, one whom he considered little more than a Jessamy Smart. Forgetting his lisp for the moment, he muttered "'Ware skirters!" *sotto voce.*

Rachel also witnessed the new arrival from her place on the ballroom floor. For once made clumsy, she missed a step in the country dance just playing and was at pains to recover her position. She didn't fully regain her composure until the baron's gaze passed over her without any sign of recognition. Still, she thought, she would have a care to keep out of his path. And with above three hundred guests crowding Almack's rooms this night, she feared it would be difficult to keep up with Lord Ripley's movements.

Indeed, the task so occupied her that she quite failed to see yet another guest admitted not ten minutes later. The Marquis of Tynsdale entered a scant half minute before the hour.

Severely elegant in beautifully tailored silk evening dress, replete with white waistcoat, white cravat, and with a brushed-silk *chapeau bras*, correctly positioned under one arm, he paused for a few moments to look over the company. And although nothing in his expression gave him away, the fact of it was, Marcus hadn't really wanted to come tonight. However, since he'd already convicted himself once of neglecting family obligations—his gross inattention toward his middle sister still pained him most particularly—he was doubly resolved to fulfill his duty to make a suitable marriage. In any case, he was obliged to remain in town until either Lady Susan or his nephew returned to the city before he could tend further to his sister's affairs. For this reason, he had decided to use the occasion to look over the unattached young ladies currently appearing at Almack's.

Somehow he failed to enjoy the prospect of tonight's venture, though. His responsibilities to the Tynsdale marquisate suddenly seemed endless.

Surveying the select society before him, Marcus first recognized Lydia in animated conversation amongst a small group to his right. He could have a word with her later, he decided. Continuing his perusal, he then noticed his friend Harry moving toward the tea room, giving escort to a lovely woman in a soft, flowing blue gown, a lady who appeared vaguely familiar. Curious, Marcus followed their progress as they passed under the last of the room's three great chandeliers. But as the bright glow lit the lady's face, all questions of identity disappeared. It pierced Marcus's unwilling brain that he beheld his own middle sister. Susan *was* out in the social world, and looking rather splendid, too. But if Susan was here, that meant. . . .

His fears increasing rapidly, Marcus narrowed his eyes to make a thorough sweep of the room. He did not see his nephew, who was likely not yet returned from Salisbury, nor Lord Ripley, who had gone into the card room, but soon enough, his concentration was rewarded when his eyes beheld Miss Rachel Doune.

It's just not possible! he cried silently in horror. Yet without a doubt, it was she. Miss Doune had somehow gained entry into this citadel of the elite, looking as serenely poised as any who belonged in the company.

Her heavy golden hair was tightly braided into a coronet accented by an elegant headpiece, while fine, curling strands were allowed loose to tease at her temples and down along the curve of her neck. As she twirled through the steps of the dance with her partner, the sheer silk gauze of her gown outlined a changing procession of altogether alluring and markedly feminine contours. A dark green sash was tied just beneath her full breasts, its trailing ends flowing smoothly down to the hemline, and the dark green length swung gently to and fro in graceful, undulating movements as she danced.

Battling the distractions of these several enticing details, Marcus held to his place until the music stopped. He then straightened his back, squared his wide shoulders, and forced himself onto the ballroom floor. If no one else realized she should not be here, *he* certainly did. And he must, really must, get her out of here!

Certainly, he had an idea that Miss Doune would not be best pleased. To be sure, he'd learned to rather dread her knack for using any opportunity to overset him. But he could not allow probable unpleasantness to act as a deterrent. He could not just stand idly by while she breached the walls of the ton.

This time, Marcus took care not to startle her. He made certain that she saw him approach. Notwithstanding that he'd twice seen her demonstrate her own odd brand of composure when challenged, he watched her carefully for any indications of nervous distress.

There were none. Almost none, that is. A slight, nearly imperceptible tilt to Miss Doune's chin did not escape his notice.

Politely acknowledging her partner, the marquis made

201

her a short stiff bow. It was the best he could manage under the circumstances, and while a thousand questions, most born of outrage, jolted through his mind. "Miss Doune," he said softly, still struggling for control, "how, ah, *extraordinary* it is to find you here. But since you are here, you must allow me your company during this intermission." He looked up to the overhanging balcony where Mr. Gow's orchestra was relaxing for a space. He forced a smile to his lips. "Surely you will not deny me the prospect. Oh, believe me, I do insist."

Marcus watched as she drew in a quick breath as if preparatory to refusing him. But before she could speak, her dance partner unwittingly interfered with her intent.

"Oh, I say, Miss Doune, please feel entirely free. I am delighted to defer to Lord Tynsdale." The young man beside her was all elation. He turned to the marquis and said excitedly, "I'm Evelyn Halston, don't you know. You may remember me as one of the fellows at Jackson's Saloon last fall? I was there that day when you had him on the hip, and what a capital set-to that was! Why, I've never seen anything to equal it. What a Go! What superior science!"

Not in a mood to appreciate these encomiums, or any other diversion, come to that, Marcus sought to hasten the young man on his way. "Yes, yes. So gratified to have your acquaintance, Mr. Halston." He shook the young man's hand with no more than the slightest degree of reserve. "But Miss Doune and I—"

From the corner of his eye, he noticed Miss Doune glancing about the room as if she were searching for someone. *Not yet*, he thought to himself. *Susan is my concern.*

"But the pleasure is all mine!" Mr. Halston enthused when Lord Tynsdale paused. "Not many can slip past the Champion's guard: only two others that I know of. And you did it in prime style, too!"

"Indeed, Mr. Halston," Marcus said dryly, returning his

202

attention to the young gentleman. "An occasion for sticking plaster, I think?" He considered Mr. Halston's mouth rather purposefully.

"Oh? Oh, indeed!" gushed Mr. Halston. "You mean the eye he gave you. Ha, ha! Very good, my lord! But you gave as good as Jackson delivered, didn't you? Well, of course, you did, for I saw the whole thing myself. And after you'd shaken hands with the Champion at the end, all of us fellows gave you a three-times-three, if you'll recall. You'll not make me believe a little sticking plaster meant anything compared to that!"

"Sticking plaster?" Rachel interrupted, rolling her eyes toward the ceiling. "I can think of rather a good use for it at the moment myself, but I don't suppose any is near to hand." Apparently she had realized that reinforcements were not available for the moment, but had decided to join battle unassisted.

"Yes, it's a shame not to have the needed items when they are wanted," Marcus agreed, then stared at their loquacious companion until Miss Doune's cheek began to twitch in amusement.

"Er, as you say," Mr. Halston agreed, without quite comprehending. "But you should have seen it, Miss Doune! Gentleman Jackson had to make a flush hit just to slow Lord Tynsdale's advance, and what a marrow-bone stop it was! But the marquis didn't go to grass after all; he took the blow on the roll."

"Oh, yes, Mr. Halston," she mused softly, turning her gaze to examine Lord Tynsdale's brow with every evidence of the greatest interest, "that does sound most satisfying. I rather think I might have liked being witness to that. Come to think of it, I'm sure I would have enjoyed it very much! But then, you say that his lordship didn't go down, if I understand you correctly? How very disappointing."

Marcus had every difficulty in discouraging a smile from forming. He knew he should bring this discussion to an end, especially since *Boxiana* was not a fit subject for mixed company. Still, he couldn't help being amused at the by-play.

"Well, no, I wouldn't say that," objected Mr. Halston. "What I mean is, Miss Doune, that Lord Tynsdale resisted a leveller issued by the Champion himself! No small feat, let me tell you. It was a tremendous, punishing blow!"

"Oh? But how very nice!" entered Miss Doune sweetly.

Evidently, Mr. Halston wasn't satisfied that she had the proper appreciation. "Well, I don't know if that's how I should put it, Miss Doune." He sounded rather disappointed with her conceptual failure. "For you must know that it was a prime turn-up. First rate!"

Again Miss Doune intervened. "Well, perhaps it is time, after all. Yes. Definitely some sticking plaster is wanted." She eyed Mr. Halston's mouth in turn. "I do wonder how it can be managed, though?"

Marcus had no hesitation in responding. Turning to the young gentleman, he said, "Miss Doune must be grateful to you for this wholly edifying account, Mr. Halston; however, this is hardly the place for it. And, I believe," he added gently, "that you were about to excuse us, were you not?"

Upon the reminder, the young man blushed slightly, then assured his lordship that he was more than happy to give Miss Doune into the keeping of one who was, by every acknowledgement, one of England's foremost amateur fighters. And her startled look at Lord Tynsdale's choice of words, a look which left Marcus grinning widely, made Mr. Halston sure that Lord Tynsdale had been pleased with their converse on matters pugilistic. As for Miss Doune's rather strange comments, Mr. Halston was left to conclude that they were due to her not yet being quite up to snuff.

After he had taken himself off, Rachel muttered under her breath, "Presumptuous prig."

"Oh, surely not that bad, Miss Doune," her new escort disagreed. "Just very young and inclined to ebullience, I think."

"I was not referring to Mr. Halston. You failed to comprehend my meaning, Lord Tynsdale."

"Did I?" he asked softly.

She stared up at him, and saw the laughter in his eyes. Then she sighed, and with a little shake of her head made a question of her own. "Could you tell me something? Do you always draw the wrong conclusions—and is it deliberate or merely done from ignorance? Though I cannot think you are a stupid man, whatever evidence to the contrary."

"And you, Miss Doune," he retorted, feeling a bit stung, "do you always turn everything into an argument?" At her frown, he continued. "Perhaps you aren't aware of it, but whenever we meet, you seem to positively delight in making the occasion contentious by picking apart everything I say to you. And when things don't go quite to suit, you resort to name calling. 'Vicious rakeshame,' 'scaly brute,' and now 'presumptuous prig' come to mind."

"No, no," she at once demurred. "'Brute' was your word, remember?"

"Oh, so it was," he said, disconcerted.

"And it still rankles, does it?" She chuckled. "Then, suppose we add 'jolter-headed nigmenog,' or possibly 'blockheaded booby'?"

"Why, then I might be inclined to commit to calling up a few accounts myself," he said meaningfully. "'Dashing deceiver' and 'lampooning ladybird' seem to me appropriate."

"So, we're back to that already!" She rounded on him, lifting her square little chin. Her eyes sparkled up at him in anger.

That outraged glare almost proved his undoing.

Not green, nor yet truly blue, he saw, bemused. He'd wondered about their color before, but now that he had a chance to restudy the matter, still he wasn't sure. Right now her eyes seemed more blue, the crisp, sunlit blue of an October morning sky. But such truly beautiful eyes, he decided wistfully. Then, there was her hair to consider. He felt a strong desire to feel the silky texture of its satin smoothness, and to feel his hand glide over the warmth that was surely her skin.

Abruptly, Marcus called himself to order. *Oh, no, not this again!* He stepped back, recollecting his proper rôle.

". . . so my acceptance here at Almack's indicates nothing to you?" she was just saying in her frank and altogether compelling way.

His answer came readily enough. "Indeed it does, Miss Doune. But come, we cannot stand here glowering at one another. Let's walk about a bit and see if we cannot reach an understanding." After she nodded a somewhat reluctant agreement, he pasted an appropriately bland sort of look on his face so as not to draw attention from those others in the room. His intention was to convince Miss Doune to leave Almack's on her own, without raising a fuss. He offered his arm, then commenced an easy stroll away from the refreshment area where the majority of guests were currently gathered.

Satisfied that they should not be remarked, and relieved not to have to face those limpid eyes while trying to make his case, he proceeded. "You came here under Susan's aegis, I take it, Miss Doune? I saw her as I came in, you must know." His voice came low and deep.

Miss Doune, following his lead, donned her own mask of vague but polite interest. "How good of you to finally recognize her," she said, the sarcastic notes at variance with her pleasant mien.

"Ah, yes. The Opera House." With effort, he maintained his carefully disinterested manner. Sternly, he squelched his ire, reminding himself that he must have Miss Doune's cooperation, no matter what the cost. "Well," he said as amicably as he could, "let us leave consideration of that for later. I think, first, we must go to the beginning to establish our facts, that is, if we are to prosper by this discussion. Do you agree, Miss Doune?"

"Yes, certainly," came her prompt response.

"And these facts must include your background, which is not such as would find its way into the pages of *Collins' Peerage*. Am I correct?" He quite casually gave the nod to an acquaintance who caught his eye in passing.

"That is true," she replied, without a sign of compunction.

"Ah. So may I also assume that you have deliberately acquainted yourself with my sister in order to expand your reputation among the upper ranks?" Without breaking stride, he skillfully guided Miss Doune around a chattering parcel of debutantes.

This time her answer was much more hesitant, even cautious. "Well, I think you could put it that way," she owned. "I came to London with the intent of establishing myself in Society, and I am very much in Susan's debt for helping me. But if you still think—"

"Well, then!" he quickly interposed. "There is no problem in our coming to an accord, Miss Doune. Since your masquerade as a lady born is now discovered, you will have no trouble understanding why I must insist that you leave here, quietly, and at once. You may trust me to see Susan home, for I intend to bring her to my house, where her *real* place lies. It's where she belongs, you understand."

Marcus was actually very pleased by the reasonable way he was managing the thing, despite Miss Doune's disquieting presence. He had withstood the temptation of Beauty and, quite naturally, felt very proud of himself.

But he had reckoned on a victory too soon.

Miss Doune's teeth clamped shut, her jaw lifted, then she spoke. Her voice was by any description frosty, as if she had resolved to not merely match, but to exceed the example he'd set her. "Unless I am very much mistaken, Lord Tynsdale," the words came cool and crisp, "we had a similar discussion once before. You warned me off from another member of your family—I recall the occasion quite clearly—though at the time, I didn't realize Mr.

Cheeves was your nephew. But I put it to you, my lord, which is worse? The supposed evils of my influence, or these unwanted attempts of yours to dominate your family, and after who-knows-how-many years of neglect? Where were you when Susan needed you, I ask? And why, pray, an interest at this late date?"

"Impertinence," he growled, feeling his control starting to slip.

"Oh, hardly that," she said, looking up at him. "I daresay that for all your talk of peerages and ranks, none of my family would ever have ignored their responsibilities to a dependant as you have done. And *that* is a fact I find very pertinent indeed!"

She was royally incensed and no denying it.

Looking down at her, Marcus rigorously held his mind to what he saw as the point. Or, at least, that's what he tried to do, for he couldn't quite prevent himself from appreciating the beautifully upright posture and the haughty, scornful countenance before him. No cringing, no wiles or wheedles from Miss Doune. Instead, she faced him steadily and without sign of fear. Her outward calm, her impossibly feminine features, cloaked the proud heart of a rampant lion.

"Miss Doune," he ground out, ruthlessly smothering an absurd inclination to admire, "you have absolutely no right to criticize, when you are yourself guilty of perpetrating this—" he looked around the room at the elegant assemblage of England's finest—"this *fraud!* You must see why such a thing is impossible."

But her response to this piece of logic left him completely nonplussed. Unbelievably, Miss Doune stopped dead in her tracks to loose a silvery shower of laughter.

"Oh, but this is all so silly!" she said at last when she could catch a breath. "Here you are, finally committed to Susan's support—which makes me very happy, of course —but, Lord Tynsdale, just how can you continue to be so excessively civil to me, when I know what you think I am!" She broke off to stifle another surging gurgle of laughter. "It's charming. Really! And while you can't possibly realize it, when you look at me *so*, you do put me in mind of what Fullerton said about you."

"I beg pardon?" he said stiffly.

"Fullerton. That's our butler." Still mirthful, she seemed undeterred by his tone.

"I know *that*, Miss Doune. But I'm waiting for you to explain how that is anything to the point. Please!" He could scarcely contain himself.

"Ah-*ha*. That's just what I mean!" she trilled, pointing up at him. "Fullerton said—well, actually Susan started it—but anyway, what they were talking about was whether you could ice a jug of water merely by a look. And indeed, your face does get all sort of frozen-looking, rather like a very fierce snowman!"

"Miss Doune!"

"There, there, now." She patted his arm reassuringly. "I didn't mean to tease you past bearing." She sighed deeply as a pensive look overtook her fine features. Holding his eye, she said seriously, "You really cannot like me, can you, Lord Tynsdale? I mean, we seem to get on famously at times, until something puts one of us back on the high-ropes. An odd sense of propriety, that," she added quietly.

He couldn't help forming a smile, a somewhat rueful one. "Miss Doune, I do have a position in this world, remember; never can I forget it. And I remind you that Susan does not deserve the embarrassment your unmasking will bring her. I cannot have her further involved. I positively will not permit her to suffer! You must see why I have to insist that you leave here, and without further ado."

Miss Doune's little chin inclined a notch.

Before he could urge further, however, a slight cough revealed another presence come upon them. Lord Petersham appeared at Miss Doune's side, striking up an Attitude of "A Gentleman Dismayed." "Do excuth my untimely interruption," he said with assumed naivete, "but Almackth's isth hardy the place for the type of converthsation you two are holding. And, really, Lord Tynsdale," he scolded with mock severity, "you should know better. Too therious for our little group, don't you thee."

The Dandy seemed unconcerned by the two indignant pairs of eyes that whirled to meet his own. He very politely reached over to take up Miss Doune's free arm, amiably motioning toward the dance floor. "The musicians are ready to begin playing again, and *I* will be the one embarrassthed if we do not find our places beforehand. Misth Doune? It won't do to be late in joining our group, you know."

Marcus could hardly protest this piece of interference, coming as it did from such an *arbitre* as Lord Petersham. Yet a deep scowl marked his features as the young viscount, with marvelous decorum, led Miss Doune away. Marcus stood unmoving for some minutes, puzzling over his closely felt obligations and wondering what next to do about them.

Only one other guest noticed the incident. Finding himself unwelcome in the card room, Lord Ripley had reentered the main assembly room in time to see the marquis engaged in a rather intense conversation with a young beauty who looked familiar. Taking a closer look, the baron recollected that he had seen the chit before—and the circumstance of that meeting.

Vastly interested, Lord Ripley watched next as Lord Petersham came upon the couple and then drew the young beauty out onto the dance floor. He thought Lord Tynsdale's subsequent frown simply due to the disappointment of the lovers at the disruption of their little *tête-à-tête;* the corresponding inferences interested the baron thoroughly.

Lord Ripley had found himself virtually shunned these past few days. Never a very popular fellow, he had lately discovered himself to be in even worse case, an *on-dit*, in fact, and he angrily blamed the Marquis of Tynsdale for his accumulating ills. Recognizing the pretty chit as

Tynsdale's *inamorata*, the same who had helped thwart him with the little servant girl, the baron now eagerly questioned a bystander about the young woman's identity. Learning that the chit was a great heiress under Lady Susan Kinsworth's protection, he immediately saw that there might be a way to gain his proper revenge.

However, he had no intention of confronting either of his adversaries head on. That way had led to his previous disgrace. But there was another way to even the score, with the interfering blond heiress thrown in for good measure. Unnoticed, Lord Ripley gathered his cape from the doorman and made his way out into the night with a malevolent, self-satisfied grin.

Lady Susan had not seen her brother's arrival, being entirely absorbed in a world of Lord Beaumont's making. The earl had guided her about the assembly rooms, introducing her to his particular friends with an unmistakable aura of pride. He saw to her every comfort and was all consideration when the music recommenced, seeing to it that she was seated comfortably, even making an adjustment to the nearby potted palm so that it wouldn't restrict her view of the dance floor. Saying he believed the tartines of bread and butter with which they'd refreshed themselves earlier were now in need of some accompaniment, Lord Beaumont then begged her to await him as he went back into the tea room to fetch her a glass of lemonade. Acknowledging his thoughtfulness, Susan sat, tapping her foot softly in time to the music while thinking this the loveliest evening in memory.

"I take it your 'houseparty' was sadly flat, dearest sister?" A low voice intruded upon her respite.

Susan started and looked up in dismay at the man who had so silently approached her chair. *What is* he *doing here?*

"Marcus!" she croaked. She quickly shot a glance around the ballroom, noting that Lord Petersham was just

211

handing Rachel safely into Lady Jersey's care, and that Lord Beaumont was already on his way back from the refreshment room. There was no time for Susan to feel much relief, however, for her brother readdressed her in a too-soft voice, a voice with a distinctive edge to it.

"Surprised, Susan?" he said mockingly. "No more than I, I do assure you. In fact, if your message had not specifically informed me otherwise, I would find myself suspecting that you had never left town at all. Or could it be—" he gave her a fulsome look—"could it *possibly* be that I am misled?"

Lord Beaumont arrived just in time to catch this last. Swiftly, he deposited the glasses of orgeat at the base of the planter and moved to interpose himself squarely between Susan and her brother. "Marcus," he said pleasantly, while Susan leaned slightly to one side so as to better see what went on, "I didn't expect to see you here tonight, man. I had assumed that—"

But the earl was cut off by an indisputably forbidding expression. "So it would seem," came Marcus's stinging rebuke. The marquis then took one lateral step and pointedly directed his attentions back to his sister. "Perhaps you would care to explain, my dear?" he said, his words still soft.

Those who knew him could not mistake his anger; nonetheless, Susan held her features tranquil as she reached out to accept Harry's arm. Gracefully, she rose from her seat, stepping forth to face her brother. She realized that Lord Beaumont would take over her defense, did she but allow it, and yet, she felt it was time she ran her own course. Marcus must learn that she might just have a temper of her very own.

"Can this actually be my brother?" Her tones were as soft as any. She paused, as if to examine the face of some stranger come upon her. In the most detached manner possible, she continued. "My brother, the Marquis of Tynsdale, who, in one breath, would defend his poor, defenseless sister from depredations to her purse—and that by the only kinsman who really cares for her!—and, in another breath, would prey on innocent and unprotected young ladies?" Her light brown eyes turned nearly golden with indignation. "Oh, no," she said as quietly as to make nearly a whisper, "I think this cannot be anyone I am related to." Turning to the gentleman beside her, she said, "Harold, I fail to recognize this person."

In an act unprecedented for such a gentle lady, she then brushed past her brother with Lord Beaumont firmly in tow. Unbeknownst to her brother, she was bent on removing to the refreshment room before her legs turned completely to jelly . . . leaving Marcus, stupefied, feeling very much as if he'd been bitten by a hutch-raised bunny!

What the deuce was going on here? Just what did Susan mean? Surely she could not be so trusting of that little upstart of a Miss Rachel Doune! And Harry? Was he, too, taken in? Marcus was sure he had heard the beginning sounds of rolling male laughter as Harry passed him by.

Watching them move away toward the card room, Lord Tynsdale, despite the many shocks of the evening, became aware of significant improvement in his sister's stride. Only the barest trace of a limp remained; not at all noticeable, unless one had watched her halting steps, year after laborious year. Neither could he fail to note the improvement in Susan's looks. Artful curls surrounded her sweet face, bringing out an appealingly piquant aspect, one which he couldn't remember Susan to have had before. For the second time that evening, Marcus remarked with astonishment his middle sister's attractions.

He pushed aside these thoughts. He bent his mind to a more important matter—the staggering change in Susan's *manner*. That Miss Doune was the cause of the alteration in Susan seemed sure; that interfering, brazen young miss had evidently infected his timid sister with her bold and insolent ways. And it wasn't such a bad thing either, Marcus had to own. Susan was the better for having a shade more confidence.

However, there were other things, and not nearly so admirable, that Miss Doune must answer for. She had somehow tricked the naive and overly generous Susan into providing sponsorship for her entry into Society. Bruton Place could also boast of a new staff of domestics, for the estimable Fullerton was certainly not the same butler who had greeted Miss Doune's arrival in London. Then, too, there were those exquisite gowns Miss Doune wore, both tonight and at the Opera House. Were they something else provided by Susan?

Yet, in all honesty, Marcus couldn't deny the apparent benefits to his sister. It seemed that Susan had gained as much or more than anyone had from her association with Miss Doune. "Oh, God, what a muddle," he groaned softly.

He began to realize that extricating his sister from Miss Doune's clutches was going to be an extremely delicate undertaking, especially now that Miss Doune had such adherents as seemed so ready to stand up in her defense. First it was Gilbert who was taken in by Miss Doune, then Susan. Marcus must add Lord Petersham to the list, who-knew-which Almack's patroness, and, apparently, to complicate matters further, even his own best friend.

Only one thing would answer. . . . Marcus carefully scouted the room.

"How very delightful to have you with us tonight!" Lady Jersey greeted someone over her shoulder.

So apparent was the countess's coy animation that Rachel didn't even need to turn round to assure herself that a member of the opposite sex had joined them.

"Dear lady," came the deep-voiced response.

Rachel froze. She couldn't believe his audacity. She could hardly mistake the distinctive timbre of *that* voice, though, and sure as check, when she looked over to see who stood on the patroness's other side, she beheld Marcus Kinsworth. Again.

The marquis executed his bow to the countess with courtly finesse, making the barest of nods in Rachel's direction. Immediately returning the whole of his attention back to Lady Jersey, he said, "May I then hope for your kind forgiveness, Sarah? Oh, I know I have too long been absent from these premises to expect you to indulge me, but I wouldn't wish to add neglect of my sister's protégée to the list of my other sins. I had the thought of introducing Miss Doune into the intricacies of the waltz, though, considering it my bounden responsibility, you understand. Will you favor us with your permission, my lady?" By neither tone of voice nor overt movement did he give away what must be his real feelings; he appeared wholly serene.

Rachel, on the other hand, had to struggle mightily to contain her own reaction! She'd no sooner felt herself secure than she'd found herself again under siege. Like the gentleman, she was accustomed to disguising her private upsets as needed, certainly, although these repeated assaults on her dignity were nearly more than she could withstand.

Consciously, she alerted her brow, lips, and eyes to hold themselves steady before this latest attack.

"Oh, you are quite, quite incorrigible!" Lady Jersey twittered, obviously unaware of the shifting currents of distrust. Her dark curls flounced animatedly while she tapped the marquis flirtatiously with the ivory tines of her fan. "You Corinthians ignore us for months on end, then have but to show your handsome faces for all to be totally forgiven. And, indeed, how should I be the one to refuse you?" She sighed, looking happily resigned. "Of course, any girl old enough for six-button gloves must be flattered to have your attention. Am I not right, Miss Doune?"

"Indeed?" Rachel responded, deliberately vague, since she was rather more aware of his lordship's game. Then, acting as though she had suddenly recalled herself, she said in stronger tones, "Oh, yes, most assuredly you are correct, my lady. Why, any suggestion that I had failed to be pleased by his lordship's notice would not do. Not at all! But then . . ." she again let her voice trail off, as if her thoughts drifted idly, "some men's self-consequence quite depends upon our participation in these little conceits, I think."

The countess laughed quite gaily, her eyes brightening with interest. "Now that is most what I like about you, Miss Doune. No missish airs and graces. But come, my dear, you must put yourself forward in his lordship's esteem just a little! Surely you've no cause to doubt my Lord Tynsdale's sincerity?"

"Nor do I." Rachel answered the question honestly. "Instead," she said, looking Lord Tynsdale straight in the eye, "I am inclined to believe that his lordship is, if anything, over-inclined to take his self-assigned rôle too seriously."

"But what could be of more import, Miss Doune?" he put in gravely. "The first waltz at Almack's marks an occasion of the utmost importance. Your opinion, Sarah?" he asked, turning to the countess.

"But of course!" Lady Jersey happily agreed. "We do not grant our permission for the waltz to just anyone, you know. So, off with you two. Enjoy yourselves!"

With no recourse after being as good as commanded by Queen Sarah, Rachel accepted her designated partner with as much grace as she could. She allowed herself to be escorted onto the waxed parquetry floor with no show of her very real misgivings. Neil Gow's orchestra launched into the melodious strains of a waltz, and with the first musical note, Lord Tynsdale took up her hand and turned her to face him.

Unwillingly, Rachel absorbed her impressions of his breathtakingly handsome features, now sternly set with purpose. Encountering the marquis' oak-dark eyes, she thought he looked more like a man resolved to some unpleasant duty, rather than a gentleman proposing to enjoy himself. She supposed he must be preparing to rip up at her again.

She held herself stiffly through the primary steps, waiting for whatever it was his lordship had in mind to say. She felt greatly inclined to resist the press of his fingertips at her back, and more especially after she noticed an unwanted tingly sort of feeling crawling its way languorously along her spine. Inexplicably, Rachel found herself suddenly reminded of the smooth lengths of muscle that surely rippled beneath his elegant evening clothes, the thought making her lower her face, her eyelashes dropping in shamed confusion.

Within moments, Rachel realized she was acting the coward. She forced herself to look up and meet her partner's eyes, eyes which now seemed oddly uncertain, a mirror to her own unsettled thoughts. Without knowing why, she at once gave up all resistance and deliberately relaxed into his hold. Rewarded for her decision, she basked in the immediate warmth of Lord Tynsdale's small, pleased smile. She instantly felt a complementing heat speed through her veins with gently insistent pulsations.

Neither one spoke a word. It was as if the fragile strength of the musical notes, linking them together, was something too extraordinarily precious to break. The firm hold of his guiding hands gently suggested the directions for her steps, and she responded easily, naturally, reacting to each changing pressure as though it were the most important thing in the world for her to do. Music washed away anger while the concurrency of their movements forbade any further teasing or exchange of words.

They circled the room to the measures of the dance. Rachel felt herself whirled skillfully around the floor, until the colorful gowns surrounding her became unrecognizable, blurry streaks of brilliant rainbow hue. She grew giddy in the circular patterns, until she felt that her only attachment to reality was the strong arms of her partner, holding her close and swinging her around and around. A small smile gradually formed on her own lips as tensions continued to ease. For the moment she left off worrying about his lordship's vile and fallacious suppositions.

His steps were long and sure. They seemed a part of the music, part of the light and color twirling endlessly about her. Rachel heard only the violins urging her on, as the marquis guided her in time to the rhythmic flow of sound.

Lord Tynsdale, too, was beguiled by the music and by the supple sway of the golden-haired beauty he held within his arms. She was of such a delicate size in contrast to his own heavier masculinity; she was fairy-slight in comparison. Strange, he hadn't noticed that before. But now he realized that the crown of her head came just as high as the top of his shoulder, making him feel taller and stronger somehow. Her fair skin glowed in the fiery lights of the ballroom fixtures, and looking down at her, Marcus watched, pleased, when her lips softened by degrees into a smile. Thick, dark lashes shielded her eyes, but he recalled their clear, green-blue fire as she had so calmly, so fearlessly faced up to him earlier. *Fearless*, he decided, reflecting on how well the word fitted her.

This last thought had the unfortunate effect of leading Marcus on to another, however. His lips thinned and tightened as he recollected his purpose in drawing Miss Doune into the dance; the dictates of conscience once again compelled him. "I think I should warn you, Miss Doune, that your game is almost up," he said through the violin's stirring notes.

The air between them seemed to quiver and vibrate with the rumbling sound of his voice. To Rachel, the sound was naught but another aspect of this beautiful, magical waltz. Lord Tynsdale's wide chest, just inches from her cheek, radiated warmth and, curiously, a solidly reliable sort of strength. She felt wonderfully secure, hardly noticing it when he continued to speak.

"However much money you have extracted from my sister, I intend that she be repaid."

He twirled her around, the words still not registering in her mind.

"I will call at Bruton Place early tomorrow, and this time I expect Susan to be there. I will have a few last things to say to you then, as well, Miss Doune."

Rachel's senses gradually returned as the dance ended on a single, fading note. She looked up to stare into his dark eyes, eyes which were no longer welcoming, but determinedly uncompromising, instead. Slowly, his meaning penetrated her consciousness. Yet, she had no time to think, no time to reply before Lord Tynsdale bowed and left her. He exited the building without uttering another word.

Chapter Fourteen

As the Marquis of Tynsdale stepped out into the night on King Street, Lady Susan and Lord Beaumont were at the same moment hurrying over to Rachel's side. They had returned to the ballroom as the waltz ended and had seen Marcus abruptly desert his partner and leave the assembly.

"I should never, never have left you!" Susan cried out in dismay upon reaching the younger woman. "How came it that Marcus contrived to get you into the dance?"

"Oh, with his usual high-handedness," Rachel grimly replied. "He just marched up to Lady Jersey and soon had me commandeered onto the floor, all before I had the veriest chance to protest. And before that, Susan, during the orchestra's intermission, there was an exchange of words in which your brother very politely said I was to leave Almack's, and at once, if you please, since I have no right to be here and masquerading as a 'lady born.' Yes, that's how he put it," she said at Susan's expression of disbelief. "Thankfully, though, Lord Petersham rescued me before we quite came to blows. Then, however, your ever-so-noble brother somehow talked the Countess of Jersey into letting me take the dance floor with him for the waltz. All of this, without caring a jot for my permission, mind, and during which, he said something about my taking your money, and how I should be made to repay him."

"Masquerading? Taking my money? What can he mean, Rachel? You have not let me spend a penny of my own funds, not even for this dress I have on!"

"Well," said Rachel somewhat acidly, "I certainly do not care to try to explain anything to one so puffed up in his own consequence. Honestly, Susan, the man has me not knowing my ups from my downs." She shook her head in confusion. "One minute he's apologizing as if my acceptance were the most important thing in the world to him; then he goes on with some sort of nonsense, until he makes me to laugh, even while he smiles at me right from his eyes. And then? Then he ices up and won't listen to a word I say! But one thing is certain. The man is determined to believe that I am a . . . a Phryne." Rachel stumbled over the term as she caught Lord Beaumont's look. "Well, he does!" she muttered, looking down as if to study the drape of the green satin sash adorning the front of her gown.

At the sound of throat-clearing, both women turned to Lord Beaumont, who had been interestedly listening to Rachel's tirade. "I think," he began, "that Marcus has drawn some rather nasty conclusions based upon the available evidence."

"Evidence?" Rachel squeaked. "Well, I'll tell you what he cited as evidence! He so much as told me that anyone not listed in his precious *Peerage* was beneath all consideration. Ha! Allow me to tell you that I think he is beneath all *contempt*."

"No, no," the earl said mildly. "Attend me, Miss Doune. Susan's brother meets a young woman when she climbs uninvited into his curricle. Now, I know it for a fact that Marcus has never allowed a female—any female—to ride with him behind his creams. Next, according to what you've told me, this woman—that's you, Miss Doune—sends him chasing after a coach containing a notorious loose fish of a nobleman and a young servant girl. Not exactly good ton, what? Then, when Marcus later sees this same young woman at the opera with his nephew, a boy whom Marcus thinks a rattlepate, by-the-by, and they are together with another beautiful creature he mistakes for a Cyprian—?" He turned a fond look upon Susan's enticing ringlets. "Well, it's all perfectly understandable, what?"

Pure disbelief met this discourse! Nonetheless, and with a satisfied smile, the earl insisted once again that nothing could be plainer. He patiently explained that even though Marcus had decided that Miss Doune's behavior marked her as someone outside the pale, his friend was so smitten that he couldn't resist any opportunity to come to blows with his ladylove. "In any other case, Marcus would simply cut you dead, Miss Doune. There would be none of these repeated, and if I may say so, these rather *involved* run-ins you two seem so prone to. Why, it's all clear as glass!" he maintained.

Disgusted by such convolutions, Rachel expressed herself in decided disagreement, then dutifully returned to the ballroom floor to finish out the dances she'd already promised. No one, positively no one, was going to put her off from her purpose tonight! Still, she had to feel it unfortunate when none of her other partners danced quite as smoothly or had shoulders quite as broad as she liked, and that their several conversations were less provocative or interesting than she could have wished. All the young men seemed to have nothing to offer but a series of overdone compliments. Lord Tynsdale, in comparison, had at least been demanding of her abilities. Trying to discern *his* meanings was a challenge.

Before they left Almack's, with unusual timorousness, Lady Cheeves approached Susan wanting to know if she might come to Bruton Place for a visit. Susan expressed herself in every way delighted by the suggestion. She hugged Lydia, helped her to untangle a wristlet caught in her ecru-colored shawl, and set about assuring her elder sister that she and Rachel would welcome her at any time. It being nearly two of the clock, Rachel's party then called for their wraps and their coach, and Lord Beaumont instructed the driver to return them to No. 12.

The night air was seasonably fresh, so the drive home should have been pleasant. Instead, Rachel found the air decidedly warm. Almost before the coach could start them on their way, she renewed her arguments against any excuses for Lord Tynsdale's behavior. The earl, shaking his head with laughter, would only say, "Think it over." More than a trifle miffed, Rachel rode the rest of the way home in silence.

After being tucked into bed by Mrs. Tully, Rachel waited only for the abigail to leave. She then climbed out from the covers and fumbled her way across to the cushioned, channel-back writing chair which she dragged over to the partially opened window. Seating herself, she disconsolately rested her elbows upon the window's sill. She tried to make some sense of the evening—and of her contradictory feelings about Susan's brother.

On the one hand, Lord Tynsdale invariably left her almost speechless with anger. The man held her in utter contempt, that was sure, beginning from the time she had refused to ignore Flora's pitiful cries for help. In retrospect, Rachel admitted that she could have sent Duncan off in her stead, but then, she remembered the tilbury that had become entangled with their coach, a situation which would have cost too much precious time to remedy. Besides, it was ever her way to see a thing done herself, and however impetuous, her actions were hardly sufficient reason for his lordship to think her less than respectable. *Weren't they?*

On the other hand, and most confusing of all, was her reaction to the man himself. Oh, it was not so surprising that she had succumbed momentarily to his kiss on that first evening, for it had come as such a surprise! But her subsequent willingness to tease him, and even to participate in a lighthearted repartee, left her feeling a touch uncertain. His lordship thought the worst of her, based upon mere nothings for evidence, so why, then, did she persist in twitting him like she did? She must conclude that contrary to what Lord Beaumont thought, it was *she* who should cut Marcus Kinsworth and not the other way round.

So why on earth don't I? she plaintively wondered.

Stubbornness was the first answer that came to mind. She hated to be bested in any dispute. Years of spirited discussions with her grandfather had always been a thing she enjoyed, for controversy stimulated her, giving her opportunities to hone her wits against a worthy adversary. It was a fault in her, she knew—one really shouldn't argue just for argument's sake—still, the subjects of her converse with Lord Tynsdale could hardly be considered unimportant.

Was there just a wee bit more to it than that? Had she not deliberately tweaked Lord Tynsdale for another reason? Honest to a fault, Rachel accepted the answer: she wanted him to smile at her. She wanted to make him laugh, particularly in those moments when he was trying his hardest to keep an aloof and detached manner. And each time she succeeded, she was rewarded with that marvelously warm, rumbling laughter that only he could make. There was such a joy in the sound of it that she wished to hear it over and over again. Contrariness, indeed.

And tonight at Almack's, she had lost herself in the waltz as if being held in Marcus Kinsworth's arms was the most marvelous thing in the world. He, too, had seemed to forget about his wrong-headed assumptions and about the angry words spoken between them in the past. He had held her with gentle, protective strength, held her till the warmth from his big body flowed right through to her very own limbs, until. . . .

"Rachel, may I come in?" Mired in her thoughts, Rachel had not heard Susan's knock.

"What? Oh! Yes, please do, Susan. I'm not asleep, so just let me set us up with a lamp." Rachel was glad for any interruption to her troublesome abstraction.

While Rachel prepared and lit the lamp, Susan entered, wearing a quilted dressing gown and closely followed by a huge, square-footed, gray-and-black-striped tom. The big cat surveyed the room in the oil lamp's light, then proceeded to the bed, which he invaded with a heavy thud. Bubbling with laughter, Susan joined him atop the covers

225

and commenced to scratch the animal under the chin.

After setting her pet into a purr, she peeped over at Rachel and said, "Rachel, I've been giving what Harold said some thought and am beginning to understand what he meant. I came to see what you think."

Rachel noted the older woman's familiar usage of Lord Beaumont's given name but made no comment on the liberty. She had more to concern herself with at present.

"Well, any light shed would be greatly appreciated," she entered dryly. "This situation has me quite cock-a-hoop. Try how I might, Susan, I cannot see how anything I have done should have brought me into such distressing predicaments as I've found myself sharing with Lord Tynsdale. Yet, in all, I keep wondering if perhaps I've misjudged, and really should be holding myself up for blame."

Susan looked thoughtful, then rejected the idea. "No, Rachel, you aren't in the wrong, for Marcus was ever full of his consequence, I own." She frowned a moment longer, before hunching slim shoulders beneath their quilted covering to muse, "I've many times wondered if things might have been different if Mother hadn't died while Marcus was so young. Six years before Father, in fact. However, as it was, Marcus was left to pattern himself after the man who, now that I look back on it, was not a very loving parent, only a very proud one."

"Ugh! Proud indeed," Rachel interjected.

"True enough," Susan agreed, absently stroking the tom. "But with the old marquis, blood was everything, you see. He was a strict disciplinarian with rigid ideas about class. I can well remember how he insisted that Marcus excel in every sport, telling Marcus that it was the way a nobleman showed his natural supremacy. Though held to be of lesser importance, my brother's fine academic progress was also extolled by our father as proof of our family's superiority."

At Rachel's patently skeptical look, Susan continued. "Oh, I know it sounds horridly condescending, Rachel, but do consider. Marcus was given the title of earl at the time of his christening, and then, by the age of fourteen, he became a marquis. The world has always ranked him high, and my brother would have every reason for accepting our father's ideas as being entirely appropriate."

Rachel couldn't keep still a moment longer. "Well, it seems he's forgotten that high stations require fulfillment of heavy responsibilities. A sad business he's made of caring for you, I'd say!"

"But I've already explained how that came about, Rachel, and the fault was at least as much mine as his. And the fact that Marcus is now attempting to rectify matters must speak well for him, don't you see? Oh, his outward manner may be like Father's, but I believe them much unalike. Why, I can't imagine the old marquis bothering to debate points with anyone! He would have just snapped his fingers and had you removed from Almack's without caring how much humiliation you or I would have suffered. Father would neither have understood, nor appreciated, how we might have felt."

Rachel remembered her own virtually unfettered, happy childhood, and contrasted it against Marcus Kinsworth's. Ian Creagh had praised her strength and took great pride in her achievements, too, but he had never dictated her judgments for her. Instead, Grandfather had seemed to enormously enjoy their disputations and disagreements, always leaving Rachel to come to her own conclusions. Nonetheless, Grandfather was her teacher. He constantly encouraged her to judge ideas from principles and people from particulars. The elder Tynsdale apparently had done the reverse, and the absurdly preconceived notions of his son showed the result.

"Well, perhaps that explains why Lord Tynsdale finds me so objectionable, and why he does not want you in my company," Rachel finally agreed, "but I still don't see what this has to do with your brother's accusations about money, nor with Lord Beaumont's theory." Rachel felt an unusual self-consciousness at these words.

"Actually," said Susan slowly, stroking the gray-striped

tom in concentration, "I don't perfectly understand everything, either. However, it would appear that Marcus is lately behaving quite out of his established character, and all appearances to the contrary, Marcus has ever prided himself on acting as befits a nobleman of the realm. Why, I know for a certainty that he's never missed a single session of Parliament since he reached his majority! Yet lately, he has interfered with a fellow peer's pursuits—an unpardonable social solecism—and then, later, caused that same lord grave embarrassment at White's. He isn't *indifferent*, don't you see, dear?"

Rachel chose to ignore this last for the moment. She at once begged for the details of the contretemps at the exclusive gentlemen's club—Susan's having had the story from Lord Beaumont, and Rachel's not having heard about what had happened there. When Susan finished, she and Rachel both fell into a bout of the giggles at Marcus's now-famous *bon mot*.

Thence reminded of Lord Ripley's subsequent appearance at Almack's, Rachel next related to Susan how she had seen the baron this night and how he had not seemed to recognize her. Shrugging her shoulders against making bugs into bears, Rachel then returned to her previous complaint.

"But if your brother thinks so little of me, why does he plague me so and accuse me of all manner of odious things?" she asked unhappily.

"And why have you not told him that you are an heiress, educated and properly genteel?"

This question stopped Rachel cold. "Well . . . well, I shouldn't have to explain," she sputtered in defense. "I mean—"

"Yes?" asked Susan in a knowing sort of voice.

"He ought to realize—"

"Indeed?"

"But—"

"Pride. Pure and simple! That's what it is, Rachel, and you know it. But don't you understand it yet? That's just what Harold was talking about." Susan stole a look to gauge her friend's reaction. Gently, she added, "And forgive me, Rachel, but I am beginning to agree. You aren't acting with your usual good sense either—no more than Marcus. Why, the mere mention of his name is enough to send you straight up into the boughs. You and my brother really are very much alike, you know."

"Oh, you are all about in the head, Susan!" Rachel jumped up, startling the tom cat, who had been stretched out quietly with his eyes half-closed. Indignantly he raised his great head and rounded his yellow-green gaze at the cause of the disturbance. Equally indignant, Rachel's aqua-bright eyes probed Susan's as she exclaimed, "First Lord Beaumont, and now you, Susan! What could possibly make you even consider such a thing?"

Susan replied in her soft-voiced way. "Well, perhaps I'm wrong, dear. Don't give it another thought." Susan's expression then turned uncharacteristically grim. "But be that as it may, I cannot regret my actions toward Marcus tonight, though I do know that I hurt him."

Rachel immediately insisted upon hearing about Susan's meeting with her brother. "Oh, Susan," she whispered at the end, "I am sorry for it. From what Lord Tynsdale said to me tonight, I think he truly regrets his treatment of you. I must beg your pardon. This is all my fault!" She swallowed a sob with difficulty.

"No, it is not," Susan promptly rejoindered. "It's nothing to do with you. I had an opportunity to get a little of my own back, and I tell you frankly, dear, that I quite enjoyed taking it. Don't you worry your head on my account, for unless I am grossly mistaken in my evaluation of my brother, we'll come about in no time, you'll see. Furthermore, if Harold is correct, you and Marcus may have your own reconciliation." This last came quite cheerfully.

"Ha!" cried Rachel, immediately taking exception. "While I may hope that you and your brother can make amends, I'd rather stay entirely away from his Most Honorable lordship. But more to the point, Susan, how are we to manage his coming here tomorrow?"

229

Susan paled at the question. *"What?"* she wailed. "Marcus is coming here? Oh, I should have guessed it!"

"His parting words to me were that he would be here early in the morning, and he expected me to be here to greet him," Rachel supplied.

Distracted by this new information, Susan sat very still. Apparently displeased by the show of inattention, the big housecat stood up on the covers and poked his wide, bewhiskered head rather forcefully into her hand, insistent in his demands that she return to his care.

Looking down at her pet, a slow smile lit Susan's features—a smile that on any but her sweet face would have been termed evil. "Leave my brother up to me, my dear," she said quietly, "for I know just what to do."

Greatly puzzled, but willing to concede a sister's superior knowledge, Rachel turned down the lamp's flame as Susan returned to her own bed, leaving with the big tom cat draped neatly over one slender arm. While Lady Susan fell into a peaceful sleep almost at once, Rachel's dreams were haunted by the harmonious strains of a waltz and of a certain tall, dark lord.

After leaving Almack's, Marcus Kinsworth began making the rounds of London's many and varied gambling dens. Most were open throughout the night, and some of them never closed, excepting Christmas day. It took him more than an hour of searching, but the marquis finally found his nephew amidst a group of young sprigs at Boodle's. Easing his way through the clustered groups intent upon their various wagers, he motioned the Honorable Gilbert Cheeves to his side.

Dressed in a short, wine red velvet coat with enormously wide lapels and a stiffened, seven-inch-high collar, Gilbert was no match for his uncle's fastidious elegance. And so the young man quickly realized. He'd thought himself quite top-of-the-trees, until a mental comparison forced him to admit of his uncle's surpassing polish, while even his newly styled, black-and-red-dotted necktie seemed somehow too flashy—tawdry!—to Gilbert now.

The marquis bade the young man follow him to an unoccupied smoking parlor. Taking brandies from a tray proffered by a servant, Marcus requested that they not be disturbed. Gilbert took a chair.

"Nephew, you will be so obliging as to tell me what you know of Rachel Doune," his lordship began very quietly after the manservant had left them. "You will also tell me what you know of her connection with my Lady Susan."

Gilbert felt as if the fit of his new neckcloth had suddenly become altogether too tight; the room seemed to grow over-hot. He gulped at his brandy, seeking relief, nearly choking on the fiery liquid in his haste. He met Lord Tynsdale's sardonic expression with extreme mortification. His uncle was in a rare taking and no doubt about it.

"She is an old friend of Aunt Susan's," he finally got out. "Heiress to a fortune—from coal, don't you know. Worth upwards of sixty thousand a year, as I hear it; what's more, she's the prettiest girl I have ever seen!" He spoke this last admiringly, but his voice lost strength as he became aware of his uncle's increasing glower. "Well, she is a choice one, I do say," he added gamely.

"Perhaps. But, Gilbert, I don't think that's entirely the way of it. I do not for an instant believe Susan met Miss Doune until very recently, and that heiress story is nothing but farrago of nonsense, for it is Susan who supports them."

"No such thing," Gilbert cried exception. "Aunt Susan went to Bruton Place right after quarrelling with m' mother because she and Miss Rachel are long-time friends. And if Aunt hadn't stayed to attend her, Miss Rachel would have had to return to her home off in Scotland someplace, since she'd lost her chaperon. As for all the blunt they've spent, why, even those rum-flashy jewels Aunt has been wearing are what Miss Rachel has loaned her! I didn't find out about Aunt's even having a use for the mint-sauce till much later. Y' see," he added sheepishly, "until I slipped her the needful, Aunt couldn't

231

have had much more than a guinea or two to her purse. She'd loaned me a rather large sum over a period of time. It was to repay her that I went to you for a loan, remember? Not that I haven't long since come to realize it wasn't very well done of me, Uncle Marcus."

The look he received after giving this information made the young man wonder if he wasn't sickening or something! At first the room had seemed too hot for comfort, yet now, he found himself shivering with chill. He thought it likely caused by his uncle's darkling look.

"Are you saying that Susan was totally without funds? She left Lydia's with pockets to let?" Lord Tynsdale's voice was low, barely audible to his listener.

"Er. Yes, sir. That's just what I mean to say. Don't mean to try to excuse it, either. But I didn't know Aunt was going anywhere—don't think she knew it herself! And I made good the amount as soon as I could; I never intended it otherwise."

As if harking back to another concern, Lord Tynsdale suddenly said, "Tell me this then, young man, was I wrong, then, in believing that you considered it my responsibility to frank you? And would you really have repaid Susan if I had given you the money you requested of me?"

"Well, of course, I would!" Gilbert was quite frankly appalled by his uncle's sordid insinuation. "I never really believed you intended to let the Kinsworth titles come to m' father's family. Uncle Marcus, you cannot believe me so wholly sunk as all that! But I had thought that if you saw it otherwise, more fool me not to take advantage, that's all." He grinned self-consciously. "But as for Miss Rachel's credentials, they aren't subject to such question. Surely you've seen those big delivery chaldrons: Creagh Coal they are marked."

"Oh, my God. Not *that* Creagh. Not from Ayrshire," his lordship groaned.

It upset Gilbert no end. He'd never seen his Uncle Marcus look so put about. He hastened to reassure. "Ayrshire. Yes, that's Miss Doune's home. Aunt Susan told me Mr. Creagh still resides there."

Since it appeared his uncle had stopped paying him any heed, Gilbert allowed himself to relax just slightly. He would have been surprised to learn that his uncle was feeling not a little proud to hear that his nephew had chosen to repay his lady aunt at the first opportunity, rather than consider her money as his due.

To be sure, Marcus was also extremely mortified to learn that he might be the one indebted, rather than Miss Doune, for he most certainly had seen the coal chaldrons his nephew referred to; they'd been around forever. They were a part of the city, those black containers of fuel for heating and cooking. How could he have been so stupid not to have made the association before? *That* Ian Creagh?

Not so naive as his nephew, however, Marcus did not accept such glib explanation as to how Lady Susan could have met persons like the upstart Scots. He knew now that he was horrendously mistaken about Miss Doune's prospects, and he had erred to suppose that Gilbert had effected Susan's introduction into Bruton Place, but the fact remained that his sister was playing ape-leader to some climbing provincial. And it seemed that she had been driven to do so in her need for a place of shelter. That thought galled Marcus worse than had his earlier speculations.

Gilbert jerked back to attention at his uncle's next question, though it seemed not to be directed to him.

"So Miss Doune's on the lookout for a title, is she? Well, whatever else may be, she'll catch cold at that." With not another word of leave-taking, Lord Tynsdale got up from his chair and quickly left the club, unaware of his rudeness or his minatory look which sent the gamblers scurrying to get out of his path.

Marcus returned to his home and scowled unseeingly at his man while the innocent valet went about the evening's routine. He was furious that his sister had been reduced to such straits, and furious with himself for so having failed his family. Why did it have to be that pert-eyed miss who came to his sister's support? A picture of the golden-haired beauty taunted him, and a memory of flashing green-blue eyes tortured him. But how could a man of his stature be so drawn to a woman like Miss Rachel Doune? Apart from the Creagh money, the girl had no background that he knew of—no breeding, no illustrious family tree—and yet, his features grew thoughtful, almost pleased, as he remembered her dauntless ways. The winsome little creature *did* have a certain courage, he had to admit.

Chapter Fifteen

Susan rose early the next morning filled with energy, a purposeful gleam in her otherwise-soft brown eyes. She spoke first to the butler, and after completing their little business, she took a somewhat lengthier conference with Mrs. Fullerton. When these last two separated, it could be seen that there was a similar answering light in that good woman's eye as well. At half-past nine, Susan was ready to send Mrs. Tully up to awaken her mistress, who hadn't yet come down. Susan then went humming into the breakfast room to fill up her plate, quite as though she was without a care in the world.

Shortly thereafter, Rachel joined her in the breakfast room, prettily attired in a bright, willow green morning dress daintily sprigged with tiny white flowers. She had allowed her shining locks with their guinea-bright highlights to flow unimpeded down her back—a morning's luxury which she especially enjoyed—with only a matching embroidered ribbon tied about her head to keep the long strands away from her face. Her cheerful attire did not match the glum cast to her countenance, however.

"Couldn't we just be 'out' or something when he calls?" she asked across the table. "It worked well enough before."

Laughing gaily, Susan replied, "No need. You must trust me to see to it that my brother does not stay overlong. It will not be so bad, I promise you."

Rachel toyed with her meal while Susan kept up an

235

innocuous chattering about one thing and another, mostly praiseworthy references to "Harold." Rachel finally had to smile as her pleasure in Susan's newfound attachment won her from the doldrums. Rachel really did like the handsome earl, whatever his strange notions. She looked forward to wishing Susan happy before very much longer.

Glancing at the clock, Rachel realized that she mustn't prolong her stay at the table. With a hearty sigh, she asked Fullerton to bring the chocolate pot into the drawing room, there to await her nemesis. She wondered if she should have bound up her hair in order to present a more imposing appearance, then shook her head at such folly, for the weight of its length was less burdensome when loose upon her shoulders. Besides, she did not need Lord Tynsdale's approbation. If he was determined to look for details to disapprove, there was little she cared to do about it at this late date.

Susan would not join her, instead saying, "Go along, Rachel, and don't you worry your head for an instant. I'll be close by, but for now, you must excuse me. I have a few things to do," she added mysteriously.

Rachel could not imagine what her friend was up to, but admitted that for herself, coming to cuffs again with the arrogant lord had its own attractions. His many deeds were so very reprehensible, his misconceptions so incredible and monumentally wrong, that she looked forward to making known her opinion of his errors. This desire was the only possible reason for the fluttery, excited sort of feeling she endured—signs of anticipation for exacting what was, after all, her due.

Soon enough, she heard Fullerton's knock on her drawing room door. Without reluctance, Rachel permitted her visitor's entrance.

The Marquis of Tynsdale promptly came through the doorway, presenting Rachel with an image of the ideal in masculine elegance. A jacket of midnight blue Bath coating fitted smoothly across a fine pair of shoulders, and as Rachel well knew, only Mr. Schweitzer of Cork Street,

Beau Brummell's own tailor, could have provided such glove-perfect construction. Buff pantaloons were displayed above Hessian-style boots, while a snowy white cravat revealed a complicated knot, one which would be envied by the veriest Tulip. Soft yellow gloves and a smart, curly-brimmed beaver finished the picture, each item worn with such an air as marked the true Man of Fashion.

Pointedly not rising, just as she had done once before at Lord Beaumont's more precipitate entry, Rachel continued to measure her adversary over the edge of her cream-glazed cup. Taught the fine points of bargaining by Grandfather Creagh, she refused the proper acknowledgement of a titled lord, since she knew it would weaken her position if she were the first one to speak.

Lord Tynsdale merely cocked an eyebrow, saying nothing. He moved into the room and, without asking leave, lowered himself onto a nearby sofa. Crossing his highly polished Hessians at the ankles, gold-tasselled tops winking in the light, he seemed unaware of the stretching silence as he viewed a rather indifferent landscape mounted above the fireplace. Notably, he did not remove his chapeau.

As Miss Doune so-casually sipped at her chocolate, Lord Tynsdale took no apparent notice of the enticing sight she made. She was seated before a window where the morning sunlight streamed through polished panes of glass, making her rich, honey-blond hair seem to sparkle with a life of its own, as it spread in bright ripples across her shoulders and down the length of her back. The clear, aqueous color of her eyes contrasted with the willow green of her gown, forming a picture far more beautiful than any painting hung on a wall. Nonetheless, his lordship kept his eyes firmly fixed above the hearth.

As the tension mounted, Rachel realized there was nothing to be gained by continuing her pose. The irritating man seemed quite capable of taking his ease on her sofa all morning! She carefully set her cup down and opened her first salvo.

"I believe that you asked for—or, I should say, you

demanded—this interview, Lord Tynsdale. Something about a repayment, I believe?" she said sweetly.

Having learned last night of his error, and having this morning received a somewhat tardy confirmation of the facts from his solicitor, Lord Tynsdale had already accepted that he did indeed owe an apology for his previous false assumptions. Moreover, as Lady Susan had so rightly surmised, he was as yet a fair-thinking man. Directing a level look into blue-green eyes, he rose with a graceful movement to make her a neat leg, sweeping his hat almost to the floor.

"My sincerest apologies," he rumbled in his deep, oddly soft voice. "I now understand that you came to Lady Susan's aid when she most needed assistance. For that, I am in your debt. I distrusted your claims from the beginning, Miss Doune, but I want you to know that I regret my error."

Rachel was greatly taken aback by this confession. This voluntary admission of guilt! "Well, I don't suppose any great harm was done," she said with somewhat discomfited candor. Impulsively she added, "And I must beg your pardon also, my lord. I judged you rather more harshly than you deserved, for it's been pointed out to me that I could have told you my circumstances sooner. I am truly very sorry for it." Was it possible, she wondered, that acceptance was so easily won?

But the possibility proved small. Lord Tynsdale answered her in softly clipped accents. "Apology accepted, Miss Doune. Now, if you will be so good as to give me an accounting of my sister's expenses, I will write you a check straightaway. I want Susan to feel free to leave with me today."

Astounded by his presumption, his arrant rudeness even after he had the truth, Rachel quickly gathered her wits and looked to her own fusillade. She returned fire without hesitation. "How very like a man of your background, my lord, to think you can put a price on friendship. Well, let me be the one to inform you that persons of *my* background find such actions objectionable in the

238

extreme! I recall that once before you misconstrued a debt," she continued in pointed reference to their first meeting, "and I must say, you gentlemen of rank do seem to have no end of trouble in making your measurings! Can you really not understand that Susan is my friend? Truly, my very dearest friend ever? And since she has expressed no interest in leaving this house, you may be assured that she will not be forced into doing so. Not by you. Not by anyone at all!"

Lord Tynsdale took a step forward at these wounding words. "Forced?" he gritted out, making another step, his eyes darkening in righteous anger. *"Forced,* you say? What makes you to think that I would—"

He started to take a third step forward, but before he could complete the move, he felt something hindering him just at ankle height. Looking down, he discovered a silver-satiny-gray cat, with white-tipped paws and bib, rubbing itself affectionately against his pristine boot. He wanted nothing so much as to take himself out of the way, and yet, incredibly, his planned backward movement was prevented by the appearance of a second member of the feline species, now behind him. And this one a fluffy orange tabby!

"Good God!" he expostulated in surpassing alarm.

Twisting about in almost comical dismay, he noted that a massive, gray-striped tom was even now taking over his own place on the sofa, while a white, long-haired cat with pale yellowish green eyes had commenced a circle of the room, preparatory to a leap onto Rachel's lap. More! Through a crack in the panelled drawing room door, there entered *two* more yellow-eyed beasties, slinking slyly ever nearer. These proceeded to approach him while he stood motionless, caught in the middle of the room.

Lord Tynsdale's dark eyes opened wide in certain horror. Before he could think how to extricate himself, however, the dignified butler tapped at the door, followed by a petite, dark-haired woman who appeared to be the housekeeper.

Effusively expressing their apologies, the couple came

in and began urgent bustlings about the room, apparently trying to contain the felines, thus to facilitate their removal. Their collective efforts were somehow less than successful, howsomever. It seemed that the harder they tried to lay hands on the cats, the more the animals jumped and raced about! Fur floated through the disturbed air as the housekeeper vigorously flapped her apron amidst her cries of "Shoo! Shoo!" until the cats seemed to bounce off the walls!

Marcus could feel his eyes start to itch and burn. He managed to extract his handkerchief just in time to collect a resounding sneeze. That first was immediately followed by a second, and soon he could hardly catch a breath.

Through his watering eyes, he missed seeing Rachel's attempts to cover a broadening grin, and he was so caught up in his own distress that he did not hear her disguised gurgles of laughter. At once comprehending the whole—Susan's mysterious plot—Rachel plucked her own lacy square from her pocket, using it to choke back the further whoops that threatened.

Without begging pardon of his hostess for making an abrupt departure, Lord Tynsdale snapped, "The bloody hell is in it!" as he decamped to his waiting curricle out in the street.

He stumbled once or twice on the steps, so swollen had his eyes become. Leaving his tiger to hold his horses' heads, he sneezed and dabbed with the handkerchief for several minutes longer before taking up his reins.

The mysteriously absent Lady Susan Kinsworth peeped through the curtains for this view of her brother: he was bent over almost double, attempting to clear his head with a final violent exhalation. Her eyes dancing merrily, Susan waited at the window until curricle and driver were safely out of sight. She then joined the group in the drawing room, wearing a look of undeniable—altogether *wicked!* —satisfaction.

At the sounds of hilarity erupting from the open drawing room, Flora and young Will came in to see what was to do, and Mrs. Fullerton tried to explain the prank

240

through her hearty cries of laughter. Even Sujit dropped his culinary pursuits to investigate the commotion, and upon finally being given the whole to understand, he, too, added his bright laugh to the others.

"I think we will not be disturbed by further visits on any pecuniary account," Lady Susan told Rachel later, "but if I am right, Marcus will come again with another, very different motive."

While appreciating Susan's efforts, Rachel dismissed this last idea with an airy wave of her hand.

Chapter Sixteen

An additional caller was received that day at No. 12 Bruton Place. Lady Cheeves came to see for herself exactly what was her sister's situation. She brought her eldest daughter with her, and Susan warmly welcomed them both. Everyone, it seemed, had sorely regretted the estrangement, feeling that their family was too small to lightly break ties with any single member.

Edwena, for once, was silenced by her aunt's stylish mien. And so, after observing the amenities, Rachel led the girl out of the room, better allowing the two sisters privacy while coming to terms. Rachel immediately found Edwena to be a tiresome child, for Edwena was not so shy about suing for favors from her hostess, but a visit to Sujit's kitchen, where a plate of warm sticky buns awaited, soon had Edwena appropriately entertained. Rachel's efforts were rewarded by the pleasure the reunion brought dear Susan.

While changing her attire some hours later, Rachel reflected on Susan's comments about expecting her brother to return. She poohed the intimation that Lord Tynsdale should be drawn again to her house for any reason, and yet, strangely, she also found herself dissatisfied at the thought that he would not come. Surely, she had more sense than to believe the man top over heels with herself, *didn't she?* It must be noted, though, that Rachel took unusual care with her toilet as she prepared for the evening's diversion.

They were engaged to the Right Honorable, the Earl and Countess of Guinness for their supper, to be followed by dancing in the Guinness family's newly remodeled grand ballroom. Their house in Mayfair was well known for its fabulous hospitality, and everyone agreed that the party was sure to be a wonderfully sad crush.

When the clock warned that it was time to finish dressing, Lady Susan had decided on a lovely beaded lustring of soft lemon yellow, while Rachel chose a dramatic French cambric dyed to an old gold color which perfectly matched her high-dressed hair. She'd added a triple-row choker of pearls with a diamond clasp worn to the front, and small diamond drops fell from dainty ears. For Susan, Rachel insisted that a delicate parure of tiny yellow sapphires, lying about unused in her jewel case, was just the thing to enhance the soft silk of the older woman's gown.

Susan's nephew was to accompany them this night, as well as Harold Beaumont. On the carriage ride over, Susan regaled the gentlemen with the story of the morning's entertainment. Young Gilbert quite stared to hear how his uncle had been brought to book. He didn't mention his own meeting with Lord Tynsdale at Boodle's, of course, since no gentleman would divulge such a privately held conversation.

Lady Guinness sat forty-eight to dine, and Rachel found herself between an older gentleman who was retired from the Admiralty, seated on her left, and a baronet of rather determined charm on her right. The baronet, a loose fish, Rachel decided, kept her occupied with tidbits of scandal about various personages seated down the long table. She was twice almost put to the blush, and so, as the first course was removed, she transferred her attention to her alternate companion with relief. When the next course was brought, the baronet perforce regained her attention, but with some skill, Rachel managed to hold the conversation within comfortable channels.

After a sumptuous meal—Rachel lost count of the

number of dishes provided—the company adjourned to the ballroom where great lengths of opera pink gauze swathed the ceiling, suspended and tied a discreet distance away from each of the three gargantuan crystal chandeliers, high overhead. The fabric continued down along the walls, spreading into streamers and giving a rosy glow to the room, a room which was further lined with spaced pedestal tables with tall, cut-glass vases overflowing in masses of richly scented red roses. The doors to the slabbed stone terrace stood open to the night. There, fairy lights nestled among the trees and bushes lining the garden walks.

Their hosts greeted the guests who were just arriving for the dance. As the orchestra struck up an old-fashioned opening minuet, Rachel took her place in the set with Mr. Cheeves. He made a face as he concentrated on the steps, but he executed the complicated dance patterns in creditable form.

"I say, Miss Rachel," he addressed her as the last notes were played, "m' thanks for the dance. But, er. . . . Well, some fellows I know are here, and—"

"Certainly, Gilbert." She smiled at the young man, long since come to the use of their christening names. "I quite understand you, rest assured. Here is my next partner just come, so you've no need to remain here with me." Rachel chuckled to see him trot off in such obvious relief to have his duty behind him.

Over the succeeding two hours, the press of humanity grew greater and greater as more guests arrived. The perfumed air accumulated in near-overpowering strength, and many couples sought the out-of-doors to recover in the cooling night breezes. But with every line on her dance card filled, Rachel could only gaze longingly at the open terrace doors and their gently billowing pink streamers.

All through the evening, Rachel fought against the temptation to look toward the ballroom entry. After the little incident this morning, though, and despite Susan's prediction, she knew better than to expect that the marquis would seek her company. Still, each time the orchestra struck up a waltz, she found herself glancing about, longing for a very different partner.

She did remark one unwelcome addition to the party. Lord Ripley came in just before midnight, his heavy cheeks shining in the glow cast by the huge chandeliers. He seemed to stare right at her, before issuing a rather knowing smile in her direction. Caught on the dance floor, Rachel pretended not to see him. She hoped she was mistaken in thinking his acknowledgement was for her.

An intermission followed the dance set, so after first making sure that the detested peer was nowhere around, Rachel excused herself and began to make her way to the room set aside for the ladies to repair. The public rooms were over-warm, making her wish for a splash of fresh water to rinse her face with before the next set started. She kept a sharp eye as she made her way out of the crowded ballroom, but a repulsively familiar voice interrupted her progress down the hallway.

"Looking for me, girlie?" Lord Ripley stepped from behind a white pilastered column where an enormous arrangement of roses had effectively concealed his presence.

"Sir? I do not believe we have been introduced." Rachel made to brush past him and continue on to the retiring room.

"Eh, but we do know one another, don't we now." At that, the baron took up her arm and clamped it tightly under his own.

She moved to pull herself free, yet he easily held her hand in place with one beefy paw. "See here," she objected, tilting her face to meet his look. "We do *not* know one another, nor do I wish to remain in your company. You will allow me to proceed on my way."

"Oh, no indeed. No indeed, Miss Doune," he sniggered. "You and I are to further expand our acquaintance. Oh, we are well met tonight."

Rachel discontinued her struggles to look up at her

246

adversary in genuine astonishment! "What*ever* gives you to think I should care to acknowledge you?" she questioned in near-stupefaction.

"Because I know exactly what you are after, my girl." Lord Ripley looked tremendously satisfied at some secret cleverness.

"Oh? And what is it that you think I am after?" she asked him coldly.

The baron's broad face shone with a nasty sort of pleasure. He said, "Not to crack a queer whid, my fine miss, you're looking to make a match as high as you can, of course. But if you presume to conclude that Lord Tynsdale intends to bestow upon you his name, you build your castle out of air. Now I, on the other hand, *will* make you such an offer. A place as my wife, Miss Doune. Consider me well." He paused as an ugly expression crossed his features. "It's a deal more than one such as yourself can usually hope for, no matter how deep your grandfather's pockets."

Rachel squared her small chin, giving him back a perfectly level look. "Your opinions are a matter of complete indifference to me," she said in freezing accents. "However, I will say this: You have storage to let in the space above your ears if you think any inducement can persuade me to align myself with you!" With renewed vigor, she increased her efforts to extract her arm from his hold.

"I do believe," a deep-pitched voice broke in, "that the young lady declines your tender bid."

The startled baron loosed his grasp, and turned to meet the solidly dark eyes of the Marquis of Tynsdale. Silently, he cursed the ill luck that had brought *this* acclaimed Corinthian so imposingly near, and just at this particular moment. Lord Ripley gauged his adversary's unrelenting eye and began to wish himself elsewhere.

"Lord Ripley?" came the voice, whisper-soft. "Have you more that needs saying? I shall be glad to hear it, if you do. Perhaps, though, we should step outside for a more, um, *settling* discussion?"

By this time, however, the baron had already decided upon making a timely retreat. Unaccompanied. Better to await more promising conditions for what he had in mind. He scowled across at Lord Tynsdale, then turned toward Miss Doune. In ominous tones, he said, "Well, just you remember that I made you a fair offer, miss. You'll soon wish you'd taken me up on it, too! Count on't!" With a look full of menacing promise, the baron wheeled about and actually swaggered his way down the hall.

Rachel was unimpressed by the show. Turning to her rescuer, she produced a blinding smile. "Oh, well done, sir!" she enthused, her eyes sparkling in the light from the ormolu sconces.

"Then, mayhaps I should give you lessons, Miss Doune," he drawled in his deep-voiced way. "But, on second thought—" he pulled out a finely monogrammed handkerchief and pointedly dabbed it beneath his nose— "I clearly recall that you have managed, unassisted, to elude *me* more than once."

"Oh, you mean about the cats?" She hid her grin. "Well, that was Susan's idea, I'm sorry to say. While I might have liked to come up with such a thing on my own, I fear I must give your sister the credit—this time."

Marcus looked down on a face positively glowing with mischief. He couldn't prevent himself from smiling as he replied. "*Touché*, Miss Doune. A home thrust! And, so," he amended thoughtfully, "it was my sister who provided this morning's entertainment."

"But you mustn't be angry with her," Rachel pleaded, her face solemn. "She only did it on my behalf, and I wouldn't like to be the cause of your further estrangement. She and Lady Cheeves are well on their way to a reconciliation, and I know Susan hopes for the same with you."

Lord Tynsdale observed Miss Doune's earnestness. He was no little amazed she should dismiss the unpleasantness with Lord Ripley so easily. Indeed, she showed far more concern for his relations with his sister. He said merely, "Are you so sanguine, then? Susan delivered me the cut direct last night, then beset me with cats today. Certainly, you may not appreciate it, but for a man of my reputation to be brought down by an absurd sensitivity to the common, domestic feline is very, very *lowering*. And yet, you say my sister wishes to be reconciled? Whatever would happen should she really wish to do me an injury, I wonder? I quite tremble at the thought!"

The canny Scots miss was apparently undeceived by his rejoinder. "Well, you'd best take every care, then," she quipped. "Although, and I tell you this in all seriousness, Susan has quite terribly missed having proper contact with her only brother."

"However infrequent that contact?"

"Yes, even so." Miss Doune did not mince words. "My lord," she then said, laying a confiding hand on his arm, "if you would but approach Susan with some of the genuine consideration that I know you to feel for her, I am certain she would be more than glad to renew relations forthwith. Also, I think it is your part to make the first offer."

Her eyes turned dark with sincerity, making their appeal impossible to deny. Lord Tynsdale sighed and nodded once. "Very well. I will begin my amends tonight. I don't expect that she will accept me right away—the years will hardly be erased so quickly, I know—but I mean to remedy our situation as soon as possible."

"Bravely said!" the young beauty cheered. "And you may count on me to assure Susan as to your intentions. I have been your worst detractor, I think, but I mean to assist you in this if I can."

A note of harmony thus established, crooking his arm, Lord Tynsdale smiled as only a very handsome man can do. He was oddly proud that Miss Doune appreciated his concerns, pleased that her sentiments marched so well with his own. He was happy when Miss Doune lightly placed one kid-gloved hand on his sleeve.

Together, they made their way back to the ballroom. They didn't stop there, however. He led Miss Doune on through the room and then out of doors, taking her to the

249

terrace, now gleaming with the light of a rising moon. They encountered several other couples as they strolled beyond to reach freshly raked gravel paths, walking for some minutes without further speech between them. They felt themselves remarkably comfortable, in fact.

Rachel forgot the strict rules of behavior that forbade an unattached young lady to walk alone outside with a gentleman. She was so relieved at her escape from Lord Ripley, so delighted by the turn of humor displayed by her new escort, that she ignored the social niceties that Susan had so carefully prescribed. Rachel was too immensely relieved by the friendly terms offered, happy that for once, she might meet Lord Tynsdale without being at daggers drawn.

It was Marcus who broke the silence. "I believe I've you to thank for the exceptional change in Susan, Miss Doune. I should have mentioned it this morning, first thing; I had that intention before things began to get so, er, complicated. You see, Miss Doune, I may be slow—presumptuous, too—but I do try to give credit where it is due. And in the case of my sister, I admit to owing you the most tremendous debt of gratitude for whatever sort of magic it is that you have performed on her. I don't mean just the physical improvements, either—although, heaven knows, the easy way Susan walks now is something of a miracle. Rather, I refer to the . . . oh, I don't know, I suppose I'd call it a 'rise in spirits.' She seems gayer, less . . ."

"Don't you dare to say 'mousey'!" Reading his mind, Rachel made a mock fist beneath his nose.

Marcus chuckled deep in his throat. "No, of course not. But she is beginning to shine, isn't she?"

Rachel heard the deep note of pride and was glad. "Yes, it is rather wonderful," she allowed. "But don't applaud me for it, for I did no more than give her a few opportunities. It is Susan who decided to take the needed steps." The unintended pun set them both to mingled, gentle laughter.

Then the gentleman seemed to remember another matter. Puzzlement coloring his voice, he said, "But why is it you won't allow me to reimburse you for Susan's expenses, Miss Doune? It cannot be right that you should bear the continued cost of her upkeep. Oh, I realize that I put it rather badly this morning, and I beg your pardon for it, but why can you not allow me to at least do this one thing for my sister?"

She answered him quietly. "I will remind you that Susan has no debt to me because we are friends. Your own arrears must be repaid to her in some other way, for in this instance, money is altogether the wrong currency."

He appeared to think it over. "You mean that debts should be settled in kind? Yes. Yes, I suppose you're right." He sighed deeply, saying nothing more.

By the time the orchestra returned and tuned up for a waltz, their stroll had taken them beyond the near gardens and out to a deserted corner of the Guinness town property. At this distance, the filtering musical strains held a hauntingly sweet, alluring sound, and Rachel was unsurprised when Marcus next pulled her into his arms and easily moved her into the steps of the dance. Amongst the trees and night-flowering bushes, he swirled her around to the rhythm of the beautifully flowing music. And, with the playing of the final note, Marcus looked a silent question. Willingly, she raised her lips to meet his.

Overcome by the magic of the night, Rachel gave herself up to his care, giving up all sense of time, place, or persons, save one. She spared no thought to propriety, nor to the partner inside whose dance she had missed; nothing seemed more important than maintaining the wonder of this spellbinding moment. His mouth, so warm upon hers, seemed very right—completely natural, and all-compelling. Velvety soft, his lips guided her into pleasures she wanted never to end. At length, he slowly raised his head.

He gently led her to a low, stonework bench. Seating himself close beside her, he began to place slow, feather-light kisses over her eyes and glowing cheeks. The tiny diamonds in the clasp on her pearl neckpiece next caught his interest in the moon's inspiring light, so he transferred his attentions, stroking the hollow of her throat just below. Her skin seemed to quiver in expectancy at his least touch.

"Enchantress," he murmured. "You need never to settle for a mere baron. Why, you deserve a belted earl, at the very least. I am committed to marrying soon myself, so it is a shame that you cannot aim for a marquis." Rachel could just see the quizzical tilt of one dark eyebrow.

"Oh, a marquis would be much nicer, my lord," she teased, "but a mere viscountcy would do." She sighed, moving closer into his embrace.

But Marcus pulled back with a slight frown gathering upon his wide brow. "Would do? Do for what, Miss Doune? Will any title satisfy you, then?" With a single smooth movement, he drew himself to his feet, where he stood towering above the stonework bench.

"Yes, it's true that I must marry a nobleman," Rachel ventured, comprehending neither his stance nor the sudden change in his manner. "I must engage a peer, it's true, but the actual rank is of no particular import."

"So you *are* on the catch for a title!" Anger deepened his voice. "That's what you've been after all along, admit it!"

"Well, you could say it like that, but—"

"Mayhaps then, Miss Doune, you should regret spurning your earlier suitor," he said cruelly. "For Lord Ripley was definitely right about one thing: a marquis is quite beyond your reach!" Stiffly he offered his arm, saying bluntly, "Take my arm and I will escort you back inside."

"Thank you, no!"

Rachel sprang up from her seat to face him. If he thought she was going to meekly accept his cold dismissal, he would soon learn better. She tilted her little chin and delivered her own command. "Take yourself off, Lord Tynsdale, if you wish, for I certainly want nothing more from you. Nothing at all! I will find my own way back when I am ready." She swung her face away from him, folding her arms resolutely. The rising moon highlighted the determined angle of her jaw.

Lord Tynsdale, thinking himself nine kinds of fool to

be almost caught in such an obvious trap—and by a conniving *climber!*—turned on his heel and immediately left her. Forgotten was his gratitude for her generosity and care to his sister. Forgotten were the moments she'd seemed as close as his very own soul. He stormed back to the house and entered the long doors, charging through the gauzy streamers without once breaking stride.

Rachel stood alone in the nighttime gardens.

Seeing his lordship disappear through the Guinness's terrace doors, she gasped aloud at the complete and utter arrogance of the man. She hadn't really expected him to just walk off and leave her! When she and Grandfather had had one of their tiffs, no one had ever walked away from the field of battle. Or, no, that wasn't quite true. In all honesty, Rachel had to recall that she most usually was the one to get in the last word, and hadn't thought a thing of leaving after its delivery. She had to bite down, hard, on the words of malediction that came springing to her lips. Perhaps she had been well served. Hoist on her own petard, so to speak.

But Lord Tynsdale's refusal to allow her to explain did frustrate her so completely! It was beyond bearing that he should actually think her so attracted by a crest that she would consider going to the highest bidder and with never a care about the man himself. Did his oh-so-stiff-rumped lordship think of nothing but his vaulted rank? "Beyond my reach!" she hissed.

"Oh, but he is wrong, girlie," came a horridly well-remembered voice from out of the shadows. "You and I shall 'aim for a marquis,' and together we will bring him down."

She whirled around to see Lord Ripley's bulky form step forth into the moonlight. He was followed by another familiar figure who wore a black tricorn hat pulled low. Rachel recognized the coachman by his stance, but before she could cry out, a blow to the chin sent her sliding down into the cool grass alongside the pathway.

*   *   *

Much later, Rachel regained consciousness to find herself face up on the floor of what she muzzily deduced was a moving carriage. She had no idea what measure of time had passed, so she lay perfectly quiet for some moments longer, trying to think what had happened. As she finally struggled to reach a sitting position, she discovered a wide, booted foot planted on her shoulder, forcing her back down to the plaited grass rug covering the floor of the coach.

Rachel's eyes widened in shock. Memory came rushing back. She realized that Lord Ripley had once again managed to trap an unwilling female . . . and this time, it was herself! How could anyone be so *ruthless*, so entirely without merit as this? She could not remember ever having been deliberately struck before; the thought made her feel quite as ill as had the actual blow.

The jarring of cobblestones beneath the wheels, along with an occasional glimmer from a passing streetlight, somewhat encouraged her as they passed through the dark streets. It meant that she was still within London's limits. Briefly she wondered if anyone would hear her if she were to cry out.

Watching her expression from the single lamp burning inside the brougham, the heavyset baron interrupted her with a definite warning. "Don't even think to scream; I would hate to lay on my fives again. Just you be a good girl now and no harm will come to your pretty face."

Rachel was not at all reassured! Gingerly, she raised a hand to her cheek and carefully massaged the bruise she could feel just starting. "Why are you doing this?" she demanded. "It's not as if I am some poor serving girl who will not be missed. My friends will raise the alarm at any time!" Rachel recalled her similar words spoken in the box at the Royal Opera House just short weeks before. But with dreadful clarity, she knew that on this occasion, she was in actual danger.

"The watch won't be called because of a note my man passed along to the Lady Susan. You were in her charge as I understand it?" The baron smiled with strong satisfaction when Rachel nodded agreement to his facts. "How nice that you are on such close terms with the family, then, since it can only enhance my expectations. After your little quarrel with Tynsdale, Lady Susan will believe that you did indeed return home with the headache I offered as your excuse. And by the time it is discovered that you are not in your bed, I will have accomplished my purpose."

"What purpose? What is it you hope to gain from all of this?" she said more weakly than before. The rug on the coach floor was none too thick, and the bumps and jars were beginning to make her head ache in earnest.

"I've snatched away Tynsdale's plaything, haven't I? Just as he once did to me. And when it's learned that you went off in my company—which it surely will be, and soon, too—the Kinsworth family will be left to suffer the most intense embarrassment. Why, it'll be the talk of the ton for weeks to come!" He laughed unpleasantly. "And by tomorrow, you will gladly accept my proposal."

"Never in this world, sir!" Rachel stated clearly, and in forthright tones. Her headache seemed rather minor under these prescribed circumstances.

"Oh, yes. You will. You'll be glad to do so." Lord Ripley leered down at her in the dim light. "Though until I see how you please me tonight, you'd do better not to count on my renewing my eleemosynary offer."

Appalled, and not a little disgusted, Rachel barely restrained herself from kicking up at his jowly face. But she prudently withheld her efforts until they might be put to better effect.

The brougham soon stopped on a quiet street, and Rachel felt the slight rocking motion as the coachman stepped down. Through the window of the carriage, Lord Ripley instructed his man to pack their traps, leaving Rachel to conclude that he intended to be gone from town for some time. She tried to squirm to the opposite door while the baron was thus engaged, but he callously kicked her back down to the floor without a word.

After the driver returned and loaded up the boot, Rachel

heard the snap of the reins which sent the carriage rumbling over the cobblestones. After a space, she felt the brougham pick up speed, and she realized that she could no longer see any light from the streetlamps through the half-drawn shades of the coach windows. They were leaving London—on their way to who knew where?

Rachel knew that the baron was right in that she would have little choice if she could not escape before the morrow. No matter how great the lure of her fortune, no nobleman was likely to offer for her if it became known that she had spent a night in another man's company. It would not be only the ton who would deny her, either; no decent commoner would take a woman to wife who had been so compromised.

But I won't marry him, she swore silently to herself. *No matter what happens, I will* not *marry him!* The thought of the gross man on the cracked leather seat enjoying her grandfather's wealth—not to mention her person!—was one Rachel refused to consider. Prudence dictated that she withhold this decision from his knowledge, however, as there might yet be a way to retrieve the situation. With this thought, Rachel spoke up. "My grandfather will pay you well if you release me," she advanced. "You already are informed that he is a very rich man, so you must know that he would not like to see me harmed."

But Lord Ripley seemed unswayed from his aims. "Oh, he'll pay all right and tight," he answered with complaisance. "Though I've a notion he is not the sort of man to give in to anything less than a wedding, now that you remind me. No, my pretty. Marriage it must be. And after tonight, no one will dispute my claim. Then it's off to the border for us."

Rachel knew that he referred to an odd quirk in the law that allowed a legal union between a man and underaged girl, when the marriage took place in Scotland. Scottish law permitted such contracts. In an unwanted thought, she then suddenly recalled another similarity in cases with the great Lady Jersey: Sarah Sophia and the fifth Earl of Jersey had spoken their wedding vows at Gretna Green.

But theirs had been a love match, so analogies were not at all to the point!

Traitorous homeland. The journey overland would take days upon unending days to complete, but even one single night in her present company was more than Rachel cared to contemplate.

Chapter Seventeen

As the black brougham sped through the night, Lady Susan returned to the Creagh town house with Lord Beaumont as escort. Her nephew Gilbert had left the ball some time ago in the company of his young friends, after he first, and very properly, requested her permission, of course.

Susan had been perplexed when Rachel had departed on her own with only an untidily scrawled message written by way of explanation. But the thundering look on her brother's face, seen shortly before Rachel had sent her note, had given Susan to suppose that those two had crossed swords again. And she hadn't felt comfortable about staying much longer after that herself. The Guinness mansion was scarcely large enough to breathe in for all the hundreds upon hundreds that were in attendance; moreover, Susan was left feeling somewhat uneasy over Rachel's desertion.

Wishing Lord Beaumont a good night, Susan bid Fullerton lock up the house as she climbed the stairs to her room.

"Did you have a fine time this evening, my lady?" Mrs. Tully asked as she bustled in to help Susan change out of her gown.

"It was a lovely party," Susan replied. "I just hope that by morning Rachel will feel more the thing."

"And what is the matter with Miss Rachel?" The stocky

maid looked up from the cupboard where she was folding the paisley shawl that Susan had just discarded. "By-the-by, my lady, where is she?"

"In her note she said she felt a dreadful headache and that she was coming home to an early rest. Did she not tell you?"

"Oh? And when was this, my lady? For Miss Rachel has not yet come in, never think it! And she has never in her life claimed a headache, what's more."

"Well, of course she is here!" said Susan, fumbling for her wrapper. "She must be in her room, Mrs. Tully. You just didn't hear her come in, that's all."

At the abigail's answering stare, and without further ado, Lady Susan darted swiftly across the wide upper hallway and tapped at Rachel's door. When no answer was forthcoming, she pushed the door open and entered, closely followed by a worried-looking Mrs. Tully.

But in the light of the silently burning bedside lamp, it was clear that the room was unoccupied. The bed was turned down neatly, and Rachel's slippers and bedgown were aligned just so, offering no sign of disturbance whatever. Mrs. Tully swore that she had tidied the chamber after Rachel had dressed for the evening, and that everything was as she had left it.

"Mrs. Tully," Susan said with a calmness she could not feel, "please check this room thoroughly while I go down and speak to Fullerton. There has to be some explanation."

But when the butler was questioned, he denied that anyone had come to the town house ahead of her ladyship. He told Lady Susan that no one could have entered without his being aware of it, as he had left his pantry door open all evening while he sat and cleaned the silver. Mrs. Tully overheard this last as she came rushing down the staircase after having completed her hurried search.

"He's right," the abigail confirmed. "I was up and down the stairs several times, and I could see him working there all along. Oh, my lady," moaned the redoubtable maid. "Whatever are we to do? The only gown missing is that nice cambric she had on when she left here, and not another thing in her room has been touched!" The abigail gulped noisily, and tears started coursing down her plump cheeks.

Susan wanted to cry herself! Her years under the Cheeves' protection had not prepared her to deal with a situation like this. What could have happened?

"Excuse me, my lady," Fullerton interrupted Susan's rising panic. "If I may make a suggestion? It might be presumptuous of me to advise it, but I think that perhaps Lord Beaumont should be called. He seems to me to be a man who would know what to do."

"By all means, Fullerton," Susan breathed, much relieved by this offer of a solution. "That may answer very well!"

"However," she next owned unsteadily, "I have no idea where we are to find him at this time of night. Even though it's not so long since he left here, it's scarcely past midnight, and it could be hours before he goes home."

Fullerton seemed unperturbed by the obstacle. "If you will allow me to be of service, I believe that I can locate his lordship without too much difficulty," he said, standing before her with such calm assurance that Susan could only beg him to set off at once.

Having long familiarity with the favorite haunts of town gentlemen, the butler whisked back into his pantry to don a well-brushed hat and black tailcoat. After rousing his good wife from her slumbers so to go to Lady Susan's support, he stepped out briskly into the night and headed toward White's Club. And as he reached the appropriate address in St. James's Street less than fifteen minutes later, the dignified butler was bidden to enter by the doorman, who rightly supposed that Fullerton bore a message for one of their esteemed members.

The club's rooms were crowded, for the evening was just beginning for most of those inside. However, Fullerton had the fortune to immediately discover not only the Earl Beaumont, but Lord Tynsdale as well. The two lords were taking their ease in a pair of high-backed leather chairs within sight of the front entryway.

When Lord Beaumont spotted Miss Doune's man, he motioned Fullerton over to them.

Lowering his voice discreetly, Fullerton informed the gentlemen of what little he knew to tell. He was immensely gratified when both their lordships instantly called for their capes and hastened outside to Lord Beaumont's carriage, where it stood awaiting the earl's pleasure on a nearby street.

By the time they reached Bruton Place, the lower windows were all lit up, and they found themselves met at the door by an anxious party of four. It seemed that when Mrs. Fullerton had gone to the kitchen to prepare a soothing tea, her preparations had aroused Sujit. These two, together with the overwrought abigail, had all then gathered with Lady Susan to think how to aid their mistress.

Harry went to place a supportive arm around Susan's shoulders and took the lead in bringing the assembly into the drawing room. Glistening tears shone in Susan's soft brown eyes, as she produced Rachel's note for him to study. She kept a tight rein on her composure, though, describing the undisturbed state of Rachel's room with only one small break. It might have been a hiccough, but it sounded more like a sob.

She looked from one lord to the other, then cried out softly, "Marcus? Oh, I'm so *glad* you're here, too!" Her feelings quite overcame her.

Without hesitating for a second, her brother went to her and gathered her into his arms. "Not to fret, Susan," he murmured quietly. "Everything will be well, and soon, you'll see. She probably just left with some friends and has been detained."

"No! No, Rachel would never do that!" Susan protested quickly, conviction firming her voice. "Besides that, Marcus, after this length of time, I should have had a message if that were merely the case. She made me that note right after you came back into the ballroom from the terrace, so she left the party well over an hour ago!"

Marcus frowned, feeling the first stirrings of fear. When Fullerton had initially divulged the purpose of his errand, he had not been particularly worried. Yet Susan was right: after this length of time, the possibility of accident became ever more likely. "Susan," he said, setting her back so that he could search her face, "did you see Rachel come in after me, then?"

"No, I don't think she came back in through the ballroom. I assumed she had reentered the house through one of the lesser doors."

He drew in a sharp breath, but didn't speak. A pair of deep creases sliced the space between his brows. Absently, he observed as Harry returned Rachel's note into Lady Susan's keeping.

Mrs. Tully suddenly shrieked. "But that's not Miss Rachel's hand!" She pointed to the note with a shaking finger. "She never wrote her letters nigh so big and ill-formed. I tell you, she never did!"

Susan stared down at the scrap of paper and jerked as if it had suddenly wriggled within her fingers of its very own accord.

Marcus could barely restrain himself from snatching for the note, and at once. He had to mentally rebuke himself for the absurd inclination, realizing that he wouldn't know if it was in Rachel's handwriting or not. And yet, oddly, he actually believed that he could recognize it, were it really hers.

Susan swiped at her tears and looked more closely at the paper in her hand. She stared at the uneven pen strokes. "Of course, you are right, Mrs. Tully," she said thinly. "I should have noticed before, for the letters are shaped all wrong, the slant isn't hers. . . ." A fresh flow of moisture collected in her eyes as she looked up in mute appeal.

"Oh, it is the worst of bad karma," broke in a mightily downcast Sujit, silent up until now. "Yes, oh, yes, very certainly it is! Evil is working most diligently this night and threatens the missy who is so very, very good. I wish I did not have the misfortune to be knowing what is happening here around me."

263

He stopped speaking before the looks of amazement spreading around the room. "I am begging pardon," he appealed. "I am truly sorry to be speaking out of my turn; you will everyone please to be excusing me?"

"But, what is it, Sujit?" Susan softly inquired. "Can you tell me?"

The little cook's shoulders slumped further, and he answered in mournful tones. "Oh, my lady, I am feeling in my bones that some vicious person is at work and preventing the missy's return home. You are before having a great anger at my missy, sir—" he turned to Lord Tynsdale with a soulful look—"but you are not having the vileness to want to hurt her in this way. There is someone else she must be knowing. Some very bad person indeed!"

Susan gasped in horror. "Ripley!"

Not fully understanding the little Hindu cook—*what had the man said, anyway?*—Marcus nonetheless agreed that his sister could be right. The baron was known to be shy of the blunt, and with the added fillip of revenge, he might feel justified in forcing Miss Doune into a marriage, will she or no. Hadn't he as much as threatened that very thing just tonight? Perhaps Miss Doune was in danger, after all.

But hard upon this thought came another: Miss Doune was committed to ensnaring a peer. She had boldly admitted as much, and on this possibility he spoke out. "Sister, perhaps we should consider another interpretation. Miss Doune may well have left willingly with someone—quite possibly the baron—but merely wanted to delay your knowledge of her plans."

"Never." Susan rounded on her brother. "How can you believe such a thing?"

"Ah, but she is most anxious to acquire a title, is she not? That *is* why she came to London and sought entry into our circles. She admits it! So, if no better offer came her way...."

"Oh, Marcus, you do not understand her at all! Rachel has to take a husband from our ranks because her grandfather ordered her to it. Coming to London was not her idea. Mr. Creagh laid the charge on her from his very deathbed! She had no choice but to agree."

"You say Ian Creagh is dead?" Marcus scoffed. "I hadn't heard it!"

"Not dead, Marcus, *dying*," Harry cut in. "He took ill a few weeks ago—in his seventies, don't you know. And from the letters he sends, I understand that there's been almost no improvement. It scared Miss Rachel half to death when he first took to his bed. Mr. Creagh then made her promise to find a husband to his liking before June was out, or she would be left out of his will."

"But the money isn't the main reason why Rachel agreed to come," Susan insisted. "She apparently had argued with her grandfather for ages over his insistence that she have a title. The matter of her inheritance was Mr. Creagh's final point, but his abrupt decline in health was ever Rachel's greatest concern. She determined to meet his requirements because of her fears for his recovery, and because she knew it to be her duty. Really, Marcus, you've no right to criticize her! From what Harold tells me, it's little different from your own reasons for choosing to marry."

"By Jove, she's got you there," Harry snorted. "You intend to marry to fulfill family obligations—and so does Miss Rachel! Admit it, Marcus. You've no reason to censure the girl's aspirations."

"But it's not the same thing," Marcus ground out. "She seeks personal gain, while I—"

"Oh?" Susan interrupted in low tones. "Just what, exactly, do you think she has to gain? A husband who will have complete control of whatever fortune Mr. Creagh leaves her? A man who may sneer at her birthright as he freely takes over her life? What, Marcus, *what* has she to gain?"

At these telling words, everyone—including the servants—turned to search Lord Tynsdale's face for his answer.

But Marcus didn't see their accusing eyes. He saw

nothing outside of his own inner thoughts. *"No matter what Grampa says . . ."* he recalled her as once saying.

Remorse smote him mightily. But not by the tiniest change in his expression did he allow anyone a clue to his thinking.

Abruptly, he spoke in quiet, but strongly determined tones. "Right then. I'm after her. Harry, are you with me?" He moved with swift grace toward the door, striding rapidly out to the earl's waiting carriage.

Anxiously, Susan detained Lord Beaumont. "You will find her, Harold, and send me back word?"

"Without a second's delay," he reassured her. "If it is the baron, those broken-down nags of his will be easily overtaken. We'll be back here with Miss Rachel in no time, you'll see." The earl set a quick kiss on Susan's trembling lips before heading out the door.

Marcus tersely directed Harry to make for Grosvenor Square. In unemotional tones, he then apprised his friend of the reason for his particular fears that Lord Ripley was responsible for Rachel's disappearance, briefly explaining about the baron's earlier "offer" to Miss Doune. He instructed Harry to drop him at his house, then sent the earl off to go to his own lodgings. They must both change into more suitable attire. Silk knee breeches would hardly stand the pace, after all. They agreed to meet at a certain inn on the Hampstead Road.

Once in his dressing room, Lord Tynsdale crisply instructed Cummings as to his needs. The fussy valet tisked quietly at such goings-on, for the room was thrown into unprecedented late-night turmoil while his lordship ripped off one set of clothing and speedily changed into dress more suitable for the road. Cummings would have been still more disturbed had he seen his lordship next detour through the library, where Marcus paused to select two gleaming pistols.

The lightly built racing curricle and the leggy, deep-chested creams stood waiting at the door by the time Marcus was ready. He waved to his tiger to release the bits, and the little groom barely made it onto his platform before the horses were set-to at a fast-paced clip. They swept through the city at a wonderfully brisk rate, as fast as eight strong legs and two over-sized wheels could go.

Desperation urged Marcus onward. He should never have left Miss Doune alone! He should have waited and heard her out instead of making those stupid, cruel accusations. He should have listened—could have asked the right questions, and without blundering in with his own allegations. So why hadn't he? He moaned softly as the answer worked its way to the surface.

He'd thought her an amazingly brazen young woman from the first and had accorded her the usual low-set status reserved for females with forward ways. But he now had to conclude that just because the respectable ladies of his acquaintance would have been inept in the business of rescuing housemaids, it did not make Rachel less than they. In fact, as he considered it, most women, even including the *demireps* and street slatterns, would have quailed at Miss Doune's intrepid actions. Rachel was far, far more than any of these. Actually, she had a deal more to her than any other lady he knew of.

Even Susan had bloomed under her influence. To-night's events had shown him proof positive that Rachel Doune had done enormous good with her sturdy, unafraid attitudes; she was a better influence than a Queen's Drawing-Room full of peeresses. Why, Miss Doune's very servants showed remarkable sense . . . well, with the possible exception of that rather strange Indiaman. And the little Hindu might be sensible enough, too, but his use of the language was beyond comprehension, for all that.

Grimly suspending further reflection, at least for the time being, Marcus drew his horses to a halt upon reaching a certain rooming house in Lincoln's Inn Fields. There, after a brief exchange with the proprietor—a nosey sort who appeared most anxious to earn the bright coin his lordship extended—Marcus satisfied himself that he was on the right track, for the proprietor gave out a detailed description of Lord Ripley's earlier stop, making mention of the travelling bags collected.

Cracking his whip smartly over his cattle, Marcus recommenced the journey northward at speed, and with a velocity likely dangerous were any other man at the reins.

Some twelve miles out of London, another carriage was at that moment being brought to a standstill. With the full moon at its zenith, the brougham's black bulk could be seen positioned in front of a small inn, two hundred yards or so off the main road. Clumps of scraggly weeds surrounded the building in disorderly, unkempt fashion, and the sounds of rough voices issued from the front door, marked by a single burning flambeau.

Lord Ripley had chosen his stopping place well. Few would notice the narrow road leading to the tumble-down, thatch-roofed building; only area residents were likely to even know of its existence. And, since its reputation was that of a favored haunt for highwaymen, there was not a local man within. Yet, remarkably, the taproom was filled with nighttime revelers.

An unshaven ostler shambled up to the carriage. After a brief exchange of words with the baron, the grizzle-cheeked servant then went inside the inn to alert the proprietor to their presence.

Lord Ripley next jerked Rachel up beside him on the seat and wrenched her arm back savagely. "Not a peep out of you now," he snarled. "You don't want the likes of these to take an interest. Just you be a good girl, and we'll have you inside without the tobymen being any the wiser."

At this reference to criminals, Rachel bit down hard on the scream she had been considering. Maybe it was best to bide her time! She didn't even offer a struggle as Lord Ripley hustled her out of the coach; she did, however, take a good look around.

The door to the taproom was closed while they came in through a small side door, and Rachel saw when her captor passed on a small purse to a man who seemed to be the owner. She didn't get a view of the man's face, since it was darker inside the building than out, but she did notice that he arrayed himself with a large bunch of keys hung from an enormously wide leather belt, worn outside a long, smock-type shirt.

With the baron's coachman right behind, she made no move of protest when led up a rather rickety-feeling wooden staircase.

They brought her to a tiny chamber in the rear on the second floor. The hunched coachman inspected the room from top to bottom while Lord Ripley kept her arm twisted tightly behind her. At the servant's nod of approval, the baron released her with a warning against her trying to call out for assistance. "For the only help you'll bring is those fellows below," he guffawed, "and we don't want that now, do we?" His eyes crinkled in horrid amusement between his fleshy lids.

Promising to return after refreshing himself with a tipple or two taken below, the baron finally left her alone, giving Rachel a rather wonderful sense of relief. She heard the hard click of a lock in the thick wooden door when it closed behind her captors, so after checking its pull and finding it firmly set against her, she could see no immediate way to escape from her prison. Even the shuttered window was nailed securely. Her repeated pushes and pulls didn't budge it an inch.

Sounds of merriment filtered up through the bare plank flooring. A woman's shrill laughter lofted up from time to time, and a particularly crude expression once followed, causing Rachel's cheeks to burn. In this thieves' den, she knew that Lord Ripley was right: Nothing could be gained if she cried out.

Finding a pitcher of fairly fresh water, Rachel splashed a portion of the liquid into a cracked basin so to rinse her face. There was no mirror, which left her to straighten her rumpled gown and repin her hair as best she could without one. The throbbing at her temples had thankfully lessened, so she sat herself down on the hard edge of the room's none-too-clean bed. Definitely, she needed to think!

The simple bed and washstand were the room's only

furnishings, except for a spotted chamberpot shoved underneath the former. There was no place of concealment, not even a fireplace, and Rachel found nothing that would serve as a weapon. She felt chilled in the late evening air; still, it was not without some little distaste that she took up the rather dirty wool blanket covering the bed ticking to wrap around her shoulders. Her own pretty shawl was left behind at the Guinness party—hours, or maybe, it was years ago.

Feeling altogether abandoned, Rachel fought down a sob. She had never felt so alone in all her twenty years!

Then, memory of a tall, dark-haired marquis came unbidden into her thoughts. Eyes wide open, she could still feel the echo of Lord Tynsdale's low-pitched voice within her mind, and an answering reverberation deep inside her chest. No matter how much the man aggravated her, she wished for nothing so much as that he should be here now.

Why, I do believe I love him! she thought with some surprise. "I love Marcus Kinsworth," she next whispered aloud.

Rachel realized that she had been so busy chafing at his lordship's misconceptions about herself, so angry at his haughty ways, that she had never really taken the time to examine the facts before. Nor her own feelings. She had somehow, amidst all of her complaints and protestations against Lord Tynsdale, forgotten what it was she had been seeking in the first place. While many of her suitors had claimed to be drawn by her beauty, most had seemed more interested in her grandfather's money. Not greatly flattered by either endorsement, Rachel suddenly understood that she had been so on the defensive that she had not really considered any man she had met to have had a genuine interest in her for herself.

And Lord Tynsdale *had* tried to determine who and what she was; he'd taken the trouble to learn that she really was an heiress and a true friend to his sister, rather than merely the light-skirt he'd at first thought her. So if he'd made a few, well, more than a few, wrong judgments—at

270

the least, he had cared enough to make the effort to correct them.

In arguing against Lord Beaumont's idea that the marquis was interested in her, she had, at the time, angrily recalled only that previous, unasked-for kiss and the sharp words that ever seemed to pass between them. Yet here was no fop, no wastrel, no peer on the strut for a fortune! Lord Tynsdale was just such a man as she'd dreamed of, a man who undertook his obligations as he saw them and who defended that which was his to protect. And remembering his wafting handkerchief, one who could even laugh at himself.

Then, tonight, outside in the fairy-lit garden, Lord Tynsdale had known that she was no woman of loose virtue. Nonetheless, he had shown no hesitation in kissing her again. She had encouraged him, true, but he was not one to compromise an inexperienced young miss—no matter how common her background—as witness his protective treatment of the little housemaid. The only reason he'd insulted her with his attentions after they'd rescued Flora was because he'd thought that Miss Rachel Doune was already a "soiled dove."

"Wrongheaded booby," Rachel grumbled.

So what did it all mean? She hoped that it meant that Lord Tynsdale would discontinue his belief that she could not truly care for him, the real man she knew him to be. But would she ever have the chance to explain about her grandfather's trust and about why she must marry into the nobility? Rachel heaved a small sigh, her mouth twisting wryly. Wonderful to know that *she* loved *him* . . . but perhaps he would never love her in return.

Or, could Lord Beaumont possibly be right?

But to learn that answer, she must first set herself free.

It was in all ways unthinkable that Marcus—she savored his name in her mind—be made to endure the shame that would inevitably accompany her downfall. When it was learned that she'd gone off with Lord Ripley like any common trollop, the gossips would say that the Kinsworths had harbored a vulgar miss, foisting her into their own

Select Circle. Oh, unforgivable, unforgettable offense. Lady Susan's good name—Marcus's name!—would instantly be on everyone's sneering lips.

Pulling her thoughts away from such dismal conjectures, at last, Rachel set herself to reasoning out her problem as her grandfather had taught her to do. She decided it was likely that Susan would have discovered the baron's forgery, and that Susan might, just might, notify her brother of what had happened. But in remembering Lord Tynsdale's parting words earlier this evening, Rachel's none-too-strong confidence about the marquis' feelings left her wondering forlornly if he would even care.

"Oh, *botheration!*" she next exclaimed softly. She dare not allow these constant, senseless diversions. Whatever his lordship's feelings, he would at least tell any searchers of Lord Ripley's possible interest. Someone might guess the baron's intentions and look along the roads to the north.

Would anyone find her in this out-of-the-way place? When she had been brought in from the coach, no lights from neighboring houses had been visible—although, from the relatively short time elapsed since her capture, she suspected that she wasn't all that far from London. She'd seen the flicker of streetlamps up until only an hour or so before arriving at the inn, meaning that if someone were searching for her, and in the right direction, she might try to gain their attention. But how was she to do that? Rachel shuddered as she realized that she didn't have much time either. Lord Ripley might return at any moment.

The room's single candle was of crude, smelly tallow. It slowly released a black, greasy smoke which curled upward from its pale yellow flame. Watching the smoke rise to the uncovered rushes high above her head, Rachel conceived the inkling of an idea. Ian Creagh's granddaughter in more ways than one, she clamped her bruised jaw with determination.

"So be it," she muttered.

There was only one way of redeeming the situation. A

272

means whereby she could save Lord Tynsdale and Lady Susan from the scandalmongers . . . and it was a way to save herself. It was risky, and Grampa would never recover from it should she fail, but at another burst of loud laughter from below, Rachel firmed her resolve.

She pulled the wooden washstand over to the outside wall and hiked her gold-colored skirts out of the way. She removed the pitcher and washbowl, setting them down on the floor, then climbed up onto the teetering furniture-top, tightly gripping the smoldering candle in one hand. Taking a deep breath, she positioned the taper just beneath the thatch. The dust-laden straw showed gray-tinged and dry with age.

At first, the rushes refused to catch. They blackened and crinkled without sparking. Bits of smutty charring fell to her arm, but Rachel willed herself to ignore the hot droppings while she held her hand steady. Just as her arm began to tremble and shake from the strain of her reach, her exertions at last produced a tiny, red-orange flicker. Almost at once, bright yellow flames leaped forth as the cool outside air drafted the thatch into burning in earnest.

Satisfied that the roofing was well and truly caught, Rachel leaped to the floor and ran to her door. Fear of meeting her parents' fate urged her to cry out, but she knew it would be disastrous if she gave the warning too soon. She used the time to douse her blanket with the water remaining in the cracked bowl and pitcher, before wrapping the soaked woolen length around her. She forced herself to wait, however impatiently, until she thought it was time.

But she waited for too long a space! Her breath started coming in shallow jerks. Already she could feel herself breaking into a fine sweat—and not from the heat of the fire.

The awful sight of the long, licking tongues of destruction, spreading their way outward, brought Rachel, round-eyed, to a standstill. She felt a slow, creeping apathy steal over her, induced by the shimmering image of weaving flames, with nothing between to protect her.

There came a terrible whooshing sound from overhead as the thatch was rapidly consumed ... numbing her, paralyzing her. She couldn't seem to breathe.

Think Rachel! she screamed in her mind. *Act, or you will die!* Even as she stood there, mesmerized, the flames reached the central beam above.

She clenched her jaw till her teeth hurt. She pulled in one deep breath through her nostrils, then another. "Fire," she gasped, forcing her voice to function. Louder: "Fire!" She hastened to beat on the door with her fists, screaming, *"Fire* up here I say!"

Rachel continued shrieking at the top of her voice until she was rewarded by the sound of heavy footsteps pounding up the uncertain stairs. The smoke was thick in the room by the time a key turned in her lock, and she quickly moved behind the door as it opened.

Men, a motley assortment as ever was seen, gathered out in the hallway to gape at the spreading flames. Through a crack behind the hinge, Rachel identified the proprietor with his keys dangling from his belt. She thought the men might try to enter, but as the smoke billowed forward, they quickly dispersed, giving forth their own shouts of "Fire!"

Clutching the dampened blanket, Rachel moved into the now-deserted hallway, fairly flying as she charged down the narrow wood steps. At the foot of the staircase, she turned toward the back of the building and threaded her way out to the empty kitchen. Peeping through a window, she saw that the stables were not too far away, and so, silently cursing the bright moon overhead, she crept out of doors.

One little item was forgotten, however. There was more than a moon to consider. She had been imprisoned in a room at the back of the building, and the burning roof was just above her head. She darted out anyway, even after realizing her predicament, heading for the shadows of a small stand of trees. But in the growing blaze from the fire, Lord Ripley easily spotted her.

"So, you have more tricks, do you?" he sneered as he grabbed her fleeing form. "Well, you've only made it

274

harder on yourself, girlie!''

Rachel wriggled free from his grasp by twisting out of her blanket, necessarily coming round to face the baron in the process. Without thinking, she bunched up her fist— and let fly! Howling with rage when her punch landed square on his so-tender nose, the baron threw up his hands to his face.

Not one to miss such a grand opportunity, Rachel snatched up her skirts and ran. She frantically searched the darkness ahead of her, ever mindful of her footing as she fled on into the night.

The heavyset baron gave a hearty curse and took off after her. He could not keep the pace for long, though, so he shouted to his coachman to bring up two horses from the stables. The innkeeper was busy organizing a chain of buckets amidst his doughty patrons, thus, none were to notice when the two men rode out minutes later.

With the orange-red glow of the inn's roof to give her direction, Rachel circled around to where she thought the road must be. Weeds slapped at her unprotected legs, slashing her stockings to ribbons. Her thin satin slippers were soon in shreds, and even with the moon's light, small rocks found their way under her flying feet. Her breathing became labored, but she dared not to rest. She must keep on running until she found that road!

An excruciating stitch developed in her side. Panting for air, she nevertheless forced herself to keep moving, until at last, she came to the narrow avenue leading down to the main road. Checking its length to see that she wasn't being followed, the exhausted young woman permitted her steps to slow. She stayed on the side of the rutted drive, hoping to reach the pike before she was discovered.

The sound of galloping horses coming up from behind reached her ears. Without stopping to turn and look, she dropped to the ground and crouched amongst the tall clumps of grass off to the edge of the drive. She was all too aware of her vulnerable position, but there were no trees nearby to offer other shelter. Rachel knew that her only chance was to remain low and still.

Yet luck was no longer with her. The gleam of her satiny gold hair gave away her position. With an ugly curse, Lord Ripley sharply pulled up his horse at the verge, the animal's hooves scant inches from her head. Reluctantly, she rose from her squatting position.

"You'll pay for this, you stupid chit. See if you don't!" He swung back his hand.

From somewhere, Rachel found the strength to dodge his planned blow. Then the drumming sounds of more hoofbeats reached her ear, and a shot next rang out; its warning whistle passed just over Lord Ripley's head. A deep bass voice carried easily through the night. "One more move and you're a dead man!"

A pair of silvery-light horses drew up alongside, and Lord Tynsdale jumped down from his seat. The deadly shape of a second pistol could be seen, pointed directly at the baron's chest.

Rachel slumped to a seat on the ground, holding her back stiffly upright only by the greatest of effort. She was surprised to see the baron's coachman suddenly wheel his horse about, and keeping his master between himself and the marquis' weapon, he galloped off in the opposite direction! Lord Ripley looked as if he would like very much to join his servant, but Marcus flicked his pistol in reminder. "You will oblige me, Lord Ripley, by coming down off that horse," he ordered.

The marquis' tone invited no argument. Warily, the baron dismounted, and Marcus passed his pistol to his tiger without taking his eyes from his adversary. "Ripley," his voice came on a low, savage growl. "This time you've gone too far. Miss Doune was—and is—under the protection of my family, never doubt it. So, and you have my word on this, if I should hear of you being in England after week's end, I will have you up on charges before the House. Terribly embarrassing when a fellow peer is sentenced, but I do assure you I shan't mind it. And do you give my avowals your most careful attention. You might just find that you prefer a long visit to the Americas . . . so much more healthful, don't you think?"

Knowing his man, Marcus expected the fist Lord Ripley promptly delivered. He shifted and took the hit off-shoulder, rolling smoothly with the punch. The blow that the marquis returned was not so easily avoided, however, as with admirable science, he sent the baron crashing to the ground. Without even bothering to examine the now-inert figure, Marcus turned to give aid to Miss Doune, still sitting upright on the verge.

Miss Rachel Doune was indeed a sorry sight by the light of the moon up above. Her once-neat topknot had fallen off to one side, and her delicate cambric gown hung un-evenly as a result of its numerous small rips and tears. But she had never looked so fair to any admirer as she sat there, tilting her little chin high into the air.

She tried to rise. Her legs, obviously over-tired and trembling, would not support her. Marcus reached down and scooped her up with no effort at all. He hugged her tightly against his thick chest, and his voice rumbled close to her ear. "Are you quite all right, love?" he asked.

Suddenly shy, Rachel could only nod her head in assent. She was overcome with a feeling of belonging, as if she had already made it home. Marcus carefully carried her over to his curricle and gently lifted her to its high seat, then removed his driving coat to wrap it snug around her. Tucking her head into his wide shoulder, he turned the curricle back toward London.

"Thank you for finding me," she said simply, peeping upward. "I wasn't certain how many hours were left to the night, so I wasn't sure of reaching home before dawn's light."

Marcus settled his team into a smooth, ground-covering trot before making comment. "You mean that if I'd not come along, you could not only have bested Lord Ripley but made your own way back to London?"

"Well, Grandfather says I am resourceful," she answered. "Although," she said in more rueful tones, "I'll admit that without your help, my chances were less than even. Still, needs must, I'd have thought of something," she added rather more optimistically.

Rachel felt it when his lordship gave a deep, rumbling chuckle. "Somehow, I rather think that you might have done so at that," he said softly. He then tucked his coat more securely around her before returning his attention to his high-mettled creams.

They met up with the earl on the turnpike. From their exchange of words, Rachel gathered that both men had been questioning anyone still awake for information on the black brougham. Learning that no one had seen it in the last village, Lord Beaumont had gone on ahead in case it had passed unnoticed, while the marquis worked his way back. Marcus had then seen the fire, and found the weed-choked turnoff to the illicit inn.

"The baron?" the earl asked, after being assured that Miss Doune was safe.

"Sent to grass for the moment," Marcus answered, "and out of the country by the morrow, if he knows what's good for him."

Harry pursed his lips in a silent whistle of approval.

Satisfied that Miss Doune was well secured, Lord Beaumont left them, anxious to carry the news ahead to Bruton Place. Having come on horseback, he could make good time, and certainly better than his friend's vehicle with its exhausted passenger. The earl was especially impatient to get word back to Lady Susan so that he could put that dear lady's worries to rest.

On the curricle's high, narrow seat, despite her best efforts to do otherwise, Rachel dropped off to sleep with her head resting beneath her champion's chin. Reducing his team to a walk so as not to disturb her, Marcus pondered his strange relationship with the young Scots miss, now leaning so comfortably, so trustingly, up against him.

He had felt so tremendously responsible for her predicament tonight, so horribly afraid that he would find her too late. Then, the sight of her valiant little figure, sitting uncompromisingly erect in the grass by the roadside, had made him expand with pride. She seemed to fully expect him to succeed in his rescue. Although, *I'd have thought of something,* she'd said. Marcus chuckled yet again.

That notwithstanding, she was still a complete little termagant. He recalled the various epithets she had thrown at him, and the way she positively defied him. What was it about Miss Rachel Doune that made her so wholly infuriating—and so alluring!—both at one and the very same time?

At length, coming to a conclusion, Marcus smiled broadly into the darkness.

Chapter Eighteen

It was four of the morning before Lord Tynsdale pulled his horses to a halt in Bruton Place. Although only a single light showed from the street, the entire household was awake and waiting inside. Even little Flora and young Will Slats had been aroused from their night's slumber— not by any particular sound, but by a strong feeling that something was not quite right at No. 12.

When the marquis came in carrying their mistress bundled up in a carriage robe, the servants responded with excited questions and muffled exclamations, for Earl Beaumont's earlier explanation to them had been unsatisfactorily incomplete. Fullerton soon put a stop to all the concerned importunings, cautioning the staff that not a whisper of this night's piece of work must get out; the scandal would be ruinous to their mistress, he reminded. Marcus passed the sleepy girl into their care; then he and Lord Beaumont left to find their own beds.

As for Rachel, she did not awaken then, nor till long after lunch the next day. And when she finally did stir, pushing herself out from between the covers, she very nearly returned to her sheets. She was stricken with the most ardent desire to cower underneath her very bed!

This, after beholding an altogether unlovely sight in her mirror.

Upon her arrival home, she'd tumbled into bed without doing more than pull the pins from her hair, dropping her jewelry—amazingly still with her—onto her bedside table. Tully had barely managed to keep her on her feet long enough to get her into a nightdress, in fact.

Now Rachel observed a quantity of soot still smudging her face and arms, and she saw that her legs were positively covered, knee to ankle, with fine scratches. One arm and hand were liberally speckled with tiny, shallow burn marks left from where smoldering thatch had fallen while she had held the fateful candle aloft. But these were as nothing compared to the awesome bruise that purpled one whole side of her jaw.

She rang for her maid, and that good woman verily goggled at seeing her mistress's damaged face. Young Will was shortly called to bring up the tub; his bulging eyes confirmed to Rachel that she was not at her best. While she had never been particularly vain regarding her appearance, neither did she enjoy being looked upon as if she were an absolute *antidote*.

After much scrubbing and rinsing, the smoky smell was vanquished, and Mrs. Tully helped Rachel into a fresh muslin day dress of rich periwinkle blue. The abigail insisted that the burns on her hand and arm be treated and wrapped in soft linen, so that after this last was accomplished, despite her fine dress, Rachel resembled some battlefield invalid. And even with careful powdering, the lower half of her cheek still showed a royal tint, adding to the pathetic picture. Only the brilliant color of Rachel's eyes belied her apparent state of ill-health.

Little Flora rapped at the door—she, too, had to stare!—before telling miss that the Lords Beaumont and Tynsdale were just come, and that Lady Susan was with them in the drawing room below.

They were all of them waiting to learn the details of her abduction, Rachel did not doubt. Much as she wished it otherwise, after everyone's help, she could not deny them, either. She was extremely reluctant to show her face but knew she must go down and extend them thanks. But, oh, how she wanted to remain in her room.

It was Marcus Kinsworth, her own love, who had come

to call. And with this thought, a hope that he returned her feelings burgeoned and grew. She hadn't missed the absolute fury with which Lord Tynsdale had confronted the baron; his deadly serious tone had sounded so wonderfully protective, as if he felt her to be the most precious thing in the world, whom he would not tolerate being offered the least threat. Then, his tenderness when lifting her up to his carriage, his sweet words of inquiry into her well-being, these made her smile softly to herself.

Oh, I just can't go down now and let him see me looking like this! she wailed silently.

Not the one to seriously consider such a pusillanimous act for long howsomever, Rachel resolutely straightened her posture and marched downstairs, wearing a look that defied anyone to disparage her appearance. Although more than slightly sore and stiff, she made a passable curtsy to the gentlemen. Gratefully, she accepted the cup of hot chocolate Susan extended. "Good morning everyone," she offered brightly. Her wide turquoise eyes smiled warmly in Lord Tynsdale's direction.

Marcus was totally stunned! He'd not examined Miss Doune closely when he'd carried her in so many hours ago; the moon was on the wane by the time he got her home, and when he'd brought her inside, Mrs. Fullerton had extinguished all but a few tapers so as not to alarm the neighbors. He'd seen that Miss Doune was a trifle rumpled and mussed, of course, but a good view of her swollen cheek with its vivid color in the day's light was truly a shock to his senses.

"It is a fine day, indeed, with you home and safe," Susan said softly, trying to keep the dismay from her voice. She couldn't help but add, "Though if I'd realized the extent of your injuries, Rachel, I would have insisted that you keep to your room! Are you in very much pain?"

"Good gad, Miss Doune!" Lord Beaumont put in. "I never realized—!" He seemed at a loss for further words.

"I assure you, it is nothing. Nothing at all," Rachel airily denied. "I look much worse than I feel. Tully insisted on wrapping me up like a mummy, but the burn marks are really very minor. Why, I'll not have a single scar to show for all my adventures."

Susan looked suddenly ill. "Great glorious heavens," she exhaled. "I just realized. Fire! Of all the things to have happened to you, that was surely the worst! You must have been utterly terrified, dear Rachel. I am so sorry!" She hastened to Rachel's chair and carefully hugged her about the shoulders. "Were you very frightened, dear? And your poor face, how did that come about?"

Rachel chuckled, grinning up at her friend. She winced slightly when her smile travelled too wide, but she quickly recovered, saying. "Actually, I have Lord Ripley to thank for that, and a good thing it was, too. You see, if I hadn't had its discomfort to distract me—well! by now, I would be little more than cinders and ashes."

From this, Rachel proceeded to detail the events of her capture and subsequent release, her narration causing one attentive listener to kindle to a very personally felt, slow, deep burn. Marcus's temper was ignited by the telling, progressing by steps into a rage quite without bounds. That the baron had shown the temerity to make off with the unwitting miss was bad enough, but that he had struck her—! Marcus burned white-hot in his wrath and briefly regretted that he had not aimed his pistol more to the purpose. Then, to learn that Rachel had set the inn afire herself, even while locked in a room with no escape—what might have happened did not bear thinking on. Last night he had been so proud of her intrepid spirit. She'd kept her head in the face of danger. Or so he'd thought. Now he wasn't so sure Rachel's solution wasn't worse than what Lord Ripley had proposed.

As the crux of her tale was reached, whereby the thatch was set alight, Susan impulsively interrupted. "You . . . you set the fire?" she gasped in anguished tones. "But, Rachel! I've seen you freeze at the sight of a rubbish pile burning uncovered. You go all over white and still, and can hardly draw breath when you so much as *see* a fire. And didn't you tell me that the awful fear stemmed from when your parents died in an inn that burned down when you were little? Merciful heavens, Rachel! How could you possibly have managed it?"

"Well—" With this reminder, Rachel did look a trifle shaken. "I'll admit that it was rather more of a challenge than I'd bargained for." She felt slightly sickened when she recalled the roaring flames busily consuming the roof overhead. "I actually had quite a time of it for a few minutes, but when I bit down on my sore teeth, it reminded me of what I had to do. So," she said more brightly, "I really dealt very well!"

"Unquestionably, you did, Miss Doune!" The earl spoke up. He, too, went over to give Rachel an awkward, but reassuring little pat on the shoulder. "My sister-in-law, Maria—I don't think you've met her yet—gets a tremendous case of the ghastlies just thinking of being shut up in any small place. Can't stand the idea of confinement. She says she once accidentally locked herself into a cupboard when she was a girl, and wasn't discovered for several hours. Ever since, she's had a horrendous reaction at the mere thought of small, dark places."

"It's a wonder I don't fear horses," mused Susan. "Perhaps it's because I was older when I fell and hurt myself, so it didn't affect me as strongly."

"Oh, enough of this," Marcus cut in. "Miss Doune—Rachel, if I may—?" She nodded in pleased acceptance of the familiarity. "I'm sure we are all very glad to have you returned to us safely."

"And I am enormously grateful to you, particularly since—"

"*However*," he overrode her, "there are a few things I would say to you in private. Sister, if you and Harry would be good enough to permit me a few moments alone with Miss Doune? There is a matter or two that we need to discuss between us." Speculating hopefully on the import of this request, Susan and the earl took themselves off with alacrity.

Marcus scarcely waited for the door to click shut.

"Rachel," he ground out. "You are, without a solitary doubt, the most damnable woman I have ever had the misfortune to meet."

Rachel started at his hushed, accusing tones, and at his choice of language! She was practically shivering with anticipation at being alone in his company, but this pleasurable response was immediately arrested.

He noted her reaction but was obviously undeterred. He continued. "Last night you thoughtlessly put yourself into a situation that no young lady should ever find herself in. Disregard for the conventions seems to be becoming a habit with you, although any dim-wit could see that it's brought nothing but trouble—to you, and to everyone else around you. That's why we have rules of deportment; they are meant to keep things like this from happening! And I am not impressed by your imaginative escape, not when there was no reason for you to be in danger in the first place. Your hey-go-mad ways are inexcusable. Completely unconscionable! You have caused intolerable distress to those who most care for you!"

Without an idea of how tightly his lordship was holding himself in check, Rachel at once took exception. "You *dare* to criticize me!" she snapped. "I'm the one who was dragged off through the night, after you went hotfooting it back to the Guinness's ballroom, leaving me alone and stranded!"

At this, he gave her *such* a look.

"Well," she muttered, "you cannot expect that I'd be pleased to continue in your company. And it should have been safe enough!"

His lordship shook his head and mumbled something incomprehensible which sounded suspiciously like a certain word in French. Dark eyes fixed sparkling aquablue. "Rachel," he finally said, "if I agree that I was wrong to leave you, will you admit that you should not have dismissed me in the first place?"

His tone was severe, arrogant even, but Rachel found his question encouraging. "Agreed," she replied instantly. "You took me at my word, no more. But . . . but you cannot expect me to like it when you become so imperious and take to ordering me about. It's not as if you, and only you, knew the right of a thing!"

Again he shook his head, this time as if enormously puzzled. He looked away from her as if to gather his thoughts. In a low voice, he asked, "Oh, Rachel, whatever is it you bring me? I used to know my world and had no doubt about my place in it. I enjoyed a simple, uncomplicated life, where everything stayed neatly patterned and entirely comprehensible. And yet, since our first meeting, things seem to have shifted and changed all around me."

"Have they? Or is it that your conceptions have changed?" she asked steadily. She longed to reassure him but felt her point too important to be ignored.

He sighed and stared off into some unknown distance, seemingly in a struggle for the words he needed. "It's more than that," he said, almost as if to himself. "I had always assumed that Susan was comfortable living with Lydia . . . but she wasn't. I believed Gilbert to be a wastrel—when in fact, he is no such thing. As it turns out, even Lydia is not quite the shallow creature I had thought her. And then you," he said with more strength. "You disregard all decorum, ignore the standards set for proper behavior, and in the most flagrant manner. It's as if such things were of no account whatsover—while I? I end up apologizing to you for it!"

She was surprised into a gurgle of laughter. "You find *that* confusing? I have been threatened by a thoroughly nasty man, then kissed by a marquis who impolitely informed me that a man of his distinction was beyond my grasp as though I really cared a jot for the stupid title. I was knocked unconscious, threatened some more, and then nearly burned to death—all in the space of a few hours. How is that for confusion!"

He stepped closer and reached over to run a light finger over her bruised and swollen cheek. "I should have killed him for that," he opined.

In seriousness, she counseled, "He wasn't worth the effort, you know."

He tapped his finger softly against the uninjured center of her chin. "No. But you are. Also, 'grasp' is the wrong word. I said, 'beyond your *reach*,' remember?" Brown eyes gently quizzed her.

But it was her turn to sigh at an inescapable truth. Her own eyes dark with emotion, she said consideringly, "We do seem to practice turn-and-turn about, don't we? First you mistake me; then I miscomprehend; and so on, and so on."

"Yes but, you see, I had always thought—" He hesitated, then said with a trace of exasperation, "Well, I just wish you had explained to me sooner: about your grandfather's directive, and about who you really were, I mean. And speaking of whom"—he scowled darkly—"I want to see Mr. Creagh's letters."

"Letters?" she asked. The question completely baffled her.

"All of them," he insisted.

"But why would you—"

"Never you mind that for now. Just bring them. Please."

To her it sounded more like a demand than a request, but she felt disinclined to argue, since it seemed so important to him. Shaking her head, she hurried out of the room to fetch the requested material. He accepted the letters from her hands, then sat himself down and read them with obvious care.

"What can you be looking for?" she asked after a few moments, her curiosity growing apace. "Why should you wish to read Grandfather's letters?"

"Because," he said absently, seeming to find particular interest in the progression, "I'm taking your advice and learning to ask the right questions before drawing conclusions."

"Questions? Conclusions? What—?"

"Not now, Rachel," he answered, rising only after he finished with the last of Ian Creagh's scrawled notes. "There is something I must see to before I say another word. Oh, I know you won't understand, and I shall not ask you to trust me; but I want you to believe that it is a thing which I must do." He looked down into eyes, darkened now to a lake green color in her distress. "It's another complication, I fear." His mouth quirked in a humorless smile.

Her look of redoubled doubt brought him to say, whisper-soft, "Please, Rachel. There is a reason I must leave you for a time, but I promise to return and provide you with due explanation."

"Then, you are leaving? For how long?" The serene, well-controlled young miss who had left Ayrshire just weeks ago looked anything but composed.

He seemed to study her bruised and swollen cheek. He winced slightly, as if he himself had been struck. His expression became unreadable as, with infinite softness, he said, "Have a care for my sister whilst I'm gone, won't you? I shall trust you to behave yourself, Rachel, but I remind you to a proper regard for the proprieties."

Truth to tell, the discussion had taken a direction that she could not like at all! She had expected to hear something quite different and was most painfully disappointed. "Oh, a pox on your stupid proprieties *and* your much-vaunted distinctions of breeding," she spat. "You think you can speak to me so, just because I cannot boast such ancestry as you? Well, mistake me not, I consider nothing in my origins inferior!" Hurt, she struck out at him with the first words that came into mind.

His answer to this rebellion was simple. In the same quiet tones as before, he warned, "Do not even consider ignoring my instructions, Rachel. You will be a perfect model of circumspection until I see you next. And learn this from my example: stupidly stubborn, *willful* pride is of no particular virtue. You must learn to have a care for your friends. Yes?" A wry half-smile lit his face. "But I think that until *this* has time to heal—he brushed the tip of one long finger gently to Rachel's bruised cheek—"I shouldn't need to worry about your getting into any more mischief. Oh, and another thing," he added, "that last remark about ancestry? It was completely unworthy, Rachel."

With that, he left her, pulling the drawing room door

closed behind him with a snap. Minutes afterward, Rachel heard the sounds of leave-taking coming from the front hall, the thump of the street door's closing told her that the gentleman had taken his leave.

"Well, that was certainly a telling encounter!" Rachel sniffed, her eyes filling with tears.

Just a few minutes later, Susan came back into the room. Marcus hadn't given a clue as to his converse with Rachel. He'd merely made his *adieux*, surprised his sister with a hug, and left. Lord Beaumont had taken leave soon after, making Susan anxious to learn what was going on.

She was astonished upon reentering the drawing room to find her intrepid young friend sunk down on the edge of a chair, with tears coursing hotly from her eyes. These splashed down unnoticed, marking Rachel's pretty muslin gown and the damask upholstery indiscriminately.

"Oh, Rachel, what can be wrong now?" she inquired gently. It was the first time she had ever seen Rachel weepy, and she was dismayed when her question only brought on a positively drenching outpour.

"H-he . . . he thinks me careless of my fr . . . friends and said that I have no sense of propriety," the younger girl wailed between great explosive sobs. "He said I r-recklessly caused my own problems, and the worst of it is, he's right. Even you came in asking me what was wrong 'now,'" the younger woman cried brokenly. "And, Susan, just last n-night, he called me *love!*" Inconsolable for the moment, Rachel then buried her face in her hands, rocking back and forth as tear-filled convulsions overwhelmed her.

Susan tried to comfort her distraught friend, but Rachel was beyond hearing or speech. Finally, she led Rachel off to bed, still shaking with sobs, crying as if her heart would break.

By the time dinner was announced, though, Rachel was apparently ready to dry her eyes, freshen her appearance, and come down to make her meal. She had even collected herself enough to go around to each of her servants, thanking them sincerely for their concern and care—*after* muttering to herself that she didn't need his high-and-mighty lordship to remind her of that particular duty. It was, in truth, an impulse born of her very real gratitude to those who served her. At dinner, she unhesitatingly encouraged Susan to discuss the events of the previous night, seemingly anxious to hear Susan's side of the story. The description of Sujit's prognostications even occasioned an appreciative gurgle of laughter.

While sipping her after-dinner coffee, Susan cleared her throat and made an announcement that brought Rachel up from her chair in delight. It seems that while at White's and before Fullerton's intrusion Harold, Lord Beaumont had acquired Lord Tynsdale's approval to make his addresses to that old spinster aunt, that erstwhile chaperon to young debutantes, my Lady Susan Kinsworth! He had made his proposal after returning with the news of Rachel's deliverance, and tonight, Susan reported her acceptance of his offer with pride shining forth from her eyes.

"I can certainly see why Almack's is called the 'Marriage Mart,'" Rachel trilled happily. "It was but two nights ago that we made our first entry there."

"And so much has happened since," Susan said, much struck.

Going to pull the cord to summon the butler, the golden-haired miss gave her a great smile. "Nothing we haven't deserved," she said cryptically.

When Fullerton answered her ring, Rachel promptly ordered champagne, shoving the last of her miseries behind her. "For Susan is promised to take the name of Beaumont, Fullerton," she explained. "And make that *two* bottles, I say. Everyone in this house shall raise a glass on this momentous occasion."

Nodding with majestic approval, Fullerton set off to bring up the vintage requested. He popped the cork for the pair in the parlor, and with no less ceremony, he opened a like bottle for those in the kitchen. But upon learning what he was about, Rachel stopped him, insisting that the servants be brought to the parlor to share in the joyous celebration.

When all were gathered round, with a merry grin, Sujit proclaimed, "I am being very gladdened to be participating here with you all!" Then he frowned, the fragrant wine bubbles striking up at his nose. "But necessarily," he begged, "if it is not displeasing the missies too much, I will be preferring to drink plain and ordinary water. Shall this be giving very great offense?"

"Certainly we do not mind," Rachel reassured him. "It is the gesture of goodwill that counts here."

The little cook, looking much relieved, bobbed his head and chimed, "Oh, indeed, you are having all of my amity."

"Best wishes," next said young Will shyly, blushing beet red as he accepted a crystal wineglass from the butler's tray.

"O-oo, my lady! What wonderful news," Flora cried, much awed and nearly as impressed by receiving her first glass of champagne as by Lady Susan's glad tidings.

"I couldn't have wanted better for you," Mrs. Tully joined in.

Mrs. Fullerton just quietly took hold of Lady Susan's hand and squeezed it. Looking over at her husband, she smiled.

Rachel, her spirits wholly restored, beamed at dear, sweet Susan. "To love and a lifetime of friendship," she advanced. "May we always give both due honor!"

Six crystal-stemmed wineglasses and a water tumbler lifted high in toast.

And the next day, Rachel came down early. She had dressed herself for riding, bent on carrying on with their established custom of taking to the parks before the bridle paths became too congested. She was determined that her own activities should return to normal as soon as possible, and a resumption of the usual habits was the best way she knew to proceed. She was more than a little ashamed of previous errors, and felt chagrined that dear Susan had had to bear with her grievous outpourings yesterday, so today, she wanted all such poor-spirited behavior behind her.

Certainly, she knew that she should remain in the house until her bruised face had healed to at least a somewhat less violent shade, but she'd covered her hair, trusting that she might go unrecognized. She had no intention of letting Lord Tynsdale learn she'd moped about in seclusion. She was set to prove that she bore him no malice for his telling words; she accepted the truth in them. But she was in no wise willing to be cowed into hiding, no matter his lordship's expectations.

For this morning's outing, Rachel had chosen a nicely concealing, wide-brimmed hat of canary yellow felt with a broad white ribbon that she had snugged under her chin, then tied off to one side. It had the felicitous effect of obscuring the greater part of her discolored jaw. Confident in the effectiveness of her costume, she had then jauntily tilted her headgear to an impudent angle before easing on her gloves of York tan. She met Susan in the front hallway, where they were ordinarily joined by Lord Beaumont.

And this fine May morning was to be no exception. If either the earl or his betrothed was surprised to see Rachel set to go out with them, neither one made any protest, being too impressed with Rachel's good cheer. "Come on, you two!" Rachel twinkled infectiously. "A pity to waste such a perfect morning."

And over the next several days Rachel stayed as busy as ever. She couldn't accept social invitations just yet, of course, but she used her time well, diligently shopping to replace the worn items in her wardrobe. When she went out on an errand, she merely affected a concealing veil, which, fortunately, was considered quite acceptable for fashion.

Maintaining her cheerfulness became more and more of an effort as the days went by, however. Rachel began to worry. She had fully expected Lord Tynsdale to return by this time—but he had not. By the time another week had passed, she had to conclude that he still couldn't quite make himself approve of her, might even have come to despise her! But he had promised, she sternly reminded her uncertain heart. He had promised, and so he would come.

Finally, her patience left her. Rachel taxed the earl over his friend's disappearance. She could scarcely believe it when Lord Beaumont, looking vastly discomfited, admitted that his friend had left town. Under further questioning, the earl told her that he didn't know the marquis' exact or even approximate whereabouts; he could only say that the message he'd received told him not to expect his friend back for some time.

Rachel *was* shaken by *this* revelation. Right down to her new kid slippers! Despite his last words upon leavetaking, though, she had presumed Lord Tynsdale would shortly return to plague her, like he always did. "Should I write a note of apology?" she wondered in painful perplexity.

Oh, she accepted that her last jab at him had been uncalled for, but had it been so very bad? No, she decided, assuredly it was not. And no young miss with a particle of claim to gentility could even think of writing to a bachelor address; he likely wouldn't be there to receive her message, anyway. So, she must wait till he came to her.

She reminded herself that when she and Grandfather had experienced a disagreement, they had argued all they pleased—held splashing debates, in fact—but, win or lose, no one had ever *pouted* over the results. But Grandfather had never brought her to tears, either, which thought recalled her to another: Marcus had advised her she needn't trust him. Was there some particular significance to that?

By the end of the third week, the last, greenish yellow tint faded from Rachel's cheek. She returned to the mad social whirl, as much sought after as ever. She insisted on accepting every invitation that she was offered, sometimes attending four, or even five parties in one night, before exhaustedly falling into her bed at dawn. She danced almost every dance, treating each partner to a smile, showing impartial enthusiasm for one and all.

Her feverish gaiety began to concern her two friends,

though. Susan and her new intended felt there was something very wrong in so much frenetic activity. They suspected Rachel of missing a certain marquis, much more than she would say. She never was seen to cry again, but Susan noted that neither did she bring up Marcus's name. Harry noticed, too, but could only shake his head in sad puzzlement at Marcus's apparent desertion. Harry soon remarked something else: Rachel never waltzed.

Chapter Nineteen

The month of June was well upon them. Nine weeks had passed since Miss Rachel Doune had arrived in London. And although she had by this time received no fewer than five fervent requests for her hand, two came to her motivated by greed, and two other gentlemen came merely because Lord Petersham had placed her in Fashion's favor. Or so Rachel judged it.

Only one man seriously tempted her to make him an acceptance. Strange though it might seem, the offer that flattered her, touched her, was the one she received from the Honorable Gilbert Cheeves.

Rachel was surprised when Gilbert had called on her to make his declaration, and when he'd gone down on one knee in form, she'd been hard pressed to withhold expression of her amazement. She took great care to be gentle in her refusal, however, telling him very kindly that she thought they would not suit.

"M' aunt said you'd not accept me," he had light-heartedly replied. "But the thing is, don't know anyone I like better. I don't suppose I'll ever like anyone half so well as I like you, Miss Rachel, so I just thought I'd put it to the touch." Gilbert had then patted her hand reassuringly, as if *he* should console *her!*

His prosaic attitude made Rachel wonder if she was foolish to turn him down. She didn't know anyone she liked better either—or at least, no one who would have her.

In a few years' time, Gilbert probably would become just such a man as she most approved of, but it was too late to think of that now. Her affections were already given.

Somehow, she realized, returning to Ayrshire in defeat was no longer the spur it had once been. Truth to tell, she wanted to leave London's gay scenes, scenes which only served to make her feel more and more isolated amidst ever-surging crowds. She was lately aware that she was now only going through the motions of searching for a husband; no one could replace the man already established firmly in her heart.

Plumwood House called her back like an old and trusted friend. She would go home and be with Grandfather, she decided. And when he was gone, she would take a small cottage, perhaps with Mrs. Tully. Two hundred pounds per year would keep her in comfort . . . and with that she must be content.

It was arranged that Susan would take on the Bruton Place staff, cats and all, when the time came. Lord Beaumont was in the process of relinquishing his bachelor rooms and had purchased a spacious new home in Cavendish Square. Will Slats would continue his training under the earl's valet, and when that elderly man retired, Will would be ready to take the position. The Fullertons, Sujit, and Flora all agreed to the move, happy to serve the new couple.

Rachel wrote these plans to her grandfather, longing for her home. The Social Season of 1814 didn't wind down for the usual close, however. Great events on the Continent culminated in Napoleon's abdication, bringing renewed gaiety to England, and to London in particular. If anything, there were more ton parties planned for the summer months than had marked the calendars in May. No one who was anyone dared to make plans to leave the city.

Besides any number of parties planned for June, a grande fête was to be held the third week in July at Carlton House to honor the newly acclaimed Duke of Wellington. The Emperor of Russia and the King of Prussia were already arrived and quite taking London by storm, and even a People's Jubilee was planned for the first of August. The Prince Regent had architects busily constructing all manner of fantastic castles, bridges, and pagodas in the city's royal parks for all of his subjects to enjoy.

But Rachel would not be there to see it. Susan's wedding was set for Saturday, the twenty-third day of June, and Rachel planned to leave for Scotland the following Monday. She saw no reason to continue her stay, even though, strictly speaking, she had until the final day in the month to obtain a husband. Neither did she long maintain her interest in attending ton parties, for there was no sense in denying the truth. She loved a man who despised her, so that was the end of it.

Rachel recalled that she had once vowed—how long ago it seemed!—that she would never marry without love. Nor would she. She had also promised herself to find a man that she could respect. She had done so. Unfortunately, her fears that she would then be measured and found wanting had come true, as well.

The middle of June saw Rachel sitting quietly curled up on the cushions of her favorite parlor window seat. Susan had gone out to Hyde Park in Lord Beaumont's carriage earlier in the afternoon, as the earl seemed never to tire of showing off his bride-to-be. While they were gone, Rachel settled herself in the parlor. She held a copy of Scott's latest poem, a long narrative that was full of romantic drama and exactly what she most enjoyed.

While Rachel attended to her reading, she absently stroked one of Mrs. Fullerton's cats, come to lounge across her lap. So engrossed was she, that the sounds of entry coming from down the hall barely pierced her concentration. She merely thought that Earl Beaumont must be returning with his intended. She continued undistracted, turning to the next page of her book, even after the cat beside her ceased its purring and swivelled its triangular head to fix narrowed eyes on an intruder.

"You will oblige me by getting rid of that menace, love." A well-deep voice rumbled nearby.

Rachel sprang up from her seat, spilling her book and a forgotten and disgruntled feline onto the floor. Waiting until the cat was safely away, Marcus Kinsworth, the Most Honorable, the sixth Marquis of Tynsdale, moved forward to pull her close into his arms. His greeting kiss was long and deep; he enveloped her senses with his presence even as his arms gently tightened around her. She wondered if she'd fallen asleep over her reading, for she surely must be dreaming. After an eternity of waiting, wondering, despairing—?

Warm, velvety-soft lips soon convinced Rachel that this was not the stuff of imagination, however. Oh, most definitely not. Each gentle change of pressure on her mouth sent her mind whorling upward to reach ever new heights of awareness. "Can you really be here?" she murmured long minutes later.

"You did then doubt it?" One dark eyebrow lifted high in admonition. "I told you I would come back. Do you still not know me well enough to understand that I would keep to my word?"

"But after so much time, Marcus?"

"I had a long way to go."

"Go? Why had you to go anywhere?" She struggled to disguise the heartache threatening to enter her voice.

"Well, that *is* how these things are usually done," he said softly. Then, before she could question him further, he nuzzled her lips softly to open to him again.

A wealth of meaning passed between them, leaving Rachel short of breath and uncaring of explanations offered in any other language.

A meaningful "Ahem!" from the doorway returned Rachel back to her senses. She peered over Marcus's broad shoulder and inhaled sharply in disbelief. There, standing upright and hale at the doorway, stood Mr. Ian Creagh.

"Grandfather! Grampa, how. . . ?" Rachel swung her gaze wildly from one man to the other.

Mr. Creagh came farther into the room, his words

sounding much aggrieved. "It be a fine thing, child, when this rare lord ye've found maun come and drag me awa' from my home," he complained. "An auld man like me should nae be hustled and hurried off on long trips wi'out a decent stop all the way. I gae him my blessing—what more could he want? Whist! I hae suffered greatly at his hands and been hard-used, I tell ye."

"That will do, sir." Lord Tynsdale fixed fierce dark eyes upon the white-haired old Scotsman. "We can discuss the particulars of our journey at a later time."

"But I told ye we had till June's end," the irrepressible septuagenarian excepted. "We'd nae need to be rushing about so."

"Enough," Marcus growled deep in his throat.

Rachel could scarcely credit it when the crusty old Scotsman at once subsided and took himself a seat. Ian Creagh merely pursed his lips as he made himself comfortable, with scarcely a reproachful look in Lord Tynsdale's direction.

She made to go to her grandfather's side, but Marcus firmly restrained her. He regained her attention, turning now-gentle eyes to her bewildered, upturned face. "Oh, Rachel, love," he sighed softly, "it would seem that you are the one most sadly used. This crafty old devil has much to answer for, since the fact of it is, he's no more likely to die this year than I am. But until now, I hadn't realized that I, too, had misled you; I thought surely you would have guessed my errand! Between his fakery and my callousness. . . . Oh, Rachel, forgive me. It never once occurred to me that I had left you thinking that I had abandoned you. Between your grandfather and me, I think we have caused you no end of trouble."

"Then, you are saying that—?" Confused, Rachel looked to her grandfather. "And you were never really sick?"

"Ah, but he was," came Marcus's sardonic assurance. "He was ill for all of a day or two! But, being a wily old scoundrel, he saw a chance to use your care for him to bend you to his will."

301

In truth, the old patriarch had not hesitated to disclose his imposture to Lord Tynsdale. When Marcus had arrived at his home, Mr. Creagh had promptly confessed that his illness had been largely feigned. Knowing his love, Marcus had inwardly concurred that it had, perhaps, all been necessary; he knew better than most how she placed her own judgment first, sometimes to the exclusion of pertinent facts. But he was not about to let the old scamp off lightly.

"Oh, no. No," Rachel choked. "How can you accuse Grandfather of so deceiving me?" But with a closer look at the old man comfortably seated on the sofa, Rachel felt a first stirring of suspicion.

"Grampa?" she directed on a cautionary note. The tilt of her chin further warned the old man, but his clear blue eyes fearlessly spoke the truth. "Then, you *were* pretending all this while!" she declared.

"Aye, ye're in the right o' it," agreed Mr. Creagh, determinedly unrepentant. "Mind ye, I ne'er actually gave the lie—a wee mite o' exaggeration, that's a'." Sincerity lent emphasis when he reminded, "But, child, I dinna wish to see ye wither into an auld *cailliach*, a lonely woman, wi'out a good man to gi' ye the home ye should hae."

"Oh, Grandfather," she moaned softly. "You made me to fear for you so!" Her pained disappointment shamed Ian Creagh as nothing else could have done.

"Aye, mayhaps it was wrong," he said gruffly. Then he grumbled out his own complaint. "But 'twere the only way I knew, Rachel! Can ye nae see that? Ye're an iron-headed lass as e'er there was. But ye'll forgive me?" he asked hopefully.

Unexpectedly, the marquis took the old man's part. "He did mean it all for the best, Rachel." Marcus had decided that if assisting in Mr. Creagh's exoneration helped his love's feelings to mend, he would facilitate the reconciliation. He wasn't going to let anything prolong her least discomfort.

Thus, she had to forgive her dearest grandfather, since

he surely had only her welfare at heart, but Rachel remained unsettled in considering Lord Tynsdale's rôle. Obviously, he had left for Scotland right after ripping at her, but why had he gone? Surely not just for the purpose of uncovering her grandfather's fraud. After all she'd been through, she was afraid to place any reliance on her expectations, either; she needed more explicit affirmation.

Before she could put her questions, however, Grandfather Creagh stood up. Casting a mightily pleased look at the couple still standing together by the window seat, he announced that Fullerton had promised to ready him a room. He left the parlor, saying "Aye, it's a fine and clever lass I raised. Beat the clock with two weeks and more to spare!" The sound of his delighted little chuckles could be heard through the open door as Mr. Creagh climbed the staircase.

Alone once more, Marcus read the uncertainty in Rachel's eyes.

"I once offered you a convenient arrangement," he said quietly. "I cannot regret the impulse which made me offer, neither do I regret your reply. Oh, Rachel, do you have any idea how unusual you are, love?" he suddenly asked, warmth coloring his tones. "You rake me down easily and without quite losing your—oh, I still haven't hit on precisely the word for it—your own inner *calm*, as I call it. Indeed, you are as unalike to every woman I've known as diamonds are to the merest trumperies. And you are also," his voice deepened further, "the most beautiful, fearless, and intriguingly wonderful lady that was ever my fortune to know." He looked down, plunging his gaze boldly into her eyes, now dilated to the deepest shade of loch green. "Tell me that you love me, Rachel," he whispered, "for you must know that you are my dearest love. I love you beyond all words, more than I once would have thought possible."

Obedient to his soft command, she responded, "Oh, yes, I love you. Ever and always, I love you." Her heart showed true from depths of aqueous green.

His answering kiss contained all that Rachel had ever

wanted. A man who would accept her, care for her, believe her precious. Even so, as their kiss ended, she thought to ask, "So, for all of this time, you were gone to seek out my grandfather?"

"What else?" he quizzed gently. "I would hardly speak of my desire to have you to wive, without first obtaining Mr. Creagh's permission. More especially after the lecture I delivered you about preserving the conventions. Then, too, I'd come to suspect the terrible way he was misleading you. You see, there was nothing in his letters that actually *said* he continued ill; your cunning old grandfather merely implied that he was 'not much improved.' Knowing the easy way you play with words, I suspected at once where you might have learned the art."

"That was so wrong of him—" Rachel started.

"So it was. But, who am I to complain? It brought you to London, to me."

Rachel probed the darkest-brown depths of his eyes. "But are you so very sure that you want me, Marcus?" she asked. "I'm not the highborn wife you'd intended for yourself, as I well know. I'm a commoner, a perfectly ordinary girl."

"Ah, but you are to be my marchioness, love," he reassured her, nuzzling her smooth cheek in a manner delightful to them both. "And from what I can see," he growled deep in his throat, "there is nothing at all common about you."